# MAELSTROM

## THE RETURN OF THE ELVES
### BOOK NINE

# BETHANY ADAMS

eBook design/illustration by The Illustrated Author Design Services (www.theillustratedauthor.net)

ISBN 978-1-953171-05-4

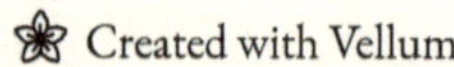 Created with Vellum

*To the "odd" ones out there,*
*those who feel out of step.*
*You're perfect*
*just the way you are.*

# ACKNOWLEDGMENTS

I have so many thanks to give that it's always tough to remember. But first, I owe so much to my husband and children, who put up with all my deadlines and grumpiness. I couldn't do it without you!

Many thanks to my critique partners, Catherine and Shiloh. Seriously, there aren't ample words. Without you two, this book wouldn't be out today, so thank you.

Thanks also to my cover artist, Melissa Stevens at The Illustrated Author Design Services for my lovely new cover. The last year has been wild, but we've made it through!

Thank you to Stefan Rudnicki, Gabrielle de Cuir, and everyone at Skyboat for your amazing work on my audiobooks. I hope you enjoy recording this one.

And a special thanks Charlotte, Laura, and Stephanie for answering my questions about the Tube in my Facebook group. If I got anything wrong, just consider it an alternate dimension. Hehe.

Of course, many blessings and thanks go to all my readers. You have no idea how much I treasure your support and kindness. Thank you!

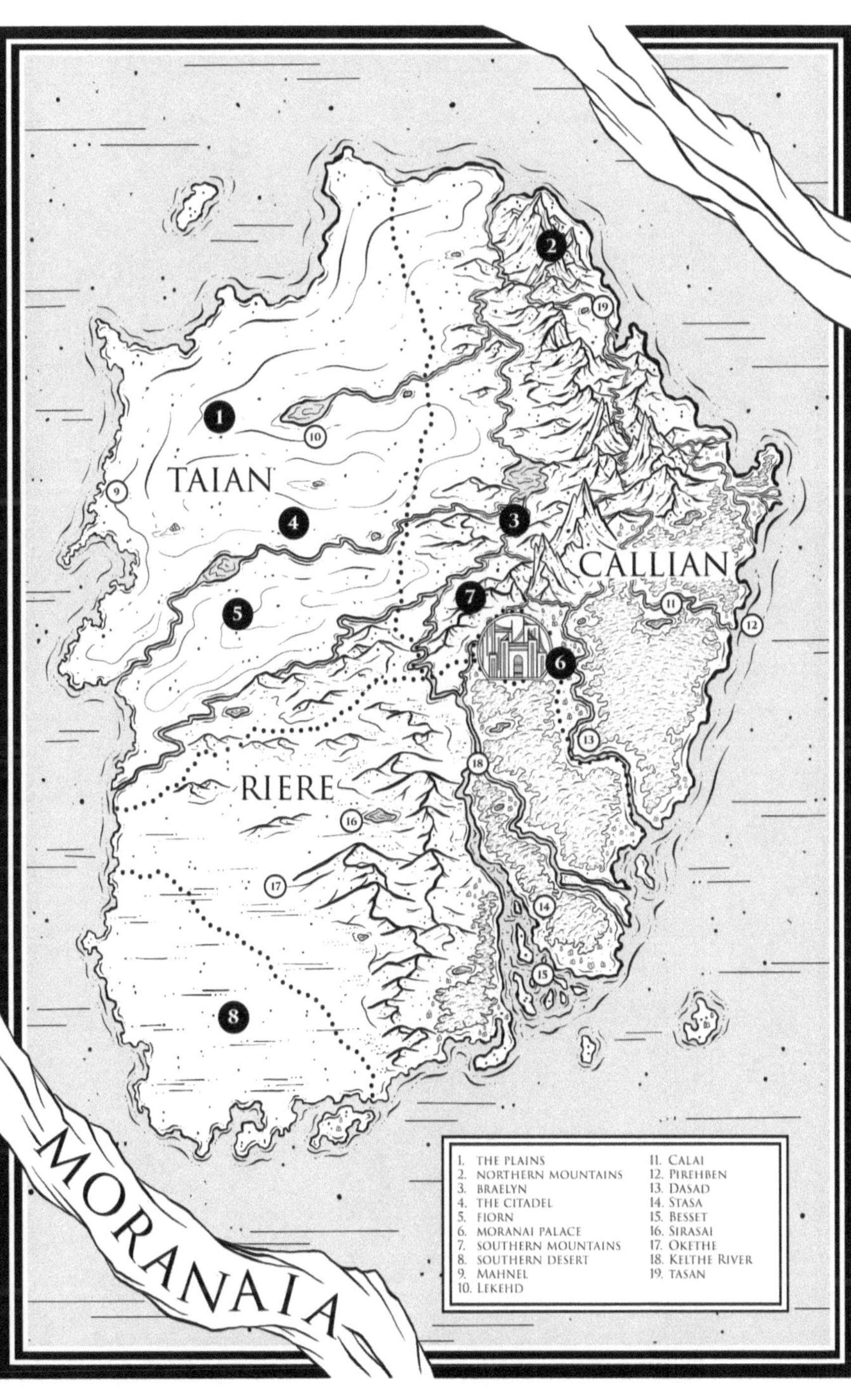

TAIAN
CALLIAN
RIERE
MORANAIA
1. THE PLAINS
2. NORTHERN MOUNTAINS
3. BRAELYN
4. THE CITADEL
5. FIORN
6. MORANAI PALACE
7. SOUTHERN MOUNTAINS
8. SOUTHERN DESERT
9. MAHNEL
10. LEKEHD
11. CALAI
12. PIREHBEN
13. DASAD
14. STASA
15. BESSET
16. SIRASAI
17. OKETHE
18. KELTHE RIVER
19. TASAN

# PRONUNCIATION GUIDE

**Main Characters:**
    Kezari (ke-ZAHR-ee)
    Tynan (TIE-nehn)

**Secondary Characters:**
    Baza (bah-zah)
    Caeregas (CARE-IH-gus)
    Caolte (KWIL-chuh)
    Egrenneth (ee-GREHN-NEHTH)
    Iskedai (IHS-keh-dai)
    Lial (lee-ahl)
    Naomh (NAY-om)
    Osieren (OH-see-EHR-ehn)
    Zevie (ZEHV-ee)

**Other:**
    Deyriglair (DAY-rih-glare)
    Orlayak (OR-lay-ahk)
    Sbezie (SBEH-zee)

# AUTHOR'S NOTE

I've done my very best to make each book in my series capable of being read alone, but now that we're on the ninth book, I thought I'd give a brief summary of the previous books. I'll also include a character list and short dictionary in the back. If you're new to the series, only read the rest of this section if you're okay with spoilers!

In SOULBOUND, half-blood Arlyn confronts her elven father, Lyr, after traveling to his world. He's surprised to find that the woman he left on Earth bore him a child, but he welcomes his daughter. But things are far from easy. Not only is Arlyn drawn into a soulbond with her father's friend, Kai, but her arrival prompts Kai's father, Allafon, to hasten his plot against Lyr. Arlyn only has time for a little training with new magic teacher, Selia, before she, Lyr, and Kai are taken captive. In the end, Allafon is defeated, but Lyr is injured, and Arlyn's grandmother almost dies.

SUNDERED continues the story from Lyr's point of view. Though Allafon was defeated, the person behind his actions was not. Banished Prince Kien is creating havoc amongst the fae with poisoned energy, and the Neorans, vassals of the Seelie Sidhe, petition Lyr for aid when their city is overrun by disease and madness. As Lyr struggles to help them, another faction of fae, the Ljósálfar, arrive from Alfheim—brought by Meli, his potential soulbonded. Lyr sends Kai to help evacuate the Neorans, but when he arrives, the inhabitants have been massacred. Eventually, Arlyn and Kai manage to destroy the spell causing the poison, but they are captured by a Seelie lord, Naomh, who turns out to be Kai's true father.

The novella EXILED features Delbin, a young elf who was sent from Moranaia to Earth when he was a teenager in order to escape Allafon. The scout Inona is sent to check on Delbin. Soon after her arrival, Prince Kien tries to recruit Delbin to join his group of half-bloods. Delbin refuses, and he and Inona eventually track down and capture Kien. Kien escapes, but Delbin is allowed to return to Moranaia and becomes the student of Prince Ralan, a powerful seer.

In SEARED, Ralan leaves his daughter Eri on Moranaia and returns to Earth to track down his brother Kien. Plagued by visions foretelling his death, Ralan is nevertheless determined to stop Kien for good. In the process, he meets his soulbonded, Cora, who owns a shop where fae can trade gold or jewels for human clothes. Her friend and employee, Maddy, is kidnapped by Kien's minions, leading Cora to join Ralan in the quest to defeat Kien. With the help of Vek of the Unseelie and his nephew, Fen, Kien is found, although he ultimately escapes to Moranaia. Ralan and Cora confront Kien at the palace. Kien nearly kills Ralan, but Cora manages to save him. The king beheads Kien, but in the process, a mysterious surge of power is released.

Though Kien was defeated, he used his death to release poison into a barrier that withheld magic from Earth. In ABYSS, the dragon Kezari senses that poison through her link to Earth and goes to retrieve her rider, Aris, only to find him being tortured by his potential soulbonded. After she saves him, Aris agrees to accompany the dragon to Braelyn, the estate of Lord Lyr. Aris doesn't know that his wife Selia, who believes him to be dead, accepted a position there a few months before. He struggles to deal with his trauma as he longs to reunite with his wife. Although a mind healer helps, Aris must overcome his darkness in time to prevent the barrier from shattering, releasing a catastrophic amount of energy at once. He, Kezari, Selia, and Kai manage to prevent disaster, but in the process, a direct portal is created between Moranaia and Earth, one that will need guarding in the future.

In AWAKENING, Ralan appoints his sister Dria to be in charge of the new outpost on Earth guarding the portal to Moranaia. In the meantime, the Unseelie prince Vek is tasked by his father to kill the leader of the outpost and claim the power stored there. Beholden to the Moranaians, Vek seeks to find a way out of this order, and while researching, he discovers that the new leader of the outpost is his mate. When the outpost comes under attack, Dria and Vek work together to find the person responsible. They eventually uncover a plot that involves the Unseelie king and the Seelie lord Meren. Dria challenges the king to combat, but Vek's sister Ara ultimately defeats him, becoming the new Unseelie queen. Meren later attempts to kill Vek but is thwarted.

Meren continues to cause trouble in ASCENT. This time, he attempts to manipulate Fen and claim the Seelie throne. However, Fen and his potential mates, Maddy and Anna, stumble into one of Meren's plans to spread poisoned energy and act to diffuse the situation. Eventually, Fen, Maddy, and Anna complete the mate bond and confront Meren. This leads to a fight in the Seelie court, though Meren escapes. Maddy, Fen, and Anna help the Seelie queen by removing a mysterious poison from her blood before returning to the outpost.

In SOLACE, Meren injects Korel, a former guard at Braelyn, with a virus capable of infecting elves. Korel attacks and infects a mage working at the estate, and while Lial heals the mage, the others search for the perpetrator. In the meantime, Lynia begins research on diseases at the request of Ralan, which throws her together with Lial. As they struggle with their feelings, the search for their new enemy intensifies. Kezari nearly kills Korel in order to help Aris, unleashing the virus and putting everyone in danger. Lial is eventually infected, and Lynia must use her research to save him. Tynan arrives to help settle Aris and to heal Lial, who recovers thanks to a potion of Lynia's creation.

# CHAPTER ONE

Kezari's wings itched—or perhaps it was her heart.

She snorted, a puff of air streaming from her nose like an errant cloud. If she kept having foolish thoughts, there would no doubt be a trail of her breath across the sky above Braelyn. An itchy heart? A patch of scales she couldn't shed or a bit of sand caught around her talon—those things were itchy.

Hearts merely beat.

Though as she pitched to the left to make yet another circle around the sprawl of Braelyn's outer lands, she couldn't deny the sudden urge to take off for...somewhere. And that was the problem, wasn't it? That sensation scratching at her insides until she wanted to gnash her teeth. Instinct called her to go, but she didn't know where.

Not to mention that she didn't want to leave Aris behind. He was still her *skizik*, her partner in magic. Not mate, as she'd had to explain to that blasted mind healer at dinner the night before. Who could confuse the two roles? A *skizik* was both friend and working partner, one whose magic was compatible. A mate was for...well...mating. That wasn't something one did with a *skizik* unless the two roles were combined.

And for whatever reason, Aris was still comfortable with being her *skizik* despite her recent errors.

Another cloud streamed from her nostrils, and she beat her wings until they ached. *Ancestors' teeth,* she muttered to herself. Recent errors? She had crushed the man they sought as though he'd been a stray *daeri* and had set loose a plague hidden in his blood in the process. One could hardly call unleashing a disease capable of wiping out the elves an error. Disaster. Calamity. Ruin. Those things, yes. A simple mistake? Hardly.

No one held it against her, of course, but that didn't stop the shame. She should have learned by now that her first instincts were always the wrong ones. This was not the Isle of Dragons, and she couldn't act as though it were. Perhaps that was the cause of her desire to leave? Yet she didn't feel the urge to head north and east to her former home.

The itchy feeling might be connected to Earth. Though the energy there had been calmer since she, Aris, and their allies had converted the wall holding back Earth's magic into a gate linking that world to this one, she *had* learned that her ancient dragon brethren still existed. The ones who had remained behind when the rest of the dragons journeyed to Moranaia—they were believed to be in hibernation on Earth. But she'd sensed one of them the last time they'd journeyed to the outpost the Moranaians kept hidden in one of Earth's mountains.

An ancient one.

Active. Waking.

Still, her body didn't angle toward the territory beyond Braelyn where Prince Ralan was building a new palace to protect the very gate she and Aris had helped to create. Nor did she feel the urge to descend upon the older portal that led to the Veil connecting all worlds. It was something else, and she might go mad if she didn't determine what.

*"Kezari,"* Aris said, a worried tone to his mental voice. *"Are you not finished hunting? If you didn't find success, there's plenty of food here. It's almost the midday meal."*

*"I do not wish to sit at a table in my elven form,"* she sent back angrily. Confusion and hurt washed back along their link, and she huffed again. At this rate, she would bring another ice storm's worth of clouds. *"Forgive me,* skizik. *That healer was particularly unpleasant last night."*

*"Lial? I thought he was rather amiable. Has been since settling things with Lynia."*

Kezari rolled over and dropped into a fall, snapping her wings out at the last moment to slow her descent. The top of the tower where Aris often slept rose toward her, and she landed on her usual spot without a sound. Cold wind rushed around her, cooling her heated body as she folded her wings against her sides.

Usually, she would take the time to bask in the frigid air, especially when it was tinged with the promise of a coming storm the way it was now. This time, there might be more snow than ice. A cushion of snow would certainly be easier to walk on when in her elven form. The lack of talons made treading on solid sheets of ice...less than ideal.

After shifting from her dragon form, she opened the hatch in the roof and climbed down into the room below. Except for a bed situated on one side and the seats built into the curve of the walls, no furniture took up space. The only thing—or rather, person—awaiting her here was Aris, who leaned against the edge of the wall at the top of the stairs. His arms were crossed, and his brows pulled down. Signs of displeasure or worry, she'd come to realize.

"Talk to me, Kezari," he said. "I can feel for myself that something is wrong."

The puny breath she exhaled in this form had no risk of causing atmospheric disturbances—far less satisfying. "I'm not sure. There is some task that needs to be done, but I have no direction as to what. Perhaps I simply have no direction."

Aris studied her silently, as deliberative as an elder attempting to divine the ways of the young—not that he was that old or she particularly youthful. He'd probably been the quiet, thoughtful type even before the torture he'd suffered at the hands of his demented almost-soulbonded. Something else Kezari could have prevented if she hadn't believed the woman and her lies.

"I'm not angry at you," Aris finally said. "Attacking Korel wasn't ideal, but you were only trying to protect me. The foul spell he carried truly threatened my sanity. According to Tynan, it was a close thing."

Kezari snorted. "Tynan. That one is an annoyance. If he wasn't so helpful to you, I would have roasted him by now."

This time, Aris's narrowed eyes held as much speculation as worry. "It's him, isn't it? He's why you're so restless. Last time, he was the one thrown into disorder by your presence, but this time, it's you."

"I see no reason for him to disturb me so," she snapped.

But her throat clenched around further rebuttal. The denial might have been instinctive, but she wasn't certain it was the full truth—and she didn't lie to her *skizik*. Yet how could she put her feelings into words? The restless, itchy feeling didn't happen around Tynan, but he *did* bother her. His presence scratched at her patience even as he drew her. She wanted to protect him and strangle him in equal measure.

Aris shoved away from the wall, but he approached with slow, measured steps. "I'm not certain that's true."

For a moment, she thought he'd followed the line of her thoughts, though she hadn't intentionally shared them. Then she recalled her previous words and the conversation she'd allowed to stall in her turmoil. He'd picked up on her lie, unintended or not.

"Perhaps not entirely," she admitted, "but I do know he isn't to blame for this restless feeling. That is a separate aggravation."

The shaky, nervous feeling that screamed at her to *Go! Fix!* felt far too akin to her distress when Earth's energy had been poisoned —yet it wasn't the same. When she sought her connection to Earth, she found no problems. But she didn't want to tell Aris, not yet. He didn't need to be burdened with more worries while he was working so hard to recover from his ordeal with Perim.

"Kezari—"

"I prefer not to speak of it anymore," she interrupted before he could pursue either issue.

He stared at her for a moment.

"Fair enough," Aris finally said, gesturing toward the stairs. "But are you really going to neglect the midday meal?"

Kezari edged her mouth into a smile at the awkward change in subject. At least she hoped it was a smile. Elven facial expressions were a strange thing, one a chronicler might spend decades researching. She, alas, was no chronicler, but today's attempt must have been close enough despite her poor study. Instead of lowered or quirked eyebrows, Aris smiled in return.

"I suppose I could enjoy some *daeri*," Kezari allowed.

Truth be told, she could always go for *daeri*.

TYNAN KNELT in front of the small altar he'd set up on his bedside table. The display was sparse, only a cube of incense and a few borrowed candles arranged across the smooth wood, but it didn't have to be fancy. Of the nine gods of Arneen, Bera was the most practical. She oversaw both good health and affliction, life and death, and there was nothing orderly or simple about those. An altar cobbled together during an unexpected healing assignment might be one of the best—or at least truest—tributes to give her.

*Or so I hope.*

Smiling at the thought, Tynan lit the incense and watched the tendrils of smoke as they curled their way upward. The scent of flowers and dried leaves, sweet and bitter, eased through him, and his shoulders lowered as the morning's stress faded away. No matter where he went, he kept a cube of this incense in his pouch. One sniff carried him back to peaceful childhood days with his tutors at the temple. He'd never been more in control than then.

Tynan took a few deep breaths to center himself before lighting the first candle, the one for Bera. Another candle for

Leres, God of the Between Seasons, followed. Then a third for Dorenal, whose sacred tree grew here at Braelyn. Should he light a fourth for Meyanen? With a sharp sigh, Tynan lowered his hand without doing so.

He would have to know what he wanted before he asked a question of the god of love.

Closing his eyes and lowering his head, Tynan began his prayers. First were those of thanksgiving, for Bera's aid and for the good graces of Leres and Dorenal in this time and place. Next, he said prayers for his patients—those he'd treated this day and those he'd helped in the past. *Especially a certain healer who won't admit that he has completely recovered, except when there's a case he insists on handling himself.* It had been, what, three or four weeks since Lial's illness? The man clearly needed divine intervention.

Tynan snorted softly at the thought, but a sudden presence filled his mind, the resounding hum of energy drowning out any other sound. *"YOU WILL HEED HIS WORDS."*

Light filled him, pure and holy, but in a heartbeat it was gone, not even the hum left behind.

Pain seared Tynan's knuckles, stone rubbing skin against bone. He blinked his eyes open. When had he braced himself against the floor? Swallowing down the knot of awe and fear, he straightened until he sat on his heels once more. Several drips of the clock passed as he stared at the strangely different altar. What—

Little tendrils of smoke danced up from the three candles he'd lit, and the incense sat cold in its little bowl.

All of them extinguished.

And not by him.

That voice hadn't been his imagination. The goddess, Bera. He'd heard of priests blessed to be in the Lady's confidence, but he'd only heard Her voice a couple of times, the last at his ordination decades ago. Why now?

*You will heed his words,* she'd said. But whose? He'd been thinking about Lial, but the man said a great many things in a day, most of them corrections or complaints about how Tynan handled a healing. Surely a goddess wouldn't concern herself with that. Perhaps She meant Ralan? The seer prince was said to speak to Lady Megelien Herself.

Arneen help him if the goddess of time and seers wanted to pass along guidance.

Tynan stood on suddenly shaky legs. He pulled in a deep breath, held it, and then let the air out in a long, soothing flow. All would be well. Lady Bera had never guided him wrong, whether she spoke to him directly or nudged him to action with energy alone. Besides, she'd said *will heed*, which implied future. If it was important enough for Her interference, he would almost certainly recognize the words when he heard them.

Though his legs still trembled a little, he did his best to shake off his worry as he left the healing tower and headed toward the main estate for the midday meal. After all, he would need all of his composure if Kezari happened to be there. She was his soulbonded—or could be. He was certain of that now, but he hadn't dared mention the possibility to her. Bonding was likely a poor choice for him, especially with her. Besides, she'd become bafflingly hostile to him over the past month.

Such as last night. He'd meant to inquire about the differences between a mate and a *skizik*, but his poor phrasing had led her to believe he conflated the two. That was his fault, of course, but she hadn't given him the opportunity to say so. Only after dinner—and her blistering explanation—had he quietly explained to Lady Selia that he had not meant to imply that her husband Aris was sleeping with Kezari.

Tynan shook his head at himself as he navigated the curved halls of Braelyn's main house. He was a mind healer who helped others through traumas and provided insight on tricky social situations, yet he inevitably fumbled the latter when Kezari was around. His control hadn't slipped—this visit—but the possibility concerned him. The sooner he could get Lial to dismiss him, the better.

The dining room table was already half-filled by Tynan's arrival, though there was always a lack of consistency as to the number of occupants here, especially at the midday meal. And there was also no telling who one might meet. In addition to Myern Lyr, third duke of Callian, and his bonded, Myerna Meli, Prince Ralan and Princess Cora sat farther down the table holding a casual conversation with Lady Selia, a renowned magic teacher, and Aris, a life mage who'd explored most of the continent over the centuries. Not to mention Kezari, their resident dragon in elven form.

Yet they dined more casually than even the priests.

It was a sharp contrast to the few meals Tynan had attended at Rekela Inai's estate, although it was true that Lady Inai had planned those as formal events from the beginning. He wouldn't know if that was how she usually dined. Despite Calai holding both the home of the second duchess along the Callian branch and a religious enclave for healer-priests, the two communities interacted less than one might expect. They certainly didn't dine together on a daily basis.

Rather than offer formal greetings to Lord Lyr as he'd attempted to do during his first visit, Tynan offered a simple "good day" to both him and Lady Meli before rounding the table toward his usual spot. He curled his fingers into his palm as he passed Prince Ralan and Princess Cora, but he didn't stop to tap his chest in salute to them, either. Ralan had made it scathingly clear that he didn't want to see such formality outside of the royal court unless his father was present—and even then, it was questionable.

*At least the children aren't here,* Tynan thought as he settled into the seat beside Cora. Not that he minded children in general, but Princess Eri in particular made him uneasy. She was a seer like her father, except she was more obviously goddess-touched. Sometimes, the power of it sparked in her eyes when she spoke, sending a frisson of unease down his spine. Megelien was not his personal goddess and was thus an even greater unknown than he was accustomed to.

He didn't like it.

Aside from that, the absence of Eri and Iren—Selia's and Aris's son—provided another boon. Tynan could avoid sitting beside Kezari. When the table was full, the only open spot was at her right hand, with Lyr's mother, Lynia, seated at the foot of the table to Tynan's right. Without the children here, he was across from Kezari. She could still pierce his heart with her angry glances, but at least he didn't have to worry about brushing against her in the process. His emotional control strained alarmingly with every touch.

Today, she resolutely ignored him, her eyes on Aris as she spoke of her latest hunt. They were the last two at the end of the table since Lial and Lynia hadn't arrived yet, so the slight was more pointed than usual, especially when Cora gave him a polite greeting. Tynan forced his gaze away from Kezari before he was trapped by the mesmerizing dance of her golden hair flowing around her thinly clad body with her every motion.

"Good day to you, too, Princess Cora," Tynan said, his voice rougher than he liked. He grabbed his water glass and took a sip. Not that dehydration was remotely the problem. "I trust that you are well?"

The lady smiled. "Just Cora, remember? And I am indeed well thanks to the excellent healers here."

As Lyr passed the first platter of food to Meli, Lynia and Lial entered, both looking a touch disheveled. Tynan's lips twitched. *I fear I'm not fully recovered,* Lial had said only two days ago. *Too much of my energy is consumed by creating these potions.* Such a flimsy excuse. Yes, Lial spent a great deal of time distilling and infusing the tinctures capable of curing the disease that had almost killed him—and could kill many if it were unleashed—but no small amount of that energy was clearly used...elsewhere.

"Forgive us for being late," Lynia said as she took her seat at the end of the table. "I wanted to get another set of potions started."

Tynan caught a hint of a sly grin from Lial as he sat to Tynan's left. It was a good thing that Lyr had found an old storage building for the distilling machines the healer had borrowed or bought from other estates, otherwise there was no telling what Tynan might have walked into on a daily basis. Kissing probably would have been the least of it. He felt lucky enough that they'd installed a short wall with a door on Lial's bedroom level so that those climbing the spiral stairs didn't have to avert their gazes and move faster.

"How goes the distribution to other healers?" Lyr asked.

"Well enough here," Lial answered calmly, but his scrunched brow foretold trouble. "However, if I am to dispense these potions outside of Moranaia, I will need assistance. I dare not travel far afield right now."

Tynan tensed, almost missing the platter of bread that Cora held out as he awaited the healer's next words. He knew without reason that this would be what he was supposed to heed, and he had to breathe through the tightness gripping his lungs. He wasn't going to like it. Why would the goddess Herself have warned him to listen otherwise? The sick, shaky feeling he'd stifled after Bera's proclamation returned in full force.

But his potential fate was unexpectedly waylaid.

"You aren't going yourself, cousin?" Ralan asked, the surprise in his tone catching the attention of the entire table. "When last I checked, you did so in at least half of the future strands. I thought those most likely, considering your disposition."

With all eyes turned toward their end of the table, Tynan leaned back so their attention would better focus on Lial. Rightfully. Tynan had never seen the other healer literally squirm before, but Lial did so now. The man's throat worked as he glanced at a blushing Lynia.

"Ah," Lial started, then coughed into his hand. "I have many tasks here that need my attention."

Arlyn, Lyr's daughter, chuckled. "When don't you?"

Though her face was still red, Lynia straightened and cast one of her pointed looks around the table. "If you must know, I'm pregnant."

A symphony of coughs, gasps, and sputters bounced around the table, most especially from Lyr, who nearly choked on a sip of wine. Tynan thought he heard an annoyed Lial mutter "Don't expect me to heal you if you almost die" toward Lyr, but the words were drowned out by congratulations and questions. Tynan relaxed against his seat. Whatever Lial had been about to say before was forgotten now—and likely would be for the rest of the meal.

"After all this time, I'm to have a sibling?" Lyr finally asked once he'd regained his composure, happiness now lighting his eyes more than surprise.

The annoyance eased from Lial's demeanor at that. "Two, though it is early yet."

"We wanted to make certain all is well before we told anyone," Lynia said. "But I didn't want Lial doing anything dangerous, so it couldn't wait."

Lial nodded. "That's why I was going to suggest an alternative. Kezari and Tynan should distribute the potions instead."

Every bit of Tynan's remaining calm shoved from his body with his sharply expelled breath.

He should have known his fate would not be delayed.

# CHAPTER TWO

K ezari's mood shifted from pleased to furious faster than a *dacri's* tail could twitch. "You wish for me to abandon my *skizik* and travel with *him*?"

Tynan flinched, and his pained expression trickled a hint of shame down the resolute wall of her anger. He didn't *try* to rile her emotions, so her rudeness was uncalled for. It was simply that he sparked something in her—aggravation, mostly, but an odd fascination, too. One she believed he shared. Though she did her best to avoid him, she felt his stares more often than he realized.

Had he invited this mission, then? There could be some hidden reason why his eyes followed her movements when he thought she wasn't looking. Perhaps he'd talked Lial into this to torment her. But if this was Tynan's plan, then he was excellent at pretending ignorance. The look he sent Lial had no small amount of frustration.

And maybe a tinge of panic?

"You have given every impression that you wish for me to remain here," Tynan said tightly. "As your eventual replacement, I believe. This seems...counterintuitive."

Kezari made a grumbling sound of agreement low in her

throat, and Aris patted her arm. "Likewise for sending Kezari without me," her *skizik* said. "We work as a team."

She studied Lial. No hint of his thoughts shadowed his face, but there was an intensity to his energy, one she'd only detected when he was healing someone. This was no reluctant agreement on his part—she would almost bet he'd created this plan himself.

"I have given this much thought," Lial said, confirming her suspicions. "According to the fairies, shapeshifters cannot be infected by the virus, so Kezari is the obvious first choice. But you are no healer, Kezari. You cannot detect who is ill, and you'll struggle to answer questions about the potion."

"Aris could do that," she pointed out.

"I need Aris to infuse new potions with life energy, and he has a wife and child to worry about, besides." Lial met her gaze, and though she caught a hint of sympathy in his eyes, she saw no lessening of resolve. "Having treated me when I was struck by the illness, Tynan is the best second choice. As to the other..." Lial's attention swung back to the mind healer. "You are correct. I do want you to remain at Braelyn after the healer's enclave is completed. And *this* is the kind of task I would do were my intended not expecting our first children."

Somewhere down the table, someone murmured, "I forgot there were two babies," but Kezari was too caught up in her personal misery to figure out who. For the healer's reasoning was unfortunately sound. She was the only one on this entire estate, save the fairies who'd walled themselves into their own enclave, who was immune to the virus capable of killing elves and fae. Tynan was the only one free to help. Wonderful.

"I could go on my own," Tynan snapped. Oh, yes, that was almost certainly panic lending an edge to his voice. He didn't want to do this any more than she did. "I'll be at risk either way."

"Alone, with no way to return if you are stricken down by illness?" Lial shook his head. "Then we would have to send multiple guides who might also become infected as they brought you back. Kezari can carry you to safety with no risk of spreading the virus to others."

Heat scalded her throat. Fortunately, she couldn't breathe fire in this form, or her response would have set the table aflame. For really, there was only one answer.

"He is correct," she ground out between clenched teeth.

Surprise flared in the mind healer's eyes, but his lips thinned. "I haven't accepted a position here. To assume I have agreed to replace him—"

"I will not consider this to be any such agreement," Lial interrupted. "But perhaps it will help you decide."

Kezari glared down at her plate as her insides roiled. For once, it seemed she couldn't stomach a slice of *daeri*. This would be torment, but it was inevitable. It might well be the universe's punishment for all of her missteps and misdeeds of late. Her negligence had caused Aris much trouble—now she could experience a shadow of that annoyance by traveling with the irritating healer.

"You should heed him," Kezari said, her eyes connecting with Tynan's. "Whatever the cost to us. We can avoid much chaos and pain by distributing the potion now."

His pale skin leeched whiter until he almost looked like Prince Vek of the Unseelie. "Yes. I suppose we should heed."

Too bad his tone didn't sound as certain as his words.

As LIAL AND Lyr began to discuss logistics and timing, Tynan shoved his plate away and struggled to reinforce his mental shields. Not that his distraction mattered. He might have offered arguments or input if it was any other journey, but what was the point? Kezari's comment confirmed what he already knew—he had to do this. His goddess commanded it, and he would do anything for Her. She'd saved his life, after all.

"I spoke to Kai's uncle Caolte this morning," Lial said, the worry in his tone catching Tynan's attention. "I almost had to travel there a couple of weeks ago to see why Naomh wasn't healing as he should, but then Caolte reported progress. But it seems that progress has reversed."

"My father is growing sicker, and my uncle didn't tell me?" Kai demanded.

Based on the conversation Tynan had accidentally overheard earlier, there was at least one other thing poor Kai didn't know. Namely that his long-dead mother was, in fact, actually alive. But Tynan wasn't going to step into that situation unless they requested a mind healer. He was too unversed in the social and political dynamics here despite his month residing at Braelyn.

Lial shrugged. "I assumed he had, so you'll have to discuss that lapse with him. In any case, I would like to send Kezari and Tynan to their realm first. Tynan can ensure that Naomh's relapse isn't due to the virus's return and deliver plenty of potions in case it was not as contained as we believed. After that, the outpost."

That brought a flare of interest to Kezari's eyes. "While I'm there, I wish to find the ancient dragon who is rumored to have awakened."

"Your mission—"

"Can still be completed," she said, interrupting Lial. "I do not know if the old ones maintain the tradition of finding a *skizik*, but if so, their *skiziks* will be as vulnerable as any other fae unless they happen to be a dragon. Also consider that the ancient dragons may be aware of fae communities that you are not. The Moranaian elves do not know everyone and everything, or you wouldn't be so often caught unaware by visitors."

Tynan's shields shuddered against the onslaught of mixed emotions her comment sent winging around the room. Bera's heart. His control over his empathy was thinner than it had been in decades if this threatened to get through. This meal needed to end, and soon.

Beside him, Princess Cora snorted. Then Arlyn chuckled and Lady Meli pressed her closed fist against her lips. The various echoes of amusement were from them, then. But why…? Ah, yes.

All three women had come from outside Moranaia. He'd grown so accustomed to them that he'd forgotten.

Lyr openly winced. It appeared that he was the source of the pain and chagrin. "And we are often negligent of our own...bloodlines...left behind there, intentionally or not. Point taken."

It took Tynan a moment to recall that Arlyn had arrived on Moranaia only a few months prior. What had Lynia told him? Something about Lyr having to leave his potential soulbonded on Earth years ago. She'd been pregnant, as it turned out, but he hadn't known. The flush on Kezari's face suggested that she remembered the story—now.

So it was her anxiety slamming against his mental shields.

"I did not intend to offer rudeness," the dragon said. "Nor judgement."

Arlyn smiled, and Lyr inclined his head. "Thank you," he said. "Nevertheless, it is something that must be considered. If you can make successful contact with the dragons still on Earth, that might be of aid. They are well suited to searching for other elves and fae, provided you can convince such ancient dragons to help."

Earth.

Had he thought apprehension had left him shaky earlier? It was nothing compared to the sick feeling churning through him now. This mission...it was more than delivering potions to a handful of fae realms. This would require searching amongst the humans on an entirely different world with completely foreign rules. He was struggling with control around Kezari now. What would happen when he added the strain of navigating an unknown culture to the mix?

"You cannot intend for me to accompany Kezari for that mission," he said. "I am neither a scout nor an explorer, and I'm as clueless about Earth as Kezari. That lack of knowledge could spell disaster."

Lyr and Lial exchanged frowns. "Another good point," Lyr

said. "One that I will consider. You'll need to check on Lord Naomh first regardless."

The calm reply did nothing to dispel the vine of fear twining through his gut. Stuck for an indeterminate amount of time on an unknown world with the potential soulbonded who eroded his control like no other? Easy enough for the others to wave that off as a small worry to ponder. They didn't know the risk. Tynan clenched his fists beneath the table and pulled a long breath in through his nose. Control was essential.

He would have to direct his energy toward maintaining it.

MOST OF THE TIME, Kezari did her best to avoid looking at Tynan, but as Lial and Lyr shifted their discussion to needed supplies and the best guide to escort them through the Veil, she couldn't help but cast glances toward the healer-priest. The man had a contained but confident nature and calm, pleasing energy—most days. Not so now. The color had yet to return to his skin, and air hissed in and out through his nose in a slow, deliberate pattern.

Was he so displeased about spending time with her that he had to take soothing breaths? She'd never dared ask if he felt such ambivalent agitation toward her, too, but if he did, perhaps he was as peeved about this mission as she was. Though, in truth, his stiff demeanor looked more worried than annoyed. Surely, she hadn't been that unpleasant to him while trying to avoid him.

Perhaps those lingering glances had been wariness.

She sensed Aris's energy at the edge of her thoughts. *"Is something wrong?"* he sent. *"You have that expression that bodes ill for the subject of your contemplation."*

*"I am not angry, merely unsettled,"* she countered. *"Tynan does not look like himself, though no one else seems to have noticed."*

Aris went quiet, and out of the corner of her eye, she saw him give the priest a quick, assessing glance. *"You're right. I don't think he appeared so discomposed even after my difficult healing."*

*"I suppose I will have to speak to him. This mission will be bad enough without discord between us. If there is any chance of an argument..."*

*"Do you wish for me to come with you?"* Aris asked.

*"I do not,"* Kezari answered at once. *"I would have him speak freely, and he may not with a patient present."*

She probably wouldn't, either, but she didn't want to offend Aris by saying so.

"If you'll pardon me," Tynan said, drawing her attention, "I'll return to my room and contact the head priest to inform her of the continued need of my presence. If there are any details of the mission needing my input, Lial can ask me telepathically."

Lyr's acknowledgement hadn't finished echoing across the table before Tynan stood, nodding to the group and then heading toward the door. Most days, his soothing energy lingered in the air like an errant gift, but he was so restrained today that the absence of his magic gave the room a hollow, mournful feel. Something was definitely wrong.

And she was going to figure out what.

Tynan's insides felt as raw and fragile as poorly formed glass, and his hands shook so badly he clenched his fingers into fists to still them. Even away from the relentless tide of emotions he'd suffered in the dining room, his control was a thin, thready thing, ready to snap. How could he have believed such tumultuous feelings had been banished? Desire, longing, sadness—those were the least of what tore through him now. The bulk of it was helpless anger. Not for Kezari or the others.

The fury, at least, was all for himself.

He'd spent so many drips of time in meditation and had consulted with another healer-priest after his first visit here, processing his mistakes. He'd acknowledged how finding a potential bonded had upset the control he'd spent his life working to attain. He'd dealt with the worry, self-doubt, and despair caused by his near-failure during Aris's healing and by his apparent—and unwise—bond with Kezari. If he hadn't, he never would have agreed to return at Aris's request. He would never abandon a patient, but he could have found some other way to help. A neutral meeting ground if nothing else.

It had gone well enough at first. Helping heal Lial from a mysterious illness had provided plenty of challenges, and he hadn't encountered Kezari at all. But in the weeks after? Tynan shuddered. He sat beside her at far too many meals, close but impossibly far. He would feel her soul sing to his even as she glared at him—a never-ending cycle of hope, rejection, and resignation. Too much more, and he would crack.

He didn't regret helping Aris or Lial, but he should have insisted on returning to the temple immediately after. Now he was bound by Lady Bera's command.

He had to get away, if only for a few drips of time so he could center himself without fear of interruption. Though he'd told the others that he was leaving to contact the high priest, that hadn't been entirely the truth. He needed to leash his emotions before he dared to do that. Otherwise, she would insist upon his return, and no matter how much he might prefer such a thing, he wouldn't risk disobeying Lady Bera.

He barely noticed the wretched cold as he plodded down the narrow, snow-covered path beyond the healing tower. Heavy flakes of snow swirled around him, lessening somewhat when he gained the shelter of the trees. At least it wasn't ice, which made walking a hazard, but the colder air that came with the snow settled more deeply into the bones. Not the best weather to need time away from others, but the clearing he'd found in the woods would at least allow the sunlight through.

He was nearly to his destination before he sensed Kezari's presence. What did she want now? Though his chest squeezed tight and his breath hitched, he sped up his steps. Not that she was likely to give up on following him. Dragons weren't exactly known for abandoning their prey.

"Tynan," Kezari called, her voice an angry snap in the dim light. "You might as well stop."

It was the last thing he should do. Already, her presence rubbed against that thin thread of control, tearing at each remaining fiber. If she continued... Tynan broke into a jog at the very thought. It wouldn't be her fault, but she would suffer his loss of control, nonetheless. That was the very reason he'd come to feel that the longed-for soulbond should never happen.

"Go back," he said over his shoulder.

Her low growl of frustration caught up to him a few drips before she did. As he broke through into the clearing, her fingers wrapped around his forearm, jerking him to an unexpected halt. His body half turned from the force, but Tynan didn't look at her. He didn't dare. Just one touch, and her worry crashed through his mental shields like one of Aris's life energy blasts.

One touch, and his longing and anger nearly choked him in equal turns.

"What is wrong with you?" she demanded. "You are not one to flee over a simple mission."

Tynan tugged his arm from her grip. "Leave. Please."

He couldn't keep the turmoil from his tone. Did she recognize the desperate frustration beneath the anger? Gods, he hoped not. If he roused her temper rather than her concern, she might leave him alone until he could calm his mind. Of course, then there would be the mission to suffer through.

How could Lady Bera ask it of him? For that matter, how could the gods give him an impossible soulbond? He'd always thought his complement would bring ease. Contentment. But as much as he longed for Kezari, he feared her. There was no peace in her presence, and peace was what he needed.

Her angry huff broke the silence. "You will tell me your affliction, or I will call Lial. You're clearly unwell."

He shouldn't be. He was supposed to be calm. Reassuring. Not this wreck of feeling, overloaded by the emotions he could normally shield against. So many decades spent hoping for a bonded, but now that he'd found her, she weakened him. And that brought only danger. His mother's pale face flashed before his eyes, and he stiffened. He could not go back to what he'd been then.

He would not.

Resentment and misery shook him, and he scrambled to contain the emotions before he blasted her with them. Kezari had to go. She had to.

"*You're* my affliction," he snapped as he turned away.

She said nothing, her indrawn breath the only sound indicating she'd heard. But her emotions—the wave of her hurt crashed over him, sweeping away some of his own tumult until his own chest ached with her pain. He hadn't intended to speak such harsh words. What kind of mind-healing priest was he?

Around her, a terrible one.

"As you are mine," Kezari finally responded in a voice colder than the snow. "I will refuse this mission if it is to be with you. Let Lial find another."

Fear erased everything, then. *You will heed his words,* Lady Bera had said. An order, and a rare, direct one. He was bound to obey or break his vow to serve Her. What would happen if Kezari refused? He couldn't plead innocence. He'd been the one to chase Kezari away. Even in that, he'd shattered his most important vow —to help, not cause harm.

He hadn't meant to hurt her. None of this was her fault. None of it.

Tynan spun on his heel, an apology on his lips, but wind and snow surrounded him in a blinding swirl as Kezari launched herself in dragon form into the sky. He hadn't even known she'd shifted. *Miaran.* She'd gone the one direction he couldn't follow.

He'd let his emotions free and once again brought ruin.

# CHAPTER THREE

The snow Kezari had sensed earlier danced around her, melting before the flakes touched her body. Condensation gathered like sweat across her heated scales, but in her current state, it did nothing to cool her. If not for the frigid air, the water would have no doubt turned to steam.

*You're my affliction.*

By her lost hoard, she was sick of this place and everyone in it, save Aris. No matter what she did, it was wrong. She couldn't even properly offer aid to someone in distress. Though she'd felt Tynan's upheaval in her own heart, frustrated demands were the only words that had escaped her lips. But what did she know of comfort? She hadn't been able to help Aris through his torment, and she hadn't done anything but anger Tynan.

*You're my affliction.*

Was this what she got for spending so many years in her cave, trying to figure out why her connection to Earth's energy felt increasingly polluted? She'd never been good at socializing, even with other dragons. Most of them had suppressed or excised their connections to Earth and thought her an oddity for having refused.

Well, now she wasn't just an oddity—she was an affliction.

*"Kezari,"* Aris sent sharply. *"What is wrong?"*

*"Tell the others that they'll send me or Tynan on their missions. Not both."* Her wingbeats carried her beyond Braelyn's borders and into Oria, but she didn't slow or turn. *"I'll not be near him again."*

Confused silence. Then, *"I should have gone with you when you talked to him."*

No matter what Aris might have meant, the comment only shoved the spear in her heart deeper. *"It wasn't I who spoke cruel words. Perhaps it is Tynan who needs a minder."*

*"I didn't—"*

*"Not now,"* she practically snarled. *"When I've worked off my anger, I'll return to my cave. Let me know when he's gone or when I'm needed to travel to Earth. Alone."*

Kezari cut off their communication link before Aris could respond. For one mad moment, she considered not turning. Just flying until her wings grew too tired to continue. But that would only take her west across the plains where there would only be more elves.

Elves, elves everywhere, with their nonsensical rules and expectations.

She wouldn't abandon Aris, though. Instead, she tipped her shoulder down until her path shifted into a curve. A slow circle back to a reality she couldn't deny. While Aris remained at Braelyn, she would, too. She only needed to avoid Tynan while doing so.

Kezari glided over the valley below the ridge where Braelyn sat. Even from the sky, she could sense the twin beacons of worry and distress—Aris and Tynan. She turned her head away and reached inside for her magic, shifting her body into a smaller form to dive between the trees. When she reached the entrance to her cave, she forced her body even smaller and slipped through the thin fissure, one that a determined elf would have to work to fit through.

She worked her way through the twisting tunnels she'd carved to the heart of her underground home. As soon as Kezari landed in her favorite cavern, she shifted again—only to find that she'd chosen her elven form. She growled a curse and changed at once to her full, beautiful, *preferred* dragon form. Clearly, she'd spent too much time above of late.

Meditation time in her cave would do her good.

LIAL'S MAGIC told him the healing tower was empty before he stepped through the door. He'd given Tynan plenty of time to reach his room and contact the high priest. Had the man come and gone? Lial hadn't passed anyone on the path, but with the snow falling heavily, he might have missed the priest if he'd taken the trail leading to the garden.

In her little bed beside the workbench, Emowa stretched and blinked up at him. The *camahr* had the hazy-eyed look typical of one of her long naps, which meant if Tynan had been here, he hadn't awakened her. That...wasn't normal for her. According to Maddy, Elan, and Tynan, the young kit watched them while Lial was gone as though worried they were plotting mischief.

Had the mind healer lied about his intentions?

A knock sounded at the door, and Lial opened it to find Aris. "Are you unwell?" Lial asked.

"For once, it isn't me," Aris answered, concern lining his face. "I just spoke to Kezari. She'd gone to talk to Tynan, and whatever happened... She's now refusing to go on any mission with him."

Well, that was an unfortunate complication. "She gave no hints as to why?"

Aris rubbed at his chin for a moment before nodding. "She mentioned something about Tynan being the one to say cruel words. But Tynan? Cruel? I believe her, but I can't credit what kind of argument would have led to that. Though he wasn't himself at the table."

Lial searched his memory of the midday meal. The healer-priest had been displeased by the mission, but he'd appeared resigned to the necessity. Unfortunately, as Lial had discussed logistics with Lyr, he'd stopped paying as much attention to Tynan. Aris—and presumably Kezari—hadn't done the same since the dragon had sought the man out.

Was this why the priest hadn't returned to the tower? Uneasiness slid through Lial. Aris was right—Tynan was not inclined toward cruelty. Perhaps there'd been more to the man's objections than Lial had realized. Unfortunately, the mind healer wasn't here to ask. With a sigh, Lial lifted the hood of his cloak once more. Nothing to do but to go find him.

"I'll speak to Tynan," Lial said. "Any idea where I should start searching?"

Aris shrugged. "I sense Tynan's life energy to the south, but I haven't walked those woods enough to give an exact location. I could help you track him if you need."

Though he would normally accept the explorer's help, Lial had a hunch about where Tynan might have gone in that section of the forest. Besides, there had to be a reason the healer had gone off by himself. If he wanted to be around others, he no doubt would have come in from the cold.

"Not yet." Something brushed his cloak against his leg, and Lial glanced down to find Emowa at his side. "I believe I can find him, especially since it seems I won't be alone."

"Call me if you need," Aris said as Lial stepped into the cold and closed the door behind him.

"I will." Hopefully, it wouldn't be necessary, but one never knew. "I would tell you to broach the topic with Kezari if I thought she was calm. That doesn't seem likely."

Aris winced. "Indeed not. I have never felt such...hurt, I suppose. Not from her. Anger, yes, and worry. But not that flavor of emotional pain. Whatever he said wounded her deeply."

"Lovely," Lial muttered.

After bidding Aris farewell, Lial sent Lynia a quick update about his change in plans and then told Elan to return to the healing tower in case the snow brought any injuries. It was easy enough to monitor the tower when he was close, but there was no telling how long he'd be out in the woods—or what he would find when he did reach Tynan. As Lial followed a prancing Emowa down the path, he reinforced his shielding. An out-of-control mind healer could do more mental damage than anyone wanted to suffer.

Unfortunately, the mind tended to be easier to damage than to repair.

~

ENDLESS TIME PASSED, but Tynan couldn't force his feet into motion. He could have been an icicle, frozen to the spot where Kezari had left him. Normally, he would have moved to the stones tumbled in the center of the clearing like a blessing, but he hadn't been able to find the will. If only his emotions were equally frozen.

His core blazed with feelings, and like a weary mountain, he struggled to hold back the explosion with the weight of time-honed will. No matter how it singed his insides, he couldn't yield. So he breathed against the burn and prayed to Bera with all his might.

*Don't let me slip. Please don't let me slip.*

By slow degrees, he rebuilt his mental shields enough to ensure his pain would remain his alone. *Finally.* Sweat chilled against his skin, and his legs shook so badly he could barely stand. Only then did he stumble over to the boulder where he sometimes meditated. He boosted himself atop the stone as clumsily as a child climbing onto a stool, but he no longer had the energy to care. Had it not been so cold, he would have lain back on the wide, flat rock.

Tynan pinched his eyes closed and practiced the deep breathing he'd been taught. His heartbeat began to slow and his tension eased, but that only allowed his mind to wander. Though he should have directed any stray thoughts away, he found he couldn't. There was simply too much to process. Stifling reality wouldn't help.

He hadn't been so close to losing control since he'd almost killed his mother.

His entire body shook at the hint of the memory, but he couldn't ignore that truth, either. He'd learned then, at the age of seven, that an empath had to maintain mastery over their emotions at all times. Their shields, too, for if the first failed, the second had to prevent those feelings from consuming others. And he'd nearly allowed both to slip as catastrophically as they had the first time.

Even out here, there was risk of harm. There were guards stationed in the trees, and although he couldn't see them, Tynan could sense at least one nearby. They certainly didn't deserve to be crushed beneath an onslaught of his distress, nor did anyone who might wander close. It would be unforgivable to cause more pain.

"Tynan?"

He didn't have to look to recognize that voice. "Go away, Lial."

"Would you leave if our situations were reversed?"

Tynan snorted at the only obvious answer—Lial wasn't going anywhere. But he had to at least try to discourage the man. "You're at risk here, especially if you can't keep your emotions to yourself."

Wind whipped through the trees, clattering branches together overhead. Tynan opened his eyes as more snow dusted down on them from the tumult above. Across the clearing, Lial cast a quick, annoyed glance upward, and at his feet, Emowa shook her fur to clear it. The palest blue glow lit the tip of the *camahr*'s upstretched tail. A shield against him?

If so, she was a wise animal.

"Curious that you've never mentioned being an empath," Lial said, his tone far too casual for the intensity of the gaze he turned on Tynan. "Is that to blame for your initial error with Aris?"

Tynan rubbed wearily at the bridge of his nose. "Not exactly. My shields held well enough, but I had...concerns...about how long they would do so with Kezari around. It made me rush to proceed when I otherwise wouldn't have."

"An empathic mind healer." Lial studied him for a moment in silence. "That's a blessing and a curse. How can you bear others' trauma?"

*Partly because little of it is greater than my own,* Tynan thought. But that was more than he wished to reveal. "I spent a solid century building my shields, and the priests taught me meditation methods to keep me grounded. When all is well, I'm able to help reroute others' mental channels without directly touching the emotions behind the trauma. But around Kezari..."

Lial took a few steps closer. "You should have told me this."

"Really?" Tynan straightened, annoyance flashing through him. "I was not aware that I was required to confess my every talent and personal struggle when filling in for you, especially when you haven't been the most forthcoming about your own health. Or are you going to claim once again that you haven't fully recovered?"

One side of Lial's mouth tipped up. "I have perhaps exaggerated my energy levels, but I do need you here. I could never distill so many potions while taking care of the estate."

"An argument you could have made instead of misleading me, but you feared I would refuse to stay." Tynan stood, and the glow of Emowa's tail brightened. "Why are you so determined to have me replace you? I am clearly not suited."

Once again, Lial studied him, but Tynan refused to squirm beneath his regard. They both knew it was a fair question. Although the answer might have already changed, of course. Having shaky control of one's empathy was a danger that couldn't be ignored, and Lial wasn't one to disregard the safety of others.

"There are several reasons," Lial finally said. "You have multiple skill sets that we've needed of late, and you're young, adaptable, and open-minded. This estate guards the gate to Earth and all connected fae realms. As such, the unexpected is prone to happen. We can't have someone so staid that they would refuse to treat a foreign visitor...or half-bloods like Arlyn."

Tynan wrinkled his nose. "What healer would do such a thing?"

"I haven't encountered one, but I wouldn't have expected much of the treachery I've seen the last few months," Lial said. "Which is another reason why flexibility is important. I fear there are more surprises to come, and we must adjust to meet them."

"And this day gives evidence of my readiness for such?" Tynan's chuckle sounded harsh to his own ears. "You jest. With Kezari around, I'll be the disaster that needs fixing."

Lial smiled slightly. "Not if you can discern why she upsets your control. I do not believe the high priest would have sent you here if you were normally volatile."

"As simple as that," Tynan snapped. He shoved his hand through his hair and tugged. "As though I haven't spent the weeks since my first visit trying to understand that very thing. Is it the bond? Her dragon nature? My own insecurities? I have no answer. It would be better to leave."

Something dark and sad shifted in Lial's gaze. "Don't be so quick to give up on a bond. There are some regrets that take centuries to heal."

"An interesting observation."

Lial shrugged. "Take it or leave it. But consider the mission to Naomh's realm, at least. Being alone with Kezari for that brief task might clarify things."

"Or end in disaster," Tynan protested, though the suggestion had merit. They wouldn't be entirely alone, of course, but they would be away from others on the estate. They could talk without fear of well-meaning interference. Except... "Of course, you forget that Kezari won't go anywhere with me now. I...might have called her an affliction. I meant in that moment while my control was so unsteady, but it was a poor thing to say, regardless."

The other healer winced. "I wish you good fortune with that apology."

"It seems unwise to offer one now." Tynan sighed. "As tenuous as my hold has been on my shields..."

"Oh?" Lial's smile was wider—and perhaps a bit smug—this time. "They seem to be fine now, as do you. Even Emowa agrees."

Tynan blinked down at the *camahr*, only then realizing that her tail no longer glowed. He took stock of himself and his shields and then chuckled wryly to find them in order once again. It seemed that Lial had helped with his words more than it had seemed. Distraction. A time-honored healer's technique.

"So they are," Tynan admitted. "But unless there's urgency to the task, I'll not seek out Kezari yet. I wouldn't blame her for the roasting, but I have no desire to be dinner. Besides, I'll need time to formulate the proper words. I'm not certain she will forgive me."

Lial gestured back toward the path. "How about some potion distilling to clear your head?"

"Not my favorite task, but in this case, it's a good choice," Tynan said before heading to the trail.

He wouldn't have believed it possible a mark or two ago, but his mood had lightened. A twilight glow, perhaps, but a welcome improvement from the darkness of before.

LYR REREAD the same paragraph for the third time, but by the end, he still couldn't recall what it said. Sighing, he leaned back in his chair and rubbed his fingers against his temples. He'd feared his attempt to return to work after the midday meal would be a futile one, and he'd been right. How was he supposed to focus on the weekly report on the food stores in Telerdai after learning he was going to be a brother?

It wasn't something he'd considered in centuries. Even before his father had died twenty-two years ago, he hadn't thought much about the possibility of a sibling, not since he'd learned how long his parents had been bonded before his own birth. Really, he'd been focused on his training and then on traveling to Earth and other realms to help his father. Being an only child was one of those things that technically *could* have changed but mostly felt like an immutable fact.

Now he was going to have two siblings.

Two.

Gods, life was a strange thing. Just a year ago, he and his mother had both been muddling through life—only surviving, really. He'd buried himself in work to avoid thinking about the bonded he'd had to leave on Earth, and his mother had spent long hours reading in the library or sleeping. They'd rarely bothered to have dinner together unless they had visitors. The long, empty table had been too depressing to face on a regular basis.

Twenty years of pretending that their lives hadn't been shattered.

Then Arlyn had arrived, stunning him with her very existence. The daughter he hadn't known his bonded had carried. The blessing he didn't deserve. Now she was soulbound to his friend Kai and expecting their first child. And Lyr's lost bonded had been reborn as Meli—another bit of fortune he didn't deserve.

He had Ralan, the crown prince, here with his family, and Selia and her son had come to help train Arlyn to use her magic. Then trouble with Earth's energy had brought Aris, Selia's lost husband, and the dragon Kezari to Braelyn. His mother and Lial had fallen in love—though Lial might argue that it was Lynia who'd needed to catch up. Now they had a visiting mind healer and a plague to finish thwarting. Each day held the promise of new chaos.

Surprisingly, he loved it.

Not the negative aspects, of course. He could do without assassins, betrayals, and mystery illnesses. But the rest of the upheaval was the best kind, more than worthwhile if it chased away the dull, sad monotony of the previous twenty years. If he could resolve the worst of their problems, life would be perfect. Perhaps he and Meli would be blessed with more children, too, and Braelyn would echo with the laughter its walls had too long been denied.

But as Kai had once succinctly put it—first, they had to get their shit together.

Based on what the fairies had told Kai, their current difficulties stemmed from unresolved mistakes. Unfortunately, they hadn't been willing or able to give details. Lyr could infer what some of those were. He hadn't checked to see if Aimee was pregnant before leaving Earth, thus accidentally abandoning Arlyn—an error hopefully resolved. Allafon's perfidy had gone too long undetected, and they were still finding victims of that.

However...Lyr had a feeling the fairies referred to deeper, older problems. The ancient war with the dragons had led to the dragons sequestering themselves on a distant island. Instead of maintaining their connection to Earth's energy, they stifled or severed the link. If not for Kezari, they might have missed the poisoned energy on Earth. And Meren of the Seelie claimed to be the former king's lost heir, a person who'd almost caused a war in that realm once. Had it been in Lyr's father's time? His grandfather's? What had the Moranaians done during the conflict?

He made a note to speak to his mother about the matter.

The communication mirror chimed, and Lyr stood to face the tall, smooth glass. With a flick of his magic, his reflection was replaced by another—Tarah, guardian of the London gate. He'd only spoken to her a handful of times, one of those during his only trip through her gate a couple of hundred years ago. He hadn't understood why she'd wanted to live in the overcrowded, stinking city teeming with pollution and refuse, but according to Kai, the place had improved greatly in the last two centuries.

"Good day, Tarah," Lyr said. "I hope all is well."

Her smile held a curiously wry slant. "Good day. Things are

fine enough, but I'd call them more interesting than well. I don't suppose you've read my recent report?"

Had he? Lyr did a mental calculation of the papers stacked on his desk. "No, not yet. I should do so today or tomorrow. I take it I should do so sooner?"

"Eh, well..." Tarah's voice trailed off, and a man moved to her side. Even through the mirror, his energy pulsed. "It depends on our diplomatic status with the dragons."

*Miaran.* Perhaps their problems had decided to present themselves.

## CHAPTER FOUR

After a solid mark's time of measuring potion ingredients, Tynan had regrets. Agreeing to this particular task for starters. It wasn't that he hated making potions—he'd done his fair share of that at the temple. Lately, however, he and Lial took turns in the workshop creating as many cures as they could until even the excitement of refining a new treatment had worn down to dull monotony. And what did monotony allow?

Thinking time.

That would be a boon if not for his other, greater, regret—his harsh words to Kezari. No matter how he considered an apology, he couldn't think of anything he could say to atone for lashing out like that. Not without admitting the full truth about his talents and his past. But he couldn't do that without ruining any possible chance of a bond.

Tynan scoffed. *There's hardly a chance regardless.* Even so, he couldn't release that sliver of hope that whispered *maybe* despite it all. Part of him knew he shouldn't let go of it. If a patient were telling him of this situation, he would have advised them to maintain their optimism in the face of potential rejection. Unfortunately, he couldn't convince himself. Why was it always simpler to help others with their problems than to handle his own?

Suddenly, the door to the distilling room opened, but instead of Lial, Aris walked through. Tynan barely managed to hide his grimace. There was a certain awkwardness to a patient witnessing one's bad behavior, and though Aris hadn't been physically present for the confrontation, being connected to Kezari was close enough. But despite the embarrassment, Tynan wouldn't hide from his actions.

He'd never claimed to be perfect.

"Good afternoon, Tynan," Aris said, no hint of his mood in his expression. "Do you have a moment?"

Had his control not been so fragile, Tynan might have lowered his shields enough to discern the other man's emotions— or at least a hint. But not today. "I suppose you want to rebuke me for hurting Kezari."

Aris shook his head. "I will not step so deeply into a conflict I know so little about. Whatever was said between you, she didn't share the details with me, only that it was cruel. As that is not typical of you, I wanted to see how you fared. And that was before I spoke to Lyr."

Was Lord Lyr involved now, too? Sighing, Tynan set down the flask he'd finished preparing and dusted his hands off before turning. "I was...overcome."

"So I suspected," Aris said. "But you needn't explain. Of all people, I am the last to demand the details of another's pain. I am merely relieved to see that you seem well-recovered now."

"Well enough." Tynan couldn't say whether it was the other man's quiet support or unfortunate, intimate acquaintance with trauma, but Tynan found himself continuing. "I told you once that the mind doesn't heal without scars. I have...reason to know. Unfortunately, Kezari unsettles me without even trying, and that has stirred emotions better left buried."

Aris leaned against the workbench. "Curious. I could have sworn there was something besides disharmony between you."

"She is my soulbonded," Tynan blurted. *Now I've done it.* But at the admission, cool relief rushed through him, and he blinked at the surprising sensation. He hadn't felt any such thing when he'd told Lial a few weeks back. "I have not mentioned the possibility of a bond to Kezari. Her feelings toward me appear complicated enough."

"I'd wondered." Aris's lips pursed. "But isn't that a good thing? You were eager to find someone, a potential bonded or otherwise, on your first visit here."

Heat crept up the back of Tynan's neck. "So I was. But that was before I spent so much time around Kezari. We spark against each other in ways that threaten my control. I'm a maelstrom of emotions, and if I lose myself again, I fear I will never recover. Not this time."

"Interesting." The life mage's regard settled over Tynan like a heavy winter cloak. "I'm curious to know if your current plan is to ignore the situation. I do believe it was you who told me that our thoughts and emotions need tending the most, lest our foundation crumble."

Tynan's breath hissed out at the well-deserved remark. He had said that very thing before healing Aris's trauma, and he'd meant it. Unresolved pain led to more hurt, for oneself and for any who happened near. It built beneath the surface of a person's mind and chipped away at parts unseen. It didn't tend to disappear on its own.

Returning to the temple right now would solve nothing. Gods. Hadn't he essentially tried that very thing when he'd gone back after Aris's initial healing? He might have worked through some of his own emotions, but deep inside, he'd known the situation wasn't settled. It wouldn't be until he spoke to Kezari about their potential bond.

"You're right to point out my inconsistency," Tynan offered. "Thank you."

Aris inclined his head. "It is the least I can do. Unfortunately, though, I can't advise you to take your time settling things with Kezari. She has blocked me from reaching her telepathically, but she is needed at the estate. Lyr sent me to find both of you."

That gave Tynan pause. Was it not the argument itself that had caught Lord Lyr's attention? "I cannot imagine he has settled upon the details of the mission so soon."

"As far as I know, he has not," Aris said. "However, it seems he heard from one of the portal guardians on Earth. She had one of the ancient dragons with her, and he wants to speak to the queen of the Moranaian dragons. It seems he wishes to know why the barrier holding back Earth's energy was allowed to fall."

A chill fear lifted the hairs on Tynan's arms. Kezari had intended to find the ancient dragons, but he had no idea what she'd planned to do if she succeeded. Had it occurred to her that they might be angry? Suddenly, even time alone with her on a foreign planet paled against the worry of what the coming confrontation might bring.

One thing was certain—this was too important to allow their argument to interfere. A conflict between dragons on two different planets linked by a mere two portals? Not good. Especially if both sides viewed the Moranaian elves as obstacles. This would require careful negotiation.

"It might be best for you to accompany Kezari if this meeting takes place on Earth," Tynan said. "I suspect the discussion will be tense enough without our current disagreement."

Aris's brows shot up. "You want to send me into a difficult situation with the promise of violence? Even if my mental channels weren't saw raw from my...trauma, I am an explorer. I have little talent for diplomacy."

"I am hardly a diplomat, myself," Tynan argued.

"What is a mind healer if not that?" Aris's lips took on a wry twist. "Gods know I was at war with myself, but you've helped repair that. It's your greatest strength. You find the discord within your patient's mind and smooth out those conflicts. If you can point out false thinking in a single mind, why not misunderstandings between two?"

It made more sense than Tynan wanted to admit, but he couldn't ignore the logic. "I'm still not certain how to apologize."

Aris shrugged. "You'll figure it out. You can think it through while I show you the entrance to the cave she's taken as her own. Bundle up."

Resigned, Tynan walked over to the hook by the door and shrugged his cloak around his shoulders. He secured the hood over his head and gathered the fabric close in front of his body as Aris opened the door. Snow drifted around them in a slow fall, the flakes light enough that they almost appeared to float. The drifts along the ground almost reached his ankles now, deeper than when he'd entered the building.

It was going to be an interesting hike—especially since the sun had already gone down. With only three weeks until the winter solstice, dark fell far too early. Good thing for him that Aris had volunteered to guide him. Otherwise, Tynan wouldn't relish attempting to hike down into the valley and along the cliffs in the cold dark.

"Let's go," Tynan said.

*Here's hoping I don't get eaten.*

～

KEZARI SHIVERED with awareness the moment Tynan stepped into the tunnel leading to her private cave. It would take some time for him to reach her, provided he didn't give up at some of the narrower fissures. Did she want him to give up? Her tail flicked against the stone floor, scattering a few stalactite fragments she hadn't bothered to smooth away. She had no clue if she wanted him to give up.

He brought her far too many mixed emotions.

Her anger had mellowed to embers in the peace of the cool cavern, but the hurt remained, as persistent and painful as a poorly grown scale. Now there was this discomfort—this restless, anxious waiting. It crawled over her like a swarm of insects searching for a vulnerable place to bite. Not usually a problem for a dragon, but Tynan had left her feeling raw and exposed.

Kezari closed her eyes and sank her awareness into the ground until she could almost feel Tynan's steps atop her own body. Unlike during their last encounter, his energy wound so tightly around him she was surprised that he could bear it. Had he always been so contained? She'd tried so hard to avoid him that she'd never looked beyond his calm façade.

That had clearly been a mistake.

Now that her ire had lessened, questions poured in. What roiled beneath Tynan's surface so stringently that he would lash out with such callous disregard? Did darkness lie beneath his apparent affability? Had her own inexperience with elves and their mannerisms led her to misread his true nature?

Why did she care so much?

Even as she stored away each question, gems she could take out and examine in more detail later, Kezari followed his progress through the tunnels. Her heartbeat accelerated until the floor trembled slightly beneath her body from the force of it. She unfolded her wings enough to shake them, then tucked them against her side once more. Her tail twitched away a few more stone fragments.

Heavens above. She was nervous—maybe even eager—for him to arrive. A hint of steam curled from her nostrils. He'd called her an affliction, and she awaited him like a lover trembling in anticipation of her first mating flight. Had life with the elves stolen her pride? He deserved nothing but scorn for the way he'd treated her.

Kezari curled her tail around her legs and relaxed her wings. She could turn her energy toward smoothing away those crumbled stalactites. And it might not be a bad idea to create multiple rooms in this cavern system. How satisfying would it be to force Tynan to wait in an antechamber until she was ready to see him?

Very.

∼

TYNAN STUDIED the narrow fissure he would undoubtedly have to slide through. Somehow. Had this always been here, or had Kezari created this to punish him? She was certainly capable—he could sense her energy linked with the stones around him, and he'd heard how she'd reshaped the outpost on Earth. But whether a regular defense or a moment of spite, it was an effective deterrent for any who couldn't shapeshift.

Unexpectedly, a chuckle tickled its way up his throat. He created inner protections and she outer, both designed to prevent others from getting too close. Perhaps it was that which called their souls together. Would she react as poorly to an incursion of that defense as he had? Considering all that had passed between them, it seemed likely.

Sending the mage globe hovering above him into the fissure, Tynan approached. He'd only made it a short distance before he had to turn sideways to fit. Naturally. The rough stone grabbed and picked at his heavy cloak with each sidling step, and best he could tell, the way would only get narrower. He eased back out long enough to remove his cloak and fold it to the side of the fissure. It was unfortunate that he wore his robes, but he would have to make do. If the stubborn dragon wouldn't even answer her *skizik*'s call, Tynan would have to force his way through.

Once again, he slid into the breach. He sidled his way through, sometimes twisting in almost painful ways to make it past awkwardly shaped gaps. More than once, the long fall of his robes tangled around his legs, and the sharp rip of rending fabric sounded alongside a breathy curse as he sucked in his stomach to squeeze through a tight spot. Drops of water plopped down from above, tiny icicles needling his scalp when they slipped through his short hair.

Tynan gritted his teeth and pressed onward.

Finally, he freed himself from the strangling fissure. Hunching over, Tynan rested his hands on his knees and sucked in air. His skin stung in a thousand little places from tiny scrapes, and his lungs burned. There had been too little air and too little room to draw more than a shallow breath. Gods. Was this what it felt like to be born? If so, he was happy not to remember.

Tynan used a touch of healing magic to ease the ache, though he didn't bother to repair every scrape. He would only earn more on the return journey from the cave. Instead, he straightened and studied the passage where he now stood. It was far broader, but he couldn't see very far before it curved abruptly to the right. He could only hope there wasn't another fissure around the bend.

He stepped over and around murky puddles formed by the water dripping from above, but his robes grew damp around his ankles despite his best efforts. Tynan sighed. He should have been considering his apology, but his mind was too focused on the twin beacons of discomfort and survival to form coherent words. How did Kezari bear it down here?

With each step through the twisting tunnels, the hum of her energy strengthened. His skin prickled, but he couldn't tell if it was from anticipation or fear. And wasn't that the very nature of their shaky relationship? He couldn't divine his own emotions, much less hers. No doubt it was much the same for Kezari.

The air began to warm, as much a sign of her presence as her magic singing around him. There was nothing chill about *her* nature. Tynan found himself smiling at the thought. She was expressive enough that it was rare for a person to need to hunt down her opinions on anything, so in that, he supposed he was unique. With good fortune, he wouldn't be the first elf to feel the bite of her sharp teeth.

Let another have that distinction.

But how to avoid it? This passage remained clear, if twisty, finally freeing his mind to mull his apology. How much could he bear to tell her? Outside of the temple, Tynan didn't speak of his parents, and rarely there. But surely it wouldn't be necessary to go that far. He didn't often share that he was empathic, either, but that would be the least painful choice.

Then the tunnel opened up into a large cavern, and abruptly, Kezari was there. Very there. In the open air, her dragon form was huge, but nestled in the cave, she appeared massive. She faced away from him so that the sweep of her tail, her side, and one wing were the first things he saw. Her golden scales glistened in the light somehow imbued into the walls, and for that moment before he had her attention, he let himself admire her sheer beauty.

Her tail swept around, the tip barely missing him as she turned. The ground trembled beneath his feet, and his heart jolted with instinctive fear at her size. Her power. A single one of the claws clacking against the floor could rend him open so thoroughly not even Lial would be able to repair the wound. Then she shifted enough for her head to snake around, and he shuddered.

Unblinking, Kezari stared him down like a predator scenting an easy meal. Her mouth was slightly parted, revealing teeth the size of his leg—or maybe his entire body. Uncanny. The thin, protective spines framing her face and the twin horns at the top didn't exactly bring comfort, either.

But despite all that, the visceral dread didn't consume him. It was instinct, not knowledge or belief. The emotion of fear didn't threaten to shake his control. Somehow, with a certainty he couldn't credit or define, he knew she wouldn't hurt him.

If only he could be so sure that he wouldn't hurt her.

# CHAPTER FIVE

*Elder's bones,* Kezari snarled to herself. She hadn't had time to complete the new chamber. There would be no waiting now, not while Tynan stared up at her like a brave but foolish *daeri*. Didn't he fear her? Under the circumstances, she would have expected such, but although there was a wariness to his stance, he hardly cowered. She couldn't resist letting out a slow, hissing stream of smoke.

But instead of flinching, Tynan chuckled, one side of his mouth curving up in wry amusement. "Really, Kezari?"

She bared her teeth in a dragon's grin. *"So confident that I won't eat you, then?"*

"Not precisely." He shrugged. "But the steam suggests that you won't. You're not the type to give warning when you're already certain of your intent."

Kezari's wings twitched at the blow. Wasn't it that very tendency that had caused such trouble for Aris and the others? But she detected no hint of maliciousness in Tynan's demeanor— no indication that he'd meant his words poorly. He was all calm coolness now, no sign of the turmoil that had surrounded him when he'd called her an affliction.

Well, his aura was composed, at least. His physical appearance certainly didn't match. Had she ever seen him in such a miserable, disheveled state? His robes were tattered and torn in multiple places, snagged bits of the fine embroidery sticking out like the spines of a desert plant. She spotted a few scrapes and smears of dirt on his hands and face. Only his short, pale hair looked the same, complete with the lock that tended to slip down against his forehead.

He gave the lock an absent flick, but it refused to smooth in with the rest of his hair. "I want to apologize," he said softly.

Of course he did. Even if he'd meant what he said earlier, she doubted a mind healer would allow such a conflict to go unaddressed. *"It is not necessary,"* she sent. *"We can avoid each other well enough."*

Tynan took a step forward. "No. Our earlier reasons for going on those missions still stand, but more... You deserve an apology."

*"Do I?"* Her tail whipped against the floor with a snap. *"If I truly cause you distress, then you were only being honest."*

And it was clear that she did cause him irritation. She had from the beginning. Hadn't he begun Aris's healing in haste because he'd wanted to complete it while she'd been flying far from the estate? He avoided her at every turn, much as she'd begun to do for him.

Though Tynan's lips thinned, he didn't respond with anger. "I would not call it distress, not the way you probably mean. Can you not feel what I do, Kezari? The link between us?"

Her heart pounded hard at his words, and the flick of her tail drummed a rain of tiny stalactites down from above. She grabbed them with her magic before they hit Tynan and melded the fragments back into the ceiling. Far too close. As he frowned up at the averted disaster, Kezari shifted to her elven form.

She blinked hard, adjusting to the change in perspective. Her snug home was now a massive cavern, and the man she should be arguing with had her feeling everything but anger. She wanted to call it mere confusion, but that would be a blatant lie. So would a denial of a link between them.

The nature of that connection...that was what confounded her.

Kezari crossed the now vast space between them until he was almost in reach. "There is no reason for anything to tie us."

Tynan rubbed at his cheek, smearing another line of dirt across his pale skin. "When I said you were my affliction, I didn't mean *you*. It's this connection that draws me toward you even as it throws my emotions into turmoil. The effects of that are the cause of my trouble. You... You're like the world's fire, a core of beauty and light it might kill me to touch."

It wasn't her smaller lungs that drew her breath short. "Am I so dangerous?"

He muttered a string of expletives worthy of Fen. "No. It's... Do dragons not have soulbonds, Kezari?"

"What?"

This time, she was the one frozen like a *daeri*. Was he suggesting that she and he...?

"The draw I feel toward you." His throat worked. "You're my soulbonded. I'm certain of it."

What he said had to be impossible. Oh, not technically. There had been rare instances of bonding between elves and dragons in the past, though she'd never known anyone who'd linked in such a way, not even dragon to dragon. Many believed the method to do so was lost. For such a thing to happen to her, and with Tynan? He had to be wrong.

For once, she felt cold.

NORMALLY, Kezari's skin was a golden tan, much like the elves of the plains, but at his words, she went decidedly...pasty. His heart twisted, and the pain only speared deeper when she shook her head in denial. But what had he expected? His declaration would have been difficult to face even when they hadn't been arguing.

"You needn't address that now," he hastened to reassure her. "But it is relevant. When I'm around you, my feelings tangle and snarl. It isn't your fault. It simply is. However, control is vital for me. When you found me in the forest, I was on the edge of losing it."

She studied him in silence, her body so still it was uncanny. Then she tilted her head in a bird-like manner—or dragon-like, he supposed. "And if you lose control? What happens then?"

Memory flashed behind his eyes. His mother, curled into a ball on the floor, her voice a strangled mess of broken cries that never ceased. "Pain."

Her head tilted the other direction, and the imitation of her dragon form's movements amused him enough that he could push away the dark memories. For now. Maybe one day, he would learn how to put them to rest—gods knew he'd already tried.

"You did well delivering that pain to me earlier," she said.

Her words were calm, but the ache threading her tone told another tale. Regret tightened his voice. "I'm sorry. But in this case, that's not what I meant. I'm...I'm an empath. If my control slips too far, I'm flooded with others' feelings. I drown in them."

"Is that so?" Kezari's flat expression revealed nothing of her thoughts as she studied him. "Well, I am no peaceful oasis. You must be mistaken about a soulbond, for there is no way we would ever suit. Leave me to my cave, Tynan. We'll have to seek another solution for distributing the potions."

If it was Lady Bera's wish that he work with Kezari and he'd ruined the possibility... Once again, fear pecked at his restraint. "No. We are needed. You have a right to your continued anger, but if—"

"I am no longer angry," Kezari interrupted. "I understand. For whatever reason, my presence threatens your shielding, and it is that which becomes affliction. My connection to Earth has caused me similar troubles. We cannot solve it, so we must avert it."

She retreated a few steps, and her power began to gather as

though she was preparing to shift. Somehow, he knew that if she did, he would never convince her to come back to the estate with him—or to speak with him at all. Tynan darted forward and grabbed her wrist. The heat of her—body and spirit—singed him to the core, shaking his foundation.

But he couldn't let her go.

"Don't," he said as she bared her teeth. "Don't be so quick to abandon everything."

Lady Bera help him, he wanted to say "me."

"You make no sense," Kezari hissed. "My solution is the reasonable one."

"It isn't the right one." Tynan couldn't resist stroking the soft inside of her wrist with his thumb. Just once. "My goddess told me to heed Lial, or so I believe. We all decided this plan is best. Now that you know about my trouble, you need only give me space if my empathy threatens to slip from my hold."

Her eyes narrowed, and she tugged at her arm. "Tynan—"

"You're needed at the estate, Kezari." He released her wrist but not her gaze. "And not just for our mission. Lyr heard from one of the ancient dragons on Earth, and he's demanding an audience. Think on the rest if you must, but at least return for that."

She didn't immediately answer, at least not with words. With a flare of her magic, she shifted into a smaller version of her dragon form. An adorable version, truth be told. His lips twitched at the thought, but he didn't dare voice it. Even a tiny stream of fire would burn.

*Let's go,* Kezari sent. Her tiny head bobbed as she looked him up and down. *I'll broaden the passage through before your robes become shreds.*

Though Tynan grimaced at the state of his appearance, there wasn't anything he could do about it at the moment. He merely nodded. "Thank you."

Sooner than he might have expected, he was slinging his cloak back over his shoulders. Caving with a dragon apparently had its advantages.

~

QUEEN ARA SLID her fingertip over the rough scrap of paper, but her frown wasn't focused on the words scribbled on top. She had those memorized well enough: *M.R. moves to gather more fae descendants even as he riles them to action. They'll try something on Earth soon, but I have heard no solid plan.* A worrying report from her spy, and for more than one reason.

M.R.—Meren Rianehd, the Sidhe lord who claimed to be the rightful king of the Seelie court. While that was mostly a problem for Queen Tatianella, it affected the Unseelie court, too. Particularly since Meren had been led to believe that Ara was an ally and now sought retribution. He'd already attempted to sway her son to his side, and on Earth, he was seeking humans with Unseelie blood.

The question now was what Meren hoped to accomplish.

Fen, her son and heir, had somehow managed to form a fragile accord between the Unseelie and Seelie courts, but the connection was shaky enough that Ara hesitated to contact the Seelie queen with this new information. Fen and his mates might have chased Meren away during the conflict, but that aid only brought so much cooperation between their peoples. Besides, Tatianella surely had spies of her own after Meren had named himself Rianehd, the true king, in front of her court.

But there were two people she *could* contact—Vek and Caolte.

Her half-brother Vek had mated with Princess Dria of the Moranaians, and they now lived at a Moranaian outpost hidden on Earth. He'd largely absented himself from the Unseelie court after their father had tried to murder both his mother and his mate. Though Ara had killed the king for his crimes, she couldn't blame Vek for the distance. However, he did still seek out those with Unseelie blood if they were near enough to the outpost, and he'd had multiple conflicts with Meren. He would want to know.

Caolte, though. He was more complicated. Until Meren had

revealed the deception of his own parentage, Caolte had believed himself to be the half-brother of Meren and Lord Naomh. Unlike Meren's and Naomh's mother, Caolte's mother had come from the Unseelie court, a point of scorn amongst the Seelie nobles. Then Meren had revealed that they didn't share a father at all—while also dealing Naomh a near-fatal wound.

As far as she knew, Lord Naomh hadn't yet recovered. But if there was anyone in this world who wanted Meren dead more than Naomh or Tatianella, it was Caolte. He would aid in any maneuver against his erstwhile half-brother. But Caolte was fire, and she wasn't sure she wanted to handle the burn.

The unpredictable made her uneasy. Contacting *him* could certainly wait.

Out of reflex, Ara scanned her surroundings, but neither magic nor blood connection revealed any unwelcome listeners. Only then did she remove the small hand-mirror from the locked, hidden drawer in her desk. She held it up until she could stare at her own frowning reflection. This wasn't her preferred method of communication, but Vek had grown craftier with his shielding, making it more difficult to teleport to him. To get near his house, she would have to appear too close to human habitations.

Ara smoothed a few stray strands of her elaborately braided hair and then activated the link. The mirror flashed and shimmered, but there was no immediate answer. Of course. Her brother could be anywhere in the outpost or even wandering the surrounding region. Who knew how much of her time he would waste, and that after leaving her the kingdom to rule.

Of all of her most recent failed plans, naming Vek king of the Unseelie while she left to pursue her own interests—finally—was the one she hated messing up the most. He'd spent most of his life travelling all over at their father's request, while she'd been stuck at court with all its manipulations. Very rarely had she ventured out, since doing so brought its own drama. Case in point? The last break she'd taken had given her Fen—then taken him away again.

Truly, *that* was her greatest failure. Ever. If she'd had the slightest inkling that Jonathan would be so terrible at guarding Fen, she never would have left her son on Earth. But she couldn't have brought Jonathan here, and he'd begged to raise their son. It had seemed to be the best solution with her father's madness. The ways the former king might have used Fen...

The mirror flashed again, and Vek's annoyed face replaced her reflection. His hair, as pale as her own, stood in disarray, and the flush of color to his skin suggested she might have interrupted him abed with Dria. Well, too bad. Ara hadn't taken a lover in over a decade. Her brother could deal with a few lost minutes.

"What is it?" Vek snapped.

She kept her expression serene. Didn't she always? "I have received intelligence concerning a certain former noble of the Seelie who has caused you much trouble. As his plans appear to pertain to Earth, I believed it to be relevant to you. If I am incorrect on that last point, I would be happy to disconnect this link."

"It is very relevant," Dria said, though the mirror was too small for Ara to see her face. "Stop being rude to your sister, Vek."

Vek glanced to his right. "I will recall that advice when next you speak to your own sibling," he muttered before returning his attention to Ara. "Forgive me. We welcome any information you are willing to give."

Nodding, Ara gathered her thoughts.

Then she told them everything she knew.

CHAPTER SIX

By the time Kezari shoved open the door to Lyr's study, her anger was all but gone. The situation with Tynan was a problem, yes, but time would show them the way through that, for good or ill. One of the ancient dragons demanding an audience? That could bring trouble to Moranaia for centuries if not handled carefully.

She was perhaps not the best choice for that reason. Her recent foibles aside, she had so many questions for the ancient one that it would be difficult to focus on a single issue. He would know why her ancestors had left for Moranaia while some remained on Earth. He could tell her about the old customs of their kind, things forgotten by the complacent after millennia of indolence on the Isle.

Even if she weren't the best choice, she would demand to be the one to meet him. She couldn't allow one of the useless reptiles on the Isle to waste such an opportunity.

"I will go," Kezari announced as she skidded to a halt in front of Lyr's desk.

Lyr blinked up at her for a moment, the pen he held dripping a splotch of ink onto his paper. "I see you've been rousted from your cave. However, I wanted only to speak to you about the issue

53

and formulate a plan, not send you through the portal right away. If at all. Caeregas asked to speak to the dragon queen."

Heat traced up Kezari's arms and down her spine. If she looked, she would no doubt find a hint of scales beneath her skin. "The same one who refused to heed my warnings about Earth's energy? Queen Zevie knows nothing about the barrier, or she would not have ignored the threat. If she speaks to the ancient one at all, she will no doubt avoid the issue."

"Perhaps." Lyr replaced the pen in its holder and blotted up the drop before turning his full attention to her. "But there is also a chance she will know something you do not. The Unseelie king acted as a pillar for the wall and used that connection to his own benefit. Queen Zevie might have done the same."

"She would not have failed to note the poison," Kezari argued.

Lyr leaned back in his seat. "Unless it perverted her as it did King Torek."

Kezari frowned at the Myern in thought. Why did he defend the queen? "If you have already decided to contact that reptile, then why did you wish to speak to me?"

"You misunderstand." He held her gaze steadily. Impressive for an elf. "I am merely considering all arguments, for if we are to make a case to send you to meet with Caeregas, we'll need counters to his possible complaints."

"Then tell him this," Kezari began, anger and resolve trembling in her voice. "Our queen has abandoned the old ways. She tells our young to stifle or sever their links to Earth's energy and has banished me for attempting to solve the problem he wishes to discuss. He will receive no truth from her."

Lyr studied her for a moment before nodding. "I agree. With luck, I should be able to convince him, but it may take time to have everything arranged. Did you resolve your disagreement with Tynan?"

At those words, she sensed a tiny flare of energy behind her. Tynan. She'd been too intent on learning about the ancient one to realize he'd followed her. But she didn't turn to look at him. What could she say? He believed they could still work together, and she thought avoidance to be best.

She'd caused enough people distress in her life.

"For the most part, yes," Kezari replied. "However, I think it best we make an alternate plan for these missions. There is the chance of a repeat conflict, and that would not do when away from Moranaia."

Tynan rushed forward, halting beside her. "No. We *must* do this."

The heat along her spine increased, right where her wings wanted to spring free. "Why?" She half-turned to better glare at him. "Why do you need to do this so much? Because you think your deity told you to?"

"Yes," he said through clenched teeth. "I'm a priest. Listening to my goddess is part of my job."

Something about his harsh tone of voice combined with his rough, disheveled appearance sliced a new kind of heat through her body. But it was irrelevant. *Irrelevant.* "I am not a priestess. Your dilemma is not mine."

His eyes flashed. "Since when has that stopped any deity from making Their will known? The gods direct us all, whether we wish it or not."

"I am no elf to—"

"Enough!" Lyr commanded, his voice hard enough to give even Kezari pause. But after gaining her attention, the Myern merely studied her and Tynan for a long moment before shaking his head. "With no disrespect for the goddess Bera, Tynan...I find myself curious as to your reasoning, as well. You and Kezari clearly do not get along. Surely, you might consider consulting Lady Bera in meditation to see if you might glean an alternative. As things stand, I'm not inclined to send either of you anywhere."

Panic gripped her throat. She could not be stuck here. Could. Not. Ancient dragon or no, there was something on Earth she needed to deal with. Or Moranaia. *Somewhere that isn't Braelyn.*

As soon as she figured out the source of that unpleasant restlessness plaguing her, she needed to be able to follow it. But the elf brought discomfort, too. She might not be able to bear his presence for so long, either. What should she do?

"Kezari." Tynan's hand cupped her shoulder, his slightly cool skin a balm to her spiking heat. "What's wrong?"

A hint of his energy, gold like the morning sun, drifted over her. He'd calmed her with his magic before, just after they'd met, but this was hesitant. Tentative. Even so, the panic dulled its hold until she could suck in a solid breath.

"Something is wrong," she whispered. "This sense of unease has been growing in me, but I wasn't certain of the source. Now, I'm wondering if there is something on Earth causing it. But no matter where it comes from, it's there, and the thought of being cut off from travel..."

Lyr cursed. "More poison?"

Kezari closed her eyes, delving deep inside herself for her connection to Earth. When she found it, she smiled—there it thrummed, a solid piece of her heart. Nothing seemed wrong. But just in case, she examined the energy as thoroughly as she knew how. No poison. No darkness.

And yet.

"I don't sense poison, but..." Kezari shook her head. "Something is off, but I can't determine what. I need to go there to see if the problem is on Earth."

Lyr's lips pinched tight for a brief moment before he sighed. "Then I suggest you find a way to work with Tynan, and delivering the potions to Caolte would be an excellent start. Expectant fathers do not go on dangerous missions any more than mothers, so I will not send Lial. And Aris... The scouts of Oria are still monitoring the area where he lost control to ensure no wildlife was warped by his release of life magic. Until he has had more time to heal, Aris goes no farther on Earth than the outpost."

"But the potion delivery," she began.

"Do you think Aris will fare well at the sight of Naomh's

battered body?" Lyr asked harshly. "I have read Lial's report on the Sidhe lord's condition. You have not. I would send Tynan alone first, though it is not ideal."

The trap closed.

Kezari snarled against the helpless feeling swamping her, but there was nothing for it. Lyr was right. Aris was too fragile to involve in this, in no small part because of her own foolishness, and Lial had to stay here. She'd already accepted the need for this at the midday meal before her interaction with Tynan had wiped away all logic.

Stuck with the man who hated that she might be his mate.

Wonderful.

∼

TYNAN HAD BROUGHT this on himself, but her reticence still hurt.

Time stretched and warbled in his heart as he stared at the side of Kezari's face. So much depended on what she would say—that certainty mingled with the ache of her hesitation, even if he didn't understand it. Was it merely Lady Bera's order? Some instinct undefined? He was no seer to have an actual foretelling.

"When would you have us leave?" Kezari asked through clenched teeth.

Lyr glanced at the water clock on the wall. "It is nearly dinner now. In all honesty, I would prefer you complete the errand this evening, but that might be a bit too late for them. I'll need to check with Lord Caolte on the timing to be certain."

"Is his condition so dire?" Tynan asked.

"Not to my knowledge," Lyr replied. "Otherwise, Lial would have been far more insistent on sending you at once, and Caolte surely would have contacted Kai. Unless something new arises, I suggest you spend the night preparing what you'll need. And calming any remaining temper."

Kezari gave a sharp nod. "I will be atop the brooding tower. Brooding."

She didn't wait for dismissal the way one of his people would have, merely spun on her heel and strode out the door. She was not pleased to yield—but then, she never was. Going with her to a Seelie lord's realm had all the makings of a diplomatic disaster. Fortunately, that was Lyr's problem. Tynan only had to survive it.

Lyr blinked at him. "I don't want to question a goddess, but..."

"Perhaps a minor calamity is Her intended goal," Tynan quipped. "One never knows what good might come of such things, after all."

Not that Lady Bera was wholly good in the way most would perceive the concept. She might be a benevolent goddess, but she reigned over life and death. The average person never considered how often the latter was necessary for the former.

"That is so," Lyr agreed, though an unexpected hint of amusement lightened his expression. "I hope you find good from your obviously difficult expedition into Kezari's cave. You appear rather the worse for wear."

Tynan glanced down out of reflex, only to be confronted once more by the sorry state of his robes. And the scratches and dried dirt on the back of his hands. Good gods. He'd appeared before the Myern looking like he'd tumbled down the ravine and landed in the muck. It hadn't been an emergency, either—just an overly impatient dragon charging ahead.

"Forgive me, Myern," Tynan said, his cheeks growing warm.

Lyr waved a hand. "I am accustomed to worse. You're not dripping blood, so all is well. However, it does beg the question of how dire your conflict with Kezari might have been."

"No more than was warranted," Tynan admitted. "I'm afraid my physical condition is my own fault, however. I was not prepared to go caving."

After a quick nod, Lyr considered him for a moment. "Did you bring simpler clothing?"

Had he? Tynan catalogued the few pieces of his wardrobe he'd packed in the small trunk he'd brought. He hadn't expected to stay so long at Braelyn, but he'd included several robes just in case. Two for formal occasions, a handful for daily use, and a couple of plain ones he reserved for messier duties.

"I have other robes better suited for caves," Tynan said.

"You are welcome to consult with our seamstress if you decide those will not serve after all." Lyr picked up his pen, a subtle sign that he was ready to resume his work. "You'll need Earth-appropriate clothing if you and Kezari prove capable of working together, so you should probably speak with Telia regardless. I'll send her advance notice."

Tynan forced a smile. "Thank you, Myern. If that is all, I will begin my preparations."

"Thank you," Lyr said. "That is indeed all."

After tapping his chest twice in salute, Tynan followed Kezari's example and fled. Not to the brooding tower, though. He needed to ensure that his portable medical kit was stocked and enough potions packed to deliver to Lord Naomh's underhill realm. Anything to delay the worry waiting to settle in. He couldn't even process Lyr's comment about Earth clothing. First, he had to make it through a meeting with the Seelie, all with an impetuous dragon as his escort.

He would *not* ask what could go wrong.

ANNA PLOPPED down on the bench where she had once confronted Meren. *Hah. Once.* It hadn't quite been two months since it had happened, but it already felt like a lifetime ago. Since then, she'd become an Unseelie princess and helped—however minutely—stop an elven plague. On another planet, no less. It was nearly incomprehensible.

Her gaze trailed lovingly over the river lapping against the bank a short distance away. Her heart seemed to pulse with each slap of water against stone, a pleasant rhythm that resonated with her soul. It was the peace of that which allowed her to sit here so calmly when she'd worried that she wouldn't be able to return to this place after their confrontation with Meren.

But she'd made it. Yep. Here she was. Totally not procrastinating.

She was going to do it. She would summon the Gwragedd Annwn lady who had claimed to be her grandmother and ask her for training. It shouldn't be a big deal. Just a potential shift in everything she knew about herself, right? She'd already learned she had fae blood. What was a little more craziness in her life?

Anna snorted. Not even she bought that casual attitude, and it was her own mental voice. Well, it was time to show herself who was boss. As soon as she figured out how, that was. She'd been told to speak her grandmother's name into the water, but she was at a loss as to the best method. Dive in for a swim? Duck her face close? Bring a handful of water to her mouth?

Hey, that had promise. This was a public park, and though it was currently empty of people in the middle of a school-and-work day, someone could come along at any time. The air held enough chill that she would look even more strange taking a swim or sitting on the bank. But she didn't have to do anything as obvious as that, thanks to her time with Lady Selia.

The Moranaian woman hadn't been able to teach Anna a great deal, since elven magic apparently differed somewhat from Gwragedd Annwn powers, but they'd worked together a little. One of those techniques had helped her manipulate water vapor with more control and intent than instinct. Maybe she could pull a little of the river to her and then send it back.

In short order, the soft tickle of water vapor caressed her upturned palm, and she smiled before lifting her hand to her face as though scratching her nose. Then ever-so-softly, she whispered, "Torlahn." A slight push of power, and the moisture in her breath melted with the name into the vapor from the river.

Anna sent it back and then prepared to wait.

And wait.

For a while, she admired the river and the assortment of passing boats. Would she learn some kind of magic to avoid those? There had to be some method if the Gwragedd Annwn survived in the river without being detected. Maybe they simply transported themselves instead of actually swimming. That curious thought kept her occupied for at least fifteen minutes.

A couple of joggers and a bicyclist passed by on the River-walk. A mom brought her preschooler to play on the playground behind Anna's bench, and that was a solid half hour of laughter and funny comments punctuated by the inevitable tears of departure. But still no sign of Torlahn of the Gwragedd Annwn.

Had she done it wrong? Anna tapped her fingernail against the edge of her phone case and frowned at the water. There might be some trick to it that she should have known. Then again, it might just take time. Her grandmother could have been doing anything when she called. Eating lunch. Having sex. Completing a secret mission in a far-flung fae realm.

Hard to tell, really.

A man and woman approached, probably college students based on their University of Tennessee hoodies and the neon flyers they taped at intervals along the railing, trees, or light poles. Anna wrinkled her nose. Wasn't there some kind of ordinance about that? If there wasn't, there should be. Most of those papers would end up dissolving in the river.

"Oh, hey," the woman said when she neared. She grabbed a paper from her stack and shoved it toward Anna. "Take this. Spread the word."

Out of reflex, Anna accepted it, giving the woman a quick smile before the pair walked on. But when she finally read the bold text on the bright orange paper, shock froze her. It took her a couple of read-throughs to fully process the words.

*Power outages. Freak lightning storms. Disappearing bridge*

*jumpers. Magic isn't just a rumor! Why won't the government admit it?*
*Join the MARCH AGAINST MAGIC as we take over Downtown Chattanooga to demand the truth!*
*NO witches or other magic-users allowed!*

A shiver of fear shook through Anna. Not because of a protest—that was becoming increasingly common around the country as more rumors of rogue magic popped up. There were countless theories being posited on the news every day, but no one really wanted to come out and say that it was magic. It was always some kind of weather anomaly or potential technology.

But this flyer...not only had they dared name it, but they also called out anyone who did magic. Not good. Even passing knowledge of history suggested it wouldn't go well for human magic-users or any of the fae—or part-fae, in Anna's case. Same for both of her mates.

"As I feared," a familiar voice said above her.

Anna jerked her head up to find that Torlahn had finally arrived, and her attention was focused on the paper in Anna's hands. "I have to tell Maddy and Fen."

Torlahn nodded as Anna lifted her phone and unlocked the screen. She hadn't been waiting for permission, but she smiled briefly anyway. No telling what social expectations the Gwragedd Annwn had, nor what they knew of technology.

Something, perhaps. Torlahn didn't appear shocked when Anna snapped a picture of the flyer and dropped it in the group text with a note that her grandmother had just arrived. Maddy and Fen would probably blow up her phone discussing the news, but at least they wouldn't expect a prompt answer.

Anna had a feeling life was about to get far too interesting.

CHAPTER SEVEN

Snow danced outside the windows as Kezari paced circles around the top floor of the observation tower. Dark had long ago fallen, and dinner was surely over. She hadn't bothered to join the group. Instead, she'd flown out and hunted her own food before returning to the tower to think. And while she normally would have lingered in dragon form on the roof, it seemed best to practice being in this form even when she was agitated. She couldn't afford mistakes while on Earth.

Kezari thrust out her arm and peered at the skin. Good. A warm gold, but a normal one—for an elf. No sign of scales wanting to break free. If nothing else, her time with the elves had aided her in mastering her second body. She'd neglected it in her youth, preferring to remain in dragon form while many of her peers enjoyed the novelty of shifting. Some had even mated as elves, but she hadn't remained in this body long enough to recognize what desire would feel like.

Thanks to Tynan, she now had a better idea.

It...wasn't dissimilar to what she'd experienced as a dragon. A warm, inviting pleasure-ache-longing. Hunger but not. She'd felt nothing like it for Aris or any of the others here, male or female. Was it because most of the people she encountered were life-mated? That wouldn't make a difference to any physiological attraction, would it? Tynan claimed a bond between them, but even if that were true, it wouldn't stop her body from responding to others.

Too confusing. Was it any wonder she'd spent decades holed up in her cave? Rock and stone and earth—those made sense. There was reason to their composition, order in the seeming chaos of their birth and growth. She could delve deep enough to discern why the ground shook or a volcano erupted, but she couldn't divine why sentient beings did anything.

It was one reason Aris made a perfect *skizik*—his energy dealt intimately with living creatures, intelligent or not. Their magics were complements. But that wasn't emotion. As a mind healer, Tynan understood those motivations that she couldn't fathom, and his empathy would leave him in tatters after being too near her chaos. Any desire they felt for each other would be foolish to pursue.

Wouldn't it?

"Debating what you'll say to the ancient dragon?" Aris asked.

With a jolt, she spun around and let out an instinctive hiss. He'd been smiling, but that bit of good humor dropped—along with his color. Kezari closed her eyes and gathered her composure. He hadn't intended to startle her, just as she hadn't meant to scare him with her reaction. She forced herself to relax before she looked at him again.

"Sorry," she said. "I was too deep in thought to sense your arrival. I had no idea you were there."

Pink flooded his cheeks again as he relaxed. "Even in this form, you looked ready to eat any errant intruder."

"These teeth are hardly sufficient," Kezari muttered.

Fortunately, he laughed instead of balked.

"I'm glad you're brooding here instead of your cave." Aris stepped away from the top of the stairs. "I wasn't sure Tynan would make it out when I sent him in after you."

Kezari settled her hand on her hip. "An interesting observation from an explorer. Why didn't you come in yourself instead of sending the priest?"

She realized her mistake as soon as the words left her mouth, but she couldn't call them back even as Aris paled again. Of course he would not go into a cave unless he had no other choice, not after he'd been held captive and tortured in one. Mind healing had helped, but he still struggled greatly when missions took them underground.

"I should have thought," she whispered.

Aris released a short, breathy growl of frustration. She couldn't help but approve.

"Do not take my trauma upon your own shoulders. I appreciate your consideration, but I hate the constant apologies. Everyone does it, and I just..." He ran his fingers through his green-streaked hair. "It becomes tedious, I suppose. I much prefer the 'give an apologetic smile and change the subject' approach at this point."

What exactly was an apologetic smile? Did it have a different curve? A slant? Why did elves have to contort their faces in so many ridiculous ways? But if it would help Aris, she would try to observe one so she could recreate it. Laughing at her failed attempts would certainly be another distraction if nothing else.

"I will try to remember," she merely said.

No need to tell him she had no clue what he was talking about.

"So," Aris began—the changing the subject portion was clear, at least. "What are you planning to ask the ancient dragon?"

Sludge and muck. She'd better come up with something quick. Otherwise, she'd have to tell him she'd been thinking about Tynan. And sex. Then she would never hear the end of it from Aris. She had enough annoyances, thank you.

BEING a substitute healer on a major estate was an unusual experience to say the least. Usually, a visitor would be given privacy by the residents and would meet few if any who lived there as they conducted business. If said visitor were to stay long term, the head of the household would formally introduce them, and more normal contact would begin. But Tynan was in the nebulous mists between those two realities, so he was often left treating patients who would avoid him outside the tower.

Such as the blushing young man in front of him.

"My knee let out a pop when I landed on it," the man said.

Should Tynan ask his name? He was rarely so forward, waiting for patients to give it on their own, but this one seemed particularly flustered. Was it his youth? Tynan judged him to be somewhere around two decades based on his appearance and demeanor. He could be younger, however. That might require input from the lad's parents.

Tynan sat on the stool beside the bed. "Forgive me for my forwardness since I am technically a visitor to this estate, but might I ask your name and age?"

The man's skin flamed even redder. "Of course. My name is Eniom, and I am thirty-two years."

Older than he'd expected but still quite young—though treatable without permission. Tynan lowered his hands to just above Eniom's knee. "Are you a new recruit to the guard, then?"

"Ah, no." The man jumped slightly when Tynan activated his healing magic, but the peace his energy often brought seemed absent in Eniom's expression. His heartrate was a bit elevated, too. "I'm apprenticing in the kitchens. I hope to train with the cook if I prove skilled enough."

"Excellent," Tynan replied absently as he began to explore the young man's injury with his magic.

Kneecap intact, no sign of fracture. Muscles and tendons a little strained in places, but nothing was torn. Even the swelling was mild. If there'd been a popping sound, it probably hadn't come from the knee. This kind of slight sprain would be healed without aid by morning with rest. Why had Eniom come to the healer for this?

Though it wasn't strictly necessary, Tynan repaired the sprain and let his magic fade. The man's heartrate hadn't gone down, but there'd been no physical injury responsible for that. Excitement, most likely.

"I didn't find a cause for the sound you heard," Tynan said. "It seems to be nothing more than a sprain. However, I am happy to summon Lial if you would like for him to confirm my diagnosis."

Eniom shook his head so quickly that his hair danced around his shoulders, but there was a curious, almost eager, glint in his eyes despite the rapid denial. "I didn't come to see him. That is... I meant to say that I don't *need* to see him. You're surely correct. It must have been the sound of the ice beneath the snow."

All at once, epiphany dawned—the man was attracted to him. If Tynan hadn't locked his empathy down so tightly, it would have been clear at once. Now, he was caught somewhere between a sympathetic grimace and a self-deprecating chuckle at his own obliviousness. But he wouldn't hurt Eniom by doing either. It wasn't the man's fault that Tynan wasn't attracted to men, nor that Tynan had found his potential soulbonded.

"An easy enough mistake," Tynan said, infusing his voice with as much impersonal cheer as he could manage without it sounding forced. "I do hope you'll take greater care on the way home. I would not wish to see you return with another such injury."

He'd intended there to be a hint of rebuke in the statement, but Eniom didn't appear to notice. Instead, the man's smile widened as he stood. "Thank you for your care. I receive it kindly."

Good gods. Was this why Lial affected such a grumpy countenance amongst his patients? The other healer was certainly attractive, but no one came to see *him* just to gawk. How did he avoid situations like this? As Eniom headed toward the door and bent down—slowly, by Lady Bera—to grab the spikes for his shoes, Tynan searched his brain for something to say. Anything to discourage the flirtation before the man truly injured himself coming up with ailments. Unfortunately, he had nothing that wouldn't sound ridiculous to a stranger, especially if he'd mistaken the situation.

The door flew open, and Kezari marched through, stony resolve hardening her expression. Eniom yelped, then quickly smothered the sound as Kezari turned a piercing glance his way. As she drew to a halt, her gaze moving between them, Tynan had to resist the urge to smooth the wrinkles from his robes. He'd cleaned up after his little caving adventure, but he still felt the echoes of the grime.

Eniom cleared his throat. "This is a private healing session."

Kezari's eyes narrowed on the brave but unwise man. Her lips tightened over her mouth as though she was trying not to bare her teeth. "Is that so?" she asked. "It is a strange healing that takes place while the patient is preparing to leave."

"Ah." Eniom dropped his gaze, but he foolishly persisted. "How do you know I didn't just arrive?"

"Because I've sensed your energy in here for some time, and Tynan's healing magic ceased several moments ago." Once again, Kezari glanced between them. "Is there more to this than a basic healing?"

Eniom reddened once more, but Tynan merely sighed. With her head slightly tilted at an inquisitive angle and her expression unbothered, Kezari gave no indication of jealously. Why should she feel such? She had no care for a potential bond. But his young patient appeared a bit worried by the question.

"Would that bother you?" Eniom asked. "It's not that unusual, lady dragon."

Kezari snorted. "Lady dragon?"

Goddess save him, but this could go...poorly. For many reasons. "Since your healing is complete, Eniom, I should speak with Kezari. We have a task to complete for Lord Lyr."

"Oh. Of course," the young man said. "Thank you again for your care."

Eniom shot him a quick, flirtatious smile before grabbing his cloak and hurrying out the door. Kezari stared after him before turning her frown on Tynan. There was something off about her, both a tension and ease to her demeanor that confounded his instincts. But of course, her body language was rarely easy to read.

"An admirer, I see." Kezari's chin tipped up. "Did he actually need healing?"

He could almost fool himself into thinking she cared. "Yes, though he would have healed well enough without my help. Do you have an ailment, *lady dragon*?"

This time, she did bare her teeth. "I have resisted eating you too many times today already. Call me that again at your peril."

Tynan chuckled. "I am merely curious as to your arrival. I thought you'd planned to brood?"

"I did that." Kezari took a few steps forward, and her thin dress glided and swirled around her body, clinging lovingly to her breasts and—No. He forced his eyes resolutely upward. "But if we are to do this task tomorrow, we should be in accord. Also, I would like to know what I should pack. I am not accustomed to traveling in this form."

"There is no discord on my end," Tynan replied. Except, of course, between his body's interest and his mind's avoidance, but she didn't need to know about that. "As to what you should pack...Not much, I would think. You create your own clothing when you shift, and we'll hardly need to camp during a visit to a Seelie lord's private underhill. Do you foresee some other problem?"

Kezari rolled her shoulders, but he'd come to realize that the gesture wasn't exactly a shrug. It was more a nervous tic akin to twitching her wings. Was he misreading her emotional state? Tentatively, he lowered his shields enough to let a tendril of his power free even as he prayed the move didn't backfire. He didn't find a clear answer. Either instinctively or out of consideration for him, her emotions were well-guarded behind her mental shields.

"What is an apologetic smile?" she blurted, rendering his effort moot.

Definitely nervous.

But what was behind the question? It clearly had nothing to do with her supposed reason for being here. "That is difficult to answer," Tynan said.

Her hum of annoyance vibrated between them. "I should not have asked."

"No," he insisted quickly, before the exit he saw in her demeanor became reality. "I'm not bothered by the question. I merely lack the context to answer it."

The tension in her shoulders eased a fraction. "I am not an elf, though this is one of my forms. Culturally...there is much I do not understand."

Tynan almost smiled at the obvious statement, but he resisted lest he cause her pain. In truth, he found her quirks endearing—when they didn't clash dangerously with his own. "And an apologetic smile is one of them?"

"Yes." Pride and defiance fired in her eyes. "Aris said he tires of verbal redress for any insensitive comments. He wants an apologetic smile and a subject change. But facial expressions... I thought to observe one, but it is such a specific thing."

Unexpected tenderness slammed into him with a force not generally connected to such a soft emotion. It stole his breath and pounded in his heart. Beneath her pride, he could practically feel her embarrassment, but he didn't need to use his empathy to find it. Her shame echoed in her hunched posture and fierce expression, one ready to devour the slightest hint of mockery.

He wouldn't give it. "For a natural example, you need only watch Kai. Such smiles quickly follow his overprotective moments with Arlyn. But I'll try to explain."

Tynan paused to consider the action before twisting his face into a rough approximation.

"A bit like that?" he said. "It's somewhat between a grimace and a smile, I think. The brows lower a little with it, and upturned lips turn to a wince before the expression drops entirely. A shrug might or might not accompany it."

"A shrug? Isn't that confusion or lack of caring?" Kezari huffed. "Gestures should not be so ambiguous."

"I suppose body language is much like verbal language. It all depends on how it's combined." Tynan thought back to the times he'd seen her in dragon form and smiled. "Don't you bare your teeth in both threat and humor?"

He'd meant it a touch flippantly, but Kezari blinked, her head tilting as she considered the question. "You are correct. I suppose it is instinctive."

"Perhaps, though much is learned. Parents and babies spend more time than you would think making faces at one another." One of Tynan's few memories of his father was just that, in fact. A bittersweet remembrance. "You're welcome to practice your apologetic smile with me. I promise I won't consider it an actual apology."

Kezari stiffened. "I will not. I feel enough like an oddity without your laughter."

"I would not—"

"No," she insisted. "I will meet you at the portal tomorrow."

Just like that, Kezari hurried from the room as though one of the ancients awaited her outside. He stared at the closed door in surprise while the quiet wrapped around him, nothing but the drips from the distilling machine filling the sudden emptiness. Curious. Very curious. Kezari generally avoided him of late, but she'd come here to ask him such a sensitive question.

She'd allowed him to glimpse a deep vulnerability. Why? Was it because he was a mind healer, or could there be a deeper reason? Maybe—No. It was best not to assume a softer reason beyond his role as a healer-priest. He was simply the logical choice for such a query.

Nothing more.

~

VEK WAS RAPIDLY LOSING patience with his mate's brother. Prince Ralan was a seer, and a powerful one at that. So as Dria disconnected the communication spell for the third time without response, Vek could only assume that either her brother hadn't Seen anything of concern, or he didn't care.

"I'm going to kill him," Dria muttered. "The only question is how."

"I believe that's treason, *ahmeeren*." Vek bent down to kiss the side of her neck. "A specialty of mine, but something I suspect you might regret. *Might* being the key word."

He caught sight of her eye roll in the mirror before she turned to face him. "Don't pretend you're not happy."

Vek shrugged. "As far as I'm concerned, we can handle Meren however we wish. My sister gave *us* the information, after all. Not Lyr or Ralan. Unless we find evidence that he's plotting against Moranaia, I see nothing wrong with gathering more information without your brother's blessing."

"This outpost is considered Moranaian, and you agreed to follow my orders," Dria argued. But he didn't miss the hint of mischief in her eyes. "That being said...I agree that we can't let this go too long. I don't want Meren to build an army because Ralan wasn't paying attention to his communication mirror."

Vek snorted. "Indeed."

Shrugging past him, Dria strode over to the huge map of Earth affixed to the wall. He'd helped her place tiny crystals in various spots, marking the portals to the Veil scattered around the world—information she'd gained from Lyr, not the brother who was technically in charge. Dria had been working on visiting the most important portals so that she could teleport there if necessary, but so far, she'd only managed a few.

"The difficult part will be finding out where he's hiding." Dria tapped the spot near the outpost and then ran her finger along the connected mountain range. "I marked the places Ara's spy mentioned seeing him. He's been moving up the Appalachia all the way up to the northeastern section of this country."

"Inconvenient," Vek said.

Blasted inconvenient. There were cities everywhere along that range, though they were sparser in the higher mountains. Vek hadn't traveled extensively on Earth for decades, but according to Delbin and Inona, there were a great many cities larger than Chattanooga, the nearest to the outpost, and no few were close to Dria's markers. Meren would be much harder to track, and it wouldn't be easy for Vek to go himself without abandoning his mate.

Unless, of course, they made use of the network of portals.

A surge of power from the transport room tingled along his senses, but the resonance of his nephew's blood revealed the newcomer's identity long before Fen rushed in, his phone clenched in his hand. Worry and anger were unmistakable in the crease of his brow and the set of his jaw. Damn. What now?

"Do you ever look at your texts?" Fen snapped as he drew to a halt in front of them.

Vek suppressed a grin. "I sent you one just yesterday."

"Yeah. A fucking chain text," Fen scoffed. "With angels. Where did you even find something like that?"

Not even torture would get Vek to reveal that Anna had sent it to him for just this purpose. He couldn't think of anyone on any world who was as delightful to troll as Fen. "I do hope you sent it to the requisite five people lest your luck turn bad."

Fen released an inarticulate groan of pure frustration, one very much worth the elbow Dria directed into Vek's side.

"I have our phones in the charging field I set up," Dria said. "Is something wrong?"

"Probably." Fen ran his free hand through his hair, and some of Vek's humor fled. "Anna was beside the river trying to contact the Gwragedd Annwn, and she sent us a disturbing text. I bet she sent it to you, too."

Vek straightened, the remainder of his humor gone. "Did they hurt Anna? Are we to cut a swath through the Gwragedd Annwn colony, then? It shouldn't take long to find, not with—"

"Hold up, Killer." Fen turned his phone so that Vek could see the screen. "It's nothing like that. She saw this weird flyer. Read it."

Vek's eyes narrowed on the bold splash of orange in the picture, text printed on the surface. It appeared to be a formal announcement. But once he read the words, he couldn't stop himself from baring his teeth. A march against magic? The humans might as well protest air. Or water. It was a bit of foolishness he might have ignored, if not for the last part.

No witches or other magic-users allowed.

That type of statement never boded well for their kind. Never. If there was anything that would truly prevent the fae and elves from returning to Earth, it was this. For whatever reason, a fair number of humans struggled to accept those outside their race. They'd hunted dragons, warred with the Sidhe. Begged for magical favors while turning the fae into villains. It was partly for that reason that the Unseelie and dragons had walled off some of Earth's energy in the first place.

No amount of magic would cure that. The question, of course, was how many agreed with this protest—and of those, how many were merely scared or confused. Reports of magic grew every day, from once-mocked rumors to news features. The human governments had no idea how to respond, and none of the fae had stepped forward to speak to them. There was Meren gathering half-bloods—

"Oh, fuck," Vek muttered. "Meren."

Dria blinked at him. "You think he's organizing the march?"

"No," Vek replied. "I think he's organizing an actual army. I'd wager a chest of diamonds that he's about to approach the humans. As himself."

Fen's brows shot up. "You mean...?"

"He'll openly claim to be king of the Seelie to the humans."

# CHAPTER EIGHT

Not even an hour spent in prayer and meditation had calmed Tynan's nerves, but at least he hadn't received any other orders from the goddess. The first was…challenge enough. As he waited beside the portal for Kezari in the pale light of dawn, he tried not to catalogue all the things that could go wrong. Like, say, offending a Sidhe lord. Or getting stranded in the Veil. The former was the most likely, but he couldn't shake thoughts of the latter.

He'd never left Moranaia. From time to time, he'd traveled to other estates for healings or to visit the sacred trees, but the local gates weren't the same thing at all. They were fixed-point teleportation spells, not connections to the Veil between worlds and dimensions. Without a guide with the appropriate magic, it truly was possible to wander lifetimes in the mists. There were probably dead bodies in there somewhere.

Tynan shuddered. Deep breathing—he needed lots and lots of deep, meditative breathing. With shaking hands, he lifted the small pouch he wore around his neck and held it beneath his nose. The tang of herbs wafted through him, soothing some of his nerves. Lady Bera would not have sent him on this mission if he wasn't capable, and the temple herbs were a good reminder of that.

Kezari marched between the trees in her elven form, her bearing stiff and regal. As usual, she wore only a thin dress despite the snow covering the ground and sprinkling from the trees above with each gust of wind. Her sole concession to the weather was a pair of sturdy boots. She hadn't even tied back her long, golden hair, leaving it to fall around her like the cloak she refused to wear.

It wasn't anxiety that quickened his breath now. He craved the right to pull all that beauty and fire close, regardless of the danger. But then, she'd always drawn him. From the moment he'd first seen her—naked, no less—kneeling at Aris's side, Tynan's very soul had longed to claim her. Not because of her appearance, either. Just...her.

A frown creased her brow as she stopped in front of him. "What are you clutching? It is pungent."

"Herbs used in our temple incense," Tynan replied, unable to keep the defensiveness from his tone. "It calms me."

Her frown deepened. "If I upset you so thoroughly, then why—"

"It's not you," Tynan rushed to say. He waved toward the portal. "It's that. I didn't expect to be so nervous, but the stories I've heard about the endless mists..."

"I see." Kezari's expression smoothed. "Whatever you're expecting, it's likely not as spectacular as that. The Veil is a little more difficult than the direct gate to the outpost, but it's quickly traversed."

He didn't bother to remind her that he'd never been through the direct gate, either. Kezari and Aris had been part of the team who'd converted the broken wall holding back Earth's energy into a fixed gate between their worlds, but Tynan had been here. Happily. He'd never thought it might be otherwise.

But he was saved from attempting to explain by the activation of the portal, heralding Inona's arrival. As the stone arch filled with the image of gray, creeping mists, Tynan's heart slammed and skittered. The expanse appeared both flat, like a picture, and as fathomless as the sky. He couldn't see anyone, either. If Inona was supposed to be activating the spell to open the gate, then shouldn't she be visible?

Then he blinked, and she was there.

"Tynan. Kezari," Inona said with a smile and a nod for each. If the journey had been difficult, there was no sign of it on her face. "Are you ready?"

Kezari stepped up to his side. "I am, but I am uncertain about Tynan. He may need extra care."

His cheeks heating, Tynan cut his gaze Kezari's way in annoyance. "I am prepared to leave at once."

Although Inona's eyes narrowed slightly on him, her expression remained easy. In fact, her mood seemed lighter than he was accustomed to seeing. He'd previously noted her often solemn demeanor and the way she sometimes ran her fingers across the scar on her throat with a haunted pain in her eyes. More than once, he'd nearly offered his services as a mind healer but had decided it would be more intrusive than welcome.

The only thing he'd heard about the wound was that Cora and Lial had been involved in the healing. As such, if there were concerns about her emotional recovery, Tynan would almost certainly know. So long as treatment was welcome, of course. Lial might be pushy, but he was too experienced to try to force it. The mind was too tricky for that.

"If you are sure," Inona finally said, "Then let's go. I have a date with Delbin later, and I'm hoping the return trip won't interfere."

A what?

"You are spending a certain day with him?" Kezari asked, echoing Tynan's confusion. "I thought you were together most days."

One side of Inona's mouth lifted. "It's an Earth term. According to Delbin, 'a date' is something couples do to solidify their relationship. It seems we'll be eating a formal dinner together and watching a movie. Which is a type of play, if you're wondering."

Dinner. Tynan held back a shudder. Considering his recent experiences, that didn't sound like the most appealing way to spend time with one's love interest. Perhaps it was different with only two people? Though the lack of distraction had its own problems. Kezari glaring at him for the entirety of a meal did not make for a pleasant mental picture.

"An interesting custom," Kezari said, and her dry, doubtful tone made him grin.

Inona smiled. "I suppose I'll find out. Now. Come over here, and I'll wrap my energy around yours for the journey through."

Tynan tried not to look at the swirling mists behind the scout as he and Kezari approached. If he'd thought it was safe to proceed with his eyes closed, he would have, but he wasn't certain if Inona's magic would prevent him from accidentally wandering off. He'd rather not find himself lost.

Or on another world.

The hum of magic surrounded him, but it didn't bring comfort. Tynan took another deep sniff of the herb pouch. Also not much help. His heartbeat thrummed in his ears with each step as they followed Inona through. Why had Lady Bera insisted—

A warm hand wrapped around his chilled one, and he jerked his gaze to Kezari. Was she trying to comfort him? *Him?* She stared straight ahead, no sign of her thoughts reflected in her expression.

But as they entered fully into the Veil, she didn't let go.

TAKING Tynan's hand turned out to be a terrible mistake, and yet it was perfection. Of course, that uneasy perfection was the bulk of the problem. It...stirred things in her. It made her nervous. It had her longing to sidle closer for better contact. And this time, she couldn't claim it was the soothing tone of his energy. Although a hint of that was still there, his fear scrambled the effect until her own heart pounded a touch faster.

Luckily, the Veil didn't appear to be turbulent. The mists rolled around them in calm complacency, and it felt like only a matter of moments before Inona pulled them through to a new world. They drew to a halt atop a stone platform in the middle of a sad-looking forest. Ahead, a path stretched between the trees, and a pair of warriors waited where platform met trail.

Tynan shifted beside her, jostling their joined hands, and Kezari froze. What was she supposed to do now? She'd taken his hand impulsively to offer comfort, but what was the protocol for keeping it? Would it be an insult to release him—or *not* to release him? There had to be some kind of code of etiquette for this. There always was.

Well, he would have to forgive her lack of knowledge. She was following her own personal comfort, and that did not include making herself uneasy in a Sidhe lord's stronghold. As Inona spoke to the guards, Kezari slowly disentangled her fingers from Tynan's. She sensed his gaze on her face, but she kept her focus straight ahead.

Soon enough, they followed one of the warriors down the path through the most pitiful forest she'd ever seen, and for the first time, she was actively grateful that Aris hadn't come. He would be greatly disturbed by the denuded life of this place. Everywhere, leaves drooped, some to the point of wilting, and the more distant trees had gone brown and sparse as though autumn was half-done. And there was barely any underbrush.

Here and there, a sad flower poked up from the dull grass as though searching for spring. Kezari couldn't blame the confused little plants, because she couldn't divine the seasons, either. The air was warm and humid like summer, but the crystal she spied at the top of the cavern cast fitful light more akin to the winter sun. At this rate, she wouldn't be surprised if snow started to fall.

"This is..." Tynan began, his voice trailing off.

Kezari knew exactly what he meant. "Indeed."

Just as a structure became visible in the distance, another man strode toward them, his flame-red hair dancing with each step. Lord Caolte. She'd interacted with him somewhat when she'd traveled to Earth to deal with the poisoned energy there, but she had little firsthand knowledge about him. From what she'd heard and seen, the fact that his hair only looked like fire was a positive.

Sparks of flame would not be a good thing in this denuded forest.

They halted in the middle of the path, and the guard stepped aside with a bow. Inona and Lord Caolte inclined their heads toward one another, but Kezari didn't bother. If he disapproved of her manners, she would be happy to take herself elsewhere. It wasn't as though she was vital for the process.

Inona launched into the bizarre dance of formal introductions that never failed to make Kezari's eyes glaze over with boredom. She barely recognized her Moranaian name in time to nod and offer something resembling a smile. If he said anything polite in return, she honestly couldn't have repeated it.

"You'll notify me when it's time for them to return?" Inona finally asked. "Until Tynan ensures that there is no sickness in your realm, I'd rather not stick around."

Caolte nodded. "You needn't linger in the Veil, either. I'll see that you are properly summoned."

That seemed unusually kind of him; in fact, his manner was more relaxed than she recalled from previous encounters. He'd been intense then. As fierce and deadly as a dragon in full rage, complete with fire. But perhaps that had been situational. Perhaps this was his demeanor when his flames were banked.

After Tynan scanned everyone for signs of illness, the scout returned to the gate, leaving them with Lord Caolte. A strained but not unfriendly silence descended for a moment before the Sidhe man gestured for them to follow.

"Forgive the state of this place," Caolte said as they neared the house. "I was a poor choice for its steward."

"Is that why it's a muddled mess of seasons?" Kezari asked without thinking.

Caolte winced, and Tynan let out a choked-sounding breath like a snort gone wrong.

"My element is fire, not earth," Caolte muttered, guiding them through the door. "How am I to know how to maintain such a balance? It is yet another reason Naomh needs to recover sooner rather than later."

Though she wised up enough not to say so, Kezari had to agree.

MANY EMOTIONS CLASHED within Lial at the sight of Elerie's motionless form, but the depth of his anger surprised him the most. Her current state wasn't new information. In fact, he'd had a solid three weeks to consider what Alerielle had done and how best to treat Lady Elerie. But seeing her...that shook him.

Her hair was the exact same shade of black as Kai's, and her fair skin had the same warm undertones. Even her lips had a similar curve and width. Her other son, Morenial, had inherited the shape of her eyes. To look at her, her breathing so slow he could barely discern it and her body so still, he could almost believe he was preparing her for the funeral pyre, and that combined with her similarity to her sons...

Lial shuddered. He hadn't experienced the like since Telien's death.

For more than five hundred years, many of those after Lial had arrived at Braelyn, she had lain in hiding beneath this chamber, forced into the dreaming by Oria's healer. Nearly five and a half centuries stolen. Would she be able to fully recover after all this time? He skimmed his gaze down her body, noting the bagginess of her long gown and her lack of muscle tone.

How could Alerielle have done this? It was beyond cruelty to have kept her this way for so long. After seeing Elerie in person, he could no longer deny it. Even healing her spine might not help her enough to make up for the rest of her physical decline.

"What do you think?" Alerielle asked softly.

"You do not wish to know what I think," Lial replied sharply. She might be a few millennia older than he was, but she still deserved rebuke. "And yet you'll hear it anyway. You had no right to keep her trapped like this. If I were the Dorn of this estate, I would remove you from your position. Lyr may do so if Morenial does not."

Sorrow glinted in the healer's eyes, and the wrinkles around her mouth deepened with the harshness of her frown. "Perhaps. But you have no knowledge of my reasons. Suffice it to say that it was Elerie's wish that I guard her children above all."

"It is true that you aren't required to tell me why," he allowed. "However, I'll be speaking with Lyr myself after this. Have you talked to Lord Morenial?"

Alerielle's shoulders slumped. "Not much, nor has he been here to see her. He decided to wait for Kai."

That revelation would not go well, but it was coming soon. Now that they had a cure for the virus and a plan of distribution, there was no longer danger in Kai traveling to Oria with Arlyn. Lyr was waiting only for Lial to examine Lady Elerie and render his opinion.

No time like the present. Shoving aside his emotions, Lial took a step closer, closed his eyes, and sent his energy into the unconscious woman. At once, he found the immense damage to her spine. So many fractures, most either partly or incorrectly healed. He could see that Alerielle had poured massive amounts of energy and effort into the repairs, but her ability to delve in and prompt the bones to knit was not well-honed.

If it were an arm or leg, re-breaking and setting the fracture again would be an option, though an unpleasant one. The spine? Without extensive surgery, these countless tiny fractures would be impossible to break so they could be reset properly, especially after her body had had five hundred years to attempt to regenerate itself. He might be able to manage some of the larger spots—might—but she would never walk without pain again.

Provided she managed to walk at all.

Tamping down a fresh wave of anger, Lial moved his scan onward. Her organs were in good shape, and Alerielle had apparently taken care to see that Elerie's body healed properly after childbirth. Gods, what a thought. Allafon had pushed her down the stairs days after Kai's birth. And here Lial stood, ensuring she'd recovered centuries after her son had grown to adulthood.

He had to shift his attention again before he lost his focus. A look at her legs and arms revealed more repaired fractures, but these were cleaner and well-healed. Same for a few spots on her left scapula and ribs. Her muscles, however... He'd already noted loss of tone, but the sheer amount was stunning. She would be more helpless than an infant, who was at least able to move inside the womb. Bringing her out of the dreaming would be a long, difficult task.

When he returned to himself, his stifled emotions roared back, and he had to take a few moments to get them under control before he dared to look at Alerielle. Though pale, she met his gaze levelly as she awaited his prognosis. Her faith in his ability to fix such severe damage might have been flattering under different circumstances.

"There isn't much to be done about her spine," Lial said without preamble. "I can help reinforce some of the weak spots, but it would be nearly impossible to actually reset the vertebrae. It could perhaps be done if I cut her open and used tools to crack apart every misalignment. But she would never survive such a procedure in her current state, and I'm uncertain it would provide enough benefit."

Alerielle went whiter than Elerie's pristine gown. "But for Lynia—"

"Lynia's spine was freshly broken and her body undergoing its early repairs to damaged bone," he interrupted. "And that was difficult enough. Lady Elerie has been like this for *five hundred years.* Her body has regenerated to its natural extent. The bone is solid. Perhaps if you had found a healer with the appropriate skill immediately after the fall, it would be otherwise."

"She was a scout," Alerielle whispered, her shattered gaze on Elerie's face. "If we can't heal her, what will she do? Ah, she may never forgive me. But Allafon ordered me to let her die. He held baby Kai at the top of the stairs and—"

Her voice choked off, but it didn't matter. He could see the sickening scene well enough. "You were there."

Alerielle closed her eyes. "Right after. I'd just left after checking on her and hadn't made it out of the tower before I heard her scream. When I rushed back... At first, he pretended innocence, but as I knelt down to begin the healing, he switched to threats. I thought for certain he would snap Kai's neck and toss him after her."

That gruesome visual cooled his anger somewhat. "Then how did you save her?"

"I swore an oath of silence if he allowed Kai to live. Then in the guise of a mercy killing, I sent her deep into the dreaming. So deep she almost did die before I could hide her." The glance she sent him held a world's weight of grief. "Allafon did as I asked, but he raged for days. He killed three of the servants, including a woman who resembled Elerie too closely. She was burned on the pyre in Elerie's place."

A secret like that was a terrible burden. Even so. "In five hundred years—"

"That wasn't my only vow." Alerielle's lips thinned. "After Kai's birth, I swore a blood oath to protect him from Allafon and to see that he knew of his parentage once it was safe. At any cost, including Elerie's life. You may judge me as you will, but I did what I had to."

For the first time since he'd entered the room, Lial could see that.

# CHAPTER NINE

Tynan skimmed his gaze over the prone man stretched out on the odd, stone slab in the equally unusual dirt room. The Sidhe lord Naomh, his pale hair tangled around his emaciated form, vines full of verdant leaves weaving through some of the strands to crisscross his body. If Caolte was neglecting the outside world, he was clearly focusing his energy here. Aside from the vines, various plants grew around the edges of the room, bolstering the natural energy.

Not bad for a fire mage.

At Caolte's impatient look, Tynan opened his shields enough to let his healing magic free. Green light glowed around Naomh as Tynan shifted his awareness to the injured man so he could scan for injuries and disease. He concentrated on searching for the virus first, since that had afflicted the Sidhe lord so deeply. Fortunately, he found no trace.

Injuries, on the other hand... As he'd discovered with Lial, the virus had left some damage on the man's organs that would require repair, and his body had been leeched of nutrients. Fixable with time, rest, and a bit of magic. No, the true problem was the partly healed wound in Lord Naomh's abdomen. It appeared to have been cauterized, and Tynan detected iron sealed inside.

That metal was a poison, preventing the man's body from healing and disrupting his ability to draw in energy. Of course, Caolte had reported that Naomh was worsening, but Tynan had no basis for comparison. Had the injury been improving despite the iron? He released his hold on his magic, blinked to clear his vision, and met Caolte's eyes.

"The infection is gone," Tynan said. "But you'll have to tell me what has changed to cause you concern since I have not examined Lord Naomh before."

Anger flashed in Caolte's eyes, and a tiny spark flickered in his hair. "I told Myern Lyrnis that might be a problem."

Kezari stepped into Tynan's field of vision as though preparing to defend him. "You will not blame Tynan out of your own laziness, not to mention your disrespect for the young."

"The young?" Caolte asked, brows drawing together.

"Do the Sidhe have no regard for their children?" Kezari glared. "Babies are most fragile before birth. To insist that Lial risk his offspring because you do not wish to recount your observations to another healer is beyond contempt."

Though a few more sparks danced upward from his hair, Caolte mostly stared at Kezari as though she'd gone mad.

Clearly, the man had no idea *why* Tynan was here in the other healer's stead. For whatever reason, Lyr hadn't shared Lial's and Lynia's news even though Caolte was Kai's uncle. A curious choice, since Lial himself would now have a familial connection, however slight, with Naomh and Caolte. His twins with Lynia would be blood cousins with Kai's child.

"I have no knowledge of Lial's offspring, born or not," Caolte finally said, his words slow and measured. "And I am too exhausted to analyze your words for meaning. A boon, considering the insult of your initial question."

Kezari reddened. "I assumed you'd heard of his impending fatherhood."

"I had not, but it clarifies his absence." Caolte's smile was pinched. "I will be certain not to send good wishes, as I was obviously not intended to know."

With his shields so open, Tynan couldn't avoid the clammy wave of embarrassment from Kezari. He shivered against it, and from the sharp look she gave him, he suspected she noticed. He needed to change the subject before things got worse.

"So," Tynan said. "Tell me how Lord Naomh has worsened."

This time, Caolte hid his annoyance, though Tynan caught the echoes of it. "He has grown thinner," the man replied. "And when I try to connect with him mentally, he is very difficult to reach, more so than the dreaming should cause. He can't regenerate properly with iron in the wound, and I suspect he has lost the will to fight against it."

Tynan frowned down at Naomh's stomach, though the wound was covered by the long robe he wore. Extracting iron fragments would require surgery, but the techniques Lial had told him about were beyond Tynan's skill. He'd been taught to use magic as a primary means of repair, and he'd not yet sought training on the type of stitching Lial had mastered. While Tynan didn't have a strong iron allergy, Naomh did, and that meant his body wouldn't react well to healing magic.

Not to mention the actual extraction. The blood might wash out most of it when the wound was reopened—or it might not. According to Lial, there were ways to coax the metal free, but Tynan didn't know that trick either. A shame, that. Naomh needed help. Perhaps not emergent, but soon.

"What's wrong?" Kezari asked.

"I...can't remove the iron," Tynan confessed, as much as he hated it. Not for pride's sake, but for his patient's. "I'll have to consult with Lial."

Kezari's brow pinched. "It should be no major thing to separate the iron. I can do it if the wound is open."

"You?" Tynan stared at her, searching for signs that she was joking, but she appeared serious. "You're not a healer."

She snorted. "I work with earth. Not just stone, but metal,

too. I could pull the iron out as easily as I could reshape a cave. All I need is an exit point."

Bera bless, but it was a wonderful idea. He'd never heard of a dragon struggling with iron, unlike elves and fae. But when he considered the second part of the problem—opening the wound—his exhilaration faded. He could certainly try it. If Kezari succeeded in removing every trace of iron, he would be perfectly able to close any incision with magic. However, if she didn't...

That could lead to disaster. He'd messed up once by acting in haste, and he refused to do so again.

"I will not risk it without Lial," Tynan said. "Since I can find no sign of disease, we may be able to arrange to bring Lord Naomh to Moranaia. I'll have to speak with Lord Lyrnis."

To say that Caolte looked displeased would be a terrible understatement. More sparks shot up from the man's hair, and his hands fisted at his sides as he glared at Tynan. But beneath that, there was desperation. Tynan could practically taste it on the air even without his empathy.

What was behind this level of panic? There had to be some kind of past trauma, but he bit back the urge to ask. To solve. He wasn't Caolte's mind healer, and this wasn't Moranaia. He would rather not be immolated for causing offense. From what he'd heard about the man, that was an actual risk.

Abruptly, Kezari stepped in front of Tynan. "Guard your flame or taste mine."

Tynan nearly choked on his own spit, but not even his strangled cough turned her attention away from her target. Was she seriously threatening a Sidhe lord in his own domain? Gods. As Tynan sucked in air, he prayed fervently to Bera for a peaceful resolution.

KEZARI STOOD AS STILL and unmovable as the stone where she'd formed her cave. The hectic flame sputtering from the Sidhe man's head echoed in the currents of fire magic flowing untapped around them, and if he did not gain control, more than just his hair would burst into flames. He would not threaten Tynan in such a way.

Caolte scowled. "You dare chide me—"

"Oh, no. 'Chide' is a weak word to describe my statement of fact." As a Sidhe lord of indeterminate—thus likely ancient—age, he clearly wasn't challenged often. Too bad. "Dragon younglings control their fire better than you. I promise you that you will not like the result if you do not contain your power. You may be impervious to the burn of your own magic, but the same cannot be said of mine."

Behind her, Tynan coughed again, and though she wasn't empathic, she caught a hint of his emotions—worry bordering on panic. Too bad for him, too. Kezari dared not turn from her prey to comfort him. Or to argue for that matter. She would not back down, a realization she could see sweeping across Caolte's face as she stared him down.

Then he surprised her by inclining his head in a slight bow. As a flush crept up his neck and his jaw clenched, the chaotic energy around him lessened, and the sparks disappeared from his hair. But she could tell that his power was still barely leashed. Was he keeping his magic close to threaten them?

"I fear my training was not as stringent as yours," Caolte said, the flush reaching his cheeks. "But I give my word I intend no harm to you or the healer."

It was a true lack of control, then. A curious matter, but one that was no concern of hers. "See that you maintain civility around Tynan. None of this is his fault."

A curious gleam entered Caolte's eyes as his gaze flickered between her and Tynan. Did he believe there was deeper meaning behind her protectiveness? Of course, he was wrong. She wouldn't allow any friend or companion to be burned when she could stop it. Nothing deeper to it than that.

Whatever the man thought, he didn't give voice to it. "I will do so," he merely said.

Tynan moved forward until he stood by her side once more. "Perhaps Kezari and I should hurry our return to Moranaia to speak with Lial and Lord Lyrnis."

"That would be best," Caolte replied, his nod much sharper this time. "I will have a guard escort you around the holding to distribute your potions while I contact Inona."

Hah. More likely, he wanted to avoid her presence, since summoning Inona would take far less time than Tynan's task. Kezari was certain her grin held more than the proper amount of teeth at the satisfying thought. She'd quite thoroughly protected her—

Her what? She couldn't think of a word that settled well, and the search for it plagued her as they left the strange dirt room and its odd Sidhe occupants. She'd thought of friends and companions earlier, but she and Tynan argued far too often for the former and didn't truly qualify for the latter. They didn't spend enough time together, traveling or not.

*You're my soulbonded. I'm certain of it.*

No. Absolutely not. She'd already dismissed that absurd possibility, and she had no intention of reconsidering it. So what...?

Charge! He was her charge, of course. She'd been assigned to see him safely returned to Moranaia. The intention might have been to do so in case of infection, but she was the only guardian he had, wasn't she?

No need to worry over it more than that.

To Tynan's intense embarrassment, Kezari grabbed his hand as soon as they neared the portal for their return. Was his anxiety truly so noticeable? He'd believed his reaction was better stifled this time, since his fear had been lessened by their previous trip. It was a simple thing, really—they only needed to walk a moment or two through the fog. The mystery of it was gone.

But the mind being a fickle, illogical thing, his heartbeat sped up anyway. Could Kezari hear it even in her elven form? An uncomfortable but distinct possibility. Just before they followed Inona through the portal, he darted a glance Kezari's way. Once again, she stared straight ahead, nothing in her demeanor indicating that she was attuned to the frantic thumping of his heart.

Nevertheless, she tightened her grip.

For once, he didn't attempt to guard himself so heavily against her, for the fire of her confidence warmed him as surely as her hand. The cool of the Veil drifted around them, the endless gray somehow both soothing and choking, but Kezari's heat enveloped him like a cloak. Or a shield.

What was this? He wouldn't have expected peace to come from her chaos, but it was so. He couldn't deny it. For all that her unpredictable nature had almost led them into trouble back in the Sidhe realm, it also lent a surprising sense of comfort. If something unexpected were to happen while they were in the Veil, Kezari would not hesitate to confront it, no matter how strange.

Much to his relief, they didn't have to test that theory. Inona guided them through in only a handful of steps, and before he knew it, they'd emerged from the gate back into the clearing where they'd left. As before, Kezari released his hand almost immediately. His skin tingled at the lack, but this time, he didn't glance her way. He would not pressure her about their possible bond, especially when she'd only offered reassurance.

Inona halted beside the stone arch and smiled. "I have nothing to add to any report, save that the Veil remains calm. You'll tell Lord Lyr so I might return right away?"

"Your date?" Tynan asked, his own lips curving up.

"Surprisingly, no," Inona answered. "It's not quite dawn where we're living. I'd been worried the errand would take far longer, so you have my thanks there. I'd love more sleep, though."

Tynan shrugged. "I don't mind passing along the message."

"I am certain the discussion will be focused on our actions, not yours," Kezari said, and from the toothiness of her grin, he wondered if she was looking forward to telling the Myern about her threat to Lord Caolte.

If so, it might not receive the approval she expected.

Once Inona bid them farewell and disappeared back through the portal, Tynan and Kezari started down the path to the estate. Cold wind buffeted them, but he was still near enough to the dragon that he warmed a little between the gusts. How did she bear the chill against her heat? Curious, he looked at her out of the corner of his eye, but rather than appearing uncomfortable, her face had gone soft with pleasure.

Tynan jerked his gaze straight ahead, but the image lingered. If he dared to kiss her, would she look like that? Or would she shove him away in disgust before gutting him for his temerity? With a dragon shifter—and this one in particular—he imagined it could go either way.

"Why didn't you attempt surgery on Naomh?" Kezari surprised him by asking. "You were skilled enough to have saved Lial, so I'm uncertain why you are convinced that you require his help."

"It wouldn't have been safe." Though he sensed her regard, Tynan kept his eyes latched on the snow-dusted trail. "I have only minimal skill in sealing wounds without magic. If you'd had more trouble than expected, Lord Naomh might have bled out while I fumbled."

He didn't have to see Kezari to feel her bristling. "I would not have failed."

"Do you succeed at *everything* you attempt? Without error?" Tynan asked.

Her huff condensed into a little, indignant cloud, but it was the quickly masked dart of pain that had his steps slowing. Once again, Tynan peered at her face, but this time, her features had tightened. Had she taken the comment as an insult?

"Obviously, I do not," she bit out. "Or you wouldn't have needed to heal my poor *skizik*. Either time."

Without pausing to think, he reclaimed her hand. Surprisingly, she didn't pull away.

"That statement wasn't personal," Tynan insisted. "No one has perfect success, not always. Not even if they are experts in a task. Certainly not healers. Sometimes, I think healing is as much balancing risk as anything. It's tricky, knowing where and how to push. When to try more energy and when to retreat. That is what was behind my decision. You probably could have done the task, but if you'd failed, he would have died. I could not bear a risk like that."

Kezari glanced down at their hands. "We dragons expect much of ourselves, you know. The kind of magic that can shape mountains, incinerate forests, alter seasons...it requires a great deal of control. Lowering one's standards too far or acting in too much haste risks ceding to a dangerous weakness."

A wave of comprehension had his fingers tightening around hers; beneath her brash, bold confidence, Kezari was wary of her own nature. She fought to suppress the impulses she deemed dangerous, and when she failed, her mistakes became monuments to her perceived inadequacy. Was that why she'd accepted her exile from the other dragons without an appeal?

Yet he couldn't tell her she was wrong—not fully. Hadn't he learned for himself the dangers of losing control? He couldn't deny having a few monuments of his own. He supposed it was proof that they were far too alike to be comfortable in a soulbond. They would form a veritable museum to insecurity between them.

Abruptly, her golden eyes fastened on his. "I understand your trouble around me more than you realize. Why else do you think I tried so hard to avoid you? As you said, some risk is too much to bear, and I would not wish to risk causing another to lose control."

Tynan quirked a brow. "You've looked more inclined to eat me than to spare me future pain."

"I didn't say I haven't had my moments of anger," Kezari replied, shrugging.

A lump formed in Tynan's throat at the hint of teasing on her face, and he had the sudden urge to coax out her humor. "Is that why you threatened to breathe flame on Lord Caolte?"

She let out a cute little scoffing sound. "I did no such thing. I merely told him what could happen if he continued. I would have shifted to my dragon form for a true threat."

"Really?" Tynan laughed, the lump in his throat dissolving into unexpected contentment. "I'll do my best to remember."

Kezari tugged at her hand, and he only then noticed that they'd stopped walking entirely. "Let's hope Lyr is so understanding. Not that I would have acted differently, of course. Whoever taught Lord Caolte to harness his fire did a poor job of it. I was not being rude to say that dragon younglings do far better."

From what he'd seen of the Sidhe man, Kezari was right—not that Tynan would have been the one to say so to his face.

# CHAPTER TEN

This meeting wasn't likely to go the way she wanted, but Kezari had no intention of backing down. She would never neglect the safety of others out of politeness, and if the Myern expected such, it was just as well that she knew before any other missions. Provided there *were* other missions, of course.

Lyr waited behind his desk, the usual stack of papers piled near his right hand. Were they the same ones, or did he really go through that many in a day? He seemed to be an efficient sort, so it was no doubt the latter. It would explain the tired look in his eyes when he straightened, rubbing the back of his neck almost absently.

"Good morning," Lyr said. "I trust Inona decided not to come with you?"

Tynan stopped a talon or two away from the desk, and Kezari halted beside him. Though Tynan completed the strange chest-tapping salute, she didn't bother. It meant nothing to her. Not fealty or anything else. The very fact that she hadn't flown away showed fealty enough, didn't it?

"Good morn, Myern," Tynan replied. "Inona asked that we notify you that she had little to report beyond the calmness of the Veil. I hope granting that request was not an error?"

Lyr tapped his finger against the stack of papers. "I'll take her word for it if it will save me from reading another formal report."

Since Tynan did nothing but shift uncomfortably, Kezari took a slight step forward. "I need not consign my words to paper, either, unless you require it. I see no need to do so. I am happy to tell you the results of our meeting with the Sidhe lord now."

"Indeed?" Lyr pursed his lips. "I've already spoken to Caolte, Kezari."

She stiffened, and she heard a sound just behind her that sounded suspiciously like a breathy curse. "I did *not* threaten him," she insisted.

"Kezari..." Tynan began.

Lyr lifted a hand for silence—a match to his raised brow. "Why would I believe that you did?"

Kezari went as still as prey waiting for the strike. What did he mean by that? Would Caolte not have told him of her admonishment? Curious. Even admirable. But once again, she'd caused her own trouble. Perhaps she needed an elder dragon to chastise *her*.

"It was in my defense," Tynan said quickly. As he stepped forward, his soothing energy brushed against her until she nearly sighed in relief. "Lord Caolte had...a moment where it seemed his flame might leave his control. Kezari told him to stand down."

"I see."

Beneath Lyr's regard, Kezari bristled, but she kept a firm grasp on her physical form. She had allowed herself to slip into partial shifts far too many times, even if it was only her skin. And she didn't have the excuse of the poisoned energy distracting her now. With ruthless resolve, she clamped down on her magic harder.

Even so, her arms itched.

"I would assume that since he didn't mention it, Lord Caolte took no insult from the encounter," Lyr finally said. "But it is concerning to hear, nonetheless. For future missions, I mean."

"Would you prefer that I allow someone to hurt my charge?" Kezari demanded, fighting to keep her tone as level as her magic.

Tynan sucked in a breath. "Your charge? I do not believe either of us is above the other."

"No," she argued. "But I am tasked with ensuring you return in one piece. One healthy, living piece, not a charred mass of elf. That Sidhe lord holds a dangerous amount of fire for such pitiful control. If—"

"Enough," Lyr snapped, sitting up straighter in his seat. "How did you manage to work together during the mission, only to fall apart here?"

Kezari blinked, the question catching her by surprise. It was... a good point. She and Tynan might not have been in perfect accord while checking on Lord Naomh, but they'd worked together well enough. Yet any time they stood before Lyr, they bickered. Was she the one too much on guard, or was it Tynan?

"I am uncertain, Myern," Tynan said, and there was a hint of weariness in his tone that suggested it might be her.

Ancestors' blood, but it was her, wasn't it?

Her dealings with the dragon queen must have left her with deeper scars than she'd realized. And why wouldn't it? Each meeting with the queen had been designed to pick at Kezari's resolve—to wear her down until she disconnected from Earth's energy or at least gave up on speaking of it. Being directly questioned by the Myern was too reminiscent of the queen's constant interrogations.

Except Lyr was nothing like Queen Zevie. He gave no indication that he wished to sabotage her, and his questions weren't designed to lead her into a trap. He spoke with command but also respect. There was nothing familiar about those things. Like most of the other dragons, the queen had mocked Kezari's talents. Her pursuit of the old ways. Her very nature. Receiving such consideration from a leader was a rare experience.

Her heart had expected disdain for confronting Caolte—the rest of her had only acted in accord.

Though it galled, Kezari inclined her head. "It is my fault. I will endeavor to control my temper."

And her fear, but that she would *not* admit.

Lyr sighed. "So long as your reaction isn't excessive, I *do* expect you to step in to protect Tynan when necessary, as should he for you. I will trust that your judgment was correct in this situation."

Kezari couldn't imagine a situation where a healer would need to protect a dragon, but she deemed it prudent not to say so. "Thank you."

"As for your suggestion to Caolte, Tynan," Lyr said, "Much relies on Lial's input. I've summoned him here, but he just returned from Oria."

Oria. That was the estate near the cursed bit of forest where she'd pounced on that bodyguard, nearly sending Aris into another breakdown. Wonderful. They'd been monitoring the area for any damage caused by Aris's life magic. Something might have happened with that.

"Did my *skizik*'s magic..." Kezari began, but she hesitated to complete the question. The first words that came to mind—warp, twist, pervert—weren't exactly complimentary.

Sympathy moved in the Myern's gaze. "No. Nothing like that."

"It's—"

Tynan's voice cut off so abruptly that she whipped her head around to search the area for a threat. But as far as she could tell, no one else had entered. What else could have caused the healer's sudden silence? His lips were pinched tight, and he didn't meet her gaze as she stared.

Oh, no.

"Was there some other damage caused by my mistake?"

That garnered his full attention. "No, not to my knowledge. I am simply uncertain about the...confidentiality of the matter. Lial might have allowed me to hear, but I'm a fellow healer who might be called upon to help."

A mysterious secret, then. Kezari gritted her teeth. A mystery was almost worse, for she had the inexplicable desire to unearth it like a precious gem, polish it up, and guard it in her mental hoard. Like a gemstone, secrets held power. It was all in how they were used. Though she had no desire to cause harm, well...one never knew.

"I appreciate your discretion," Lyr said, which only sparked her curiosity to greater heights. "If I'm not mistaken, I believe Lial intends to speak to you in private about this soon. The need for secrecy may end before long."

What could it be? She was so busy scouring her memory for all she'd learned about Oria that she barely noticed when the door opened and Lial strode in.

TYNAN COULD FEEL Kezari's fervent curiosity as surely as his own leaping pulse. Lady Bera help him, but he should have kept his mouth closed. Kezari was relentless when riled, and he had a feeling she would be no different when prying for information. Not that he anticipated her being malicious if she learned the secret. It was only that the more people who knew, the greater the risk that Kai would find out in the worst possible way.

With good fortune, Lial would speak to him about the matter sooner rather than later.

The man in question halted on the other side of Kezari and gave the barest of salutes. "I've much to catch up on after both myself and Tynan were absent from the healing tower for so long. What do you need?"

Tynan hid a grimace at Lial's bold words. Had the man always been so casual with the Myern, or was it a benefit of being engaged to the Myern's mother? Either way, Lord Lyr showed no signs of offense.

Instead, Lyr's lips twisted into a wry smile. "I rather thought you'd want input into our treatment plans for Naomh."

"Oh?" Lial's eyes narrowed on Tynan rather than the Myern. "I expected you to return to the tower to report."

The statement had been delivered sharply, but it wasn't anger resonating from the other healer. There was edginess, to be certain, but the overriding emotion held the solemn tang of grief. What exactly had happened at Oria? If Lial had been there to examine Elerie, it must have brought out deep feelings.

"Is it not customary to speak to the Myern first?" Tynan asked calmly.

Lial frowned. "In general, yes, but in this case..."

"You are always too harsh on him," Kezari said, a growl to her voice that boded ill for the future of the conversation.

Unless he interfered.

"We can discuss such technicalities later," Tynan rushed to say before Lial could turn his scowl fully on Kezari and further spark her anger. "I found no signs of the virus in either Sidhe lord or in anyone I encountered while distributing potions. However, I've determined Lord Naomh requires surgery to remove the iron from his wound before he can recover. I am unfortunately unable to handle such a procedure myself."

That distracted Lial like little else could. "Were you not trained to stitch an incision closed in the event of an emergency?"

"I was," Tynan countered, keeping a wary eye on Kezari's increasingly stormy expression. "But not to the extent that I would consider performing surgery on an important Sidhe lord, particularly one who is currently stable. It would be best to bring him here if you do not wish to risk a journey there yourself."

Based on Lial's pinched lips and furrowed brow, Tynan antici-pated a scathing reply, but the healer only studied him for a moment before nodding. "Better to be safe if you are uncertain of your abilities. However, there are other risks in bringing him here. With the healing we must do on Elerie and their potential bond..."

Tynan glanced pointedly toward Kezari, but the other two men didn't notice.

"What is her prognosis?" Lord Lyr asked.

"She will require a great deal of healing," Lial replied, and the earlier grief Tynan had sensed now echoed in the man's tone. "But the damage is too extensive for me to fully repair no matter how much time and energy I happen to spend. Lady Elerie has had over five hundred years of natural healing. With the way her spine has fused, she may never walk again, even if I were to attempt to rebreak each bone and fuse it again."

Lyr winced. "I'd hoped for better news from your visit to Oria."

"*Kai's mother* was the secret?" Kezari interjected. "I've known about her being alive for weeks."

"Yes," Lial replied, his lips twitching. "I assume everyone who was in the healing tower that night is aware. It is the extent of her injuries that is new information."

Ah, she'd been there with Aris. He should have considered such.

Despite the gravity of Lial's news, Tynan nearly smiled at the blatant disappointment on the dragon's face. No doubt the curious dragon had been eager for a mysterious secret, and he could practically see her huffing at discovering it was nothing new. But then the considering gleam returned to her eyes.

"Do you think Aris could help?" she asked.

"I—"

An insistent chime cut across Lial's words, but Tynan was uncertain of the source until the Myern glanced at the tall mirror positioned in front of one of the windows to his left. A communication spell? Tynan expected Lord Lyr to silence the chime in light of their current meeting, but instead, he gestured at the door.

"This may be important," Lyr said. "Lial, I give you leave to handle Naomh however you see best. Let me know what you may need, and keep me apprised of each step. And please speak to Tynan about Elerie as soon as possible. Unless Ralan storms in with another prophecy, I want Kai told now that the danger from the virus has passed."

"Presuming Tynan will accompany me to the healing tower,

I'll discuss the matter with him now," Lial said. "I'll send you notice of the rest."

"My thanks, *Orlayak*," Lyr said with a quick, wicked grin.

"Did you just—" The chime interrupted Lial's words once again, but it did nothing to erase his scowl. He flicked his hand outward in a dismissive gesture before spinning toward the door. "I'm not even married yet," Lial muttered, but only Tynan and Kezari were likely close enough to hear beneath the incessant chiming.

Though from the widening of Lyr's grin, Tynan suspected he'd caught the general meaning. *Orlayak*—second father. Oh yes, there was definitely a casual relationship between the two if the Myern would tease Lial with that. Tynan hid his own amusement as he gave a hurried salute and retreated toward the door.

The dynamics here were far different than at home—and he was starting to think that he liked it.

LYR STOOD as the door closed behind Kezari and then hurried to activate the mirror. At once, his image disappeared, replaced by Princess Dria and her bonded, Vek. It was rare for her to contact him unless there was a major issue at the outpost, especially since Ralan was nominally in charge. He dared not risk ignoring some new potential problem.

"Good morning, Princess Dria," Lyr said. "And Prince Vek."

"So our times align fairly well for once, though I don't know if the sun is up here." Dria's smile stretched into a tight, tense line. "I confess that I didn't take the time to check, but I have been trying to contact my brother for several hours now. Aside from my worry, there are some new developments that need reporting."

Of course there were new developments. Weren't there always?

"That's curious. He and Cora left early this morning to check the progress on their new home, but he was here for dinner yesterday." Lyr did a quick check of the estate's shields and detected Eri with Iren and Selia. But Ralan and Cora had yet to return. "If he's ignoring your mirror call, there's no doubt some arcane reason. I would assume it isn't too bad, though, since Eri hasn't attempted to answer in his stead."

Dria's faint, breathy laugh vibrated fuzzily through the link. "There is that. Well, whatever prophecy he might be following, I'm telling you about this anyway. Some of the humans are growing restless here, and we're worried that Meren is involved with at least one group of them."

"Not that we can't handle it," Vek interjected.

Lyr felt confident in assuming that *that* would've been the Unseelie prince's preference. "I'll provide assistance if I am able. I foresee no problems with doing so."

"It could be tricky." Dria held up a piece of paper. "Read this."

He leaned slightly forward, eyes focusing on the text through the sometimes-wavering link. But with each word he read, a chill grew within him. Though it hadn't been a serious concern in most areas in over a century, anti-magic hysteria had been a real threat almost everywhere during Lyr's earlier travels on Earth. They'd taken care to avoid places where such fears were heightened, and the wording of this new note prompted the same wrench of the gut.

Ralan or no, it would have to be dealt with.

# CHAPTER ELEVEN

Tynan expected Kezari to make her excuses and leave since the meeting with Lord Lyr was over, but she surprised him by following him out into the cold. Silently, the three of them picked their way down the trail, recently cleared but growing slick once more with the snow falling heavily. At least the cloud and tree canopy muted the mid-morning sun; as it was, he had to shade his eyes against the brightness.

By the time they reached the healing tower, snow coated Tynan's cloak so thickly that he resembled one of the white, fuzzy *bersen* that roamed the frigid north. Kezari, of course, didn't have so much as a speck marring her golden hair or dampening her dress. Somehow, she wasn't even surrounded by a cloud of steam.

The spell inlaid into the door removed the snow from their clothes and shoes as they entered, so Tynan hung his now-dry cloak on a hook and ran his hand through his hair to settle it. Thankfully, the fine-tuned spell didn't remove moisture from the body, only fabric, or his skin would be dry as dust from the constant coming and going.

Lial closed the door with a questioning glance toward Kezari, but he didn't ask her to leave. He merely removed his outerwear and headed for the small grouping of chairs situated between his workbench and the stone surgery table. Tynan had expected him to clear away the seats that Maddy, Fen, and Anna had brought down during their last visit, but instead, Lial had requested replacements for his room upstairs.

Tynan sat across from Lial, and once again, Kezari surprised him by sitting in the third seat that formed their little triangle. What was she doing? She hadn't even been aware that Lial had gone to examine Lady Elerie until a short time ago. As far as he knew, Kezari wasn't particularly close to Kai, so she would have no insight there. Though her presence didn't bother him, exactly, it seemed unusual.

Why had she stayed?

The question picked at the edge of his mind as he settled into his chair, but he didn't want to voice it. Lial's brow was wrinkled in thought, and when Emowa leaped into his lap and curled up, he stroked the *camahr*'s soft-looking fur almost absently. Tynan didn't want to disrupt the other healer's musings any more than he wanted to test Emowa's patience by attempting to pet her.

One did not touch a *camahr* without permission.

"Well?" Kezari asked, her patience the first to break. "Wasn't this going to be a meeting? You said you wanted to discuss things with Tynan."

Lial's gaze flicked toward her, and his frown returned. "You aren't Tynan, last I checked. Or a healer. If you're here out of concern, I assure you that I have no intention of chastising Tynan again. You need not continue to act as his guardian."

Her nostrils flared. "That's not what I'm doing."

"Then what *are* you doing?" Lial asked. "Do you have more to add to Tynan's report on Naomh?"

At least Tynan wasn't the only one confused about her presence, though the other healer seemed far more unsettled by it. There wasn't really a problem with her staying, not at the beginning of the discussion, but Lial's mood had been sour from the moment he'd walked into Lyr's study earlier.

Kezari shrugged. "I don't have any additional observations

about Naomh, no. I was more concerned about his brother's excessive fire."

"I see." Lial's hand went still against Emowa's back. "In that case, you must leave."

Kezari reared back, but her head tilted as though in confusion. "You are frequently blunt but not usually cruel. Your tone verged toward the latter."

And it had—even Tynan wanted to squirm uncomfortably in his seat from it.

Though tension hummed on the air, sitting near these two was largely a study in pride and stubbornness. For a couple of drips, Kezari and Lial frowned at each other, neither willing to yield. Then Lial swiped his hand across his face and grimaced, and at the tired gesture, Kezari's shoulders lowered a fraction.

"You are correct," Lial admitted. "Truth be told, my emotions are not as measured as they should be. Far from it."

Tynan had noted as much, but the other healer's shielding was impressive. He hadn't *felt* a single one of those tumultuous emotions. "Do you need a consultation?" Tynan offered.

"I may at some point, but I am managing well enough for now." Lial dropped his hand to his lap, and Emowa rubbed her snout against his fingers. "Forgive me, Kezari, for taking it out on you. I was surprised by your presence since you don't usually attend such meetings, and this one in particular has to be private. I really *must* ask you to leave if you have no additional details. We are discussing both a patient and another member of the household, and healers guard such secrets carefully."

"Understandable," Kezari said, nodding. "I doubt that would hold my interest, anyway. I merely wanted to pursue my earlier question."

Her question? What had she last asked? Before Tynan could recall, Lial shook his head. "No."

"What do you mean?" Kezari asked, her tension returning. "Is that the answer to the question or to my pursuit of it?"

Lial shoved back a strand of his auburn hair. "That is the answer. I do not believe Aris can help with this."

Ah, yes. Kezari had wondered if Aris could use his life magic on Lady Elerie, hadn't she? Something to that effect. It was a curious possibility, but Lial dismissed it without a second thought. Why? Life mages were rare, their ability to shape living things often sought-after. What if Aris *could* use that to reform the lady's bones?

"You have not had time to consider it," Kezari insisted.

"Oh, I have," Lial said. "Yes, life mages can alter and shape living beings, but the more complex the lifeform, the more difficulty. And the more energy required. Intense levels of that kind of magic can warp things in the general area. The attempt would not be worth the risk, and if you asked Aris, I have no doubt he would concur."

Kezari stood. "I will do so."

As she turned toward the door, Tynan grabbed her wrist, and the warmth of her skin tingled through him like pure sunlight. She frowned down at him until he had to clear his throat. "Kezari. Why are you so adamant about this?"

Her expression softened, though chagrin shaded it. "Partly because the secret of her survival wouldn't have been revealed so abruptly if I hadn't hurt Korel, requiring healing. But mostly because the people here have been kind to me, and I dislike the hurt the lady's injuries will cause them."

Tynan could only stare up at her, stunned by her honesty and humbled by the kindness hidden beneath her blunt façade. He tried to formulate a response, but before he could think of anything, she tugged her arm free and hurried out into the snow. Flakes still swirled in the closing door's wake by the time he'd even blinked.

"I do not understand her," Tynan muttered.

"It seems I don't either," Lial said. Then he lifted a shoulder. "Fortunately, *I'm* not her soulbonded."

The last was said with humor, but it cut, nonetheless. "Nor am I. Yet."

Lial winced. "I'm sorry. I'm beyond all tact, and it isn't even midday."

"So it's a normal day?" Tynan asked wryly.

The other man laughed. "Complete with another complicated dilemma, I suppose. Care to tell me your thoughts as a mind healer on the best way to break the news to Kai? It's complicated by his bonded's pregnancy."

As he always did, Tynan tamped down the ache caused by the careless comment about his non-existent soulbond and instead latched on to the current problem—Kai and Arlyn. It was very true that emotions could ricochet and magnify between soulbonded pairs, so Kai's pain could turn Arlyn's compassion for her bonded into extreme and dangerous distress. But there were methods to mitigate that.

"I would be happy to do so," Tynan said. "I've dealt with soulbonded couples during trauma before. A solid plan will help immensely."

As would care and timeliness.

He sent a quick prayer to Lady Bera that they could manage both.

KEZARI WOULD NOT LET her scales spring free. Nor her wings. Not even fangs. She absolutely would maintain control, from now until she finished speaking to Aris. She wasn't a youngling to be controlled by her emotions. And she certainly wasn't Caolte of the Sidhe, letting her fire loose at risk to others.

No matter how much her skin itched or her throat ached.

Snow crunched beneath her boots as she stomped along the path. *Why* did everyone consider her heartless because her view of the world was different? Was it so unfathomable that she truly wanted to help Kai and the others? As frustrating as they could be, they had listened to her and given her aid when her own kind hadn't. She would not forget it.

And Kai. While helping heal the poison afflicting Earth's magic, Kai had been injured, his mental channels damaged while shaping the permanent gate between the outpost and Moranaia. They'd been mentally linked, she, Aris, and Kai, so she knew better than most how much he'd given as part of the process. He deserved whatever good fortune she and Aris could provide when it came to his injured mother. Was it so strange for her to wish such?

By the time she reached the back entrance to the estate, a hint of mist danced across her skin, and she snarled at herself as she jerked open the door. So much for absolute control. She would have steam coming off of her in truth if she didn't reign in her emotions. If she wanted, she could radiate enough heat to warm the entire building even without its temperature regulation spells.

Or burn down the library full of books that she was about to enter.

Kezari closed her eyes and focused on her breath. Cool, not-at-all-flame-y breath. She counted the tiny beats of her current body's heart and let the calming rhythm soothe her. The thrum was much more delicate than the drumbeat she felt as a dragon, yet this body had power, all the same. Though once foreign, the duality now brought an unusual sense of comfort.

The door opened, and Aris's presence neared. "Kezari?"

She took one more deep breath before she opened her eyes to her *skizik*'s gaze. "Yes?"

"Why are you standing by the back door?"

"Calming myself enough not to burn anything," she replied at once. "Tynan is a vexing man."

Aris's brows rose. "So the mission went poorly."

"Not exactly," Kezari said as she brushed past him. She marched down the short set of stairs leading to the bottom level of the library, but she came to an abrupt halt at the sight of Selia sitting with Eri and Iren at one of the tables on the other side of the large room. "Ah, I should have scanned to see if the children were still here. I have a question that does not need such curious listeners."

"They might not be able to hear you over here," Aris said, though his forehead held more than a few concerned wrinkles.

Kezari snorted. "Those two? I would count on nothing."

At the table, Selia leaned over and whispered to the children to go play. A perfect example of how sound carried in this place since Kezari had heard the low words, but she didn't point that out to Aris. She could sense his growing concern through their link and decided it was best not to aggravate him further.

"Should I be worried?" he murmured.

"I don't think so," Kezari replied.

Their books in hand, Iren and Eri hurried by them, Eri casting Kezari a grin that suggested the girl knew perfectly well what the discussion would be about. And the young seer probably did. Interesting that she showed enough restraint not to comment, though. Kezari watched her until the door closed behind the two.

Just in case.

They crossed the room in uneasy silence, one Kezari wasn't certain how to break. As she stopped beside the table, Aris sat beside Selia, but Kezari couldn't stand to be so constrained, even if it was only gravity holding her elven arse to wood. She could pretend that flight was only a quick leap away in her current spot.

"I'm sorry for the interruption," Kezari finally ventured.

Aris studied her with his measured gaze. "Something *is* wrong if you're being so formal with *me*."

Or anyone. He was kind enough not to say it, but all three of them knew it to be true. "Fine, then. There's a point of debate between me and Lial, and only you can answer it."

"Only me?" he asked carefully.

Selia rubbed a soothing hand down Aris's arm, her touch light and careful even to Kezari's eyes. "Why Aris?"

"Is it possible to use life magic to repair severe damage to an elf?" Kezari asked before their concern could grow. "I know you can alter creatures, but according to Lial, it would be too risky to attempt on a person. But how much would it take to, say, remold bone that healed improperly?"

The color leeched from Aris's skin. "I am content with the healing I've received, Kezari."

"Oh, elders' dangly..." Kezari huffed. "Not *you*. Remember when we were at Oria? Kai's mother? Lial examined her today, and it seems a great many of her bones set poorly. He can't do much after so many centuries, but with life magic, perhaps—"

A thud cracked the air behind and above her. "What?"

Kezari spun, her hands curling like talons even as recognition hit.

Arlyn.

Without hesitation, Kezari sent a mental call for Tynan.

ARLYN STARED down at the book she'd nearly dropped on her toe, but she couldn't make sense of much beyond the words she'd just overheard. *Kai's mother. Lial examined her today.* Today. As in some time between sunrise and now. Not five hundred and forty-two years ago. Really, there was no sense to be made of anything.

She left the book where it lay and stepped up to the railing to better see over the side. Yep. Kezari, Aris, and Selia, all gawking up at her with various degrees of chagrin and/or worry. Even from several floors up, she could see the *Oh, shit* expression spreading across Kezari's face. What was going on?

"I couldn't have heard that right," Arlyn said.

Even though she'd heard perfectly clearly.

Selia's shock cleared first, but the hint of fear pinching her eyes wasn't much better. "Perhaps you should come down."

Like she would do anything else. "Give me a moment."

Her thoughts fluttered around like the pages of the book partially crumpled on the floor. *Lynia will kill me if I leave that there*, Arlyn thought somewhat uselessly, although she bent and picked it up. Carefully, she smoothed the bent paper as she circled around to the recently installed lift on the far side. She took the stairs most of the time, but now?

No.

As the lift descended, she cupped her gently rounded belly with concern. But aside from the same dance of nerves she always felt in such situations, she detected no unusual sensations. Good. So far, she'd only felt sporadic flutters and maybe-kicks from the baby. If she was panicking—was she panicking?—it wasn't affecting her child.

*Deep breaths, Arlyn. Kai's mother absolutely is not returning from the dead.*

Selia was at her side as soon as she stepped from the lift. "Tynan and Lial are on their way."

"Great," Arlyn muttered. "Just what I wanted...more orders to rest."

Her teacher linked arms with her, and together, they approached Aris and Kezari. Part of Arlyn almost felt sorry for the poor dragon, but she couldn't quite manage full sympathy at the moment. "Please tell me you said the wrong name."

Kezari's mouth twisted into a...what the hell kind of expression was that? Smile? Grimace? Eldritch horror? "You weren't supposed to hear that."

Her tone sounded apologetic. Some weird dragon grimace, then.

"Yeah, I guessed as much." Arlyn rubbed soothing circles over her stomach. Well, soothing for her, at least. "Soooo...not the wrong name, then."

If Kai's mother was alive—*please, don't let there be zombies*—he would lose his mind. Gone. But when would Kezari have been at Oria to find out? She hadn't been at Braelyn for that long, so it was probably a new secret. Who else knew?

How were they going to tell Kai?

"It was revealed during the disease outbreak," Aris said softly.

Wordlessly, Selia helped Arlyn into a chair. "Ralan ordered the secret kept, I believe."

Arlyn leaned forward and dropped her forehead into her palm, her elbow digging into her knee. That, of course, squeezed her belly uncomfortably, forcing her to straighten. What kind of universe gave her this kind of news when she couldn't even slump properly?

"Are you okay?" Selia asked. "Never mind. Of course you aren't."

"I should leave this place," Kezari said to Aris in a soft tone that suggested Arlyn wasn't supposed to hear.

Yay, elven hearing.

Suddenly, Kai's worry echoed through their bond. *"What's wrong?"*

Dammit. She did her best to shield her emotions before responding. *"I'm fine. Just learning some surprising history in the library."*

*"I'll be there as soon as I can,"* Kai replied, an edge of panic already in his voice. *"But it will take at least half a mark from this section of the woods."*

*"Really, I'm fine. You don't have to do that,"* Arlyn insisted.

But the bad thing about being bonded? Sometimes, it was the bond.

Shielding only went so far against that.

# CHAPTER TWELVE

Tynan should have guessed that the timing would be all wrong. It was simply one of those cycles—one of those inexplicable spans of time where every action seemed destined to find a chaotic outcome. "Seemed" being key. The good moments tended to become lost amidst the turmoil, but they were there. As he and Lial hurried as safely as they could along the slippery garden path, Tynan did his best to recall a single one.

"I notified Lyr," Lial said in a low voice. "He's on his way to the library, but I told him to wait outside for the moment. At least Kai was out checking on one of the observation towers to the north. We'll have a little time to speak to Arlyn."

Well, then. There was a good thing.

He and Lial entered the back door in a rush, but without a word, they both halted for a moment to collect themselves. Tynan couldn't help but smile at the shared reflex, an instinct honed by countless healings. Sometimes, calm was as important as haste, and this was definitely one of those situations.

After smoothing down his wind-tossed hair and straightening his robes, Tynan opened the library door and stepped through. Immediately, he had to tighten his shields to nearly uncomfortable levels. Not because of Arlyn—it was Kezari. Her guilt and pain filled the room as thoroughly as her dragon form would, and he was as vulnerable to it as a newborn *daeri*.

Everything within him demanded he comfort her, and the sensation only increased as he approached the group. Between his instincts and the strength of Kezari's emotions, opening himself up enough to help calm Arlyn—and eventually Kai—would be a challenge. But he had to do his best to tolerate the turmoil. After their earlier argument, Kezari wouldn't take it well if he told her to leave.

Lial eyed him as they reached Arlyn, and whatever he saw made him frown. Could he tell how tightly Tynan had to guard against Kezari? Deep inside, Tynan flinched at the thought of being so transparent, his struggles so easy for Lial to see. The man already had a questionable opinion of him after Aris's healing, and this would in no way help.

*Struggle isn't weakness, and needing help is not a mark of shame,* he reminded himself.

If he couldn't handle the current situation, he would let Lial know.

"Kezari," the other healer said, his tone kinder than Tynan would have expected. "Would you and Aris fly over to the new palace and find out why Ralan hasn't returned? Since my cousin is responsible for much of this situation, it seems fitting he should be here to provide input."

Instead of answering right away, Kezari's gaze flicked to Tynan. Would the sight of him upset her further? Her body language showed little of the chaotic emotions swirling around her, and he didn't dare open his shields enough to find out for himself. But her feelings for him, good or bad, never showed anywhere he could see. Her attention returning to Lial, she stood taller, and the chaos of her emotions receded somewhat.

"I will do so," she said.

He must look more troubled than he'd thought if she was shielding her feelings in the middle of this.

"Thank you," Tynan murmured to Lial when Kezari and Aris had gone. "I didn't want to hurt her again, but..."

Lial gave a sharp nod. "I guessed as much."

With the pressure of Kezari's emotions now absent, Tynan studied the scene once more, including the flow of energy. A pale Arlyn sat in a chair pulled askew from the table, and Selia stood beside her, her hand on Arlyn's shoulder. Not only for comfort, he noted. Arlyn was Selia's apprentice in magic, and her teacher had added an extra layer of shielding in case of magic gone awry.

Lial knelt beside Arlyn, and the light turned blue with his magic as he examined her and the babe she carried. Leaving him to it, Tynan narrowed his focus on her face, noting her expression. She appeared shocked but not *in* shock. A good sign. He noted an expected amount of confusion and worry. But when he opened up his empathy, Tynan felt what her face didn't show—a thread of anger.

Tynan allowed his calming energy to flow free, and between that and the soothing effect of Lial's healing magic, Arlyn slumped against the back of her seat. Not in absolute relief—her emotions were in too much upheaval for that without greater intervention—but enough to suggest that the situation would be manageable.

The other healer's magic winked out. "Fortunately, you are both well."

Arlyn took a deep breath, but some of her annoyance spilled out despite the calming action. "How long have you been hiding this? Does everyone know? Gods, Lial. Please tell me not-dead dead people aren't common here."

"I promise you that they are not." Lial's lips thinned into a hard line. "This was hidden from me, too. From everyone. Oria's healer kept Lady Elerie in the dreaming. Alerielle only revealed the secret when she thought she might die attempting to heal Korel."

"Holy shit," Arlyn whispered.

Wordlessly, Tynan absorbed her wave of emotions and increased his calming flow.

"Morenial was on his way to tell Kai when Ralan stopped him," Lial continued. "And Ralan urged me to remain silent, as well."

"I can't believe you kept something like this a secret." Arlyn shifted back in her chair, an unconscious retreat. "I trusted you."

Lial grimaced. "It was not my desire to break that trust. But to be blunt...Ralan's vision revealed that if you and Kai rushed to Oria that night, both of you would have likely sickened and died. I would never do anything to risk that outcome. None of us would."

When Lial and Tynan had discussed the course they should take, they'd agreed that being straightforward was best. It was almost too much. Arlyn's fear surged, and if not for Tynan's calming magic, she might have made herself ill. He knelt on her other side and took her hand.

"Please allow me to dull your emotions to a greater extent," Tynan said. "With your permission, I can keep you calmer when discussing this with the others."

Her brows drew together. "I'm upset, but I can handle difficult topics. I don't need someone to turn off my feelings."

Of course she assumed that was what he would do. Tynan sighed. *If only it were so simple.*

"To be more precise," he began, "it's mostly the physiological response I wish to dull right now. Emotions must be dealt with one way or another. No avoiding that. But stress hormones can be harmful for you and your child. When Kai's emotions crash into yours, and you're each magnifying one another, it could be dangerous. My methods reduce that rebound effect."

Tynan could also absorb some of the excess with his empathy, but that was best left unsaid. It was too complicated to explain, and patients invariably held back in unhealthy ways if they thought he might be injured. He would willingly suffer the after-effects later if it helped prevent harm now.

Some of the fierceness leeched from Arlyn's expression, but a hint of annoyance lingered. "Will you magically calm Kai, too?"

"More directly than by ambient energy?" Tynan shrugged. "If necessary. Consent for treatment is important, but not if someone is about to cause themselves or others harm. Kai works with Veil magic, correct?" She nodded. "That is not something one wants to be uncontrolled."

Arlyn huffed, but her hand relaxed in his. "Fine. But don't try to get rid of my anger at Lial. He deserves it."

"Would you have preferred I sent you to Oria to die?" Lial asked tightly. "I vow there was no harm intended. I've spent much of the last couple of weeks considering the best way to tell you both about this. It isn't easy, and Ralan hasn't been inclined to offer direction."

"More like three or four weeks," she muttered.

But Tynan could sense her softening.

Closing his eyes, he slipped into meditative stillness. Arlyn said something to Selia, but this time, he let the words go. Let everything go as he linked his mind gently with Arlyn's. It was a difficult process to touch upon the edges without alerting Kai—a hazard when one needed to work with one soulbonded alone. But finally, he connected with her mental channels.

Not as deeply as with Aris, thank Lady Bera. He had no need to access her memories or redirect misaligned mental channels. This was pure emotion, and emotion where it influenced the body, at that. Already, her heart pounded harder despite the soothing energy in the room, and adrenaline burned like fire through her blood.

As time dripped on, Tynan bent his energy to filtering those links. He had to get this established now. Once Kai arrived, the true challenge would begin.

A harrowing thought, that.

KEZARI KEPT her wingbeats as gentle as she could, but by the time they broke through the tree cover, she couldn't help wondering if they should have gone on foot through the portal. Though Aris didn't say a word, his legs clamped around the saddle at the base of her neck with more force than usual, and she could feel his uneasiness like the snow melting to rain around them.

He hadn't flown with her since she'd dived on Korel three weeks before.

*"I'm sorry, skizik,"* she sent. *"This was a bad idea."*

One misstep to add to the others. Why had she thought it would be okay to stay here?

Aris rapped his fist against her neck. *"Stop it. Yes, I'm nervous, but I'm also drenched already. I would rather not lose my grip, if you please. And what happened with Arlyn wasn't your fault."*

Kezari tipped to the right, and in the distance, she could already discern the slight break in the trees that they sought. *"It clearly was."*

*"You only wanted to help. I'm certain you wouldn't have spoken had you realized Arlyn was there."*

*"I should have scanned for others, but I was distracted."* By her annoyance at Tynan. And at Lial, of course. *"I wanted to lessen hurt, not increase it."*

Aris shifted against her neck, and she could feel his steady regard on the back of her head like a touch. *"Everyone knows that, or they will when they are thinking clearly. There's no need for the dark thoughts I sense from you."*

*"I believe I have cause,"* she countered.

His wry laugh danced on the wind. *"Are we to trade places, then? Shall I comfort you out of your maudlin thoughts as you once did me? Unfortunately, I am unable to fly you to a deserted island to gather your composure."*

Kezari snorted at the mental image of him attempting to carry her anywhere, but her thoughts circled around to his words like they were hunting prey. Did he believe she'd shifted to a place *that* dark? He'd been ready to leap from her back when she'd first saved him, but she had no similar desire to cause herself harm. Isolation? Certainly. The others would be safer without her fumbling presence, but it would be easy enough to remove herself to another location. One they couldn't reach.

*"I do not believe Selia and Iren would be pleased with such a move."*

She focused one annoyed eye on him before returning her focus to their destination. *"You know perfectly well what 'isolation' means,* skizik.*"*

*"So I would no longer* be *your* skizik?" His thighs tightened harder on the saddle. *"That feels more like a punishment than a help."*

*"A—"* If they weren't so close to their destination, she would have whipped her head around to glare again. As it was, she had to resist the urge to drop into an angry dive. *"I cannot believe you would accuse me of punishing you. I merely offer you freedom. Unlike soulbonds, our link does not have to be permanent."*

His groan was deeper than the currents she navigated. *"Kezari. I like working with you. I like* you. *I would be very upset if you left."*

She faltered a little in their descent, bobbling him awkwardly, but no fear echoed her way. Unless she couldn't sense it beneath the weight of her shock. After all that had happened, he truly enjoyed working with her? She couldn't quite grasp the thought, not and land them safely on the ground.

Unfortunately, circumstances would give her no time to process the revelation. Ralan and Cora appeared almost at once, the former looking resigned and the latter worried. Kezari snapped her wings closed. Ralan had *known* they were coming. Why hadn't the blasted prince returned on his own if he'd Seen that? She could have spared Aris the entire uncomfortable journey.

*But then we wouldn't have talked.*

Kezari crushed that errant bit of reason with a mental claw. *"Why did you force us to fly here in this weather?"* she sent, relishing her ability to shove the thoughts through the prince's strong shields.

Ralan's brows rose. "How did I force you to do anything?" he asked aloud.

Cora darted a concerned glance between them. "By my gods and yours, Ralan, if you've kept me out here this long for some damned prophecy, you'll be sleeping alone. I could've been curled up in our warm rooms while you messed with people."

The alarm crossing the prince's face brought Kezari no end of satisfaction.

"I did not intend to be out here this long," Ralan insisted to his mate. "The initial trip was on purpose for...reasons, but I didn't anticipate the error in stonework that required our attention. I didn't examine these particular strands enough to—"

Cora placed her fingers against his lips before glancing up at Kezari. "Is everyone okay?"

At the gesture, Kezari bared her teeth in a dragon's grin—surprisingly, Cora didn't flinch.

*"For the most part. But not long ago..."* Kezari hesitated. Did the lady know about Kai's mother? *"I'm not sure I should reveal the details, but no one is injured."*

Yet. There was no telling what would happen once Kai reached the estate.

Ralan captured Cora's hand in his, though he kissed her fingers almost absently before lowering her hand from his mouth. "It's Kai, isn't it?" he asked solemnly. "Most strands suggested he would not learn the truth until this evening. What happened?"

*An elf-shaped dragon with a dragon-sized mouth happened, that was what,* Kezari almost sent, but for some reason, she couldn't bring herself to expose her error.

"Kai doesn't know yet," Aris said, drawing the others' eyes his way. "But Arlyn overheard something that revealed the truth. He's headed back to the estate after sensing her distress. Because of that, Lial requested we retrieve you. He was...not pleased."

The prince grimaced. "I imagine not."

"Lial suggested we fly back with you?" Cora asked, her hand cupping her rounded stomach. Less so than Arlyn's, but it was obvious that both carried young. "That doesn't sound safe."

Kezari's breath streamed into mist with her chuckle-snort. *"Absolutely not. I'm not transporting anyone but my* skizik *after that terrible experience with Morenial. We'll go back through the portal."*

She braced herself for relief from Aris, but he emanated only amusement.

Ralan studied her, a shrewd light entering his eyes. "Then why did you fly in the first place?"

No doubt Lial had suggested it so Kezari could calm down, but she didn't want to admit that to the prince. That would require her to tell the full story, and at the moment, she had no desire to get worked up again. Then she would return to Braelyn upset, which would interfere with Tynan's empathy. But what could she say to avoid that very situation?

"I wanted to try a short flight," Aris said, saving her again.

If Kezari was in her elven form, she would kiss him. In a friendly way that wouldn't prompt Selia to immobilize her with some dragon-foiling spell, of course.

Kezari had enough trouble without adding that worry.

If Kai had learned one thing for certain, it was this: if Arlyn said everything was okay immediately after some random surge of energy or moment of fear, he should probably run to her side at once. It wasn't that she lied to him. No, it was her unfortunate tendency to protect others at her own cost, a trait she'd no doubt inherited from Lyr.

It couldn't be the baby. If something was wrong with their child, she would have called for him immediately. But some new external disaster? She would absolutely try to shield him from that. What had she claimed? She'd learned something startling in the library? He knew without a doubt that it wasn't ancient history.

As soon as he skidded through the back door near the library, he spotted Lyr. The sight was...not reassuring. His friend paced circles in the wide corridor, and as Kai watched, Lyr shoved his fingers through his hair in a sharp, frenzied motion. Oh yeah, something was wrong. That was approaching peak "there's something I want to control but can't" body language for Lyr. He hadn't started drumming his fingers—ah, no. *Tap, tap, tap* against the wall where he'd stopped to lean.

"What's going on?" Kai demanded.

Lyr's head snapped up, and for the space of a breath, panic flashed across his face. Though his friend schooled his expression quickly, Kai's heart slammed hard in his chest. When was the last time he'd seen Lyr that worried? No standard disaster would cause panic like that. No, it had to be personal. Deeply personal.

"Arlyn and the baby are fine. No one is injured." Lyr hesitated. "No one here, at least."

Foreboding froze Kai to the spot. "No one *here*? Is that supposed to sound reassuring?"

Who...?

*Oh, no.* It had to be Naomh, his father. They must have received bad news.

The chill spread through his blood. "My father is dead."

"What?" Lyr's fingers stopped their tapping. "No. I'm sorry, Kai. I should have mentioned that at once. According to Tynan, Naomh isn't doing well, but plans are being formed to help. This... Ah, come on. Let's join the others in the library for the rest."

Was that intended to calm his nerves? Sure, relief that his father was still alive allowed him to unlock his muscles and follow Lyr, but the ominous mystery of it all haunted his heart with heavy foreboding. Not even the calm he sensed from Arlyn through the bond eased the certainty that something was terribly wrong.

The sight of Selia, Lial, and Tynan surrounding Arlyn didn't help.

Kai rushed to her side. "What happened?"

"We're fine," Arlyn said quickly, her hand going to her belly. "I simply...overheard something that bothered me."

Despite his fear, calm seeped into his body, easing the frantic race of his heart. Kai shot Tynan an aggravated look. "Are you manipulating my emotions?"

The mind healer shook his head. "This calm is for everyone, but most especially for the sake of your bonded and child. If you can shield your emotions from Arlyn at all, I suggest you do it."

Kai pinched the bridge of his nose. "Someone please tell me what the fuck is going on."

"Fine. I will do so," Lial said—but not with his usual sharpness. There was a grieved tone to his voice that had little resemblance to Lial's typical impatience. "This will undoubtedly be difficult, but delay clearly won't help. When we were at Oria during the last crisis, Alerielle revealed a rather...distressing secret. It's your mother, Kai. She's alive."

For long drips of time, the words made no sense. None. Kai replayed them in his mind, hoping a review would bring clarity.

No such luck.

"Has Alerielle lost her senses?" Kai asked. "Perhaps she saw someone who resembled my mother?"

"No." Lial's jaw clenched the way it always did when he was unhappy about something concerning his work. "I examined the woman earlier today, and I can assure you that it was your mother. She was placed into the dreaming and hidden from Allafon. Gods know how long Alerielle would have waited to tell me if not for our near miss with Korel and the virus."

Kai's head spun, his body going fragile and light. This was unfathomable.

Then the pain crept in, slow at first. But like all assassins, it stabbed with sudden force.

# CHAPTER THIRTEEN

As Tynan had expected, the relative calm of shock gave way quickly to pain. "Chair," he said as he braced himself against the coming deluge.

"Steady, Kai," Lial said. Lyr slid a seat behind Kai, and Lial directed the shocked man into it.

There would be no steady, that Tynan knew. Even with an ultimately pleasant shock—a life found rather than lost—the sheer, life-changing magnitude of such news was almost always processed with an initial burst of agony. Mourning, really, for the reality that hadn't happened...and the one that had.

No avoiding it.

The first wave of pain crashed against Tynan's defenses with enough force to steal a gasp from his lungs, but he held his connection to Arlyn firm. From where he knelt, he could see the shock crumbling from Kai's expression. There would be more waves, and soon.

Lowering himself to his knees, Tynan closed his eyes and focused on the dulling shield he'd placed around Arlyn. Easing her physiological response wouldn't be enough, not as he'd hoped. If he didn't absorb some of this, they would never be able to avoid the dangerous ricochet of emotions between the bonded pair.

"I spent over five hundred years without a parent's love," Kai murmured. "And you're telling me that all that time, my mother—"

At those stark words, Tynan opened his shields wide to the flow of emotion pouring into Arlyn, grasping with his empathy and giving a soft, mental tug. Instantly, it rushed through Tynan's mind and heart. It rattled in his skull and raced with his pulse.

Lady Bera bless them, but this...this pain had a flavor. The bitter taste of loneliness and neglect proved that Kai's words were no hyperbole. Without a true link, Tynan didn't receive any memories to give context. Nothing but the concentrated agony of it. Gritting his teeth, Tynan did his best to channel the emotion into the ground as he'd been trained, but unlike lightning, this was no quick flash.

The shift to anger was nearly a relief.

"Try to stay calm," Lial said.

"Would *you* stay calm?" Kai snapped. "You said you found out about this, what, a month ago? How could you leave me in ignorance like this?" A strained pause. "All of you. For fuck's sake, Lyr, you sent me out on a mission this morning knowing where Lial was going. Didn't you? I can't believe you've kept this from me!"

A new surge of pain slipped in—this one from Arlyn. And another from Lyr.

*Miaran.*

Tynan couldn't lose control of this, not under these circumstances. Despite the tumult of emotions searing through his mind, he directed power almost recklessly into the spell radiating calm through the room—or attempting to. The spell currently had as much effect as a snowflake falling in the desert. At midsummer. In the middle of the day.

"We were ordered to," Lyr said.

"By whom?" Kai demanded. "You're the Myern. Unless—"

"It was me," a new voice called. Tynan had no need to open his eyes—there was no mistaking Prince Ralan. "As usual, I'm the only one in the whole fucking room to blame. I had a vision, and I gave the order. Now calm down before it's all in vain."

Tynan could have told him that last statement was a waste of words. If there was a least effective way to inspire calm, it was to command it.

"What is that supposed to mean?"

"If you'd gone to Oria that night, then you, Arlyn, and your child would be dead," Ralan announced. "And a few other strands...you don't want to know."

The silence that descended held no hint of peace, but it certainly hid a wealth of pain. Breath-stealing. All-encompassing. But relentlessly, Tynan pulled it through. His muscles began to tremble, and pain bloomed like a spike between his temples. But until Kai reached some kind of equilibrium, some return to control, there wasn't another choice.

Had he thought this would be easier than helping Aris?

Hah.

"I'm going to Oria," Kai snarled. "You can take your orders and—"

An uncanny shriek-snarl split the air, cutting off Kai's words. "You'll cease hurting Tynan, or you'll face my fire."

Well, then. Of course, they needed an angry dragon added to the mix.

Anger scalded her veins, and her vision went hazy with it. Even so, Kezari kept a ruthless grip on her mental shields. For once, she would not be the one sending uncontrolled emotion through her—*the* healer. Not hers. But no matter who the man belonged to, he didn't deserve to be huddled on the floor beside Arlyn, ready to crack beneath the force of the others' feelings.

She felt Aris's hand on her shoulder and fought down the urge to knock it away. "Kezari, what—"

"Look at him," she snarled, pointing at Tynan.

Surprisingly, everyone in the room complied.

Ducking away from Aris's hand and shoving past Ralan, Kezari marched across the library floor toward the mind healer. It appeared that he'd knelt next to Arlyn's chair, but now he leaned against it, nearly slumping. His already pale skin had gone alarmingly pasty beneath his white-blonde hair. And was that a sheen of sweat on his brow? Though his eyes were closed, his breathing was steady, at least.

Kezari crouched down beside him. "That is enough."

Ever so slightly, Tynan shook his head. "Not yet. I can bear far more."

"*Can* and *should* exist in different realms," she muttered before straightening again.

The gazes directed her way held a great many emotions she didn't give an earth's clod about deciphering. Not at the moment. It didn't matter if she'd been the one to start the entire mess with her slip of the tongue. Nothing would excuse the pain Tynan was suffering. If no one else would tend to the mind healer, she would.

With force.

"Your emotions should not be his burden." A lesson she was learning herself, in fact. "This goes beyond the generous bounds of the mind healer's work."

Various degrees of chagrin spread across the others' faces as though carried on the breeze—except for Kai, whose expression remained hard and closed. Then Arlyn stood, her attention directed solely at her mate. Perhaps she could stop him from causing Kezari's...friend more pain.

Tynan was a friend, right?

No time to answer that.

"He's doing this for me, Kai," Arlyn said softly. "And our child. The shock of this much emotion magnifying between us..."

Kai blanched, the hardness crumbling away as he hurried

toward Arlyn. "Oh, gods. Tynan recommended I shield, but I forgot as soon as I heard... *Miaran.* Are you well? Please tell me I didn't cause either of you harm."

"If there had been risk of that," Tynan said in a quiet but firm voice, "Either I or Lial would have rendered you unconscious. I was able to redirect the worst of it and ease her physical reactions to the rest."

"I..." Kai ran his fingers through his hair. "You have my thanks. And apologies."

Kezari frowned down at Tynan as he braced himself against the chair and stumbled to his feet. The man was swaying. She could see the muscles in his legs jumping like a *daeri* twitching beneath her claw. What was he thinking, pushing himself like this? Her unsatisfactory nails dug into her too-soft palms.

"It's my job," Tynan said.

"By the elders' rotten teeth it is," Kezari snapped. "Not to this extent. I'm taking you to my cave for some rest. None of these emotions will reach you there."

The ungrateful wretch turned a scowl her way. "Really, Kezari, that's—"

"An excellent plan," Lial interrupted, his narrowed gaze intent on Tynan. "Kai is in control of himself now, but the emotions here will no doubt remain heightened. If you don't wish to become my latest patient, you need a break."

"Going caving is hardly that," Tynan grumbled.

Kezari scoffed. "I can see you through easily. I simply didn't wish to before."

Tynan's sigh could have provided lift for her wings. "Fine."

Fierce satisfaction filled her until she longed to arch her neck with pride, and her shoulder blades itched for wings to unfurl. Why did it give her such pleasure to be carrying him to her cave when she'd wanted to chase him away only the day before? He was neither prey nor treasure.

Too bad something within her responded as though he was the latter.

~

To Lyr's surprise, even Kai was speechless for several moments after the door closed behind Kezari and Tynan. But then again, what did one say when a dragon woman half-carried, half-assisted one's healer from the room? Certainly nothing while the pair had still been present. As she and Tynan had shuffled past him and the others, her glare had burned across their group as intensely as any dragonfire.

Aris cleared his throat. "I should follow. Perhaps I can encourage her to guard her new treasure in the brooding tower instead."

"I can offer to augment shielding," Selia said. "At this point, I'll be able to monitor Arlyn through our teacher-student link. If that is acceptable?"

Lyr waited for Arlyn's nod of assent before offering one of his own. "Thank you both."

But even after Aris and Selia departed, no one seemed inclined to broach the serious topic stretched between them like a stained and tattered battle standard. Kai had his arm wrapped around Arlyn, and their heads were ducked close as though whispering secrets. Cora peered at Ralan with a narrowed gaze, while the prince studied the floor with equal fervor. And a tired Lial stood between them all, an unhappy point in the center of their uneven triangle.

"Well, then. I didn't foresee *that*," Ralan murmured, earning him a sharp nudge from Cora. "I recommend not upsetting Tynan for a while. Or ever."

Lyr couldn't hold back a glare of his own, though it couldn't rival Kezari's. "Speaking of foresight, it would have been nice if you'd told me the optimal time to share this news with Kai. Instead, you left us all to fumble our way through."

"You're right. I did." Ralan flung his hands wide. "But only because there was no good strand for this. If you must know, the best time would have been this evening after dinner. Fewer people would have been present, preventing such a heavy emotional burden on the healer, and Kai wouldn't have arrived in a near panic over Arlyn's safety."

"You had no idea this…" Lyr gestured at the room and everyone in it. "Was a possibility? Gods of Arneen. I wanted to tell them myself. I had Lial and Tynan working on a plan for doing that very thing with the least amount of trauma."

To his credit, Ralan appeared just as flustered as the rest of them. Brow furrowed, the prince blew out a sharp breath and settled his hands on his hips. "I told you I did not See this. Dragons have always been difficult to read, which was one reason the ancient war took so long. If my ancestor…" Ralan shook his head. "Never mind. The history is hardly relevant. Suffice it to say that Kezari's innate spontaneity causes problems."

That was a fact they'd learned well after her strike on Korel had unleashed the virus. Come to think of it, Ralan hadn't accurately foreseen that, either. Lyr sighed. Yet another mess, but at least one that didn't come with a plague.

One hoped.

Finally, Lyr allowed himself to do what he'd dreaded—face Kai and Arlyn directly. "I hope you will both forgive me for the silence. I could not tolerate the thought of either of you rushing to your deaths, and with the babe…"

The muscles in Kai's jaw twitched. Still angry, then. Lyr couldn't blame him. But Arlyn's expression softened. "Of course I will. I don't like it, but I understand."

Kai's pained gaze clashed with his. "You knew what this would mean to me."

"Yes," Lyr countered. "But handled poorly, this news would have brought only further tragedy. After all that has happened, you and your mother both deserve better than that."

It took far too long, but finally, some of the tension drained from Kai's posture.

"Does Moren know?" Kai asked.

Lial stepped forward. "He does, but I believe he is waiting

until you're there to see her. But Kai...she is not awake, and I am uncertain when it will be safe to bring her from the dreaming. She was severely injured in the fall. That was no lie."

Kai's breath hissed in. "She still might die?"

Recalling Lial's earlier report, Lyr's heart twisted for his friend. None of them could guess what the future held for Lady Elerie. Well, except for Ralan, perhaps, but he was unlikely to be of help. He'd held the truth of Kai's mother too close for that.

"She will not," Ralan stunned Lyr by saying. "Her future strands are varied as to what might happen, but she survives awakening in all of them."

Curious, Lyr assessed the prince, but instead of the guarded expression he often wore, there was an uncharacteristic openness there. Ralan did want to help—and badly.

Kai's eyes narrowed. "Will harm come from going to Oria now?"

"I can't believe you're asking," Ralan said, true surprise crossing his face. "Would you actually stay here if I said yes?"

Lyr couldn't help wondering the same.

"I would. I forgot myself for a moment, but..." Kai faced Arlyn, and his hand settled over her stomach. "I will not risk my current family for the sake of the mother I never truly met."

"This evening," Ralan said at once. "Let your emotions settle, send a missive to Morenial, and go after dinner this evening."

With more speed than Lyr would have anticipated, Kai agreed, but Lyr wasn't certain if the added time would be a reprieve or a minor torture.

As with most things, probably a bit of both.

THE MOMENT THEY STEPPED OUTSIDE, Tynan slumped against Kezari as relief erased the tension contracting his muscles. Her grip tightened around his waist, and a low growl rumbled low in her throat. He opened his mouth to reassure her, only to have a frigid blast of wind steal his breath. Against Kezari, his body felt warm, but even her heat couldn't compete with a gust like that.

"I should go back in there and—"

"No," Tynan gasped out before her ire was reawakened. Shifting away from her slightly, he lifted the hood of his cloak around his face. "It was the cold."

She studied him with a dubious frown. "The way you leaned on me suggested exhaustion."

"*That* was a good thing," Tynan explained. "The pressure of all those emotions disappeared, and my body reacted by relaxing."

"If you say so," Kezari replied before nudging him gently onward.

As they started down the snow-dusted path, Tynan tried to ease away. Not out of rudeness. With each step, his energy and strength returned, though a hint of his earlier shakiness lingered. Unfortunately, Kezari's grip on his waist didn't yield despite his subtle cues. A flush heated his face at the continued support. He wasn't too good for help, but it forever made him want to squirm, regardless.

He knew his emotions were unreasonable, but he could never make himself believe he deserved such consideration. *You were only a child when you hurt your mother,* he reminded himself. *You can allow yourself good things. Normal things.* But no amount of sacrifice or service ever truly worked to erase his shame. It had dug deep until it seemed fused with his soul.

"There is no need to climb all the way down to your cave." Tynan glanced up at the nearly bare canopy of trees above, but even with most of the leaves gone, it was difficult to determine how thick the clouds were. "If it snows enough, we'll be trapped."

Unexpectedly, Kezari laughed. "Have you forgotten I can breathe fire?"

The tips of his ears heated. "It seems I have. Regardless, this is unnecessary. I appreciate your concern, but I'm not that overextended. I have dealt with far worse."

It was his calling, as both man and priest, to do so. He didn't want to consider what it had looked like to the others when she'd hauled him out like a child, although if the suggestion of incompetence changed Lial's mind about stationing him here, it might be worth the embarrassment. A small consolation, that.

"Kezari," Aris called from somewhere behind them. "Tynan. Wait."

Kezari frowned over her shoulder. "I will not return him to that misery."

But she halted in the center of the path.

Tynan squeezed his eyes closed as footsteps neared. He was supposed to be Aris's healer, but it would be difficult to maintain any hint of authority after this. When was the last time he'd felt this foolish? Possibly never, since he'd never had to be carried out of a healing session before—not as the one in charge, at any rate.

Or perhaps he had his own feelings wrong. Perhaps what truly bothered him was that someone cared enough to help at all.

He winced against the accuracy of that thought.

"See?" Kezari said. "He's grimacing. I cannot countenance the way Moranaians treat their healers."

Tynan opened his eyes to find that Aris and Selia had slipped around to stand in front of them. A hint of pain shifted in Aris's eyes and brushed against Tynan's raw senses, but the life mage's posture remained relaxed. A minor upset, then, and not a trauma response.

"Emotions are not always easy to control," Aris said softly. "Or to heal. We patients rarely intend to mistreat our healers."

Kezari stiffened against Tynan. "I didn't..."

"Think about that," Aris finished for her. "I know. There is some truth to your complaint, but it is oversight, not malice."

At her lack of response, Tynan glanced over at Kezari. Then blinked and peered at her harder. Was that a smile or a frown? Selia let out a choked sound, and Tynan had to resist the urge to echo the sentiment.

"Why do you keep doing that?" Aris asked.

Kezari's lips immediately twisted into a scowl. "I have yet to master an apologetic smile, but I suppose the failure makes an excellent change in subject."

Though Aris's brows lifted in surprise, Tynan could feel the impact of those words on the life mage in the wave of stunned joy and affection. Could Kezari tell how much her attempt meant to her *skizik*? Probably not, as he detected only embarrassment from her.

"Thank you, Kezari," Aris said. "Truly."

He thought Kezari might not answer, at least not directly, but her soft sigh heralded a deeper reply. "Dragons use their faces far less for conveying emotion, you know. And not in the same way when we do. I'm afraid the only thing I've mastered in this form is a frown, though I do think my usual smile has shown improvement."

"It has," Aris replied, his own expression turning grave. "Forgive me, Kezari. I knew you had some trouble with this, but I didn't realize it bothered you to such an extent."

Selia lifted a hand, then let it drop. "Nor did I. I wish I'd known. If you ever need advice, I hope you'll ask."

"I will consider it," Kezari said in a low, grumbly voice.

Gods help them, but she was just as uneasy with receiving help as he was. How had he missed how similar they could be? Both of them were happy to rush in and offer their whole selves to any emergency, but accepting simple kindness? That was akin to torment.

"Why don't you escort Tynan up to the brooding tower?" Aris nodded in his direction. "You can't fly him down to the cave in your dragon form because you have to shift yourself too small to make it between the trees. In this weather, a hike down the ridge isn't going to be relaxing."

Was it his imagination, or had Kezari's hold on him tightened?

"I'm not sure that would offer ample protection from all those emotions," Kezari answered.

Her stubborn tone suggested a hike was in his immediate

future. He wanted to slump in resignation, but she would think he was sick again.

"I'll reinforce the shielding," Selia offered.

Most kindly, truth be told. There had been tension between them from the beginning because of his initial mistakes in helping Aris. But Tynan detected no hint of malice or subterfuge behind the offer, not in her demeanor or the emotions lingering around her. Maybe she really had forgiven him.

"You might consider staying in the tower for a while." Aris averted his gaze for a moment before gathering his nerve enough to meet Tynan's eyes. "I haven't been sleeping there, not for a couple of weeks, at the least. I'm sure you gain little rest in the small bedroom at the top of the healing tower. An empath so close to a new couple..."

Tynan hadn't stopped to consider the full impact of that, but it was true. He'd been pouring a great deal of energy into his mental shielding lately, especially at night. Lower quality sleep combined with greater magic use no doubt contributed greatly to his current struggle with control.

Perhaps he'd placed too much blame on Kezari, after all.

"If it does not cause you distress to lose the space, I would be happy to give it a try," Tynan said—and tried not to think about how frequently Kezari used the tower roof to land.

# CHAPTER FOURTEEN

What in all the worlds was wrong with her?

Kezari paced the top floor of the brooding tower as Selia did something to the shielding and Tynan and Aris spoke quietly near the window. Tynan looked perfectly fine, if a little shaky yet. Certainly not in poor enough condition for her to sweep him away to her cave as though he was an injured dragonling. Or a priceless treasure.

Or a mate.

No, no, no.

She did not think about him that way. The warmth that had made her feel pliant and flushed as she'd held him close? That meant nothing. What did she know of physical contact in this form? The same could happen with any touch. Of course, it hadn't with Aris, so...it had to be random. An odd, variable event.

*Oh, poisoned earth,* she muttered to herself. *I'm attracted to the mind healer.*

Such an impossible situation. He believed she could bond with him the way an elf would, but although she'd heard of such things happening in the distant past, it sounded more like a myth than a true possibility. Didn't the elves exchange necklaces or some other form of token? She had nothing. *Nothing.* Not even the tiniest focus gem or grain of sand.

She didn't even own her cave. The Myern had given her use of it, but it was still part of Braelyn. For all she knew, Lyr would be angry at the modifications she'd made to the space, no matter how carefully wrought. She was too much the stranger here, and with every mistake, she felt destined to lose even her borrowed life. Adding a bond to the mix only threatened more, and deeper, rejection and pain.

Of course, Tynan might be wrong about the soulbond. Feeling desire for a dragon shifter must seem like a foreign, special thing. Were they to mate—physically, not in soul—he would no doubt lose interest. Could that likewise be the cause of her unusual behavior? She did love a mystery, and this attraction would remain that unless they explored it.

"Kezari?"

At the sound of Tynan's voice, she spun so quickly she nearly overbalanced. "Yes?"

"I really am fine," he said. "You needn't worry. Unless something else is bothering you?"

She skimmed her gaze down his well-honed body and back up to his oddly appealing face. How could she test this? Ah! "I want to attempt a kiss with you."

Tynan's mouth dropped open. "What?"

Mentally, she cursed. *Why* didn't she think things through?

Beside Tynan, Aris straightened, and she could sense his alarm as easily as her own embarrassment. *"What are you doing?"* he sent.

Oh, well. She wasn't good at backing down, either.

*"I have to know what it's like,"* she replied. *"Is Selia finished with the shields?"*

The hum of the lady's magic ceased before Aris could answer. Not that it stopped him from nagging. *"You claimed to hate the man just yesterday. I'm not sure you didn't still hate him this morning."*

*"Which you didn't believe even then,"* Kezari pointed out. *"Leave me to speak with Tynan. Please."*

Although her *skizik* studied her with obvious—even to her—concern, he left with Selia without protest. Unfortunately, Kezari wasn't nearly as certain what to do once she was actually alone with Tynan. She understood the mechanics of kissing and even of sex. How many times had she run across shifted dragon pairs in her youth? How often had details slipped across her link with Aris before he'd learned to better shield it?

But *knowing* and *doing* were as far apart as *can* and *should*.

Perhaps she should have thought a little more about the second part of that analogy first.

"I don't understand," Tynan finally said.

Kezari marched across the space between them until he was within her reach. "I don't, either."

He shook his head. "Then why...?"

"Did you know that when dragons first master their shift to elven form, they often spend weeks exploring them? In *all* ways?" The widening of his eyes answered that. Kezari smiled. "I didn't, though. I was too intent on my link to Earth and the strangeness I sensed from there. Not poison then, but that doesn't matter. The point is...now I'm not sure how to identify desire. It's as foreign as an apologetic smile."

Although his expression pinched with hurt, Tynan held her gaze. "And you suddenly decided I would be the ideal person to use for an experiment?"

"No, I didn't mean it like that," she said in a rush. "When your body was against mine earlier, I... Maybe it was desire? For what I felt, I have no baseline. No comparison."

The pain she'd seen building in his eyes gave way to amusement. "Wouldn't you be comparing me to me, then?"

Could she still kiss him if she burned him a little first? "If you would prefer, I could perform the experiment with other people instead."

His hands darted forward so suddenly that she almost shifted to her dragon form out of instinct, but he simply gripped her waist to bring her closer. Kezari stared up into his eyes, full of anger and frustration and...something. But not humor. There was no sign of humor now.

"I find myself contemplating every lesson I learned on death while at the temple," Tynan muttered.

Her heart slammed, and her skin burned beneath his hold. "Death?"

"Every priest of Bera knows it is the necessary opposite of life." He leaned closer, so close their lips nearly brushed. "It would be a great temptation to deal such death to anyone who tastes your lips before I can."

Kezari's breath seized in her lungs.

Oh, she was in trouble.

So much trouble.

WHAT HAD COME OVER HIM? Hadn't he resolved to avoid her? Yet here he was, a breath away from kissing her—and practically murderous for the right to do so. He'd never been possessive of past lovers. In fact, he would warn a patient away from such a display. But it didn't seem to matter. The thought of his bonded kissing another sent waves of rage coursing through his blood like fire.

Where was his reason?

This moment had hit like one of Kezari's hunting dives, and his heart thrummed as madly as her prey's would. He couldn't get a handle on his reactions. What should he do? For the life of him, he couldn't decide if kissing her would be the deepest folly or the chance he'd always longed for.

It might be both.

Either way, things would never be the same.

"A kiss would be a mistake," Tynan murmured, setting his thoughts free for her to judge.

Immediately, she leaned back against his hold, anger and shame tightening her face. "Yet again, I do the wrong thing."

"No, you misunderstand," he reassured her quickly. "I didn't say I wasn't going to do it. I merely fear we'll regret it."

Kezari went still, and he nearly sighed in relief. The curve of her hips felt like home to his hands, and he would have been grieved if she'd pulled free. Even so, he couldn't interpret her expression now. It was unfortunate that his empathy was a raw, painful thing after helping Arlyn and Kai. For once, he longed to open himself to Kezari.

Fully.

What was *wrong* with him? Never fully. Far too much risk lay in that direction.

"Is kissing a major event to elves?" Kezari asked, her tone more solemn than upset. "It is not for dragons, though of course it is only done when shifted to our elven forms."

A mental image of two dragons attempting to kiss popped into his head, and he nearly choked on a sudden laugh. "I imagine teeth would be a problem otherwise."

Would that offend her? Fortunately, she grinned. "Most certainly."

There was something so endearing about that smile, somehow both sweet and biting. Bera help him, but he had the unexpected urge to bring that expression to her face daily. And how long had *that* desire been lingering in his heart, unnoted? Perhaps since they'd first met. She deserved far better than the self-recrimination and doubt that haunted her at every turn. What was she ever but only herself?

A kiss wasn't so much to ask, after all.

Slowly, Tynan shifted her body subtly closer and lowered his head back down to hers. Her breath turned harsh and ragged against his lips. He savored that hint of vulnerability, so rare and precious from her. Not because he'd never recognized it in her before, but because for once, she wasn't guarding herself against him.

Ah, this would be the best folly.

"Well?" she half-asked, half-demanded.

It was his turn to smile. That impatient tone, even during a tender moment...it was so *her*. "Are you certain about this?"

Her hands darted up to rest on his cheeks. "Now or never, healer. I will not suffer this intolerable suspense again. At this point, I'd wait another century before asking another to—"

Tynan claimed her mouth before she could finish that terrible statement. Unexpected fierceness filled him at the first taste of her, and combined with what she'd almost said, the instinct to claim— to devour—nearly overcame him. But she was new to this. Though his fingers dug into her hips, he kept his lips gentle.

Until his clever dragon touched her tongue to his.

Groaning, Tynan pulled her body flush against his and gloried in the heat of her. In the passion revealed by her restless squirming and by the duel of her tongue with his. *This can't be her first kiss,* he thought blearily. *I'd never survive if she had more experience.*

But suddenly, he could think of no better way to die.

THIS WAS EXCELLENT. Why had she spent so long communing with the earth when she could have been doing this? Talk about a misspent youth. The couple of mating flights she'd taken as a dragon stood no chance of comparing.

Shivering, Kezari dug her fingers into Tynan's short hair and boosted herself a touch higher so that she could deepen the kiss. His hold on her tightened, and she growled low as his almost-painful grip sent heat straight to her core. She'd wondered if a healer would be all gentleness, but with him, that was blessedly not the case.

Dragons weren't inclined toward delicate.

When Tynan finally pulled back, she contemplated biting his chin. Just a nibble. "Why did you stop?"

She could set stone aflame, but that heat couldn't compare to the fire in his eyes. "Because neither of us are ready to tumble into that bed," he said, his voice low and scratchy.

At his sharp nod, she looked over her shoulder. The bed where Aris slept during his bad nights. Neat and tidy—and ready for occupants, her body wanted to scream. But Tynan was correct. That would be no mere kiss, and the kiss alone had been a revelation desperately in need of analysis.

When she tugged against his hold this time, he released her easily, and she couldn't help the little twist of unhappiness at the loss of his grip. *His* grip on *her*. Where had this strange yearning come from?

Kezari couldn't stop the uncomfortable thought that it had lived in her all along.

"Is it always like that?" she asked.

With a wry snort, Tynan shoved his fingers through his hair. "No. I've never been that tempted from a single kiss. I've known past lovers much longer and still never experienced such intensity."

Past. Lovers.

Rage slashed through her so abruptly that her skin itched with the hint of scales before she pushed the shift back. She had the sudden, inexplicable urge to hunt down every person he'd ever slept with and rend them limb from limb. Oh, the bloody ways she could make them pay for daring to touch her ma—

Oh, no. Not that word. *Earth's dross.*

"Kezari?"

Her gaze snapped to his. "How many?"

He frowned. "How many what?"

"Lovers," she ground out.

Tynan stared at her for a ridiculously long moment. "Ah. Why? I've hardly kept count. But I assure you I've thrown none of them on a bed in haste after a single kiss, not the way I wished to do with you. Nothing so intense as what just happened. I was well enough regarded at the temple, but..."

His words trailed off into a worried whisper, which meant she must look as fierce as she felt. *What* did he mean by "well enough regarded," anyway? Kezari had the sudden mental image of burning down the temple with a single, satisfying burst of fiery breath. The dragons didn't worship the Moranaian's borrowed gods, so it wouldn't even be a sacrilege.

"I..." Tynan's throat bobbed. "I admire the effort you've put into your mental shielding, but now I'm not sure what you're feeling. And I rather suspect I should."

Oh, he did not want to know. She didn't even want to know —because it was ludicrous. Was this the result of kissing? If so, it was a scary thing best avoided. Something that could rouse her to such murderous intent was dangerous while she lived amongst the elves. They barely tolerated her dragon nature at the best of times.

Gleefully contemplating the annihilation of an enclave of priests was...not the best.

"I need time to process these emotions," Kezari said. "That is all. I believe I'll go fly until I calm down."

Though that little concerned crease had formed between his brows, he nodded. "So long as you're okay."

Was she? Perhaps not, but she had to make herself be. Tynan might have jested about killing anyone else who kissed her, but her possessiveness was not so innocuous. Dragons needed control above all things.

As soon as Kezari disappeared through the hatch in the ceiling, Tynan dropped down onto one of the window seats and stared out at the swirling snow. He heard the moment she took flight, the snap of wing-against-air reaching him through the windows. Even the snow twisted and snarled with the gust of disturbed wind.

What had just happened?

She'd been right to insist on needing time, for now that he had a moment to contemplate, the shape of her anger clarified. It hadn't been their kiss, profound though that had been. No, her fury had been born of his foolish rambling about the past. Unless he was mistaken, the same spark of possessiveness that had lit in him also affected her.

No doubt he'd been right about her regretting the kiss. Despite her assurances before climbing up to the hatch, she'd clearly been upset. Perhaps he should be, too, but Tynan couldn't summon the tiniest bit of his own regret. For in that simple melding, something new had taken shape in his heart.

Hope.

For decades, he'd longed to find a steady, peaceful love. The kind that had bound his parents before his father's death. He'd believed Kezari could never provide that, and in a way, he was right. But there was one thing he'd neglected to consider—whether he needed tranquility at all. It might be a balm for his empathy, but it did nothing for his heart.

There were so many parts of him he'd suppressed to avoid hurting others. Ironic for a mind healer, he supposed, but he'd done it with purpose. How else could he ensure that his empathy didn't become an inadvertent weapon again? The first time had been an accident, not a choice, and that would forever be a risk.

But Kezari inspired a long-forgotten fierceness in him. He'd gloried in it, and yet he hadn't hurt her—or himself. In their embrace, he'd finally understood. He didn't need a serene paragon. He needed a warrior. Someone who would fight for him, even if it meant fighting him.

He'd been embarrassed when Kezari had hauled him out of the library, but who else would have done so? No one else had noticed the depth of his pain. In fact, every time he struggled, she was somewhere near, either with comfort or a biting word. But near.

Tynan let his head rest against the glass and closed his eyes against the weather beyond. Yes, there might be hope for a bond. Except... What did he have to offer to her? It would be foul to consider only his own needs. Unfortunately, though, nothing immediately sprang to mind. This was the second encounter with her in as many days that had ended with her flying off in anger. Not even the calm he tended to unwittingly exude seemed to help with that.

Just how *did* one win a dragon for a mate?

# CHAPTER FIFTEEN

*L*yr wasn't precisely grateful for his past, but it had helped him learn to compartmentalize. Like now, when he was forced to pour over the latest report from Dria instead of spending time with Arlyn and Kai. Provided they would allow him near for a while yet. He understood the source of their anger all too well, but he longed to comfort his family, nonetheless.

Too bad work never ended. Dria's report made it clear that matters on Earth were escalating. They needed to discover if Meren was responsible for that anti-magic rally—preferably in the couple of weeks before it happened—and whether he *did* intend to go public in an attempt to gain power over the humans.

The sooner he sent Koranel, his former captain, to Earth the better. If Lyr pretended to exile the man for his part in the plan to release a virus on Moranaia, then Meren might draw Koranel into his group of renegades. But who should Lyr involve in the supposed exile? Dria? Delbin? The outpost? Fewer would certainly be better.

A trill from the mirror caught his immediate attention, forcing him to set his other thoughts aside. That was the tone he'd set for the London gate. Had Tarah's dragon already decided who he would speak to? Lyr hurried around his desk to answer.

When he activated his side of the link, Tarah's image appeared at once. "Good evening, Myern. I hope you'll forgive the interruption, but I thought it prudent to deliver Caeregas's decision immediately."

"Of course," Lyr answered, even as he braced himself for the news. "Haste is more important than formality in this instance."

She nodded. "Which is why I wanted to contact you now instead of waiting for Caeregas to return. He's attempting to find his brother, although that may prove tricky. Egrenneth is an odd one."

"So your report indicated." He'd read it immediately after their last communication, and the presence of two dragons wandering Earth had only increased his alarm. To his knowledge, they'd been dormant as long as anyone could remember. "Does it pertain to his decision?"

The scout lifted a shoulder, but her serious expression kept the shrug from looking dismissive. "Unless something was missing from his hoard, I'd say so. As for his request to you, Caeregas said he wants to speak to a proper dragon, not 'some foul wyrm who profanes our sacred connection' or some such. Which is to say... the dragon you recommended is a far better choice than the queen. Trust me on that. I thought he was going to burn down my garden when I told him what you said about the Moranaian dragons."

Well, wasn't that curious? How far had the dragons shifted in culture after leaving Earth? Although there was reason for concern, Lyr found himself a touch eager to hear whatever Kezari learned on her mission. Not that such facts would bring greater ease. If life had taught him anything, it was this: When this type of change swept through, it altered everything.

Hopefully for the better, but he was perfectly aware it could always get worse.

～

BY THE TIME Kezari's ire had eased, the snow had diminished greatly. She could almost count each frigid flake as it pricked her body with unsatisfying cold. Not a refreshing or glorious chill. *Uncomfortable.* And that wasn't a good sign. Contrary to Earth legends, dragons were warm-blooded, not reptiles, and they ran far hotter than elves did. Few things lowered a dragon's natural temperature down to where it *matched* an elf's innate body heat.

Really only two things, if it was involuntary: severe injury or a full mating.

Kezari had never experienced either. Her mating flights hadn't been serious, and she'd never been truly injured. Twisted tails, but *surely* her body didn't recognize the potential for young with Tynan. Did it? Her temperature would have to cool closer to his for that, otherwise her natural heat would interfere with conception.

Perhaps it was something else? Some great mystery?

*You can't keep claiming it's something else. You are not stupid,* she muttered to herself.

Denial only took one so far, and this was the end of that pleasant stream. Every instinct cried that he was her mate. *Hers.* Elders' teeth, the feeling was deep enough for her body to react before her mind could fully process what a bond between them would be like. The old stories told of elf-dragon pairings, but it was difficult to fathom.

Of course, there was a great deal that she didn't understand about mate bonds in general. They were practically myths, for one thing. She'd never met a dragon who'd experienced one, nor were there family stories about mate-bonded parents or grandparents. Did bonds always cause a temperature shift? When it came to bearing young these days, it was generally done with intent, not as part of some link. A few committed, loving couples had their temperatures shift spontaneously, but it wasn't common.

What was she going to do? Avoiding Tynan until the end of time was certainly a possibility, especially after her embarrassing display of jealousy, but that would be cowardly. She couldn't abide that. And it wasn't as though she was opposed to bearing young. It was simply...complicated. A tangle in so many ways.

Feelings aside, Tynan wasn't a dragon. There were also legends of children born from such pairings—in fact, many believed it to be the source of the dragons' elven forms—but legends didn't talk about logistics. Sure, dragons gave live birth rather than laying eggs like human stories said, but that didn't mean there couldn't be complications when mating with an elf. If she and Tynan should produce a child, what then? Would she have to remain in elven form until it was born? Would shifting to a dragon kill her unborn? Would her own children be able to shift at all?

She'd always had a vague image of teaching her children to fly. Someday. A far away someday. Could she give up on that ideal?

What a mess.

Aris gave her a mental nudge. *"Need I say I told you so?"*

*"No, because I have no regrets,"* Kezari insisted.

Many, many questions, but no regrets.

*"Then why are you flying circles around Braelyn in the middle of a snowstorm?"*

*"I enjoy the cold."* Usually. But not now. Burn it all. *"Do you need something beyond this sad attempt at gloating?"*

She felt rather than heard his chuckle. *"Sorry. Lyr wants to speak to you in his study. And before you can ask, not for any trouble. As far as I know."*

Excitement sent her heat a notch closer to normal. *"The ancient dragon?"*

*"I believe so."* Aris hesitated. *"He called for Tynan, too. I thought I'd tell you in case things were more awkward with him than you would admit."*

She might not regret kissing Tynan, but awkwardness between them was a real possibility.

Aris was a very good friend.

∼

Tynan hadn't expected to be summoned again so soon, but he'd barely made it back to the healing tower to collect his belongings before he received a mental call from Lyr. A simple but formal request to meet with him in his study, though Tynan supposed the politeness merely softened the order. He left the robes he'd gathered on his bed and headed down the stairs.

On the main level, Lial was slinging his cloak onto a hook when Tynan neared the door. The healer lifted a brow. "I was surprised to sense you here."

"Aris talked Kezari into taking me up to the observation tower, and at his prompting, I've decided to stay there for a few days," Tynan explained. "I'd returned to pack a few things, but Lord Lyr has called for me."

Concern shadowed Lial's eyes at that. "Has Kai—"

"No, no." Tynan lifted his hands in reassurance. "He said it involved the ancient dragons' request. Which is fortunate since my channels are still raw."

Lial grimaced. "I should have had more care for the strain you were under, both before and during."

"You would have done the same as I did." From what Tynan had heard, the man almost made self-sacrifice a weekly ritual. "Although I admit I wouldn't mind a healing session to repair the damage once I return."

"I'll be here," Lial replied. "With the weather mages antici-pating more snow, I'll no doubt remain in the healing tower instead of sleeping in Lynia's room. There are always a few new recruits from the warmer regions who get caught in the first heavy snow. It's difficult to imagine how high it can pile up if you've never seen it for yourself, I suppose."

Tynan frowned. "Should I stay here, too?"

"Not if you haven't recovered," Lial said, then shrugged. "I'm accustomed to this."

"As you say."

But as Tynan wrapped himself in his cloak and hurried into the snow, a sense of discomfort settled in—and not one born of the knee-deep snow he now had to struggle through. Yes, Lial was accustomed to working practically alone, only his assistant Elan to offer a bit of help, but that wasn't the norm. Not for an estate this size. Tynan found himself contemplating Kezari's pithy statement about *can* and *should*.

He could only conclude that Lial should not have to handle a blizzard's worth of injuries alone. If Lyr didn't send him on a mission, Tynan would return to help, empathy or not. The area he was from, Calai, didn't receive quite so much snow as these mountains were said to, but the healer-priests there still dealt with frostbite and hypothermia during storms.

And they didn't do so alone, either.

By the time he knocked on the door to Lyr's study, Tynan had a loose plan in mind: return to the healing tower to pack most of his belongings but prepare to remain there for a night or two if possible. Between whatever missions he was assigned, he could assist Lial if necessary. Then once the rush of the storm was over, Tynan would move to the observation tower. An easy enough solution.

Lyr called for him to enter, and Tynan walked in to find the Myern sitting casually in one of the chairs beneath the dim skylights. Tynan came to an immediate halt. What was he to make of this? A summons tended to be a formal thing, and in so answering, he would approach the desk and salute. Did he do the same, except at Lyr's chair?

"Please, sit," Lyr said, waving toward the seat across from him. "I've had more formal meetings than I want to contemplate this week. I would rather we await Kezari in comfort."

After a brief moment where Tynan's feet seemed disinclined to move, he made his way over to sit in the offered chair. The Myern was a friendly enough man, but Tynan still couldn't make himself relax. What should he say?

One glimpse at the window behind Lyr provided the obvious. "The snow has nearly stopped, but Lial said more is expected."

Lyr's lips curved up slowly. "Yes. My mother's packing for the healing tower already, I'm sure, though Lial told her she shouldn't."

"Why?" Tynan asked. "Will the trails not be cleared again before the next wave of snow?"

"They will be, but he worries over her after her back injury." The Myern's smile faded. "As do I, especially now that she's pregnant. It might be hard on her. Not that I know how well she handled that state the first time, being the one she bore."

Carrying twins was difficult at the best of times, but Tynan refused to worry Lyr with that. The man obviously loved his mother deeply. "I can't imagine Lial allowing anything bad to happen. He would offer himself to Bera Herself to save Lady Lynia."

Lyr's brows lifted. "Coming from a priest of Bera..."

"Just so." Finally, Tynan relaxed—a little. "I don't say that lightly. But if I might be so bold as to offer a suggestion on this matter...have you considered an addition to the healing tower? Healers' quarters on the ground floor would help immensely."

"Indeed? And what would you expect from such quarters?" Lyr asked, a curious glint entering his eyes. "Considering Lial's intentions..."

Tynan's cheeks heated. "I have no plans to accept the position simply because Lial wishes, so I can assure you that I did not make the suggestion for my own benefit. However, if I *were* to accept, I would want to bring in another full healer for Braelyn. Even with a healer's enclave nearby, the workload here is immense. A small expansion to the healing tower would help with both."

Lyr's expression turned thoughtful, and for several drips, he stared out the window behind Tynan. "It's an excellent idea, but it would be difficult to accomplish in this weather. Now that the reinforcing spells are complete, our borrowed mages have returned home, and our regular mages will be busy keeping the paths relatively clear as we approach midwinter. Then there's the season of ice and the heavy rains of early spring. She'll be halfway through the pregnancy before we can begin construction."

The weather was an unfortunate problem, one Tynan hadn't fully considered. "Too bad we can't keep the snow away before the ice and mud make things worse."

"If it wouldn't risk offense, I'd be tempted to ask Kezari to breathe fire on it," Lyr quipped.

Wouldn't that be a sight indeed? Although...what if she *could* help? She'd looked at him as though he was ridiculous when he'd worried about being snowed in with her in the cave. *Have you forgotten I can breathe fire?* And in the healing tower earlier, she'd been intent on helping them. What had she said? Because the people here had been kind to her?

Come to think of it, no small part of her troubles seemed to stem from a struggle to belong. After losing her place amongst the dragons, she'd officially joined the Moranaians, but even in his brief time here, Tynan had seen how often she made a misstep. But were they really missteps? What right did they have to expect a dragon to act exactly like an elf? Perhaps they should consider ways to appreciate her for herself.

Really, they were all trapped in a cycle of reaction.

"If I may..." Tynan began, but his words trailed off. How far could he push this with the Myern? He wasn't a citizen of Braelyn, after all. Lyr's good nature might not extend to him.

Lyr seemed to understand. "Please speak freely."

"What is Kezari's official job here?" Tynan asked, barely managing not to rush the words to ease his nerves.

"Her job?" Lyr's brow creased. "She... I suppose she works with Aris as needed, and now she's helping with the potion deliveries."

Tynan cleared his throat and hoped the Myern had been serious about speaking freely. "She has a Moranaian title, correct? An official House? I thought all citizens received housing and pay so long as they fulfill their chosen duties. But as far as I know, Kezari has none. No certain duties or true home of her own."

Lyr went so still and reserved that Tynan began calculating how quickly he could finish packing. Then the Myern released a groaning sigh. "*Miaran,*" Lyr cursed. "I have failed my own duties abysmally not to have considered such. I granted her use of the cave, but as part of the actual land, that would be difficult to simply give her outright. Even so... Thank you, Tynan. I can't believe no one else has mentioned it."

Relief unlocked the tension in Tynan's shoulders, though a hint of annoyance filled the void. He wasn't surprised that no one had thought of the same. To his shame, it had taken him too long to truly see her himself.

"In truth, I didn't intend to offer criticism," Tynan said carefully. "When you mentioned not wanting to ask her about using her fire, though, it struck me. Why *not* ask her? She doesn't know how to fit in here, but she wants to. She offered to help pull the iron from Lord Naomh's wound and wanted to give suggestions about Lady Elerie. I've heard she reshaped the entire outpost. What if she could help with the healing tower?"

Lyr shook his head, but it was more an incredulous gesture than one of denial. "And I'd intended to ask you if you thought she would truly be suited for this mission to Earth after the meeting with Caolte."

"Well. If you need the help of a dragon..." Despite his lingering nerves, Tynan kept his gaze on the Myern's. "Perhaps a dragon's reactions are best suited."

Something Tynan needed to remember himself.

# CHAPTER SIXTEEN

Thanks to the warming spells imbued in the observation tower, Kezari's landing had gone smoothly. Walking through the garden to the main building? Misery. Since the path nearest the tower hadn't been cleared, she'd had to trudge through actual snowdrifts. Although she'd been trying to maintain control of her shifting, she'd ended up allowing scales to form beneath her skin along her legs to lessen the cold.

An elf might have suggested pants, but those would just get wet, wouldn't they?

By the time she reached the cleared garden path, Kezari was shivering so hard even her bones seemed to rattle. *Shivering*, by the ancestors. And this was the normal internal temperature for elves? It was intolerable how her body reacted to the cold. With a low growl, she formed a cloak with her magic and slung it around her shoulders.

Fine. There. She would yield to the necessity of thicker clothes.

The back door opened as she approached, and Lynia slipped out. At the sight of Kezari, she halted. "Kezari?"

"Yes." She frowned at the elven woman. "What are you doing out here? The weather is miserable."

Lynia grimaced down at the path. "It is, isn't it? Looks like there's already a fine layer of snow after the last clearing. Better than the front path, but not great. I wanted to meet Lial at the healing tower since he's decided to spend the night there. But with the sun already setting, it's probably a bad idea."

Ah, Lynia wanted to join her mate. That was understandable, but it was already dark enough that the lady's trepidation was warranted. Not only had she sustained an injury, but she also carried young. There would be no wisdom in walking dark, snow-covered paths in that situation.

"I'll walk with you," Kezari offered.

Lynia's expression lightened. "That would be kind of you. Unless you're in the middle of something?"

"Lyr called me to his study." Kezari shrugged. "He can't be angry if I'm late because I helped his mother. Or if he is, I would not care."

Instead of frowning, the lady laughed. "I can't disagree with that sentiment. I would be pleased to have your company, then."

They walked in silence at first, but it was a peaceful one. The mage globes that hung from poles along the path came to life, illuminating the area as dark descended. Kezari rarely paid attention to the winding, natural-unnatural garden, but the features carefully arranged to mimic a true forest took on a special, more magical appearance beneath the snow.

"How are you faring?" Lynia asked as they turned down a side path. "I...wasn't in the library earlier, of course, but Lial told me what happened."

Kezari sent the lady a side-long glance. "Me? I was the one who caused the problem by talking about the secret to Aris without checking to see who else was there."

Lynia smiled softly. "You didn't cause this. Allafon, Alerielle... they were responsible for Lady Elerie's current state. The rest of us are merely doing our best. And no matter what Lyr and Lial might think, there would have been no gentle way to break that kind of news. In truth, it worked out well. Kai was far enough away that Tynan could soothe Arlyn before her bonded had to deal with his own emotions."

She thought it had been a *good* thing that Kezari had messed up?

"From your expression, I suspect you disagree," Lynia said before Kezari could formulate a response. "I thought you might be upset, which is why I asked how you're faring. You know...we might not know each other well, but I do consider you a valuable member of the household. I would hate for you to take your mistakes too much to heart."

Kezari was so stunned that she slipped on a slick bit of rock. As her balance altered, she instinctively shifted into her smaller dragon form, the one she used to flit between the trees on the way to her cave. But a tiny body held even less warmth, and dragons didn't wear cloaks. Her muscles contracted, the cold hitting her like Selia's paralyzing spell, and she nearly dropped from the sky. Scrambling, she shifted back before she fell.

Lynia's breathy laugh fogged the air in a thin stream. "That wasn't the reaction I was expecting."

Though she tried to grin in return, Kezari's teeth chattered too much for it to have the right effect. Instantly, she recreated her cloak, but it barely helped. How did elves survive this every winter?

Concern filled the lady's face as she stepped closer. Oh, no. Now the temperature shift would be obvious. Well, twisted scales. She wasn't the shy type, but her skin prickled at the thought of explaining the reason for this.

"It's nothing," Kezari said, tugging the hood of her cloak over her hair. "I was only startled by the near fall."

Kezari wasn't always good at interpreting facial expressions, but she imagined Lynia's current piercing frown was worn by elven mothers everywhere at some point. "I can tell you're evading. Did you think I hadn't noticed you were wearing a cloak? Now you're shivering."

"Please." She wasn't afraid to plead at this point. "It's a personal matter. Not abnormal. Not illness. Just...personal."

Lynia studied her for another moment before nodding. "If you say so, but if there is a problem, I hope you'll discuss it with Lial or Tynan."

It took all of Kezari's resolve not to release the choked sound burning in her throat. "I will consider it, but there is no need. Though I thank you for your concern."

The first part was an absolute lie—if she had her way, Tynan in particular would never, ever hear of this. He did *not* need to get any ideas.

ONCE AGAIN, Tynan glanced toward the water clock, though he tried not to show the worry turning his gaze in that direction with increasing frequency. Where was Kezari? Had she flown to the other side of the continent? If she weren't a dragon, he might have feared that she'd been caught in the snow.

"She helped my mother to the healer's tower," Lyr said, a hint of amusement in his voice. "*Laiala* just sent word. It seems the paths had already grown slippery again."

Tynan's attention snapped to Lyr. "How did you know...?"

"A guess, really, but an educated one." The Myern smiled. "Did something happen between you and Kezari? You lack much of the tension you usually carry when she is mentioned. In fact, you've defended her today."

"I am uncertain how to answer such a personal question," Tynan replied, a polite but pointed reminder for Lyr to mind his own business. Whether it angered the Myern or not, they hardly knew each other well enough for Tynan to share what had happened in the observation tower with him.

Lyr inclined his head in acknowledgment. "Understood. I hadn't intended to pry. I trust if something relevant to the mission occurs, you'll notify me."

Kezari's arrival brought a fortunate end to that increasingly awkward conversation. Relief unclenched the tight knot between his shoulder blades, but the effect only lasted a moment. As she approached the seat next to his, Tynan noted more than a few signs that something was wrong. Her face looked flushed, and though she wore her usual loose dress, she'd also donned pants and boots beneath. And her hair had the slightly tangled but flat look of someone who'd just removed a cloak.

The glance she gave him was tense and a little nervous, but she didn't avoid meeting his eyes. There was that bit of normalcy, at least. Combined with everything else, if she had cowered, he would have hauled her out of here the way she'd done earlier with him. As it was, he couldn't deny his own unease.

"Sorry," she said.

No formality, either. Some of Tynan's worry faded.

"I would rather my mother be safe than you be punctual," Lyr said easily. "Now, I'll keep this simple. Caeregas wishes to speak to you, Kezari, rather than the dragon queen. According to Tarah, he is not pleased by how matters stand with the Moranaian dragons, so I suspect you will be more informant than emissary."

"When do I leave?" she asked at once.

"Tynan goes with you, remember?" Lyr smiled. "Not only will both of you need to prepare, but we need to align three different time zones on two different worlds. You'll leave tomorrow morning at the third mark and go through the new portal to meet Dria at the outpost. She wants to create a teleportation point near the London gate, so she'll accompany you through the Veil to Tarah's gate."

How many portals would they have to pass through? Tynan's heart gave an anxious thump as he attempted to count. One to reach the outpost and then another? Then they had to return? That meant he would have to step into that swirling void of empty chaos four times. His stomach lurched.

Kezari settled her hand over his, and the surprising chill of it snapped him out of his daze. He peered down at her fingers, the tips bright red as though warmth was returning after too much exposure to the cold. Was even the heat of a dragon tempered by a snowstorm, or was this abnormal for her? He'd never paid attention to her hands after she'd come in from the snow.

"There's no need for concern," Kezari said. Had she caught an echo of his concern about her fingers? "The portal to the outpost bypasses the Veil, so it's nearly instant. You'll only have to worry about the other."

He stiffened. Not an echo, then. What if the Myern found him unfit to go? "I'll be fine."

"Ah, I see I'm not the only one who dislikes such travel." Lyr chuckled. "Kai used to tease me about it in our youth. I assure you that it does grow easier, if not precisely enjoyable."

That confession was almost as startling as Kezari's cold hand. "I hope so."

"I suggest you speak to Arlyn—" Lyr's amusement cut off as cleanly as his words. "Or perhaps not at the moment. She doesn't need more to deal with. You could talk to Cora about what you might expect on Earth. Ralan, too, though gods know what prophecy might be mixed in with the advice."

Tynan nodded. "Anything else?"

"Pack more potions." Lyr tapped his finger against the arm of his chair. "Those still need to be delivered, but if you're going to the outpost, some of that burden can be dispersed. You can hand some off to Fen to carry to the Unseelie court, and the Seelie have an emissary who just arrived to consult with Dria. They'll likely need more than one batch, but it's a start."

Kezari's skin finally warmed more against his, and the glorious feel made a lovely distraction. Until she jerked her hand away and stood. "I will speak to Aris. It seems unusual to travel without my *skizik*."

A twinge of pain caught Tynan by surprise. Was it jealousy?

He pondered that question well after they departed Lyr's study.

~

As Kezari started to follow Tynan from the room, Lyr called out, "Kezari, could I have a moment?"

She drew to a halt, her body going instantly tense. It was never a good sign when one's superior requested a private audience. But when Tynan tossed a questioning glance over his shoulder, she waved him on. Even if she were to be berated, this might turn out to be a good thing. She had a feeling that Tynan had noticed her unusually cold hands, and she did not want to answer questions about that.

"I suppose so," Kezari said, pivoting on her feet to face the approaching Myern.

As soon as the door closed behind Tynan, Lyr spoke. "It has come to my attention that you are not receiving proper compensation as a citizen of Braelyn, nor do you have an assigned task. That is something that must be remedied."

She blinked. "Compensation?"

"All contributing citizens receive necessities such as food and housing in payment for their work. The *daeri* have been handled, and you do have the cave. But the latter is only on loan since it is part of the actual land beneath Braelyn." Lyr tapped a finger against his cheek. "However, a suggestion of Tynan's has given me an idea on how to correct that, and it will give you a task, besides."

Her inquisitive heart perked up at the inherent mystery in his words. Still. "I am uncertain what task I might safely perform."

"You are an expert with stone," the Myern pointed out. "First, the healing tower needs expansion, but winter presents many difficulties for our artisans, particularly the waist-high snow. As the tower is stone, I wondered if you might be able to shape the expansion from the rock itself. Melting the snow from the construction area shouldn't present a problem."

Kezari nearly laughed at that unknowing statement. She would have to breathe fire, for the ambient heat of her body certainly wouldn't be a help.

"Second," he continued, "Is your need of a house. It occurred to me that you could form a tunnel up from the caves to the surface and form a home of your own there. The caves would still be borrowed, but you're welcome to use them when you need the escape. There are several suitable places near the healing tower, so you wouldn't need to work in two distant places."

"The house would be my payment then?" she asked, her doubt ringing in her tone. She simply couldn't hide it.

"In part," Lyr said. "Also food, as I said, and other necessities. Helping with the healing tower would be your first contribution, and I'm sure I'll call upon you for other such tasks in the future."

For a moment, her body went so cold she might have stepped back outside—but it wasn't from fear. Who would have thought that hope could make her feel like prey? But oh, how it did. This was more than working with Aris or delivering potions. These ideas, these tasks...they could only be her own. As far as she knew, no one else could turn their magic to reshaping stone with such speed.

"I will be happy to do so," Kezari said. "I can begin tonight before my mission."

Lyr smiled. "If you would like to consider the location for your house and begin on altering the cave, that is well. But do confirm with me before you do anything on the surface. We'll also need to consult with Lial, as he would no doubt annihilate us both if we started work on his tower without warning."

The very image brought a toothy grin to her lips. "That is so."

"I do hope you will forgive the delay in seeing you settled." Lyr's expression shifted decidedly toward an apologetic smile. Finally, a true one to observe. "I owe Tynan for pointing out my lapse."

Earlier, he'd mentioned that Tynan had made a suggestion, but it seemed the mind healer's involvement had run deep. How had he recognized what she needed so thoroughly? Shame and joy twisted her insides in equal measure. She hadn't always been kind to Tynan, yet he'd still seen to her happiness.

The idea was almost too hard to fathom.

~

Several marks had passed, but Kai still couldn't tame his racing thoughts—the best he could do was shield them from his bonded.

He and Arlyn had talked a little while they shared a luncheon tray, but he'd barely eaten. His words had no doubt been sparse, too. It was nearly impossible to grasp the enormity of the news he'd been dealt, but fortunately, Arlyn had understood how little he could bring himself to say. Together, they'd drafted a message to send to his brother and then curled up on the bed to nap.

Only Arlyn had succeeded at that last part.

But he didn't mind. Lying here with his bonded snuggled against him, her back tucked against his chest and her head resting on his arm, brought him the closest he was likely to get to peace for some time. His hand rested over her rounded belly where their child nestled, and his chest burned with the emotion of it.

As was his habit, he sent his energy to brush against the baby's in a gentle caress, and for the first time, he thought he felt a slight nudge of energy in return. His breath caught. Was this the magical equivalent of a kick? Temptation nearly had him sending another tendril, but he held back in case it would cause their child distress. Gods knew he would be annoyed if someone kept poking him with magic.

Would his own father have done this? At that thought, the burning ache coalesced into a jagged spear, and he buried his hair in the vibrant fall of Arlyn's hair for some semblance of comfort. Even still, he maintained the shield preventing the bulk of his emotions from leaking across the bond as he breathed through the pain.

He could not risk Arlyn or their child.

Which meant he had to release some of the pointless anger still simmering for those who'd kept the secret these past weeks.

Kai sagged against the bed at the thought. As much as it galled him, they'd been right. When his deepest emotions were engaged, his impetuous nature often won. And he would have rushed his family straight into a plague.

Gods, though. His mother was *alive.*

He'd lain here for countless drips of time, and he still wasn't certain what he would do when he saw her. According to Lial, she wouldn't be conscious. But when she woke? She would expect her son to be a baby, not a man who'd been grown for five hundred years. His own mother wouldn't recognize him—just like his father hadn't.

There was no way to prepare. Absolutely none.

Arlyn wiggled slightly, and he lifted his face away from her hair. "Kai?" she asked, her voice hoarse with sleep.

He rubbed a slow circle over her belly. "Shh. Rest."

"I'm done sleeping." Her tone took that indignant turn that warned him not to push. "So you'd better not be bossy. We need to see if you've received a reply from your brother."

She was right, but it took everything within him to pull back enough for her to rise. As she swung her legs over the side of the bed, he nearly groaned at the loss. She stood and stretched, but when she looked his way, her expression softened.

"Let me know when you're ready to talk about it," Arlyn said softly.

Kai hauled himself to his feet on the other side of the bed. "You know I will."

Just then, the mirror over the desk chimed, and he released a resigned sigh. After a quick moment to straighten their hair and clothes, they went to answer it together. Kai activated the link as soon as they reached the mirror, and the sight of his uncle was by no means a surprise. What else but a problem with his father?

Caolte's eyes narrowed immediately. "Has something happened?"

"Over five hundred and forty plus years ago," Kai muttered. "Have you heard about my mother?"

A single spark flickered in his uncle's crimson hair. "Yes."

"Excellent." How many people were in on the secret? Kai gritted his teeth, but Arlyn's arm around his waist calmed him somewhat. "Well if something seems amiss with me, it's that."

Caolte nodded. "Understood. Unfortunately, my words may not help."

Suddenly, Kai's body felt too weighed down for new fear to rise. "Just say it."

"Your father lives, but he needs to be transported to Moranaia for healing. I've spoken with Lord Lyr about that." Caolte's nostrils flared. "However...I cannot accompany him. As I am his guardian, it will leave him vulnerable, but I...I do not have the skill to maintain this realm from afar. Naomh will be furious at its state already."

Kai stared at his uncle and fought the inexplicable urge to laugh. "You're contacting me because you have to stay home?"

From the pair of sparks that drifted up from Caolte's hair, he didn't see a reason for amusement. "I am blood-sworn to protect your father, boy. This is no small matter. I am contacting you to have your promise to guard him in my stead. Not as deeply as my own oath, but I must do my best to ensure his protection."

*Someday, I'm going to learn the truth behind that.*

But he wouldn't ask today. He couldn't bear any other news.

"Fine," Kai said. "If he still bears no sign of illness when he arrives, I will watch over him myself."

Standing over two unconscious parents he barely knew— what could be better?

## CHAPTER SEVENTEEN

If Tynan had thought a casual conversation with the Myern was nerve-wracking, knocking on the door of the future queen of Moranaia was infinitely worse. But what else could he do? He would be traveling to a new world tomorrow, and he was entirely unprepared. Princess Cora had once lived on Earth. If anyone could help, she could.

The door opened at once, but it was neither Cora nor Ralan who answered. Instead, Eri stared up at him with solemn eyes, making his heart do a little twist and leap. Would she give him some dire prophecy? He didn't see the spark of the goddess Megelien upon her, but it could appear at any time.

Eri sighed, and the depth of it struck his heart in a different way. That was the sound of a person who knew how they'd be received—poorly—and had already braced for it. But the little girl was far too young for such heaviness. How old was she? Seven or eight?

"Please come in," Eri said. "*Onaiala* should be out in a moment."

"Thank you, Princess Eri," he replied politely.

Tynan followed the child into a small but comfortable sitting area. She grabbed a pair of dolls from one of the chairs and waved him over. "You can sit here."

As soon as he took the offered chair, Eri plopped down on the long sofa across from him. She held a doll under each arm, but the look she cast his way was more adult than child. "I know you don't like me. Most people don't."

He almost uttered a few automatic platitudes, but the dejected slump of her shoulders gave him pause. She was hurting, and his reaction to her was partly to blame. Heat crept up the back of his neck. No matter her goddess, Eri was only a child.

"That isn't entirely true," Tynan said. "But I suppose it isn't false, either. Really, I don't know you well enough for like or dislike. What I *am* is uncomfortable around your goddess."

Her eyes went wide. "So you dislike Lady Megelien?"

The fear and awe in her voice sent a shiver through him, but he understood it. He would feel much the same around someone who maligned Lady Bera. "No, I pray to Lady Megelien as well. I mean no offense. But as part of my priesthood, I am sworn to the goddess Bera. I am more familiar with her energy and her ways, so Megelien's power makes me oddly nervous."

Eri pondered that a moment before nodding. "I thought you avoided me because of my gift. Most people hate when I tell them their futures, even if the outcome is good."

"The future can be scary for those who cannot see it," Tynan pointed out.

Her nose wrinkled. "Seeing isn't necessarily better."

He imagined it wasn't. What darkness had this child witnessed through her visions? From what he understood, Lady Megelien blocked the worst of them from her Sight, but Eri's serious demeanor suggested that some things made it through.

Tynan made note to speak with Cora and Ralan. Eri might not need mind healing in the traditional sense, but a consultation wouldn't hurt. And if the odd spark of Megelien's power brushed against his senses in the process, he would deal with it as it came.

He would not allow discomfort to stop him from helping the child.

A door opened, and Princess Cora hurried through, her arms loaded with fabric. "I'm sorry," she said. "I didn't realize you were here until I heard the sound of voices through the door. I was too busy digging through Ralan's clothes."

The prince's clothes? Before his frown could fully form, the princess set the stack of fabric down beside Eri and lifted the first piece from the top. It unfurled into a strange, soft-looking tunic in a shade of bright blue-green. Based on the design, it had to be an Earth garment.

"Ralan didn't bring much with him, but he recently had Delbin grab a few things for any future trips." Cora wrinkled her nose much the way Eri had. "Hopefully not because of a vision. Anyway, you can borrow this for now while we find you something of your own. You're similar enough in height and build."

Wait a moment. She was loaning him Prince Ralan's clothes? As in the heir to the throne? Second only to the king? With each piece Princess Cora lifted from the pile, Tynan's pulse picked up its pace. He'd never seen those fabrics or styles. Were they expensive on Earth? He was compensated well enough as a priest, but he was too young to have accumulated much wealth. How would he replace those garments if something happened?

Tynan was traveling with a dragon to meet another dragon on a world neither he nor Kezari had ever seen. Anything could happen. A sudden caving expedition? A fire-breathing contest? A full battle?

Who knew?

"You won't ruin them," Eri said softly. Then she leaped to her feet. "I'm going to go play. We'll talk more in a couple of weeks. Maybe three."

He followed her jaunty skip across the room until she closed the door behind her. Every word had been delivered casually, but they hung in the air like a tangible thing. What had she said just a moment ago? *People hate when I tell them their future, even if it's good.* Something to that effect. And at this moment, he could understand how that happened. He couldn't decide how he felt about her offhand prophecy himself.

"What did she mean by that?" Cora asked. "Not the last part. Gods know what you'll be talking about in a couple of weeks. The thing about ruining."

Tynan wasn't precisely embarrassed about his lack of wealth, but he found his skin heating regardless. "She must have realized I was worrying about borrowing such expensive clothes."

Cora frowned down at the pile a moment before her expression cleared. "Ah, I see. These aren't as expensive as you might think. I didn't take any of the designer stuff since I wasn't sure where you might be going."

"Princess Cora—"

"Just Cora," she insisted. "I lived on Earth for hundreds of years, and right before I met Ralan, I was a shop owner. There's really no need for deference. It's my understanding that Moranaian royals aren't ranked amongst the gods, in any case."

That was true. Technically speaking, any noble or royal from the lowest branch to the top could be removed if they failed in their duty. Nevertheless, he found himself nervous around them. His family wasn't nobility, and he'd only dealt with those in charge in passing. The exasperated woman in front of him would be queen when Ralan ascended the throne. Would he ever be comfortable being so familiar with her?

"I will try to remember," he said politely. He could hardly forget, though evading made a tempting option. "As for the clothes, their cost on Earth isn't nearly as relevant as the cost to replace them from Moranaia."

"You are the exact opposite of Delbin," she muttered. "He's already bought himself a car."

A car. Tynan understood the word because of the language spell, but at the same time, he did not. What would the contraption be like in person? The question filled him with equal parts excitement and terror.

Cora sat on the sofa where Eri had been. "Trust me when I tell you that Ralan can afford it. Truly. Consider this compensation for the mission if nothing else. You're traveling with Kezari since Aris can't and delivering potions, too. Let this be the least of your problems."

It was solid advice, no matter how much his pride tried to argue against it.

"Very well," Tynan conceded. "So, what else will I need to know?"

As it turned out, a lot.

~

KEZARI PROBABLY SHOULD HAVE SOUGHT out Cora in preparation for tomorrow's journey, but she hadn't been able to resist a thorough examination of the caves beneath Braelyn instead. From the cavern she'd been using as her own, she connected with the land and studied every tunnel and hollow that branched off from her current spot. The place where she'd settled was a fair distance from the healing tower where Lyr had suggested she build her new house, but it didn't take long to find a tunnel that went in that direction.

Letting herself sink more fully into her connection with the stone, Kezari followed the trail through each twist and turn and made note of what she might alter. But how much should she change? She could keep the passage narrow and shift herself smaller to fly through, or she could build it into something she could traverse in her elven form. If her body temperature kept fluctuating, the former would be a chilly endeavor. And if she did end up bearing Tynan's young, she might not be able to shift to—

She cut that thought off with a stream of dragonian curses. *You kissed him once,* she reminded herself. *Once.*

With a huff, Kezari forced her focus back to the earth around her. She could decide about tunnels later. She needed to check on the stability and depth of the stone in the vicinity of the healing tower. Would there be enough to pull rock to the surface for creating the addition, or would that weaken the ground? Carefully, she studied every single talon-length beneath the tower.

She was so intent on her work that she almost missed the nudge against her shields. Not elven, either. Deeper. *Dragon.* Kezari hissed at the temerity of that contact even before she examined the energy to identify who'd sought her out. How dare anyone from the Isle attempt to speak to her after exiling her so coldly?

But rage flared heat back into her body when she recognized Tebzn.

Her wretched, betraying, reptile-hearted traitor of a cousin. The last time they'd spoken, Tebzn had denied all knowledge of Aris's tormenter, Perim, and had expressed happiness at Kezari's banishment. Of course the wyrm had—Tebzn had gained Kezari's hoard as part of the deal. And hadn't she told Kezari not to contact her again?

Steam hissed between Kezari's teeth. For several heartbeats, she considered ignoring that nudge. She owed Tebzn nothing, and even if there had been a debt to pay, it would have been more than settled by the theft of her hoard. But...what could prompt her cousin to risk contact? Kezari grumbled curses as curiosity won.

She blasted her cousin as soon as the connection opened. *"How dare you reach out to me! You who betrayed her entire family line."*

A jumble of emotions echoed back, but chief among them was fear. *"I'm sorry, Kezari. So sorry. You were right. I thought you'd gone mad in your cave. Baza said so. But these last four months..."*

*"Baza? What does that lazy, useless reptile have to do with anything?"* Kezari snarled. *"He's hardly one to criticize another for staying in their cave all the time. I bet his father still air-drops him his daeri."*

Frustration slipped along the connection. *"Forget Baza. It's the younglings. I thought you lied about shielding them, but it's been months since they've lost their senses. The queen has given every excuse, but it is clear the young ones will not settle. That isn't even the worst."*

The dragonlings? That chilled away the steam dancing around her mouth. *"What have you done?"*

*"I haven't done anything,"* Tebzn sent back, her mental voice a near screech. *"But any who had a remaining connection to Earth have gone nearly wild with the power. Then today, a couple of the youngest adults led the wild dragonlings to one of the other nearby islands. After attacking the fae village. Several died. Kezari, you must come back."*

Kezari went so still that she could have been an overgrown stalagmite. This sounded like a true disaster, the likes of which the Isle had never seen. Losing their dragonlings alone... What should she do? Part of her wanted to fly to her former home at once, but despite her shock and horror, it was a surprisingly small part.

They'd cast her out for the very thing they wanted her to solve.

*"What makes you so certain I have the solution?"* Kezari demanded. *"I do not know how to return reason to the young."*

Did anyone? If their own elders didn't, what hope did she have? Besides, she was supposed to meet with the ancient dragon... Wait. Would the ancient one know? Perhaps something similar might have happened before. Even if it hadn't, he might be willing to help.

The queen, the elders, Tebzn—they deserved nothing. But the young deserved aid.

*"Please say you will try,"* her cousin pleaded.

Kezari's talons dug into the stone. *"Will you return my hoard?"*

Stunned silence. Then... *"But the queen decreed it mine, and I did give a small amount to Baza. I'm not sure I could sort it out from the rest."*

*"If I do return, perhaps I'll bring the dragonlings back here with me. They'll learn nothing of a dragon's honor there,"* Kezari

snarled, though she wasn't surprised by Tebzn's answer. *"I suppose you'll just have to wait and see, won't you?"*

Before her cousin could attempt one more mewling response, Kezari cut off the connection, and when Tebzn dared another nudge, she added an extra layer of shielding to the cavern to keep the wyrm out. She would not be forced or guilted.

Not by Tebzn or anyone.

IT TOOK FOREVER to pick his way along the snow-laden trails with an armload of ridiculously expensive clothes, but somehow, Tynan managed to reach the healing tower without dropping anything. How did one even wash fabric like this? It wasn't necessarily better than the cloth Moranaians used, but the textures were so different—some almost as thin as silk and others thick and textured. Denim, Cora had called the last one. He had no desire to find out what happened to such fabric if it was dropped in the muddy slush covering parts of the path.

Couldn't Cora have retrieved clothing from *any other person?*

Though he had to admit it would make a fine story to tell when he returned to the temple.

After a brief fumble—and near disaster—at the door, Tynan made it into the warmth of the tower. He shoved the door closed with his back and then leaned against it, finally releasing a sigh of relief. Fortunately, the room was empty of all but Lial, who merely lifted a brow. Lynia must have gone upstairs to rest.

"Are you that unaccustomed to snow?" the other healer teased.

Tynan lifted the stack of clothes enough to catch Lial's attention. "Princess Cora gave me these for tomorrow's mission. They are Ralan's."

Lial's frown of confusion lasted only a moment before giving way to a grin. "And you were taking extra care. I confess if it was me, I'd drop at least one piece in the mud just to vex my cousin."

"Some of us have only been earning full income for a handful of decades," Tynan replied, but his indignant huff was more jest than annoyance. "But if there's an accident, perhaps I should blame you. You received enough offerings last month to pay for a replacement."

Inside, he winced at the ill-thought comment. Despite his time here, he didn't know Lial that well, and his humor could come across as impertinence. Thankfully, though, the other healer laughed.

"Feel free," Lial said. "Gods know I have nothing to use it on."

Tynan pushed away from the door. "You will in several more months. Children bring much expense."

Lial glanced up at the ceiling for a moment with a smile. "That is truth."

Something felt different in their interaction, though Tynan couldn't say what. A greater ease, perhaps? After the poor first impression he'd made on Lial, he hadn't expected to approach this kind of familiarity.

"Once you've carried your treasure upstairs, would you mind coming back down?" Lial asked as Tynan neared the workbench. "It seems Caolte has requested help for Naomh sooner rather than later. Since you last examined Naomh, I would like to hear your thoughts."

Pleasure warmed him at the request. "Sure. I'll return in a moment."

Tynan made quick—but careful—work of carrying his bundle upstairs to join the rest of the clothes he'd been packing. By the time he returned to the lower level, Lial and Lynia both sat in the center seats. The lady smiled at him in greeting as he took one of the chairs across from them. To his healer's eye, she appeared to be in good health, no signs of strain pinching her face.

He returned the smile. "Good eve, Lady Lynia. It seems Kezari saw you here safely."

"Of course," Lynia answered. "Though in truth, I worried more for her than myself."

That gave him pause. "What do you mean?"

"I've never seen her cold before, but at one point, her teeth were actually chattering." Although the lady's smile faded more with each word, she shrugged. "She said it happened sometimes and was nothing to worry about. Still, I wish she'd spoken to Lial about it before she hurried off."

Nothing to worry about? Just that morning, she'd walked to the portal in nothing but her usual thin dress. Even the air around her had felt warmer. And after they'd returned... His mind flashed to the study when her hand had been cold against his, and a twist of fear assailed him. He hadn't checked her for the virus because shifters were supposed to be immune. That's what the fairies had told Kai before closing their pond to visitors. But what if they'd been wrong?

"Where is Kezari?" Lial asked in a tense tone that suggested their thoughts ran parallel.

"I shouldn't have said anything," Lynia murmured. "She didn't swear me to secrecy, but I doubt she'll be pleased if you start pestering her."

Lial leaned forward. "What if the fairies were incorrect about the virus, Lyni? If Kezari is ill, then..."

Lynia's skin went pale. "Oh, no. Except...she did say it was normal. She's not the type to lie about such a thing."

"She might not even realize it," Lial countered. "As far as I know, she cannot scan herself."

Although Tynan had had that very thought, he couldn't make himself believe it was true. Wishful thinking or some instinct born of their potential bond? The latter wasn't an impossibility. If nothing else, he surely would have detected some sign of illness when they'd kissed. His healing gift wasn't as strong as Lial's, but it was more than adequate.

*When they'd kissed*—as in close contact. That would put him at risk, too. Quickly, he scanned himself for any sign of infection, but he found nothing. Not a single hint of the virus. It seemed impossible that he would have escaped illness if she were sick.

"Well, she's coming this way," Lynia said, drawing his attention. "According to the estate shields, you can check her yourself in a moment."

Tynan couldn't imagine a world where he'd be able to resist.

ortunately, Kezari's anger flared too hot for the chill to bother her as she landed on the path and shifted back to her elven form. No cloak needed, though she did keep the sturdy boots that helped guard against slipping on the snow. She sighed with pleasure as the cold air once again soothed her inner fire.

But as soon as she entered the healing tower, that heat dimmed on its own. Not as much as before, but enough for the warmth of the room to be equally pleasing. The reason for the cooling leapt to his feet, turning toward her so quickly his chair scraped against the floor. But it wasn't awkwardness or even desire that crossed Tynan's face—it was fear.

Her steps slowed as she neared, especially when Lial also stood. "Did something else happen?"

Tynan cleared his throat. "Only worry for you."

Kezari's gaze went from person to person, but it wasn't until she reached Lynia's guilty face that realization set in. "You told them."

A hint of color bloomed on the lady's cheeks. "It was a casual comment, but these two have made much of it."

"I should have asked for a promise," Kezari muttered. Then

she pinned Tynan with a fierce glance. "As I told Lady Lynia, I'm fine."

"Your hand was cold earlier," the stubborn man said. "Everyone knows that's not normal for you."

Kezari's nails dug into her palms. "So you're a dragon healer, now?"

"Enough," Lial snapped, his steps echoing against the stone as he strode over. "You'll need to be scanned for the virus at the least. Although the fairies insisted that shifters are immune, any sudden change like this is cause for concern. I will not have the people here put at risk."

And by people, he mostly meant his family. Which she understood. Wasn't concern for the young what had brought her here with such haste? Shattered gems, but she was going to have to confess. Lial wouldn't let it rest even when he confirmed that she didn't carry the virus.

"You can scan me if you wish, but I already know the cause." Kezari did her very best to avoid Tynan's worried eyes. "It is... With dragons..."

"Yes?" Lial prodded.

She let out a gusty sigh and forged ahead. "If you must know, my body recognized a potential mating partner. Usually, we dragons purposefully cool our internal temperature to something closer to yours for such a thing, but upon occasion, it is...spontaneous. Though I'm technically no colder than you right now, the shock of such a shift makes me feel the frigid weather acutely. Rather inconvenient in the winter, I have to say."

All three elves stared at her. Then Lial and Lynia glanced at Tynan, who wore both a flush and a hint of a grin, and once again, Kezari gave serious consideration to flying west until she nearly ran out of continent. At the least, her cave sounded particularly appealing at the moment. Rocks didn't peer at her with a host of unspoken questions.

"I'm sorry, Kezari," Lial surprised her by saying. "I should not have asked such questions in front of others. I'm afraid I don't know enough about dragon physiology to anticipate the more personal issues."

She shook her head. "You were worried for your family. I understand."

Tynan didn't say a word—and she couldn't decide if that was better or worse.

"So," Lynia said, injecting a hint of cheer into her voice. "Was there another reason you were headed to the healing tower?"

Kezari latched onto that topic change like prey. "My cousin contacted me, and I am uncertain how to respond. It seems the shattering of the wall on Earth has affected the young. Tebzn actually requested my aid."

Which...probably would have been better discussed with the Myern, but in her rush, she'd thought mostly of reaching Tynan. Not a good sign. She could tell herself it was because he was accompanying her to Earth, but there was no point in lying. She'd *wanted* to speak to the mind healer first. The same one who was still staring at her without uttering a word.

Maybe *he* was the one who'd turned into a stalactite.

OF ALL THE things she might have said, Tynan never would have imagined...that. He hadn't even registered whatever she said her cousin had wanted. He couldn't get beyond the "potential mating partner" thing. Was that another way to talk about bonding, or was she being literal? *Of course she meant that literally,* he chastised himself. Why else would her body temperature play a role?

From a healer's perspective, he understood perfectly. There was an ideal temperature at which conception occurred, and the amount of heat Kezari exuded on any given day was well beyond that delicate balance. He might have considered this possibility already if he'd ever considered babies much at all.

He'd only started to accept the possibility of bonding.

"Let go of it, Tynan," Kezari snapped. "You've already mangled the thoughts enough."

He ran his fingers through his hair and gave her a tentative smile. "Sorry."

For the first time since the incident in the library, he caught a hint of her emotions, and the sting of embarrassment hidden beneath her glare sobered him as deeply as her revelation. He didn't know what to make of this, but neither did she. Continuing this awkwardness in front of Lial and Lynia would help no one.

So Tynan gathered his fragmented thoughts, shoved them into a mental box, and slammed the lid closed. "I'm afraid I don't know anything about your cousin."

"Tebzn lied about Aris's torture so that I would be exiled. As my nearest relative, she was then able to claim my hoard." Her fists squeezed so tightly he feared he would have to heal her palms. "Now, she claims the dragonlings have gone wild along with a few young adults, who then led the smallest to another island. It seems they also attacked the fae village."

Lynia gasped. "Aren't those fae the dragons' ancient allies? We have very few books about dragon society after the war, so my knowledge is clearly outdated. Still, I can't imagine that has changed."

"The relationship is much more distant," Kezari said. "But not erased."

Tynan's mind locked on a single point. "Gone wild. What did she mean by that?"

"I'm not sure," she answered.

At her lost look, Tynan let himself move closer until he could reach out and touch her arm if he wanted. But he didn't dare offer that comfort uninvited. "If it is centered in the mind, I might be able to help."

Kezari shifted on her feet. "Tebzn said the dragonlings wouldn't settle. Unfortunately, she angered me enough that I didn't ask many questions."

"What will you do?" Lial asked.

"I don't know." Her brow knitted tight. "The thought of waiting makes me ill, but I'd also planned to ask the ancient dragon about the matter. Part of me says I should go now. Yet arriving early at the ancient one's habitation... I do not know if that would be cause for offense, nor if it would help."

Tynan had no idea about that, but one thing was clear—Kezari had hesitated. If his impetuous dragon was disinclined to fly off immediately, there was a reason. Whether she could identify the cause or not.

"Hmm." Lial tilted his head. "How long has it been?"

"Four months. I believe that's what Tebzn said."

With the way Kezari trembled, Tynan had to fight the urge to take her hand in his, but he didn't know if it would be welcome. "Then another night for us to prepare will make no difference," he said instead.

She nodded, but her eyes remained troubled.

"I could use your help with Naomh in any case," Lial said.

Kezari frowned. "Mine?"

"Ah, no." The other healer grimaced. "I'm sorry. I meant—"

"No," Tynan interrupted. "You do want her help with this."

"Tynan—"

"Kezari can remove the iron." Tynan met the dragon's eyes and sighed with relief at her small nod. "We discussed the matter earlier."

At the moment, even helping with a surgery would be a welcome distraction.

Lial's eyes narrowed on the dragon. "Is that so?"

"If you provide an escape route for me to ease the metal through," she replied, shrugging.

Tynan held his breath while the other healer debated—which fortunately didn't take long. It was only a couple of drips before Lial nodded. "That's one possibility, then. Go update Lyr on your cousin's warning while we finalize transport for Lord Naomh. I imagine that will occur after Kai's visit to Oria, and considering the weather by then, Naomh will have to be brought here instead of a more remote location. Which reminds me. Lynia—"

"I'm staying here," the lady interrupted. "Tynan said that Naomh is no longer infected, which means I am in no more danger from him than I am from you. However, if you *do* have extra patients because of the snow, you'll need someone to help with the less serious problems along with the rest."

At Lial's disgruntled expression, Tynan bit his lip to hide his smile. Lady Lynia was right, which Lial knew perfectly well. He simply didn't like it.

"I don't like it," Lial said, and Tynan nearly choked on a laugh at the echo of his own thoughts.

Lial shot him a glare, but Lynia's serene smile made up for it.

Kezari snorted. "You like fewer things than any elf I've met so far."

Oddly enough, she didn't receive quite as fierce of a look—apparently, being a dragon had benefits. Then Lynia laughed, and although Lial's lips were still tilted down, his sigh held resignation. Whatever tension had been building evaporated.

"Anyway, I'll return later," Kezari said. "So long as you don't ask me to *carry* anyone, I am happy to help."

With that pointed statement, his dragon strode for the door, but as soon as she opened it, he heard a muttered curse. And when she stepped out into the gently falling snow, Tynan caught sight of a cloak swirling around her before the door fully closed. She was cold again because of him.

He probably should have been ashamed of the surge of intense, possessive joy.

But he wasn't.

By the time Kezari stomped her way to the main entrance, she'd recited every curse she could think of. Not only was her body getting ideas again, but she actually had to suffer discomfort because of them. Couldn't her thrice-blasted instincts have waited until summer—or at least until she could stay inside for more than a few moments at a time?

Once the warmth of the entryway wrapped around her, she dispelled the annoying cloak and marched down the winding hallway toward Lyr's study. But she was only part of the way there when a door opened and Lyr himself poked his head out. Without a word, he waved for her to enter.

"I just heard from Lial," he finally said as he closed the door behind them.

Kezari came to an immediate halt when she saw the other two people standing across the room—Kai and Arlyn. They both looked tired and more than a little shattered, Kai especially. He didn't tend to be as lighthearted as Delbin or Fen, but Kai usually had an affable nature. There was no sign of it now. She'd never seen his expression so solemn.

Suddenly, her missing heat returned in a steady stream of shame.

"I'm sorry," Kezari said. Simply. Starkly.

Arlyn's smile held a touch of sadness. "As far as I know, no one is upset at you. I'm not."

So Lynia had said, but it was difficult to believe. "Someday, I will temper my haste."

"Hey, something you have in common with Kai," Arlyn said, directing a pointed look her bonded's way. "Gods know strong emotions ruin this one's good sense."

Kai scrubbed at his face, but when he lowered his hand, he wore the ghost of a smile. "Unfortunately, I can't argue with that. And I'm not upset at you, either, Kezari. If I can forgive the people who kept the secret, I can certainly forgive the one who accidentally revealed it. Also, you have my apologies for overextending your bond...erm...Tynan. I should have noticed his pain."

*Grr.* Did everyone believe her and Tynan to be potential bondmates? But she could only sigh at herself. Of course they did.

She'd hauled the man out of the library like the world's most awkwardly shaped sack of precious gems.

"Perhaps he'll learn to enforce his boundaries better," Kezari simply said.

Arlyn's grin flashed quick but bright. "Well said."

"Something many of us would benefit from improving." Lyr extended his hand toward a chair. "Please sit and tell us the latest news from the Isle of Dragons. Lial only told me a little."

Kezari found it surprisingly easy, but the lack of information helped in that regard. There were simply too many details she'd forgotten to consider in her anger. Even so, Lyr was frowning by the time she finished.

"Wild dragons," Arlyn mused. "That doesn't sound good."

Lyr crossed his arms, one hand lifting to stroke his chin. "No, it doesn't. Unfortunately, responding isn't so simple as it may seem. I'm glad you didn't fly off, Kezari."

He was? Kezari had the sudden suspicion that there was something she was missing. "Why?"

"You're a citizen of Moranaia now," he answered. "As part of our treaty, we are to avoid the Isle without permission of both kingdoms' monarchs, unless there is an emergency of rather severe proportions or some type of accident. We are absolutely not supposed to interfere in the dragons' conflicts."

Kezari stared up at him from the seat she regretted taking, for suddenly, she felt at a disadvantage. Instinct prompted her to stand tall, wings flared, to defend the dragon young from any harm in spite of his objections. But reason countered that he was right. She'd been banished from the Isle, so she couldn't claim the right to help her fellow dragons as a citizen. Tebzn didn't have the authority to end a dinner, much less an exile.

"You don't think this is an emergency?" Kai asked suddenly, some of the shadows leaving his gaze for a moment.

"Of course it is," Lyr snapped. "But severe enough to interfere? To risk breaking the treaty? I would need the king's approval for that. I'm not sure even Ralan's word alone would suffice, and his absence suggests that such approval is not forthcoming."

Involuntarily, Kezari glanced toward the door, but no prince burst through. Alas.

"Hmm, maybe. But remember what he told us in the library earlier," Arlyn said.

Kezari frowned. Had Ralan said something about dragons? He could have cast aspersions on them all, but she'd been too focused on Tynan to notice.

"'Dragons have always been difficult to read,'" Lyr murmured. "That's what he said. If he struggles with his Sight in such a way, he might not be aware of what's happening on the Isle at all. I'll speak to him as soon as I can. Perhaps your meeting with Caeregas will provide further insight, as well."

She was so caught up in the first revelation—that the seer struggled to See the future strands for dragons—that she nearly missed the rest of Lyr's words. He, too, seemed to wonder about what she might learn from the ancient dragon. Tomorrow. Sunrise felt far too distant considering she hadn't even had dinner yet.

"I could go now," Kezari said. "If we delay the potion delivery, I could travel alone and avoid the outpost completely."

"How long has this been a problem for the Isle, Kezari?" Lyr asked softly.

She frowned. "Four months?"

"Then one more night of proper preparations will not hurt," he pointed out, echoing Tynan's earlier observation. "Tarah said that Caeregas is searching for his brother, so he might not be there if you did go early. Not that I find this delay in any way ideal. I understand perfectly well that it is not."

Kezari longed to growl out her frustrations, but there would be no point. The Myern was right. "Fine. In the meantime, I'll be helping the healers."

And she didn't wait around to answer the questions she could see in the others' eyes about *that* turn of events.

# CHAPTER NINETEEN

Carefully, Tynan packed the vials into the crate and tucked the padding around the glass. Medicinal vials were spell-imbued against breaking, but magic could only do so much to counter the fragile nature of the material. Much like people, truth be told. He could reroute the mind's own channels, but he couldn't make such changes permanent. He certainly couldn't prevent a warped mind from shattering into madness.

"That's an intense look for packing," Lial said from his spot at the other end of the workbench. "I would ask what's bothering you, but since I can think of at least three possibilities, it seems pointless."

Tynan sealed the lid on the box before turning toward the other healer. "Very true. Are you going to dinner?"

Lial grimaced. "Not tonight. As soon as it's over, Kai and Arlyn are heading to Oria to see Kai's mother. I imagine tensions will be high at the table. Besides, I would rather not risk Lynia slipping on the paths if I can help it."

"I heard that," Lynia called, looking up from the book she was reading in her chair across the room. "You do realize I've learned which of those potions are the unpleasant type, right? I would certainly *hate* for you to be dosed with one."

"Put in my place by my own threat," Lial muttered, though he grinned.

Tynan couldn't help but smile along with him. He'd learned rather quickly that their apparent bickering was more light-hearted than it might seem and that a wealth of love was hidden beneath it. The depth of their relationship was something he'd longed for since seeing the same in his own parents. Before his father's accident, at least.

Quickly, he glanced back down at the crate before Lial could see his smile drop.

"Tynan?" Lial said with concern.

*Miaran.* He hadn't looked away rapidly enough. But more than his past weighed on him, so at least he had a wealth of choices to pull from. "I should accompany Kai and Arlyn, don't you think? He appears to have regained control, but there is a great deal of risk still."

Before Lial could answer, Kezari shoved through the door, her cloak disappearing like the swirl of snow that she closed outside. He'd never actively watched her as she formed fabric out of air, though Aris had mentioned her ability to create clothing. When she shifted from dragon to elven form, her dress simply appeared in the chaos of it. But seeing her cloak essentially evaporate? Fascinating, indeed.

He shook his head to clear it of that stray thought as she approached.

"Did I hear you mention Kai?" she asked.

Bera's blessed heart. How good was a dragon's hearing? "I was just suggesting I go with him to Oria."

Kezari nodded. "I'll go, too."

Visions of being hauled out of yet another estate, this one less familiar, flashed through his head so vividly that he winced. "I'm not sure that's a good idea."

"And why not?" she demanded, a scowl building on her brow.

"If I must take on Kai's emotions again..."

Kezari closed the distance between them and poked her finger against his chest. "I see. You don't want me to interrupt your self-flagellation. You *do* realize there's no prize for becoming a sacrifice, right? Unless I have misunderstood your gods entirely?"

He heard a choked sound from Lynia, but he was too busy glaring at Kezari to see if the sound was horror or amusement. "Well, do the dragon gods reward such a thing? You've wallowed in your fair share of self-recriminations lately, Kezari."

She dropped her hand, her expression going blank. Tynan snapped his mouth closed before more angry words slipped free. In truth, both of them were correct. He had the training to see the scars in his mind that wrought such foolish behavior, but he'd never been able to fully heal them.

It was the curse of the mind healer—understanding where one's mind went off-course but being unable to shift the thoughts oneself. He couldn't even use his power on himself, since the mind that held the talent knew precisely how to shield against it. He had to rely on the same type of behavior-correcting tricks as everyone else.

"I suppose I can't refute that," Kezari said. "But the way you were crumpled against that chair..."

His anger fled as suddenly as it had arrived, blown away by the pained, haunted look in her eyes. It hadn't been instinct, then. She truly had been bothered by the cost his gift sometimes demanded. Before he could think better of it, he caught her hand in his.

"Thank you for worrying about me," Tynan said.

Her eyes widened. "You're surprised that I would?"

"Considering you seemed to hate me approximately one day ago, yes," Tynan replied, though his memory countered those words almost immediately.

She had defended him in the past. How many times had she told Lial to back off when he'd chastised Tynan for a mistake? Nearly from their first meeting, that hint of protectiveness had been there. But he hadn't let himself examine it.

"Yes, well..." Kezari huffed. "Some conflicts I am eager to dive upon, yet I steer myself away from others. Particularly those involving emotions. My parents died when I was too young to remember, and I've drifted away from close relationships ever since. Often, it does not serve me well, but I suspect it hurts others worse."

Oh, but her shadows suggested otherwise—that melancholy beneath the harshness, the bitter tang of sorrow that tinged her other emotions. Wasn't that why she unsettled him, after all? The flavor of that pain filled his empathy with the familiar taste of his own past grief—and his own worst mistakes.

"I'm not so sure," Tynan finally said, though he kept the rest of his revelations close to his heart. He wasn't ready to tell her about the tragedy of his parents and how that affected his reactions to her. Maybe he would never be ready.

Kezari stunned him by linking her fingers with his. "That you for that." She caught his gaze, and he could do little but stare into her unusual—perfect—golden eyes. "But I'm still going with you."

The laugh took him by surprise, but the annoyed line it brought to Kezari's brow filled him with the urge to kiss her. Unfortunately, they were in the middle of the healing tower, and her kissing experiment was obviously over. Wresting his gaze from hers, Tynan glanced over at Lial, only to find that the other healer wasn't in his previous spot. In fact, he and Lynia had left without him even noticing.

Kezari tugged at his hand. As soon as his attention returned to her face, she leaned forward and claimed his lips with hers. Just like that. No doubt or debate—and impossible to resist. Tynan wrapped his free arm around her waist and pulled her close as he deepened the kiss.

She fit so very perfectly against him. How could he bear to leave her behind? He sighed against her lips and finally admitted that he couldn't.

Gods help them both.

~

AT THIS POINT, Kai hated every damned stone of the estate where he'd grown up. Though his not-father was dead and the place presumably cleared of traitors, the stark corridors echoed with more than footsteps as he and his small entourage followed his brother toward Oria's healing tower. This place was misery. It was mocking words and cruel taunts. Failure and betrayal. Nothing seemed capable of erasing that.

Arlyn squeezed his hand, her comfort a welcome balm through their bond. Behind them, Tynan and Kezari walked in silence, and Kai had to admit that the mind healer's peace was another boon. Even the dragon's fierceness seemed somehow subdued. He'd worried about her presence, but since Lial had needed to stay at Braelyn because of the storm, she'd insisted on coming to assist Tynan.

If Tynan and Kezari weren't bonded within a month, Kai would be greatly surprised.

But that errant thought evaporated as they hurried through a cold courtyard toward the outer wall. Had Allafon's ancestors really needed to construct something that resembled a medieval castle? A nicer one, no doubt, one that included a great deal of magical conveniences, but a castle, nonetheless.

His brother stopped beside a door in the outer wall, his fingers white on the handle. "Are you sure?"

Though his throat burned, Kai nodded. "I can't believe you've made it a month."

"It is...I cannot describe it," Moren said before jerking open the door.

*Gods,* Kai thought as they followed his brother in, *I really do need a new nickname for him, thanks to Meren.*

Such a random thing for his brain to fasten on, but somehow relevant all the same. It was yet another symbol of his shattered family. Why was it so difficult to decide how to refer to his own brother? Using his full name—Morenial—was too stilted somehow. It would feel like a return to formality after they'd finally come to know each other a little better. The last thing they needed was more distance, considering the valley's worth of history already separating them.

But at the same time, he couldn't bring himself to shorten the name in another way. Mor. Ren. Nial. Oren. So many possibilities, but that remaining distance kept him from choosing one. He simply had no idea how his brother would react.

And *why* were his thoughts so scattered?

Maybe it was because the world suddenly made no sense. If his mind flitted around enough, would he discover the secret to restoring his equilibrium? Now, that was a question to ask the mind healer if there ever was one.

When they entered the healing tower, Alerielle waited in the center, near the base of the stairs leading to the upper floors. Kai looked around, but of course, there was no one else on the entry level. Unlike Lial's tower, this one had benches to the right for patients to wait, and the actual treatment rooms were upstairs. The healer wouldn't have his mother on display here.

"Lord Morenial. Lord Kai," Alerielle said, inclining her head respectfully. "As Lial's words reminded me, I owe you an apology, but more than that, an explanation."

Kai couldn't find words, but Moren didn't suffer the same constraint. "I cannot imagine any excuse for this."

"So you say," the healer conceded. "But at the risk of too much bluntness... Your father threatened to snap Kai's neck and toss him down the stairs after your mother if I didn't finish the job his shove began. Elerie herself begged me to kill her if it was required for Kai's survival. And Allafon's menace didn't go away. He threatened Kai any time he thought I wouldn't cooperate with something he asked, though holding his squirming little body over the stairs was the worst."

A hiss of dragon rage sounded behind him, but Kai went cold

at the vicious truth behind those words. From past experience, he could see that scene so very clearly. Almost objectively, like a painting. What was new about Allafon wanting him dead? It made no sense for him to be shocked by something so...expected.

Then Arlyn's hand tightened around his, and her sudden, fierce anger burned away the cold. His mother had offered up her life for his. Why hadn't the healer done something sooner?

"Moren killed Allafon last summer," Kai said tightly. "Yet we're just now learning the truth? Would we know at all if not for Korel's death?"

A hint of calm floated over him, but it wasn't his own. Tynan. Though Kai still wasn't entirely comfortable being influenced in such a manner, he couldn't help but feel grateful. Especially after Alerielle's next words.

"Follow me downstairs, and you will see why."

Gods, that didn't bode well.

She led them through a door and down the staircase to the storage room, and with each step, dread screamed within him with increasing force. He shivered with it. He burned with it. Even the mind healer's relentless calm only went so far. But when they finally reached the examination table where his mother lay, the emotion leached out of him entirely.

Moren let out a choked moan and hurried to her side, but Kai's feet froze to the floor a few paces from her feet. When his brother lifted her hand to his face and wept, Kai could only watch numbly. Of course, it only made sense. Moren was three hundred years older than him. His brother had actually known their mother.

And yet...so many pieces snapped into place in a single moment. Kai might not know her as a person, but he recognized her energy. The hum of it was dim but steady—and as familiar as his own. He felt Arlyn's arm slip around his waist as his breath rushed out and pain slipped in.

His mother was so ridiculously fragile. Gaunt, little muscle tone, pale as death. Even her breaths were shallow enough that he almost couldn't count them. Was this what Alerielle meant when she'd said they would see? Ralan claimed that his mother wouldn't die, but it was difficult to believe.

"I look a little like her," Kai murmured.

Moren straightened, and every grieved moment of his brother's life was written upon his face. Their mother's "death," Allafon's madness, becoming the Dorn of an estate still shaken from so much betrayal. How did he bear it? Why hadn't Kai really seen?

"You always have." Moren's tear-roughened voice spanned the distance between them. "Except the eyes. You act like her, too."

That gave Kai pause. "What do you mean?"

"She would do anything for those she loved," Moren said, one side of his mouth tipping up. "And do it impulsively, too. It was how she ended up married to our...to *my* father. I believe she was pregnant with me."

Gods knew what Allafon had threatened her with if that had been the case. Kai shuddered.

"You have it right," Alerielle said gravely. "And when Allafon found out she intended to leave him for Kai's father, he threatened to slit Morenial's throat while he slept. He would have done it, too. That's why I swore a blood oath to Elerie that I would do my best to protect her children at any cost."

What a wretched tragedy, all overseen by one twisted man. In that moment, the anger that simmered beneath the surface drained away, and Kai let his eyes sweep closed. The elderly healer had kept that oath of protection for over five hundred years, no matter the risk. He couldn't bring himself to ask what else she had suffered—but someday, he would. Alerielle deserved to be lauded for each heartbreaking injustice.

"Thank you," Kai said.

All his faded emotions crashed back into him with such force that his knees nearly buckled. Desperately, he tightened both his muscles and his shields, lest it flow over to hurt Arlyn. In return, she sent him love. Love and peace.

"When can you wake her?" Moren asked.

Kai opened his eyes to watch the answer form on the healer's face, a truer test than mere words. The solemn tilt of her lips didn't bode well for a happy answer.

"I don't know," Alerielle confessed. "Lial does...not have good hopes for her spine. I hadn't considered a true repair until Lady Lynia's healing, but it seems your mother's bones have set for too long for that kind of work. Even so, he wants to try. If nothing else, she needs strengthening."

Perhaps it was for the best with Naomh arriving. His father had once claimed he would've sensed his bonded if he'd touched the same ground, so... Wait. Kai's eyes narrowed on the healer. Naomh had been to Moranaia a couple of times since learning of his existence.

"Why didn't my true father detect her with his earth magic during his visits?" Kai asked.

Alerielle didn't meet his eyes. "I kept her wrapped in silk to avoid detection by Allafon. Because silk insulates, Lord Naomh wouldn't have sensed her."

It wasn't a complete answer, but Kai found himself reluctant to press.

Some things were his parents' right to question.

KEZARI HAD HELD SUCH a tight grip on her emotions that by the time they returned to Braelyn, her teeth ached from grinding them together. And not only because she'd been shielding for Tynan's benefit. In truth, she hadn't expected to be this affected when she'd insisted on accompanying Tynan and the others. She wasn't accustomed to having family or even close friends, so the entire scenario had felt almost foreign until she'd experienced it.

First had come anger, a deep, burning well of it, when the old healer had described Kai's near-murder when he was only a baby. What kind of being would do such a thing to their helpless young? If that man Allafon had been in her reach, she would have separated his flesh from his bones one tiny strip at a time.

After, though...the open grief and wonder she'd seen as the brothers finally saw their mother was entirely new. That had been heavy enough that she hadn't needed empathy to feel it, but Tynan had held strong this time. Whatever had caused him to falter in the library hadn't happened again. But a shift in her heart? Apparently, that had been inevitable.

All the way back to Lial's healing tower, she found herself pondering her own lost parents. No one had ever told her precisely what had happened to them, but there'd been whispers that they'd tried to leave the island against the queen's wishes. Others said a spell had failed catastrophically. Either way, she'd never asked. She'd felt the absence of their energy so long that she hadn't seen a point in questioning. Knowledge wouldn't bring them back.

But what if there was more to it? No, she didn't think they were wrapped in silk in some hole. Mere fabric wouldn't stop her earth senses, so she would have found them in all her years communing with the earth here—and Earth across the Veil. She had no lost parents to guard. Their legacy, however, still lingered. Could they have left for a similar reason to hers?

Thoughts that would have to wait.

Kezari followed Arlyn into the healing tower, but unlike the other woman, she only had to will her cloak away. As such, she had already taken a seat next to Lynia when Arlyn shuffled over, her hand held low to support her growing belly. The elf looked pale, except for dark circles beneath her eyes, but Lial showed no sign of concern. Normal exhaustion, then?

"Are you unwell?" Kezari asked after Arlyn sat down across from her.

"I must look awful," Arlyn said, sighing. "No surprise, I guess."

Kezari stiffened. "I meant no offense."

Chuckling, the elf waved a hand. "Oh, I know. Thank you for asking, truly. If I don't look like I've been hit by a truck, I'd be greatly surprised."

"A...truck?" Kezari tried to recall the word and failed.

"Human transport," Arlyn explained. "One I wouldn't have minded having on the walk."

Lial sank down on the seat beside Arlyn. "Such a thing would help with Naomh's transport. I'm sure Selia would prefer that to standing out in the cold waiting to teleport him."

*Perhaps I should have gone with Tynan and Kai,* Kezari mused. Not that she would have carried the Sidhe lord on her back. Absolutely not. But she could have carried him with her claws if they'd prepared the proper litter. Kai would've had to walk, and Tynan... Ancestors' bones. Would she actually allow Tynan to ride her?

A question with an entirely different meaning in this form.

Heat flashed across her skin at the realization, and that desperate, liquid warmth ran through her even in Tynan's absence. Was it normal to feel such desire from such a simple thought? It was nearly as intense as their second kiss had been.

"Are *you* unwell?" Arlyn asked.

Gah, all three of them were staring at her now. Fabulous.

"My temperature has been...unreliable," Kezari muttered.

Frowning, Arlyn opened her mouth to ask another question. But if the Moranaian gods granted blessings, one was surely in the guise of Lynia, who deftly shifted the subject. "It *is* a touch warm in here for Naomh's procedure, Lial. Don't you typically keep it colder?"

Lady Lynia was quickly becoming Kezari's favorite elf at Braelyn, except for maybe Tynan.

A look of concentration lined Lial's face for a moment, but then he nodded. "They should be here soon, so I went ahead and shifted the spell."

"It felt fine to me," Arlyn said, her frown deepening.

"Ah, you know dragons run hot," Lynia replied. Then she turned in her seat to better face Kezari. "Lyr mentioned earlier that you might be remodeling the healing tower. Can it really be done in the winter?"

Then Lynia winked, and in that moment, she absolutely was Kezari's favorite.

# CHAPTER TWENTY

The tension humming in the room was far from comfortable for Tynan's empathy, and the sheer number of people also didn't help. Aside from him and Lial, Kezari waited at his shoulder for her part of the healing, Kai stood guard at the foot of the stone table, Lynia and Arlyn still sat near the workbench, and Selia and Aris lingered a couple of paces away. It made for a chaotic blend of fear, worry, and curiosity that had Tynan's stomach muscles clenching tight.

"I'm afraid your work is about to grow more complicated," Selia said, her sodden cloak dripping onto the stone floor. "The snow is really starting to pick up, so if any were caught unprepared, you'll be seeing them within the next couple of marks."

Lynia stood and hurried over to the workbench. "Have any search crews contact me first. I'll have warming potions at the ready, and Elan should be here to assist soon, too."

"Shall I notify Lyr of that, then?" Selia asked, her brow quirked.

"Oh." Lynia lowered the basket she'd grabbed with a sheepish grin. "Sorry, I'll send him the message. I snapped into emergency mode."

Selia smiled in return. "Understood. Well, I suppose Aris and I should get out of the way. If you're ready, love?"

But Aris's attention was on Naomh, who lay so still he might have been dead. The Sidhe lord was...not doing well. Tynan had thought Kai's mother looked bad, but Naomh might be worse, not in absolute physical condition but in energy. Elerie's had been slight but steady—Naomh's power was a tiny candle flickering in the wind. It was that rather than the wound itself that had no doubt prompted Lord Caolte to send his brother here.

"Allow me to give you life energy," Aris said softly, a hint of dark pain shifting in his eyes. "To both healers and Lord Naomh, I mean. You may run low, but I fear I won't be able to enter once you've...once you've opened the wound."

The last time Aris had provided Lial with life energy had been during a surgery, and the sight of the wound had reminded Aris too closely of his years of torture. Tynan's heart ached for his patient. Not only because of empathy, but because in treating the life mage, Tynan had learned exactly what the man had suffered to cause this current dread. The offer Aris made came at great cost.

"Of course," Lial replied. "Do you think life energy will bolster Naomh's natural reserves?"

Aris shrugged. "Possibly. His earth magic extends to plants, so even if he can't sense life the way I can, he's connected. The way his spark flickers..."

A new spear of pain arrowed from Kai, the unintentional dart cutting through Tynan's strained mental shields like an arrow. He shivered as he absorbed the hit, but the motion was so subtle that only Kezari seemed to notice it. When she shifted slightly on her feet, Tynan gave her a warning glance.

"Hurry, then," Lial told Aris.

The life mage wasted no time. As Tynan watched, Aris trickled energy into Naomh, whose breathing notably steadied at the infusion, and then provided extra to Lial. Then it was Tynan's turn. He swallowed nervously. During Aris's treatment, the flare of the mage's energy had nearly overwhelmed him more than once. Would this shatter his already strained mental shields?

Kezari's hand caught his. "My *skizik* will not cause you harm."

Was his worry so obvious? But no, not if the others' curious expressions were anything to go by. Even Aris's face held surprise. "Is there something I should be aware of?" Aris asked.

Ah, well. If his client could be vulnerable for him, he could do the same. "I nearly lost control of the shields around my empathy during your treatment," Tynan said quietly. "I fear I have my own ill-formed mental channel after the event."

Understanding, not judgment, lit the other man's eyes. "I see. But can't you just..."

"My magic isn't particularly effective on my own mind," Tynan confessed.

It wasn't something mind healers talked about—the last thing they wanted was a patient who hesitated to seek treatment out of fear of causing pain. But at this point, the others deserved to know. Considering how much he was taking on at Braelyn, they might be well served to hear all of his failings, for those might end up affecting his work. Not now, though. It was far from the right time.

"I will not take offense if you wish to abstain," Aris said.

Did he? Truth be told, his energy reserves were low, though not to dangerous levels. But any emotional outburst in this tense situation could suck away the remainder of his power, and he still had the mission to Earth in the morning. This would be a real benefit.

Kezari's hand tightened around his, and that bit of comfort helped him reach for what he needed.

"No," Tynan said. "I won't abstain. But proceed with care."

The connection Aris built for this was far weaker than the one they used for Aris's treatments, and the energy that flowed through was more a runnel than a stream. Tynan soaked it up, the light and vitality of the power stealing his breath. Wielded on purpose, life magic was beautiful. An echo of reality, perhaps, since life wasn't always peaceful if it hit unexpectedly.

When the power cut off, Tynan was almost sorry. "Thank you."

Aris's smile held a fair amount of relief. "It was my honor."

After bidding them farewell, Selia and Aris finally departed with Arlyn, and the glimpse Tynan got of the outside before the door closed gave him some concern. Snow was falling at a heavy clip, enough that Selia had needed to use her magic to clear a path through the waist-high drifts before they could proceed. The scouts would already be working hard to locate anyone lost in the storm.

Elan shoved through the door in the wake of Selia's magic-hewn path. "I'll put up the new privacy screen," he said before he'd even removed his cloak.

Tynan had a feeling that things would not be easy for Elan and Lynia on the other side of the screen, not if the estate's residents were heedless of the weather. But Naomh's infusion of life energy was already beginning to disperse, his body shoving away the power thanks to the iron in his wound. This surgery couldn't wait.

Lial glanced over his shoulder at Elan. "I trust you and Lynia to handle the bulk of it, but if there's any doubt about whether you can treat someone, call for Tynan. He'll be faster if I have to stitch the wound."

Pride swelled in Tynan at that, but he couldn't savor it. As Elan stretched out a divider blocking the stone table from the rest of the room, his focus shifted to the task at hand. They'd decided that since Tynan was strongest in mind magic, he would ensure sedation and numbing. It was no small task. One of the most important ones, in fact. The dreaming was too much like stasis for optimal healing, so he would have to bring Naomh out of it just the right amount.

He stared down at the pale Sidhe lord with his tangled blonde hair and his emaciated form. Tynan had never worked with a full Sidhe, and definitely not a powerful noble, so it was difficult to quell the nerves rising up his throat. But then Kezari squeezed his hand again before she moved farther down the table, and Kai caught his eye and gave a sober nod.

There really wasn't another choice.

After a long, deep breath, Tynan closed his eyes and pushed his energy toward Naomh's to create a connection. Would a Sidhe lord be heavily shielded? Probably. Yet Naomh's energy was so decimated that Tynan slipped through the meager defenses faster than a single drip. With the man already deep in the dreaming, even his consciousness was only a dim flicker.

Nevertheless, Tynan reached out, infusing himself with calm before forming the barest link. *"I am Callian ay'tor Beronai pel asebarah i Tynan Fessen nai Calai of Moranaia. Be at peace while we heal you. I believe you already know Lial, who will be the one removing the iron."*

A spark of alarm. *"Caolte?"*

*"Must uphold your realm,"* Tynan explained. *"Your son Kai stands guard here."*

*"I thought I heard..."* Confusion. Pain. *"My bonded. Where?"*

Tynan wanted to curse, but he had to keep his energy serene. If Naomh had overheard mention of Elerie, confirming the rumor would only bring more stress.

*"I'm not certain what you mean,"* Tynan settled on saying. *"You'll have to live to ask Kai, I suppose. But first, I need to bring you up from the dreaming to a more natural deep sleep. If you'll allow it?"*

In a situation like this, he hadn't *had* to make a connection to ask permission, but it would help. The mind resisted what it didn't understand—and sometimes what it did. Naomh's cooperation would aid their task immensely.

For a moment, he feared he wouldn't get it, but Naomh was too weak to struggle with his own thoughts for long. *"Do it. Tell Kai not to leave."*

Tynan smiled at the command even as he sent the Sidhe lord into a deep sleep and numbed every possible nerve. The man had no idea how adamant his son had already been about staying. No matter how tentative their relationship was, Naomh and Kai already cared for one another.

No doubt more than either of them realized.

~

KEZARI HAD no aversion to blood or open wounds—she would be a starving dragon if she did. But this...this was different. This process was meant to save a life, not consume it. She couldn't stop staring at each meticulous cut Lial made as he sought out the iron embedded deep within.

She felt Kai's concerned gaze on her more than once, which meant her stare had probably taken on a predatory glint. But she felt no desire to consume. Her kind had no instincts toward eating humanoid creatures, maybe because they could shift into that form. Apparently, her curiosity too closely resembled hunting. She almost grinned, but that would probably be too much.

Suddenly, Lial looked up at her. "I've allowed a little blood to flood the wound. Do you sense any iron that might be trapped?"

Kezari shifted to her inner sight, and each little flake filled her senses as she hunted them down. "All loose."

"Remove them, then."

She held her hand over the Sidhe lord's open wound and eased the iron upward, toward her palm. Instinct clamored to jerk the metal free quickly and shape it to her will, but she resisted. This flesh was too fragile, and if she'd mistaken the placement of a single fleck, she could rip it through tissue. Little by little, she coaxed each fragment out of the blood.

Though exacting, it didn't take long. Kezari ensured that Naomh's wound was free of iron, then turned her hand until the flakes rested atop her palm. *So tiny to cause the fae such harm.* She cleansed away the blood with a flex of magic and forced the fragments together into a ball the size of her elven fingernail.

When she glanced down again, the wound was nearly sealed. In the absence of iron, Lial hadn't needed to use thread to stitch the incisions. Kezari looked toward Tynan, but his eyes were still closed while he kept the Sidhe lord unconscious. What was she supposed to do with a ball of iron in the middle of an elven habitation?

Voices on the other side of the dividing screen caught her attention. Lynia, Elan, and...was that the same man who'd asked Tynan to repair his knee? She tilted her head and concentrated harder. Yes, it was. Frostbite, he claimed.

Hah. He no doubt longed to see Tynan again.

Kezari curled the iron into her palm and slipped away from the operating table. When Kai straightened, a questioning frown on his brow, she gestured for silence and pointed toward the divider. Though his frown didn't disappear, he nodded.

Honestly, what did the man think she could do for his father now that the iron was gone? Silliness. But she could scare away... err...help this other patient so Tynan wasn't disturbed.

*Liar. Tynan doesn't even realize anyone else is here.*

Ah well. Maybe it was for herself.

But when she rounded the divider, she spotted the man sitting on the stool by the workbench while a flustered Elan rubbed potion onto his fingers. "Honestly, Eniom. Did you do this on purpose? How could your hands get near frozen when you're working in the kitchens?"

Eniom flushed, either in anger or embarrassment. "It was an accident. I wanted to grab the last of the *oansie* leaves before the snow killed them completely, but they were already buried."

"And you dug through the snow until your skin blistered?" Elan demanded.

Kezari exchanged a confused glance with Lynia, who stood on Eniom's other side with a vial of ointment in her hand. What in the world was wrong with Lial's assistant? She'd never heard him speak so harshly to a patient. Or anyone. The man had enough patience to work with *Lial*, for goodness' sake.

"Tynan told me about your knee," Elan continued when Eniom remained silent. "If you are injuring yourself to see him, it's no use. He has a potential bonded, you know."

Eniom's eyes went wide a moment before his shoulders slumped. Kezari had to fight the urge to preen, though in truth, she couldn't fault the man for his interest. Tynan had drawn *her* attention, and she was a dragon.

"I didn't know," Eniom said. "But I promise this was no guise. I was supposed to harvest those herbs last week, but I forgot until today's dinner recipe called for them. Now, we're almost out, and I'll be in trouble."

Elan's lips tightened. "Fine. But if you have any other accidents, come find *me*."

The command was harshly delivered, but a hint of red crept into the assistant's cheeks. Ahh, he was interested in Eniom. That was handy. If they formed a relationship, then Eniom could stop longing after her...whatever Tynan was. She would figure out a word later.

Kezari marched forward, forcing enough sound to her motions to catch both men's attention. Eniom flinched, but she only smiled. A little toothily, perhaps, but he would live. Maybe someday, he would even thank her.

"I must have mistaken your intentions toward Tynan on your last visit," Kezari said. "I had no idea of your relationship with Elan."

The healer's assistant sent her a furious glare, and the other man's mouth dropped open. Even Lynia lifted a brow. "We are not in...there's no...no relationship," Eniom stammered.

Elan turned as red as a fire dragon's scales. "Kezari!"

"I'm sorry if I misunderstood. There is a certain...charisma between you, I suppose." Kezari widened her grin. "Since Tynan is my potential bonded, I'd hoped my impression was correct. You surely would not wish to pine over him."

The words slipped out of their own volition, but they felt surprisingly delightful. Like a perfectly shaped gemstone in an unclaimed cave. Like the first cool winds of autumn flowing around her wings. Like pure connection to the world's energy. A sense of lightness and joy tickled through her until she nearly laughed with it.

Possibly even giggled, ancestors help her.

Eniom and Elan didn't appear to experience that same happiness. The former snapped his mouth closed and the latter wrapped a bandage around the man's hand with unusual haste. Oh, well. She'd tried to help, and her statement truly hadn't been a lie. Self-serving, maybe, but honest. There was an air about the two men that suggested they would suit each other nicely.

Lynia's lips twitched as she held out the vial of ointment for Eniom. The man snatched the container from her hand, inclined his head toward the lady and Elan, and then hurried from the room as though Kezari had scalded his feet with fire. Really, was she that terrible for pointing out the obvious?

As soon as the door closed, Elan glared at her again. Did working with Lial make him bold, or had he forgotten that she could eat him?

Not that she would. Yuck.

"What in the world were you doing?" Elan demanded.

Her regard for him slipped up a notch at his bravery. "Helping you acquire your desired companion while freeing my own from the man's attention."

Elan's mouth opened. Then closed. Then opened again. "I'm going to go see if Lial needs anything."

Kezari frowned after him. Was he truly upset by her assistance? Why did elves waste so much time? Uncertainty happened, but once that doubt was cleared, it was time for action. Sure, they lived long enough to not really *require* haste, but why not spend more of that long time in a state of greater happiness?

Something to consider now that she'd apparently accepted the possibility of a bond with Tynan.

Shrugging, she joined Lady Lynia beside the workbench. Though the lady's grin was wide, she said nothing about the scene she'd witnessed. "Is the procedure complete?"

"My part." Kezari held out her hand, palm up, to reveal the ball of iron. "What should I do with this? The others were too distracted to ask."

Including Elan, thanks to her meddling.

"Oh!" Eyeing the tiny ball, Lynia's throat worked. Then the lady spun to grab a basket from the bench and removed a piece of fabric from inside. "Here. Wrap it in the silk and tie it tight. Maybe you can carry it to Earth and dispose of it away from the outpost. Iron is too abundant there for it to cause comment."

Hah. No wonder so many of the elves and fae had been eager to find other worlds or dimensions. But it worked out well for Kezari. Even without the draw of the ancient dragons, she'd grown increasingly curious about Earth. She hadn't seen a great deal of it, since the others worried too much about what she might do. So she couldn't fly? Fine. She'd adapted to her elven form well enough to remain in it while observing the human technology she'd heard mentioned.

If they attempted to shuffle her between portals during her next mission without allowing her to see anything of note, she would have to reconsider her opinions about elf consumption.

With a hefty amount of relief, Tynan allowed Naomh to drift into a lighter level of sleep—still deep, but not to the extent surgery required. Then he set longer-lasting nerve-numbing spells before slipping his mind free of the Sidhe lord's. They'd done it. He could feel the return of natural energy flows around and into the man. It would take a long time for him to be replenished, much less healed, but recovery was now certain.

He opened his eyes to find Lial and Elan staring at him, only

Kai's attention now on Naomh. "Did I do something wrong?" Tynan asked hesitantly.

Actual humor lightened Lial's expression. "No, but I think Elan would like it if you carried away your dragon."

His...What had Kezari done? He'd observed her as she'd removed the iron with ease, so it clearly wasn't that.

"Do I want to know why?" Tynan dared ask.

Lial chuckled. "It seems she wanted to play matchmaker for poor Elan. He's never going to round the privacy screen again if he can help it. Of course, he'll have to move it when we shift Naomh to the bed."

Shaking his head, Tynan looked at the assistant healer. "I'm afraid I have no sway there."

"Oh? She said she's your potential soulbonded," Elan muttered. Then he released a long, frustrated sigh. "Never mind. I would rather not discuss this any longer."

Lial's grin turned a bit wicked—no doubt he remembered the teasing he'd received about Lynia—but without another word, he started cleaning up. Tynan watched curiously as Lial used a spell to force the blood on the table to flow into the basin at the end, all while giving Elan instructions. The healer was halfway through his directions before the first part of the assistant's words made their impact.

Kezari had claimed a bond? The very dragon who had denied the possibility so fiercely?

*Kezari?*

If Lial told him to do something, Tynan didn't hear it. He was too busy deciding what he would say once he circled around that divider. But then new voices poured through the door, and Lynia called for his help with a patient. A healer's timing, of course. As Tynan ran a cleansing spell over himself for safety's sake, Kai caught his attention.

"While you three were talking, I heard Kezari say she was heading for the observation tower to rest up for tomorrow," Kai said softly. He glanced down at his father for a moment before meeting Tynan's gaze. "And thank you."

Tynan nodded. "He seemed relieved to know that you guard him, though he did order you to stay until he wakes."

Kai's smile was bittersweet. "Sounds about right."

*There's much I could do for these two,* Tynan thought.

For the first time, staying at Braelyn didn't seem like such a bad idea after all.

## CHAPTER TWENTY-ONE

*A*cquisition took a certain amount of planning, but more than anything, it required endurance. So after snagging a hunk of *daeri* from the kitchens, Kezari flew her dinner through the blistering winds to the top of the observation tower. The stone, at least, made a warm place to eat in peace. No one but Aris came to the roof, and he was currently reading a story to Iren in the main part of the estate.

She smiled in satisfaction at that. It was a good sign that Aris was rebuilding his relationship with his youngling. Iren had been a child of four when his father had left on a mission, but Aris had been presumed dead after his ship sank. No one had known that poor Aris had been captured and then tortured. After Kezari had brought him here from the island, her *skizik* had struggled mightily to reconnect with his now-eleven-year-old. But if a child who could read sat to listen, it was from happiness, not need.

Aris would need her less, and soon. Despite his recent relapse, his mind was growing stronger than he realized. But she could see it. How many hours had she spent connected to his thoughts in case the pain overcame him? More than she could ever count. Now, such instances were rare. Their connection was closer to that of a typical dragon and *skizik*—present but not consuming.

She'd been oddly sad about that shift. Once. But it hadn't occurred to her how much she relied on him, too. It must have been fear of losing her own support that had driven that shameful melancholy, because she wanted good health for Aris more than almost anything. The last few days had revealed a great deal she hadn't been ready to see—like the depth of her insecurity.

Maybe she *could* live at Braelyn on her own merits, though.

No longer merely Aris's dragon.

Kezari choked down the last bite of *daeri* on that last uncomfortable thought, but acknowledging it cleared away so much. Her exile had freed her from a place where she'd never quite fit, and at first, she'd expected the same lack of belonging here. Which meant that she'd found it. But these Moranaians, they were willing to open a spot for her, one shaped for her and her alone. She needed only to seize it.

Yes, acquisition required planning and endurance, yet confidence was the hidden bolster. Suddenly, there was so much she wanted here, and delaying because of past doubts would waste everyone's time. No more of that. If she wanted to live here...if she wanted to add Tynan to her family—the greatest treasure in any dragon's hoard—then she had to feel that desire in her bones.

And then act.

Lyr had offered her a way forward in the task he'd assigned her. That was clear. Tynan, though... He would accept her because of their potential bond, no question. But acceptance sounded boring. The heat that flared between them when they kissed? Not boring. That was the kind of connection she and Tynan deserved, and she would accept nothing less. Their intensity demanded it. And someday, they might even find love.

Of course, there were also downsides. Like this horrific shift in her temperature. Sex had better be worthwhile after all this.

Shivering, Kezari tightened her wings against her back, but it didn't provide much warmth. Not even the heat radiating up from the stone tower could counter the frigid bite of that. Should she return to her cave to sleep? It would be more comfortable, but she would have to clear the entrance with fire. And what if someone needed her?

Too bad she didn't already have that house with the underground tunnels. For that matter, it was too bad the *elves* didn't have any underground tunnels. That might be a good alteration to suggest, for traveling between all the towers to the main part of the estate was misery for everyone in this weather. Even dragon shifters.

Especially dragon shifters in the throes of a new mating.

After another violent shiver and a curse for her ill-timed body clock, Kezari shifted quickly and chattered her way through the hatch and down the ladder into the upper floor of the tower. Instantly, warmth surrounded her, and she released a satisfied sigh. Much better. But what about sleep?

Kezari eyed the bed, but that was now Tynan's. Even though he intended to stay at the healing tower, it didn't seem right. How did one sleep in a bed, anyway? It was so small and confining with its sheets and covers, and she would be too far removed from both ground and sky. Could she shift small enough to rest comfortably on the floor?

Only one way to know for sure.

But after noting the composition of each stone in the tower and trying to count the snowflakes melting against the window, Kezari gave up and changed back to her elven form. With a huff, she dropped down on one of the window seats. Perhaps she wasn't tired enough. Was it excitement over the journey? It could be that. Normally, she would fly until she purged such restlessness, but the snow was falling heavily now. It would do no good to get herself injured.

Apparently, she was going to spend the night staring out at the storm.

Tynan had just managed to sit down when the door opened again.

He couldn't help it—he groaned.

Lial barely glanced his way as he hurried over to help the pair in. The man was some kind of magical construct. There was no other explanation for how he managed to balance the constant stream of patients mostly by himself.

It was around five marks until dawn. Lynia had crept upstairs to sleep a mark or two ago, and poor Elan had fallen asleep in a chair at the foot of Naomh's bed. Though they'd placed the screen up, Kai stood in the corner like a bodyguard, his attention on his father. At least they didn't have to worry about the Sidhe lord worsening without anyone noticing. Kai could probably tell them how many breaths the man had taken since the procedure.

Lial directed their new arrivals toward the chairs. A female scout half-carried a snow-covered man across the room, and Tynan could tell by the way the man's head bounced periodically that he was struggling hard to stay awake. Much less shuffle forward. He leapt to his feet to help, but Lial ducked his shoulder beneath the man's other arm and lifted him away from the scout. The woman sagged in relief.

"I found him near the new recruits' barracks," she said, her voice almost hollow with exhaustion and maybe pain.

Tynan studied her more closely as Lial helped the man into a chair. The white lines of strain on her face had him opening his senses a touch, but he needn't have bothered. She gripped her left forearm and grimaced. Even still, she didn't say a word.

"How are you hurt?" he asked.

The scout blinked at him. "Oh. See to him first. He didn't even have a cloak on, and his boots were soaked through. I'm not sure there's enough frostbite ointment for that."

If Lial hadn't been there, Tynan would have done as she suggested, but there was no need to leave her in pain. Besides, he could see now that her hand and wrist were beginning to bruise and swell. "There are two of us. Please, tell me."

Her gaze flicked to Lial for a moment, but it only took her a heartbeat to nod. "I slipped climbing down from the tree. My hand might be broken. Or maybe my wrist."

Bera's heart, but the scouts and warriors here were tougher than the people who lived around the temple. The woman barely winced when he gently took her hand in his to examine it. Both a visual and magical scan revealed that she was actually right on both counts—she'd cracked her wrist and fully broken two of the bones in her hand.

"Broken," Tynan said to Lial, who looked over his shoulder where he knelt in front of the man. "We should change places, if you've the energy. I am not as good at bone work."

Nodding, Lial stood. "Elan," he called. His assistant jerked upright immediately. "Warming potions, cool water, frostbite treatment, and dry clothes."

To Tynan's amazement, Elan rushed into action as though he hadn't been asleep a couple of drips before. He was fast, too. By the time Tynan had the man's boots off, Elan had returned with a shallow bucket of cool water to slowly warm their patient's feet. Tynan had barely settled both feet in the water before the assistant was dripping some potion into it. Efficient.

But even so, Tynan had a feeling it was going to be a long night.

A NUDGE BROUGHT Tynan to full awareness, but he straightened in his seat slowly. How long had he managed to nap in the chaos? He opened his eyes to find Lial frowning down at him. Considering the lack of sunlight streaming through the window behind the man's head, he hadn't slept long enough.

"What is it this time?" Tynan asked roughly, then cleared his throat. "Not an emergency, I'm guessing, since you're not barking orders."

Lial smiled a little then. "No new patients, as luck has it. We have nearly two marks until dawn, and both snow and injuries have stopped. You should go get some real sleep before tomorrow's mission."

It was a true statement, but also an impossible one. "Did you forget that we put that patient in the upstairs bedroom until his next frostbite treatment?"

"I did not." The healer's nose wrinkled. "Gods, I hate frostbite. It takes forever to coax the skin into full regeneration, so he might be there a while."

Tynan smoothed down his hair. "Then...?"

Lial shrugged. "You already had most of your things packed to move to the observation tower. If the trails are clear enough, you could go sleep there. I imagine it will be more comfortable."

Although he nodded in agreement, Tynan hesitated. Would the isolated room be a balm or a lesson in loneliness? Moving had sounded like a nice plan when his empathy had been overwhelmed, but in general, he enjoyed being around people. Otherwise, he was left with nothing but his own thoughts and memories.

"Unless you prefer to sleep in chairs?" Lial asked wryly.

"Of course not."

Tynan shook off his melancholy musings and stood, wavering on his feet only a moment. He'd brought his stuff down after they carried the new patient up, so he only had to grab his bags from the base of the stairs. The short walk there, and then to the door, still took too much effort. He truly did need solid sleep before the journey to Earth. It would be difficult enough making it to the tower, much less traveling to another planet.

Best not to think about all the portals involved in that.

After securing his cloak at his throat, Tynan glanced over his shoulder at Lial. "Thank you. If you need me again, send a mental call."

Lial shook his head. "It's unlikely. I'm going to grab some sleep during the lull myself."

With a quick wave, Tynan plunged out into the cold. By the

nine gods, the wind had bite, slipping beneath his cloak to burn against his flesh. But at least the initial paths had been cleared, since access to the healing tower took priority. It was a frigid but easy walk until he reached the back gardens. That became... trickier. Along the side paths, he had to climb over snow drifts or push through them. Snow squeaked beneath his boots and turned the bottom of his cloak and robes into a frigid mess.

He was frozen solid by the time he reached the base of the observation tower. Thankfully, the door held the same enchantment as all the others, removing the moisture from his clothes and hair as soon as he hurried through. And the warmth... He paused to savor that blessed infusion of heat before beginning the climb up.

Tynan ran his fingers along the semi-opaque crystal of the walls as he followed the spiral to the top. Selia had transmuted this from regular stone for Aris, who'd been traumatized by his imprisonment in a dark cave. There was nothing but darkness now, but during the day, the structure filled with light, and one could see glimpses of the outer world beyond. What would it be like to have someone love you deeply enough to create such a wonder? He'd certainly never experienced it.

Once Tynan reached the upper floor, he removed his cloak and hung it on a hook by the stairs, then kicked off his boots and tossed his bags down beside them. Why was the room so dark? With all the windows...ah, but the moons had both set. He sent a trickle of magic to the mage globe above, brightening it until he could make out more of the room.

He was about to head for the bed when a glimmer of gold and white caught his eye. On the window seat...Kezari? Was she injured? Tynan hurried over, but he realized before he reached her side that she was sleeping. Why in the world was she curled up on the window seat, sleeping against the glass in her elven form? If not for the drape of her long, white dress and the fall of her golden hair, he might not have seen her.

Tynan knelt beside Kezari before gently cupping her shoulder and giving her a tentative shake. He did *not* want to startle a sleeping dragon—there was probably a parable about that very thing out there somewhere. But the way she slumped looked very uncomfortable. He couldn't just leave her here and go climb into his soft bed.

"Kezari?" he ventured.

She shifted a little, and one eye opened. "Hmm?"

"What are you doing?"

Down drifted her eyelid once more. "Roof too cold."

Too cold for Kezari? Her temperature must still be off, which meant... His heart turned over. It was his fault, if indirectly, that she'd had to find another place to sleep. He eyed the bed. It was large enough for both of them, and there was no reason they couldn't share it. He wouldn't take advantage of her—even if he *were* that kind of awful person, Kezari would be more than willing to kill him for it.

"May I carry you?" he asked.

Was she still awake enough to hear? He was about to give her another slight shake when she smiled. "Carry *me*? Hah. If you can."

Did she even realize what form she was in? Silly dragon shifter. Shaking his head, Tynan scooped Kezari carefully into his arms and walked as softly as he could toward the bed. Would she wake? He worried a little—startled dragons and all—but she burrowed her face against his chest and sighed.

It hurt his very heart to tuck her beneath the covers and round the bed to the other side. With a sigh of his own, he stripped off his robe and the tunic beneath. But he hesitated to remove his pants. It seemed too...familiar, he supposed. If Kezari woke before he did, he would rather she not get the wrong impression. And he was tired enough to sleep in just about anything.

With that decided, Tynan crawled beneath the covers and tried very hard not to think about the woman breathing steadily beside him. He needed sleep. If he had to, he could trigger a healing spell to that effect. But as soon as he rolled over, his back to Kezari, he slipped almost instantly into the soothing darkness.

~

KEZARI STIRRED awake as soon as the first ray of sunlight touched the ridge where Braelyn sat. That first brush of energy served as her constant alarm, though sometimes she chose to ignore it. Deliciously warm and comfortable, she considered doing just that now. This was far better than when she'd fallen asleep against the window. Whatever had—

*Kezari.*

Tynan's voice brushed against her memory. Her eyes popped open, but she remained perfectly still. That delicious warmth? It came from Tynan, whose back currently filled her view. Her body was pressed against his, her arm curled around his waist. His *bare* waist. What had she done? What had *he* done? Anger forced air through her teeth with a hiss.

He stirred, and she urged herself to calm. Surely, she was mistaken. She'd never mated in this form, but from what she could tell about the process, it was rather...notable. Though she'd been exhausted, she wasn't that light of a sleeper. Nor was Tynan the type to accost her while she slept. In fact, *she* was the one curled around *him*.

She still wore her dress, and now that she was calmer, she noticed the cloth of his pants against her leg where it rested against his. They weren't naked, then. There was no sign of something untoward. So he'd simply brought her here? She had only the vaguest memory of what he'd said when he woke her. Had he asked to carry her? That couldn't be right, either. She was a dragon. What elf carried a dragon?

Although she had to admit that she wasn't exactly dragon-shaped at the moment.

Tynan shifted in his sleep again, and her current form became...a problem. Suddenly, she didn't need any other heat but the fire that lit in her blood, so similar to when they'd kissed. She wanted to roll him over and wake him with another of those kisses. More, she longed to claim him like the finest treasure.

But she couldn't do that for so many reasons. For one, he was asleep, and even she knew that acting on her instincts in this situation would be wrong. They had no established rules to allow such liberties. For another...well, it could begin something rather irrevocable between them. He hadn't given her the necklace the elves so often spoke of, but what if that wasn't a requirement? Though she'd decided he was hers, this still felt monumental.

Kezari eased away from Tynan and flopped onto her back. Instantly, cool rushed over her, taunting her with the loss. She scowled up at the ceiling. There was so much she didn't know about Tynan. Namely, the source of the darkness haunting his spirit. He'd hinted that there was a reason for his lack of control over his empathy, but he hadn't trusted her enough to share it.

With a rustle of sheets, Tynan leaned over her. "I'm sorry, Kezari. You said I could carry you, so I thought it would be fine. You looked terribly uncomfortable huddled against the window. Are you angry?"

Hah. He had no idea how initially upset she'd been, but fortunately, her reason had returned before he woke. "No. I remembered enough on my own. Thank you for considering my comfort."

His smile held a playfulness she'd never glimpsed before, and a stream of sunlight glinted in his tousled hair. Her fingers itched to touch the pale gold strands, more precious than any hoard. She reached up, but instead of his hair, her finger found and traced the sharp line of his jaw, curled along his well-defined cheekbone. The fullness of his lower lip beckoned until she nearly leaned up for a nibble.

He truly was a handsome elf. Was it any wonder he received interested glances wherever he passed? Even some of the mated ladies had stared a bit when first meeting him. Once he was formally introduced here, he would have more offers than he could consider, and she would have to fight them all off if she hadn't already claimed him.

Could she risk that? A tiny snarling sound slipped free.

Absolutely not.

Tynan's smile morphed into a confused frown. "Kezari?"

"You are awake now," she pointed out.

His frown deepened. "Yes. Clearly. What—"

Wrapping her arms around his neck for balance, she darted up to claim his mouth before he could complete the question. Would this go further? She didn't know. But her very blood demanded his skin against hers. His heat. His closeness. Him. Her spirit hummed with the joy of it all.

One of his arms curled around her back. Then he rolled over, pulling her with him, and sat up. She straddled his lap lest their lips part, and he moaned against her mouth. His free hand dug into her hip just shy of pain, and she couldn't help but squirm.

Then the fool man pulled free of their kiss, his panting breaths shivering against her skin. "Kezari. I had no intent..."

She snarled from the force of the mating urge burning through her. Were she a less civilized dragon, she would press forward, but no. If he did not want her, then he did not. In truth, his hesitation was probably for the best. Elves loved discussion far more than action.

Kezari leaned back, twisting to free herself, but his hold tightened. His eyes flashed with sudden fierceness. "That was not a rejection," he said, almost sharply. "I can feel that you think so, but it isn't. I merely didn't want to take advantage."

She blinked at him. "*I* straddled *your* lap."

"And we're excellent at miscommunication," Tynan pointed out. Expression softening, he brushed a kiss across her lips. "I needed to be sure of your true wishes."

What were her wishes?

The only thing she could think in this moment was him.

# CHAPTER TWENTY-TWO

Tynan couldn't look away from the glimmering gold of Kezari's gaze. He could barely bring himself to breathe. What was she thinking? Because of her dragon nature, her expressions were often difficult to read. But her desire…that rang clear through his own soul.

Gods, Kezari felt so perfect and vital in his arms. The hand cupping her shoulder shook with the need to stroke. Or grip. He wanted to caress every bit of her skin and hold her tight against him in nearly equal measure. But although her instincts might be roused, she didn't really want *him*. She couldn't possibly.

Tynan buried his face against her chest, his lips finding her collarbone of their own accord. Her warm, spicy scent slid into him with each breath until he grew dizzy with it, and every emotion haunting his heart rose up in response. Hope for the future. Despair for what he couldn't have. Loneliness and shame and love unrequited. It took everything within him to tamp it all down behind his shields, lest she feel the bite in her own spirit.

This was why he shouldn't risk a bond, no matter how much he wanted to. For Kezari's sake, he had to let this craving go unfulfilled. Wasn't this the heart of why she really sent him to the edge of control? In truth, it wasn't her at all. It was his own foolish wishes.

Her fingers slid into his hair, and he pinched his eyes closed.

"I want to mate with you, Tynan."

His already hard body grew pained with desire at her words, yet all he could do was shudder against her. Kezari wanted to sate her desire—he did, too. But could he share his body with her knowing she had no real desire for a bond? His heart might never recover. And if he lost full control...

Kezari tugged gently on his hair until he lifted his head to peer at her. "What's wrong?" she asked.

Tynan sighed. "No matter how much I want you, I'm not sure giving in to random desire is the best thing for either of us."

Her free hand slid around his neck and along his chest. Then she grabbed the chain of his medallion and followed it down to the round pendant on the end. Her rapt gaze focused on the engravings, and when she brushed her thumb over the surface, he shivered as though she'd touched his actual flesh.

"It's this, right?" Kezari asked. "The bonding?"

His heart pounded against his ribs with sudden force. "Kai said you told Eniom I'm your potential soulbonded, but I know how much you doubt such a connection. Which is your right. I'm just not sure I should join with you without *fully* joining."

"Then give me your medallion," Kezari said, shrugging. "I have accepted that you are mine."

Tynan blinked at her. He must have heard her incorrectly. Or perhaps she misunderstood? He couldn't remember if he'd explained how the magical link behind the pendants worked, and he had no idea if anyone else would have mentioned it. Hadn't she said dragons weren't inclined to bond?

"It's attuned to me," he said gruffly. "Activating the magic within begins the literal soulbonding process. But doing that with me, that is..."

She scowled. "And what is wrong with you? Nothing. Except your self-sacrificial tendencies. And stubbornness. Didn't you say you wanted to mate? Now you're talking yourself out of any kind of link. Why?"

Annoyance poured from her, and he gasped from the additional burden on the emotions he already restrained. If this shield cracked with her in his arms, it could break them both. To actually join with her? Suddenly, he couldn't bear the thought, for he would never forgive himself if he destroyed her.

Tynan rested his forehead on her collarbone and tried not to savor the feel of her perched on his lap. "I can't. My emotions...my empathy... You should go before..."

Kezari dropped the pendant, and her arms curled gently around his head in an oddly comforting embrace. "Tell me."

"I can push emotions *out*, Kezari. Into others," he whispered. "Enough to overload a person's mind if I lose total control."

"That sounds unlikely to happen," she replied.

Tynan took a deep, shuddering breath. "I almost killed my mother when I was seven."

Though muffled against her chest, the confession reverberated with its own weight.

Her head tipped against his, and her fingers brushed through his hair. "Tell me," she said again.

And for the first time in decades—maybe centuries—he wanted to talk about it. He held his past and all his feelings about what had happened too close inside, even when he knew he shouldn't. He would have advised his own patients against it, in fact. But there was a reason he didn't judge them when they failed.

"My parents weren't soulbonded, but they loved one another deeply," Tynan began. "My memories may have grown hazy, but I'll never forget their devotion. A love that strong... But then my father died. Drowned in the Kelthe River after he slipped and hit his head."

Kezari stiffened a little in his arms, but her fingers still drifted softly through his hair.

"My mother's grief was terrible on its own. Me? I was inconsolable. I couldn't contain it." He took a shuddering breath. "I didn't try, Bera forgive me. I lost any ability to block others' emotions, too, until the world became a screaming mass of pain. When they finally found someone capable of shielding empathy, I'd nearly shattered the minds of four people, and my mother was near death. I still have memories of standing over her huddled form."

Finally, Kezari leaned back, her hold gently coaxing his head up until their eyes met. "Tynan. You know it isn't your fault."

He nodded. "Of course. I was seven. But no matter how I try, I can't forget. I studied hard to ensure it would never happen again, but now..."

Understanding flickered in her gaze. "I have become your affliction."

Tynan grimaced. "I truly didn't mean you were to blame for—"

"Yes, yes." Kezari lifted the medallion again and held it between them. "You're afraid, and I became the symbol for it. But I am not your grief-stricken mother, and you are not a child learning emotional regulation. Neither of us would be in our current position otherwise."

Considering how she currently sat, he couldn't help but grin at that, whether she meant it literally or not. Unfortunately, that amusement dissipated quickly under the weight of his worry. "A bond is a strong link. Remember how I had to shield Arlyn from Kai's pain?"

Kezari tapped the medallion against the tip of his nose. "Proof empathy isn't to blame. And if you didn't hold it all in, there would be less force. Here's a dragon saying for you. One doesn't dam off the cave stream and expect one's home not to eventually flood."

Gods above. Clearly, he'd spent too much time in caves of late, for the analogy made perfect sense.

"When I said I wanted to mate with you, I didn't mean only sex," Kezari said, a grumble entering her tone. "I've made up my mind. Now, the decision is yours. You'll have to let me know when you've chosen."

His breath backed up in his lungs. There was so much risk here, to her and to himself. But at the same time, her words had held more than a little truth.

Could he brave the danger?

And what would happen if he could not?

KEZARI HAD NEVER FELT such an exasperating blend of frustration, tenderness, and fury—the latter being the most useless. She couldn't rend apart the sadness of his past and morph it into something better. She couldn't go back and fly that little boy somewhere different. But if he let her, she could guard his future.

Annoyingly, he only stared at her while the kaleidoscope of his emotions danced over her like refracted light through hazy skies. She let his medallion drop again and leaned back against his hold, hoping he would take the hint and release her before she had to snap at him. Of course, he did not. Instead, his grip on her hip tightened once more.

"Already giving up?" he asked.

She blew out a sharp breath. "I will neither beg nor pressure. If—"

His lips cut off her words, but she didn't struggle to continue. His actions spoke well enough. With his hand on her back, Tynan gathered her closer, his touch so tender she felt almost delicate. But there was no gentleness in the way his mouth devoured hers, and that alone had her desire blazing anew. Her fingers dug into his shoulders as she pressed herself even closer.

She didn't know what to do with this craving, but she wanted to learn.

He caressed her, then, his hands exploring every curve and hollow of her body. And when his thumb traced over her heated core, she couldn't hold back a ragged gasp. Delightful. Perfect. How much better would this be flesh-to-flesh? With only a thought, she sent their clothes away, then smiled a wicked, satisfied smile at the sheer glory of it.

Tynan jerked his head back, but as soon as he saw her face, he laughed. "A fascinating skill."

Her smile widened as she ran her hand down his chest, tracing every line of muscle along the way. But that wasn't what caught her attention the most. She wanted to see and touch and taste the hard, full length of him rising against her belly. She wrapped her hand around him and stroked, and just that had him releasing a hiss worthy of any dragon.

"Kezari..." he breathed.

She didn't entirely know what she was doing, but it seemed she understood well enough.

Her gaze landed on the medallion. "Yes or no?"

He threw his head back with a shudder, and Kezari squirmed against him as her own body burned brighter. Too much longer, and she would climb him like a cliff.

"That's not fair," Tynan groaned.

"I'm happy to continue, medallion or no." She nipped his chin with her teeth. "You are the one who is not."

Though he still shivered, Tynan met her eyes once more. "It's a true bond." His hands cupped her face. "A forever bond, broken only at great cost. If you choose this in haste..."

"If I've chosen in haste, it was after a rather lengthy brood," Kezari said wryly. "I have learned that delaying action when I know something to be right only causes pain. I know you are mine. And perhaps once I gain your necklace, others will leave you be, and I won't have to think about eating them for their temerity."

His brows lifted. "You wouldn't."

"Not happily," Kezari conceded. Then she bared her teeth. "But sometimes needs must. Do you really want to chance it?"

Laughing, Tynan lifted the chain over his head. Despite how

she ached for him, she stared at the pendant with rapt attention. "We'll have to have one attuned to you to give me in return," he said, "Or the bond won't be fully complete."

She nearly scoffed, but she wouldn't hurt him by doing so. Really, this elven magic might not affect her at all. She'd already accepted him as a mate, so this was for him—and as a symbol for his culture. Her curiosity now was purely scholarly.

"We'll figure it out," Kezari said, shrugging.

The chain quivered in his hand for a moment. *"i'Tayah ay nac-mor kehy ler ehy anan taen,"* Tynan finally whispered.

A flash of light caught her by surprise—but not as much as the invisible tendrils of power that surged through her. Linking. Forming. Her mouth dropped open as thoughts and feelings and memories and magic flooded her like an overtipped cave spring. She barely noticed when he settled the chain around her neck.

For the first time in her life, she truly understood another person. Hopes, fears, dreams. And her heart ached all the more in ways she couldn't define.

Unable to resist, Kezari rose up, taking his mouth with hers as she lowered herself onto his hard length bit by bit. There was a slight pinch of pain, but she disregarded it, too caught up in the desire ricocheting between them as his hands resumed their journey across the planes of her body. Then they were fully joined, and he gripped her hips once more to guide her in the proper rhythm.

Fortunately, she'd always been a quick learner, so together they flew.

TYNAN STARED up at the ceiling in numb shock. Not the bad kind. Merely...stunned. Blown away. Rendered useless for anything resembling thought.

What in Bera's name had just happened?

Kezari lay over him, a mass of pliant, contented dragon. He

could almost imagine he heard the same kind of soft *rrrurrrrr* Emowa sometimes released when Lial scratched behind her ears. His heart could concur with the sentiment even though his mind wanted to race.

He traced her spine with his fingertips and smiled when she trembled. So responsive. He hadn't expected that. But he hadn't expected any of this. How in the world had they moved from avoiding each other to bonded in a matter of days? He felt like the happier version of one of Kezari's *daeri*.

When she acted, she acted. Her ability to simply leap awed him.

"It's rather important for flight," Kezari mumbled.

"Wha—Oh." She'd caught his thoughts through their new bond. "I suppose that's true, though I didn't mean it literally."

She propped her chin on his chest to stare up at him. "Hmm, this is a rare occurrence, you know. A dragon riding an elf."

His choked laugh nearly jostled her off him. "Kezari!"

"You're strangely shy about such things," she said. But she smiled. "I suppose I should re-form your pants. We need to get ready soon."

He grasped for the meaning behind her statement, but his mind was a perfect blank. "Ready?"

"It can't be long until the third mark, when we're supposed to leave." One of her brows quirked up. "For Earth? The ancient dragon?"

Tynan groaned, even as his skin went hot. They would probably be late, and it would be more than obvious why. How would their bonding be received? Most wouldn't care, of course, but some... Aris in particular might be upset. His patient had a different kind of link to Kezari, but it was a bond, nonetheless. Would he be bothered by the abrupt change?

Kezari snorted. "Aris already knows. He fussed at me for not shielding more thoroughly."

Tynan groaned again.

With a laugh, Kezari rose, her usual dress surrounding her

between one blink and another. "Don't worry. He shielded enough for our privacy, though I wouldn't feel regret if he hadn't. I had my own bit of discomfort when he first mated with Selia after his healing."

Did they have to go on this mission today? Remaining in the tower with a pillow over his head sounded like a far better plan at this point. Maybe if he didn't emerge for a few days, he'd be able to meet Aris's eyes without awkwardness.

Maybe.

Kezari poked him in the side. "Come on. Sex is not taboo here, so I don't understand your reticence. But if anyone *does* make you feel uncomfortable, I'll be happy to bare my teeth. A quick shift, and fire wouldn't be out of the question."

She meant it, too. He felt her earnestness like his own unreasonable embarrassment. And what was wrong with him, anyway? He'd never experienced this strange shyness over his previous lovers—though he supposed he hadn't formed a connection with any of them. Nothing beyond a night or two of pleasure.

His dragon's annoyed hiss warned him he'd better change that line of thought.

Tynan sat up and swung his legs over the side of the bed. After running his hand through his messy hair, he squinted up at her. "No need to worry about the pants. I need to wear Earth clothes, anyway. Too bad there's not a place to bathe up here. After seeing so many patients and then, well..."

Kezari grinned down at him. "If we had more time, I would make you one in recompense. Though mostly, I'd rather make you dirtier."

He couldn't resist grabbing her hips and nuzzling her belly. How much time did they have? Was there a water clock up here? Over the fabric of her dress, he kissed along the line of her hip bone. He could get dressed quickly, and there were always cleansing spells. Not as satisfying, but it would give them longer to—

"If you want the path to be clear, get moving," a voice called up the stairs. Aris. And that hadn't been an amused lilt in his tone.

Tynan drew back. "He sounds angry."

"I disrupted his sleep," she said, lifting a shoulder. "And he is upset that his mental state is too unsettled for him to accompany me."

Both of those things were probably true, assuming the man had been honest when speaking mentally to Kezari, but that might not be all of it. Tynan worried over that as he pulled clothes from his bag and rushed to don them. Instinctively, he formed a shield around his thoughts, not wanting to upset her. She would be hurt if Aris was mad about their bond.

It was a possibility, though. Tynan frowned at the thought. He hadn't courted her properly before offering his medallion, not by Moranaian standards. Quick bondings happened, but they could be more tumultuous. And considering Aris's potential bonded had been the one to torture him, the man was already aware of how wrong such things could go. He might think Tynan had taken advantage.

"What do you think?" Kezari asked, drawing his gaze.

His heart skipped and then pounded at the way the thick blue pants hugged her hips and the tight shirt stretched lovingly across her breasts. Earth clothing had benefits, though he had to admit that he'd never seen her in true Moranaian clothes, either. Her usual flowing dress was a creation all her own.

She settled her hands on her hips, emphasizing the curve. "Well?"

"Beautiful."

Her face went soft, but she shook her head. "I wasn't asking about aesthetics. Does this look similar to the clothes Selia wore on her mission? I created them from memory."

Oh, that. Tynan shrugged. "I believe so. Cora provided mine, so I'm no expert."

Kezari trailed her eyes down his body with sudden interest. "She certainly is."

He went almost painfully hard. Too bad he couldn't act on it. "We're not talking aesthetics, Kezari."

She grinned at him before darting toward the top of the stairs. Shaking his head, Tynan grabbed the other sack he'd prepared, one that contained essential supplies. At least he wouldn't have to carry the crate of potions, too, since Lial had sent that over already. He needed only to sling his cloak around his shoulders and follow his new bonded down.

Hopefully, the rest of the journey would be so easy.

# CHAPTER TWENTY-THREE

When Kezari reached the base of the stairs, Aris was waiting, a hint of a frown pinching his face. "I'm surprised you would risk being late," he said.

Snow drifted around her like little arrows ready to strike. Shivering, Kezari formed a cloak around herself, and Aris sent her a curious look. "I'm not in the mood to explain dragon biology to you," she grumbled. "And you honestly have no right to be so grumpy. You've kept me from sleep more than once."

"Do you think it's the lost sleep that's disturbing me?" Aris sighed. "Never mind. We need to get inside before the next wave of snow hits in earnest. This is almost as bad as the weather in the north."

Kezari had a feeling she needed to learn the source of Aris's annoyance, but as Tynan slipped out the door to join her, she let it pass. If it was more than just his unhappiness about staying behind, he would have to tell her later. It had to be nearly the third mark. So as they started down the snow-dusted path toward the back of the main building, she continued along with his change in subject.

"Isn't it nearly midwinter?" she asked, taking Tynan's hand in hers. "When the snows hit harder?"

"In about three weeks, I believe," Aris answered. "But large snows this early aren't unheard of, simply not as common. The timing of this mission is poor, considering Lial will have one less healer to help."

So that was why her *skizik* was discussing the weather of all things. She sent him a pointed, side-eyed glance. "Isn't Lial accustomed to working alone? Really, Aris. If you're that bothered, then come along. I'll have to stay in this form on Earth, so it isn't as though you'd have to face flying."

"The ride to the new palace didn't bother me," Aris pointed out.

She ignored the warning squeeze Tynan gave her hand. "Then—"

"It is too much risk." Aris's jaw clenched. "In truth, I would likely do fine. But until I know for certain that I won't have a flashback and end up mutating some hapless lifeform on Earth, I'll stay here."

If he was that resolved, why was he hinting that Tynan shouldn't go? He couldn't mean for her to travel to Earth alone. As much as she hated it, she was self-aware enough to realize what a disaster that could be—or at least she was *now,* after a great deal of contemplation over why the others had refused to let her chase the ancient dragons. The dangers of flying blind around a foreign world had been markedly more obvious when she was away from temptation.

Aris had understood such things far sooner than she had. He was undoubtedly worried.

"You shouldn't fret about me," Kezari said as they passed through the back door by the library and started down the long corridors to the front. "Your health is the most important."

"Thank you," Aris said, but his gaze flicked down to her hand where it joined with Tynan's.

Was that displeasure on his face? His mental shields were tight —and had been since her mating with Tynan. Surely, her *skizik* wasn't unhappy about the bonding? Tynan had claimed that Aris sounded angry earlier, but she hadn't seriously considered it. Now, she might need to reevaluate. But why would this bother him?

Maybe he had a problem with elves and dragons mating. But ancestors' blood, it wasn't as though they did so while she was in dragon form. *Eww.* That would simply be unpleasant for all involved. Though if the legends about the origins of their elven forms were true... No. She really did not want that mental image. That mystery could remain unsolved.

As they neared the entryway, Tynan's mind brushed against hers. *"I don't believe Aris is bothered by your nature, love. Remember that he has good reason to mistrust soulbonds."*

Right. Because Aris had been literally tortured by his.

Kezari's stomach lurched at the reminder, and she stopped in her tracks at the base of the stairs leading to the family rooms, blocking Arlyn from finishing her descent in the process. But the elf could wait a moment. Kezari was too busy trying not to be sick as the full weight of what Aris had suffered fell upon her.

While helping her *skizik,* she'd lived through some of his memories. But after experiencing the pureness of the link forming between her and Tynan, she understood more vividly how Aris's potential bond had been abused and perverted. Horrific. No wonder he'd been ready to fling himself from her back when she'd first flown him away—and for days afterward.

Tynan's arms wrapped around her, his calming energy surrounding her like a second cloak. *"I'm sorry. I should have thought before I spoke."*

*"It was only the truth. The wretched, disgusting truth."* A sudden rage pushed away her sadness with a rude shove. *"If I could go to the afterlife, I would yank Perim free, only to roast every inch of her with my flame. Or perhaps I would encase her in solid stone and—"*

*"Calm, Kezari,"* Tynan said, though to her surprise, there was a hint of agreement tinged with fierceness shifting through his

mind. *"Some people deserve such a fate, but it's best not to go down that path."*

She leaned back to frown at him. *"Aren't you a healer? That's an odd attitude for one."*

*"Yes."* His nostrils flared. *"How do you think I developed such an opinion? Some of the things I've helped people through..."*

A few flickers flashed into her mind before he could shield them, but it was enough to have her contemplating murder once more. How could anyone—elf, dragon, fae, human, *anyone*—treat the innocent in such horrible ways? And Tynan suffered though each dark memory with them, healing that awful pain.

That truth filled her with a powerful, nearly overwhelming tenderness—but also protectiveness. She would not let the dark world tarnish him, not if she could help it. And if he didn't find a way to purge all the horrors he witnessed, he would surely wither into gloom and despair.

"Umm," Arlyn said hesitantly from behind her. "Is everything okay?"

Awareness returned in a rush, and Kezari glanced around to find Aris and Lyr staring at her from the stone arch where the portal would be activated and Arlyn frowning down from the stairs. They had to wonder if she'd lost her senses to stop like this, considering they couldn't hear her mental conversation with Tynan.

Flustered, she pulled free of her new mate and then tugged him aside so Arlyn could come down the stairs. "Sorry," Kezari mumbled.

When Arlyn's eyes landed on the pendant Kezari now wore, the elf skipped a step, a hand on the banister the only thing saving her from disaster. Tynan hurried forward to steady the woman, who smiled at him gratefully. The tiniest hint of jealousy twitched in Kezari's heart, but she tamped it down.

She could be civilized.

"Thanks," Arlyn said. "And congratulations."

The tip of Tynan's ear turned pink, but he inclined his head. "Thank you."

From beside the portal, Lyr cleared his throat. "Is there something else I should know about?"

After striding forward a few steps, Kezari pointed proudly at the medallion nestled against her chest, and Lyr's eyes widened. He peered at her and then Tynan, with a quick glimpse at Aris for good measure. His expression didn't shift a great deal otherwise, but at least he didn't appear *more* stressed. Then chagrin colored Lyr's cheeks. So much for that.

"I need to have your medallion commissioned so that you can complete the bond," Lyr said. "I'd meant to ask if we would need to make adjustments for your shifting, but time escaped me."

She'd forgotten she should even have one, so she couldn't fault him for that.

"I'm only one among thousands here," Kezari said. "It is understandable."

The troubled look didn't leave the Myern's face, but there wasn't much she could do about that. From what she'd learned of him, she knew he would worry over the matter until the necklace was presented. So instead of offering more reassurances, she turned around for Tynan, who approached with Arlyn. He remained respectfully close in case the lady tripped again, and Kezari could understand why. Arlyn was only halfway through her pregnancy, but the swell of her stomach already looked like it would alter her balance.

Kezari frowned. Would *she* have to worry about that if she someday carried Tynan's young? It wasn't likely to be an immediate concern since it often took decades for dragons to conceive even with lowered temperatures, but she didn't relish that aspect if it did happen. Bad enough to be cold. But stumbling around at the same time? A terrible indignity.

"Have I done something wrong?" Arlyn asked when she reached Kezari.

Kezari studied the elf in confusion. "No. Why?"

"You frowned at me the entire walk over."

"Oh, that." Kezari waved her hand. "I was lost in thought, nothing more."

Arlyn relaxed, thankfully. Kezari really didn't want to explain such personal thoughts in front of an audience. Again. "I came down a little early to talk to you," Arlyn said. "I know you've been warned more than once about Earth weapons and such, but it occurred to me that you might struggle with human social cues. Do you want a quick rundown on the differences between elves and humans?"

Ah, clever. It was difficult enough to understand the elves' strange rules at times. But were they really that different? "What about Tynan?"

"Well, I suppose he can listen." Arlyn shrugged. "I hadn't considered any kind of formal lesson. It's just that since you're…"

"Ill-mannered? Untamed?" Kezari said, only to regret the teasing when the elf looked abashed. "Sorry. I meant that in jest, though I suppose some would find it true. They simply don't consider that other societies' manners differ so greatly. I would be happy to hear your insights before I leave to avoid that very thing."

Because if dragon manners weren't welcome here, they surely wouldn't go over well on Earth.

"I spoke to Cora about this when she gave me these clothes," Tynan said, his fingers tugging at the end of his thin shirt. "I'm well-enough informed, I believe. If there's time, I'd like to pay homage to Eradisel."

Arlyn glanced at one of the delicate water clocks stationed on the wall and smiled. "We have nearly a quarter mark. Enough time for me and Kezari to talk and you to pray. I think."

Tynan inclined his head. "Yes, it should be."

"Let's move over here," Arlyn said.

Kezari found her wrist locked in the other woman's grip, but she didn't resist as Arlyn tugged her over to the stairs. Would this be helpful? Hard to tell. But it certainly wouldn't hurt.

~

WITH THE WAY the estate was built around the trees, particularly Eradisel, it was no surprise that the wall curved around the ancient trunk with enough room for worshippers to walk a complete circle. However, the altar was on the far side of the tree to allow for privacy, so Tynan was only halfway to his destination when he sensed Aris behind him. He must be truly upset to disrupt someone's worship.

"May I have a quick word?" Aris asked before the altar was even in sight.

Halting, Tynan took a deep breath and then spun to face the man. "Very quick, if I'm to have my prayer."

Aris's gaze slid uneasily toward Eradisel, but he didn't relent. "What were you thinking?"

That surprised Tynan enough that he opened his shields in search of an emotional clue—and more than worry, he found anger. Just as he'd suspected at the tower. "If you're concerned that your past experience might repeat, I assure you I would never hurt her that way."

Shock flashed across Aris's face. "I wasn't implying *that*. I'm referring to your haste. How could you offer her the necklace when she barely understands our ways? I was worried enough when she randomly decided to try a kiss, but this..."

"Do you think Kezari is too weak to decide for herself?" Tynan asked, feeling out the true heart of the matter. He'd expected awkwardness, not hostility.

"Not exactly." Aris rubbed his fingers across his brow before pinching the bridge of his nose. "There's a softness to Kezari, though she'd burn the world before she'd admit it. And she might not realize this, but she's family to me. Like a sibling. Of course I'm angry that you took advantage."

There was something both absurd and touching about Aris defending Kezari's honor, but Tynan wouldn't yield on one point. "I did not take advantage of her."

"I know how much you longed for a bond," Aris said. "I recall you mentioning it during one of my early treatments. So at the first opportunity, you—"

"Please don't continue that statement," Tynan interrupted, a surge of anger making his fingers twitch with the need to curl into a fist. But just as he hid his emotions behind his strongest shield, he suppressed the action. Aris might break at such a gesture, and no one deserved that. "I can't counter it as I'd wish, for both of our sakes."

The full import of his words must have struck, for Aris paled. "I do have respect for you, Tynan. But did she even understand what the necklace meant?"

"Yes. I made sure of it." Tynan held Aris's gaze. "Did it occur to you that this was Kezari's idea? *She* was the one who asked *me*. You might consider your own preconceived notions on this matter. Now, I have little time left to commune with Eradisel. If you wish to settle your feelings about the haste of our bonding, I suggest you discuss it with Kezari."

Before Aris could counter with some other ridiculous accusation, Tynan spun away and continued toward his goal. He understood Aris's concern, but it was insulting, regardless. Not just to Tynan but to Kezari, too. As if she wouldn't have seen through any kind of trap.

"Wait," Aris called.

Tynan considered ignoring him, but there was distress in the man's tone. That, he could not dismiss so casually. Pausing, he glanced over his shoulder. "Yes?"

"I'm sorry. Truly." Aris pinched the back of his neck and sighed. "It's only...with you not wanting to remain at Braelyn and Kezari bound here with me as her *skizik*, I worried even more. If you leave her, she will blame herself."

Gods above. Aris was right about that, at least. They hadn't discussed even the most basic things about how they would live together. Not homes or family or children. Children. Oh, *clechtan*. She'd said her temperature dropped to allow for conception, and they'd taken no precautions. What if she didn't want to have a child with an elf? There was a great deal they didn't know about such a joining.

"Tynan? *Are* you planning to leave already?"

A wave of Aris's concern thudded against Tynan's shields and snapped him back to the conversation. "Of course not, but you're correct that we didn't consider such matters. Even so, rest assured that whether I take Lial's place or not, I'll stay with Kezari."

Some of the tension drained from Aris's stance, though his expression still showed worry. "See that you don't hurt her."

Tynan smiled softly at the statement. No, he hadn't liked the questioning, but he could respect it. Kezari had saved and protected Aris after his torture. It was only natural that he looked out for her now, insulting though it had been.

"No one can promise that," Tynan replied. "But I'll do my best."

Then he hurried away to do the fastest communing of his life.

SOMETHING WAS WRONG WITH TYNAN—KEZARI felt certain of it. She studied his tense demeanor and tried to analyze the muffled hints of emotion passing along their bond, but he was holding his feelings under tight shield. Could it be simply nerves? He held the smelly pouch of herbs already, even though they'd only traveled through the local teleportation gate to reach the portal located by the new palace.

Well, palace-in-progress. Not that she could tell how much had been completed beneath the waist-deep snow piled beyond the path that linked the two portals. Poor Ralan would have no reason to venture here all day the next time he wanted to avoid someone, at least not until warmer weather returned.

Inona waited beside one of the guards protecting the portal, and as they neared, Tynan grew increasingly tense. She could practically taste his unease. But was it really this little trip? Maybe he hadn't believed her when she'd said this gate bypassed the Veil with its endless mists. Silently, she slipped her hand into his.

He gave a return squeeze, but his emotions didn't shift toward relief.

What had Aris said to him? She'd seen her *skizik* follow, and when he'd returned, he'd appeared worried. Then Tynan had emerged acting decidedly strange. More closed and remote than he'd been for days. It was difficult to imagine Aris being cruel, but there'd been something off about him, too.

Kezari halted before they reached the portal, drawing Tynan to a stop with her. "Do I need to go back and have a talk with Aris?"

Tynan's brows drew together. "Why?"

"He said something about me being a dragon, didn't he?" she demanded. "When he followed you behind the tree, that is."

"No." Tynan's shoulders slumped. "It wasn't that. Most of his words were born of concern, but one of his points got me thinking..."

Her heart skipped a beat. "About our bond?"

"Kezari, I—" Pain speared her gut, and instantly, his gaze shot to hers. "Of course I don't wish to sever it. Don't let your fears wander there. But Aris did bring up one good point. We haven't exactly discussed the details. Do you wish to stay at Braelyn? Do I? Things like that."

*Aris did bring up one good point.* Which meant he had tried to interfere. Oh, she was going to have words with him when they got back to Braelyn. Gentle-ish ones, of course, with no hint of violence. It was...probably fortuitous that it would be some time before they returned.

"I'm sure we'll move multiple times over the next few thousand years," Kezari pointed out. Reasonably, she hoped. "And there is no rush on that decision unless you're wanting to hurry back to your temple."

She had to admit she didn't like *that* possibility.

Tynan chuckled low. "Not particularly, but I haven't decided about Lial's request, either."

"Eh, it's fine." Kezari grinned. "It seems I've earned us a house."

Though the second laugh was stronger, Tynan still had a worried air about him that bothered her. But Inona called out a reminder about the time, and she decided to let it rest. He seemed to have settled the worst of it. And if not?

Well, it was better not to arrive at the Ancient One's home already angry.

# CHAPTER TWENTY-FOUR

Ara let the note flutter to her desk and then scowled down at it. Once again, her spy had sent her news, but on the surface, it made no sense. *M.R. and associates abandoned camp. Tracked to Ireland. Now missing.* She pulled out the map Fen had brought her. With its bright colors and intricate lines detailing borders, it reminded her of art, but there was no beauty in this search—nor in the marks she'd already made showing Meren's known locations.

Ireland required a journey across the ocean from his last camp in the northeastern area of the United States. Had Meren used a gate? A pocket dimension? Had he taken his growing band of half-blood fae to his new destination using human means? She'd never been on an airplane, but she'd seen pictures and films detailing them during her travels on Earth. It was difficult to picture haughty Meren in such a space with all those humans.

Regardless, his journey to Ireland had implications she could no longer ignore, as much as she wanted to. Because the easiest access to Lord Naomh's realm was in Ireland—at least if the rumors she'd heard were true. Naomh's grandfather had been a paranoid man, and the vast warren of underground rooms he'd built had long been whispered about, even if not experienced. And what would a paranoid man have added?

A hidden exit.

Naomh surely knew of and guarded that weakness, but from what she'd heard, he wasn't doing well. If his brother was protecting that underhill dimension, did he know to guard against that incursion? Possibly not. Meren would absolutely count on Caolte's ignorance for the chance to finish off Naomh.

With unhurried steps, she strode toward the room where Fen studied. Sullenly, but there was no help for that. She'd deserved his dislike of her and his grudging acceptance of his role as her heir from the moment she'd left him with his human father right after his birth. It didn't matter to his heart that she'd done it to save him, and she had to respect that.

Not to mention that Fen was never at his best when he had to come to the Unseelie realm alone. But there was much he had to learn, and his mates couldn't always come with him. Not with their obligations on Earth. It wasn't something she was fond of, but she could respect their adherence to responsibility, too. Some-day, though, Fen and his mates would have to decide where they fully belonged.

Fen glanced up as she closed the door, and a frown creased his brow when she scanned the room magically for any listeners. "What now?"

His tone wasn't friendly, but that was something else she'd grown resigned to. "I need to leave the realm for a brief time. If there are any insurrections, quash them."

Though his mouth dropped open, he recovered quickly. "Wait. No. I'm *not* acting in your place while you go have fun. With all the trouble brewing on Earth, I should be there. If Maddy wasn't swamped with inventory and Anna wasn't spending a couple of days with her fae relatives, I wouldn't be here now. You can't just dump everything and go."

"I am not 'dumping everything,' Fen," she bit out. Would they ever get along? "I need to go warn Caolte of a possible attack.

Only that. Mirror communication is not always secure, and this is important. You are the only person in this entire palace who will know of my departure, though perhaps I should have left you unaware, too."

He studied her for a moment in silence before running his fingers through his hair with a sigh. "Sorry. I'm just...what do you want me to do? I've barely even scraped the surface of these history books, much less anything else."

"You marched into the throne room in full *Felshreh* armor to demand help for your mate, and you stood with us against my father," Ara said. "I have every confidence you can deal with my quick absence."

"But—"

"Those things were the heat of the moment." She studied him, noting the hint of a flush creeping into his cheeks. Perhaps having him study history and laws first was a mistake, since his lack of knowledge undermined his confidence. "One of the most important attributes in this court is strength. I give you leave to use your sword and magic in any way necessary to keep the peace. Such as it is."

Before he could argue, Ara marched from the room, heading for her bedroom. She'd formed her own hidden path to reach Naomh's realm without anyone in the Unseelie court knowing. It would ultimately drop her through the main portal into their pocket dimension, but it took a touch longer than a more direct trip.

Hopefully, no one would cause trouble. Fen *could* handle it, but she wasn't certain he would. Not as much as he worried. As she changed into a simple dress and her identity-dampening cloak, she pondered the problem of her son. Perhaps the best thing would be to have him sit beside her on the dais while she rendered judgments, much as she had once done when her father was king.

Fen seemed the type to thrive under that approach.

~

TYNAN AND KEZARI emerged within a heartbeat onto a platform in the center of a vast cavern and descended the steps to the floor. Naturally, Tynan had formed his own mental image of how the outpost would look, but that hadn't prepared him for the reality of it. The sheer enormity. He barely noticed when Inona said something about looking for Delbin and darted away. Instead, he peered up and up and up at the seemingly endless levels connected by stone stairs that spiraled around the walls.

He nearly dropped the small crate of potions he'd retrieved from Inona at the portal. Wouldn't that be a disaster? Jerking his gaze resolutely away, he settled the crate onto the ground at his feet. Even the floor was somehow stunning. What kind of rock was it? Was even the composition different from Moranaia?

Another planet...better not to linger on that.

The comforting hum of Kezari's energy permeated the stone, and if he hadn't already heard the tale of the outpost's creation, he would have known at once that she'd formed the rock into its current shape. Did his fellow Moranaians realize what an immense gift this was? She hadn't merely shifted the earth—she'd infused it with enough magic to preserve it.

"Beautiful work," Tynan said softly as two elves approached from across the cavern.

Most likely Prince Vek and Princess Dria. More royalty, of course.

Kezari paid them little mind, smiling at him instead. "Thank you for saying so. Did Aris tell you a great deal about the cavern's creation?"

"Some." He glanced around at their current level then, noting the smoothness near the center. No stalagmites in this section, only around the perimeter. "Thanks to our bond, I suppose, I can feel how much you put into this. You're truly phenomenal at earth magic."

He sensed her surprise and pleasure at the simple compliment. Were others so careless of her, then, that they rarely considered her feelings? Probably, though he would wager it was done without malice. Those who appeared strong—physically or mentally— were often seen as too resilient to require the same consideration as others. Who would look stronger than a dragon?

But such apparent strength often hid the most bruised hearts.

As soon as the approaching pair reached them, Tynan decided for certain that the man was Prince Vek. He was like a paler, harder version of Fen, who Tynan had met at the healing tower when the young blood elf had accompanied Maddy to Moranaia for her training. What other relative of the half-*Felshreh* man would be standing beside a woman with the same golden eyes as Prince Ralan?

Tynan tapped his chest twice with his fist and bowed. If he was mistaken, the courtesy wouldn't go amiss—unlike slighting the royalty of two different courts, one being his own sovereign princess. That could bring disaster.

"Thank you, but there's no need for that," the woman said. "Forgive Vek and me for not being here when you stepped through. We had...a distraction."

From the hint of tangle to her hair, he could imagine. Not that he would point that out. "It was no burden, Feraien. It gave me a chance to marvel at Kezari's creation."

The princess's smile grew a touch forced, and a tendril of annoyance flowed from her like a draft from one of the tunnels above them. "Welcome to the outpost. I am Moranai Feraien i Driathen Moreln se Vekenayeth nai Moranaia. However, I would far prefer you call me Dria rather than refer to me by title. Your sentences will surely be shorter without all the honorifics."

"Wouldn't they all," Kezari muttered beside him.

Dria snorted. "Absolutely. But to complete our introductions, I should present Vekenayeth anh Torekthayed. I don't believe you've met, have you?"

"Not that I recall," Tynan replied. And there was no way he wouldn't have remembered, considering the hint of danger that surrounded the man. Not the chaotic kind, either. *Deadly* was more the word that came to mind. "But it is a pleasure to meet you. I am Callian ay'tor Beronai pel asebarah i Tynan Fessen nai Calai."

Kezari shifted impatiently beside him, and a new thought hit with nearly painful force. He should have included her in his title. Or had it changed entirely? Their bond wasn't quite complete, but that didn't matter. Names were altered from the very first step of the process.

"Ah, Kezari?" he asked in a low voice, earning a quirked brow from Dria and a frown from Vek. "What's your Moranaian title?"

Her head tilted slightly as she peered at him. "I've met them already, Tynan. I don't think they care."

"I care," he said tightly.

Despite her obvious bemusement, she conceded. "Callian iy'dianore tenah i Kezari Baran nai Braelyn. Happy?"

He was...not exactly happy, but only because of the mental comparison he was forced to make while everyone was staring. If Lord Lyr had given her iy'dianore, Kezari was part of his household directly, and that was the third branching point. But ay'tor was off the fifth, which meant, yes, Tynan had to rearrange the entirety of his title. Wonderful. Now he would look incompetent having to correct himself in front of two royals.

It did happen, though. With new bonds. Surely even to royalty? He swallowed hard against the lump in his throat.

"We should probably go," Princess Dria said slowly.

But Prince Vek's gaze had gone sharp. "Why did you need her title?"

Somehow, there was both simple curiosity and wary suspicion in that question.

Tynan sighed, bracing himself for the confession. "Because I was wrong about my own. It is now Callian iy'dianore Beronai pel asebarah i Tynan Baran se Kezari nai Braelyn."

"Elders' musty wings," Kezari snapped. Annoyance flashed across her face as she stared at him. "Do you mean you have to tell people all of that because we mated? Ugh. As if these introductions needed to be longer. Please tell me you're joking."

He couldn't help it—he laughed. "I'm afraid not."

Even the Unseelie prince looked amused at that point.

"If we didn't have an appointment in some place called London, I would dearly love to hear how you two managed to become soulbound, but alas," Dria said, a definite twinkle in her eye.

Tynan had a feeling they were going to get that reaction a great deal.

~

KEZARI WANTED to grumble about the ridiculousness of elves, but she supposed it wouldn't be fair to do so. Not anymore. Did she find their titles to be silly? Absolutely. But the Moranaians had accepted her despite her differences, so it no longer felt right to judge them for theirs.

Someday, maybe her mouth would catch up with her good intentions.

No one had seemed offended by her comment on Tynan's new title, though. After a moment's discussion over the potions he had brought, they shifted easily to their mission without a word about the rudeness of dragons. Kezari allowed herself to relax as they took the lift Dria had created to the top of the cavern and headed toward the large room Kezari had shaped for formal meetings.

Or what she'd imagined elves might use for such. Was it sufficient?

She frowned at the long room with its plethora of support columns as they passed through. Aside from a few furnished sections, it appeared unused. Nearly the same as the last time she and Aris had been here a month or so prior. It might be worthwhile to offer to reshape the place if it didn't meet their needs.

Not that they required her help. Dria and Vek led them into a small room mostly formed by Vek's and Fen's earth magic. This was the most heavily shielded area in the whole outpost, layer upon layer of protective spells imbued into the walls, and though Kezari couldn't create the magics within, she understood why it was so guarded. For here, Dria had created a permanent, local portal keyed to the places on Earth where she'd been.

Inona and Delbin waited on the other side of the room. Where the scout had retrieved him from, Kezari had no clue, but he would be useful to have along. Since he'd lived for a century on Earth as an exile, he knew the human world well. More importantly, Arlyn had said, he possessed something called a credit card —and a fierce joy at spending Ralan's money.

*"You don't want to be without money if you can help it," she'd said. "Seriously. In cities, you might not even find water for free. I mean, it's okay to ask if you're really thirsty. Some nice person would probably give you water or even food. But don't make assumptions, and don't pick up and take anything. Anywhere."*

Why hoard water, of all the possibilities? What a foolish thing. The resource was necessary for life, sure, but it wasn't exactly rare. Unless things had changed greatly since dragons had lived here? There would be no way to know until she spoke to the Ancient One. But not simply taking things? That made perfect sense on any world. One always inquired about ownership of an item if one didn't want a claw to the face upon the grabbing.

"Return safely, *ahmeeren*," Vek said, dropping a swift kiss on Dria's lips. The words sounded sweet, but the bite beneath them suggested he'd happily rip out the throats of any who hampered that safe return.

Kezari approved.

But as usual, Dria rolled her eyes and nudged her mate back. "Come on," she said, glancing back at Kezari and Tynan. "I'll create a gate to the Veil entrance. Once there, Inona will guide us through to London."

This time, Kezari didn't merely notice Tynan tensing beside her—she felt the surge of fear, too. Had he forgotten his bag of comforting herbs? Once again, she took his hand firmly in hers. He had to realize by now that she wouldn't let him get lost.

Even if they hadn't been bound, she would have prevented that.

Dria's gate flared to life, but the image on the other side looked different than where they'd gone before the direct portal had been created. That gate had been embedded in a crevice in the middle of a small ridge, but Kezari saw nothing but sun-coated trees this time. Only after they'd followed the others through did she see the shallow indention in the side of a hill, just out of view of the local portal.

"This is Arlyn's land," Inona explained. "The Chattanooga gate is more exposed, so I brought Dria here so she could create the teleportation spell."

It was a fascinating little forest—emphasis on little. Were all Earth trees so small? Suddenly, her throat ached with the desire to ask Aris. He probably could have studied the trees minutely and shared with her the extent of their potential growth. She could only give the composition of the soil and rock beneath them.

Tynan squeezed her hand, and a wave of comfort flowed over her. She tipped her head to rest against his shoulder while Inona activated the portal to the Veil. It was only a brief moment, but it was enough to ease some of the ache. Some. What would she do if Aris *did* disapprove of her bonding with a Moranaian? It would grieve her heart to lose his friendship.

*"I told you it was not that,"* Tynan sent, his mental voice growing tense as the swirling mists appeared on the hillside. *"If you must know, it was me. He thought I took advantage of you."*

A strangled laugh nearly made her cough. *"Of me? Did you tell him I rode—"*

*"I didn't go into that much detail,"* he interrupted quickly, and she grinned. It was so delightful to fluster him. *"Anyway, he meant the bond, not sex. He worried that you hadn't known what the necklace meant. Aris considers you family, Kezari. You needn't be concerned about that."*

She'd never really thought about the term "heartwarming," but it made perfect sense now.

The feeling stayed with her as they entered the Veil, and perhaps it helped Tynan, too. Either that, or experience kept him from growing as tense and shaky as his last Veil trip. By the time they passed through into yet another location, his usual calm radiated around him like a fine mist.

This time, they'd emerged into a rather tight spot—a staircase to be exact. The others had already started to ascend. But to move beyond the mouth of the portal, Kezari had to release Tynan's hand and duck in front of him, earning her a bit of a grumble from her new mate. Too bad. He might wish to protect as stringently as she did, but he was a healer, not a dragon.

Fortunately, it was a short climb to the top, which turned out to be a strange but lovely room covered in decorative mosaics. But since the steps ended at the door, Kezari didn't linger any more than the others had. Quickly, she crossed the threshold onto the true surface of Earth.

As always, the barely repressible urge to spread her wings surged through her. The energy here was simply *right* in a way Moranaia wasn't. It was one of the main reasons she'd never been able to tolerate the idea of severing her connection to Earth the way most of the other dragons had. That little tendril sustained her no matter where she was.

"I can guess who the dragon is," a woman said wryly, her voice lilting with an accent Kezari hadn't heard before.

The slim, leanly muscled scout stared at Kezari with a slight smile. She looked as young as any elf, maybe younger with her brown hair pulled up and back, but centuries weighted the spirit behind those blue-green eyes. The gate guardian, then? Kezari didn't spot any weapons, but the wariness fit.

Except the woman was alone.

Surely, the Ancient One wasn't far. As Dria started another round of infernal introductions, Kezari sank her awareness into the ground beneath her feet, hoping to sense the other dragon. But what shrieked through her carried so much information that she swayed and might have fallen if Tynan hadn't curled his arm around her for support.

Immediately, Kezari pulled back—but only a little. What was going on in this place? The earth rumbled constantly, though it wasn't perceptible to her physical form, and the stone beneath the top layer of soil didn't extend downward quite the way it ought. Or rather, it did, but... She slipped a little deeper again, though more carefully.

*Hmm.*

There were rooms—little chambers carved out here and there. Quite a few places to transport or hold wastewater. Forgotten burials. But the most glaring? Long, reinforced caves stretched all over the place, burrowed through the deposits of sedimentary rock in decidedly unnatural patterns. Pipes and tubes stretched beside a strange, moving transport—if Aris were here, she would have connected to him so he could count the lifeforms in each long container. Through it all, there were currents of power, an energy she couldn't access but could feel all the same.

She absolutely had to go down there.

"Kezari," Tynan said sharply, his arm tightening around her waist.

"A moment," she mumbled, too eager to follow one of the speeding containers to see how far the tunnel went. Ah, it was like underground flight. She might just like humans if they regularly created wonders such as this. Could one travel beneath the surface of the entire Earth in this way? She was not going to leave without finding out.

"Kezari!"

Tynan's frantic voice cut through the haze, and she snapped back to herself all at once. The spicy-sweet scent of some kind of flower filled her nose with a sudden breeze, the crisp air combining with the distinct smell to help ground her above the earth. She blinked to clear her vision, and five worried faces stared back at her. When had the others moved so close?

Against her side, Tynan shuddered. "I'd worried that you

might fly off hastily, but it didn't occur to me that you'd become entranced."

Kezari pulled back a little against his arm so that she could study his face. The fear streaming along their link matched the lines on his brow, but neither made sense. "I wasn't entranced."

"He called your name at least five times," Dria said dryly.

"I was only exploring." Kezari shared her frown freely, but Tynan received the bulk of it. "With our bond, you should have felt that."

He brushed his thumb across her cheek. "Dragon exploring appears to be beyond my expertise."

"I wouldn't say that," she quipped without thinking the words through.

Only to worry that she might have killed Delbin with laughter.

# CHAPTER TWENTY-FIVE

Tynan couldn't feel much amusement in the moment, not with the fear still coursing through him. When he'd gone through the cave a few days ago to find Kezari after their argument, he'd experienced how she sank into the world around her, but they hadn't been bonded then. This time, he'd felt exactly how deeply she lost herself to the earth, and for a few heartbeats, he'd ached with the fear that it might be permanent.

It was foolishness, of course. She was simply using her magic when she did that, and it was that deep connection that allowed her to manipulate the stone itself. The outpost he'd admired wouldn't exist without her talent. So why had he been torn apart by the fear that she was leaving him?

Of course, the answer came immediately. It was his own trauma, not hers. So he let the humor of the others sweep around him and lift his own mood, at least a little. Even if the laughter was at his own expense for his ill-planned words to Kezari. She was here, and that was all that mattered.

"Inona said you two had bonded, but I didn't actually believe it," Delbin said when his chuckling finally waned. "Damn."

The portal guardian—Tarah, he believed she'd told Dria—

lifted her brows, curiosity lighting her expression. "You've bonded? I thought that was more myth than truth."

Kezari huffed. "It's unusual, but I'm sure this isn't the first time that dragons and elves have—"

"No, no," Tarah hastened to say. "Caeregas said it could be done, but I've never known anyone who actually soulbonded before. It sounded more like a fairy tale than reality. In fact, I left my own necklace on Moranaia."

Tynan stared at her in shock—and he wasn't the only one. How long had she been away from their world that she'd lost touch with their ways? A great deal of time, he suspected, based on her accent. They were speaking Moranaian, but her pronunciation was different than any he'd heard before.

"Is Caeregas the dragon?" Kezari asked eagerly. "I believe that was the name I was given."

Her thoughts had obviously gone in a different direction than the Moranaians'.

At Tarah's nod, Tynan could feel the excitement vibrating around his bonded. "And he said this could be done? The bond? The Moranaian dragons have lost the method to such a thing."

"Really?" The scout's lips pursed. "That's fascinating. I'm sure Caeregas will be happy to tell you about it. At least...once he returns."

Kezari took a step forward. "He's not here?"

Tarah cast a worried glance toward the sky. "Not yet. He still hasn't returned from searching for his brother. I'm starting to get a little concerned."

Which sent a new worry straight through Tynan's heart— would Kezari fly off in pursuit? The draw of this world was immense, and if she started out after the Ancient One, she might get caught up in the rush. Not intentionally. But when she focused, she *focused*. No hesitation and no deviation.

It was best to prepare for the coming ride—and not the pleasurable kind.

~

CAOLTE STARED out at the disaster of his brother's realm and cursed. How had he managed to mess this up so spectacularly? But of course, he knew the answer as soon as the question popped into his mind. He'd failed to fulfill his one solemn oath, and this was the cost.

The crystal that acted as the "sun" for the underhill realm was dim enough to leave the cavern in a state of perpetual twilight, and that in no way helped the plant life that Caolte was ill-equipped to bolster. Burn through the drying vines and parched trees with abandon? Absolutely. Return it to proper life? Hah.

*See to Naomh, Caolte. He is paramount. Swear to guard him from harm, and I will save you. Fail, and our entire bloodline dies.*

He could still see the dark, desperate look in his father's eyes as he'd made his demands. At first, Caolte had agreed to save himself, both from his step-father and from hateful attacks from a band of Unseelie who hated his Seelie-lord father. But Naomh had earned his loyalty in short order. His brother was one of the few to treat him like a person, not the fucked-up result of their father's affair.

Caolte touched a twisted bit of leaf and watched it crumble. Just like everything else. Though he'd received word not long ago that Naomh had survived the procedure and would live, Caolte's heart was barely lighter. This place was one wrong touch away from disaster. Would his brother hate him for it when he returned?

A flare of power sent the fine hair along his arms into prickly alert. Someone had entered through the portal. Was this that final nudge, then? The one spelling his final failure? As he darted down the path to the gate, fury pounded to the beat of his heart. But he had to keep a hold on it. Had to. One spark would burn this whole dry realm to the ground.

He slowed near the clearing in front of the gate, but there was no point in trying for stealth. Any reliable cover was too dead to be of use, and the path crackled beneath his feet from the sound of all the former greenery. Fortunately, the guards hadn't abandoned him despite everything—their visitor stood on the small platform at sword point.

The slim, heavily cloaked figure turned, and Caolte's breath froze in his chest before rushing out on a harsh oath. Though she was shielded, the safeguards didn't fool him this time. Queen Ara. What was *she* doing here? She might have warned them once about Meren's treachery, but she'd worked with the man for her own ends, too.

"You," Caolte snarled, rushing into the clearing. "Leave before you do more harm."

She lowered the hood of her cloak, revealing herself clearly, and swept her gaze around the pitiful remnants of the forest. "I'm not sure I'm capable of doing much worse."

His hand fell to the hilt of the dagger at his waist, but he didn't bother to draw it. He couldn't argue when she was so obviously right. "What do you want?"

Her lips curved up. "*Tarma.*"

Ah, a request for a neutral meeting. Did she think he would adhere as strictly to such rules as his brother? Not likely. He had no reason to grant her a private audience, and he could hardly trust that she would keep the peace as *tarma* required.

"Why should I allow it?"

Ara's eyes widened slightly. "Perhaps I should leave without sharing the intelligence I have gathered. I have enough troubles without this."

Inexplicable chagrin bent his face into an unwitting grimace. He owed her nothing. How long had she been aware of Meren's plans before her last visit? If she had come sooner, they might have averted Naomh's near-fatal wound entirely. And yet...she had traveled here despite the recent upheaval in the Unseelie court that had culminated with her ascending the throne. According to his half-sister, matters still hadn't entirely settled there.

"Fine," Caolte snapped. "Come."

Unlike her last visit, they didn't have to go far. It would be nearly impossible for anyone to sneak close enough to eavesdrop on the open spot where he led her. Ara didn't appear inclined to argue that point, for after the barest scan, she faced him, hands on hips.

"Allow me to tell you and go, then." The waspishness to her tone made him feel...he wasn't sure. Anger? Regret? "My spies tracked Meren to Ireland, but he has recently disappeared. If the whispers are true about a secret entrance to this place, I recommend you guard it."

A frenzied blend of Unseelie and Seelie curses created a discordant litany in his head. "Now?"

"Well, I wouldn't recommend later."

She spun on her heel, but after taking a few steps, she knelt down, her hands flattening against the ground. Instinctively, Caolte pulled his knife to stop whatever she planned, but the cross look she cast over her shoulder made him falter. Gods. The dim light glowed against her pale skin and hair, highlighting her exquisite features—and the unmistakable force of female annoyance. It was the kind of expression worn by a woman who was completely fed up with another person's foolishness.

"I can't connect with plant life like your brother, but I can contribute energy through the ground itself." Her lip curled, and he could feel that hint of scorn to his soul. "Consider it a gift in recompense for my family's recent actions."

Power vibrated beneath his feet, and immediately, the burden of supporting this place lightened as new energy poured in. Her energy. Caolte shivered, then tried not to consider what that meant. Better to focus on the way the light slowly grew brighter overhead, relieving the oppressive gloom. If there was any greenery left, it would surely appreciate the renewal of the sun spell.

The intensity of the energy cut off a moment before Ara stood. "There," she said over her shoulder. "Have a *fine* day, Lord Caolte. I will not bother you again."

He stood frozen to the spot as she marched away. His tongue

was a heavy thing in his mouth, unwilling to form the sounds that would stop her. He owed her thanks. It seemed she truly had come to help, and he... A sigh hissed out. As Kai would say, he'd been a dick.

But maybe it was better if she hated him.

~

THE LOVELY EARTH garden felt more like a cage than a pleasure as Kezari paced circles around its perimeter. Outside the fence, people strode by along walkways that bordered their streets, and atop those streets, vehicles moved. Buildings were absolutely everywhere in all their sharp-edged pride—squares and rectangles, the only curves in the decorations and carvings adorning them. Very different from the roundness of Braelyn.

Actually, it was more akin to Oria, though not as harsh as that dark fortress.

Magic danced in and around this walled-off space. Tarah had told her the garden was enchanted so that those outside could only see and hear what she wished. Exterior sounds and even the weather itself was muffled, though the day and night cycles hadn't been altered. They hadn't been here that long, but the lowering sun already gilded the trees and hedges gold. It was almost sunset on this side of the world.

And here she remained. Waiting, waiting, waiting.

Dria had already teleported back to the outpost, and the others had wanted to discuss their next steps. Kezari wanted to fly. Even a month ago, she would have, heedless of the cost. Unaware if there even was one. But she'd sensed the pain behind Tynan's eyes as he'd watched her, waiting for her to do that very thing. Everyone had stared at her with varying degrees of anxious expectation.

So she circled the gardens instead. In truth, it was the wise choice. She knew next to nothing about this planet or the people here. How large were their oceans? Where could she find food?

What was safe to eat? It would do no good to fly off in a hasty search for the Ancient One only to get lost. How embarrassing would it be to require rescue like a youngling who flew too far from their parent?

When she'd left the Isle, she'd had plenty of time to commune with the world around her in advance of the journey. She'd spent weeks making mental maps of every bit of land between the Isle and the pulsing song of the portal at Braelyn. There'd been maps, too, and legends of the journey over once the war had ended. She hadn't flown blind by any means.

Why hadn't she asked Lynia if her library contained maps of Earth? The humans surely had them, if they spent so much effort on all these roads and tunnels. Her steps slowed as memory stirred. Ah, yes—Dria had found one. Kezari had a hazy recollection of seeing it on one of the outpost walls. Hadn't there been four large landmasses? But unfortunately, she had no idea where London was located on any of them.

"Kezari?" Tynan asked, his voice a touch hesitant.

She spun to face him, and his obvious worry softened her heart. "I'm not on the verge of fleeing," she reassured him.

His shoulders lowered a notch. "That's good. According to Tarah, Caeregas is in telepathy range and expects to be here not long after nightfall. His brother was farther afield than expected."

Well, then. Her newfound prudence had actually paid off.

"So we wait here?" she asked, though an idea began to form as a passing car caught her eye.

Tynan's glance toward the outer world was markedly less enthusiastic than her excitement about the place. "Delbin suggested we go buy some dinner, but I'm not sure that is wise. The unfamiliar food could cause stomach upset, not to mention the need to navigate...that."

She grinned at the way he flicked his fingers toward the gate and everything beyond it. The gesture could have been scornful, but she could tell that it was mostly hesitation. Her healer was no adventurer. Despite that, he would go just to make her happy. And if she had any say, he would have fun in the process.

"I want to travel through the tunnels," Kezari announced.

His brows rose. "What tunnels?"

"I found them earlier." She grabbed his hand and started back down the path. "Let's ask Tarah."

But at the mention of tunnels, the guardian stared at her for a moment before shaking her head. "I'm going to assume you mean the Tube, but there are a lot of passages down there. People have been digging around beneath the surface almost as long as I've been in charge of this gate. I don't think even the government knows everything to be found."

Mysteries beneath the earth? Kezari had to shove that thought away and forbid its reentry, or she'd never get anything done. "There were moving conveyances. I don't care where we get food, so long as I can ride one of those to get there."

"That's the Tube, then." Tarah fished a card out of her pocket and handed it to Kezari. "It's not free to ride, but this will get you through. Provided the others feel confident going. I'm waiting here for Caeregas."

"Hey, the big stations have food stalls, right?" Delbin asked. "Just give us a bit of direction, and I think we can handle it."

After a brief discussion, they settled on a destination and headed toward the gate—some more eagerly than others.

Yes, her prudence had paid off.

IF LADY BERA had any intention of torturing him during the afterlife, it might resemble this. Really, one of the few consolations to be found while hurtling who-knew-how-far underground in a narrow box with people on all sides was that Kezari was nestled against him in the madness. Though he had to admit that the child-like way she pressed her face up to the glass with little chirps of excitement made the constant onslaught of emotions somewhat worth it, too.

"Feckin' tourists," he heard a man mutter from the seat behind him.

A soft thud, then a woman's voice. "Bollocks for brains. No need to be rude. Anyway, you want to give up your job at the Tower if they stop coming?"

A tower? He had a feeling this one wasn't for healing, but he wasn't going to turn around and ask. Aside from the scraping, screeching sound of the conveyance and that small, overheard exchange, it was remarkably quiet. If he and Kezari weren't huddled by the door in a clump of people, their emotions hovering in the air like a poisoned cloud, he might have thought they were alone.

Why didn't anyone converse?

Maybe their rules bore some resemblance to Moranaia, where one left strangers alone unless specifically introduced. That would be a good policy in forced proximity to so many. Too bad these humans couldn't protect themselves with mental shielding quite so thoroughly.

The conveyance squealed to a halt, and they exited to the sound of a disembodied voice advising them to "mind the gap." A good reminder, of course, but Tynan would have preferred actual directions. The long platform stretched to both the left and right. In the rush of people, it was difficult to tell which way to go, and it didn't get better when the crowd thinned.

For a moment, the strangeness of it all overwhelmed him. An acrid scent coated his nostrils with each breath, and more voices than he could process ebbed and crashed against him. Worse, his shielding was thinner than it had been in ages, threatening more pain than the simple overwhelm he'd experienced while helping Arlyn. Had he thought he was close to losing control the day he'd argued with Kezari?

At least elves and dragons had decent shields.

"Tarah said to follow the Way Out signs," Delbin said from somewhere beside him.

Tynan was too afraid to turn his head to see where. He was barely moving forward as it was.

But then Kezari pulled him over to an empty spot near the white-tiled wall and stepped in front of him. Frowning, she settled her hand gently on the side of his neck and leaned close. "Sink into our link if you need."

"I don't understand why my shielding is so...battered," he whispered.

"If you've an allergy, I'd say it's the iron." That from Inona. "That's what the tracks are made of, and gods know what else."

Kezari let out a guttural, snarly sound that could only be a dragon curse. "How bad is your allergy?"

"Minor." Tynan shook his head. "Or so I thought."

Delbin stepped into his line of view. "Hey, the next train is about to arrive, and more people are headed this way. I can try my hand at reinforcing your shields. Mine are for mind magic, so...I don't know, kind of related."

Wordlessly, Tynan nodded, and a new wall of energy formed around him. It wasn't quite right, but it helped enough that he no longer feared losing control. More of their surroundings took shape as his mind cleared. The area was well-lit, with neat white tiling and colorful images covering some of the walls. More people approached, headed for the bright yellow line painted on the platform.

It was perfectly normal yet entirely foreign, a curiosity he might have enjoyed more if it hadn't caused him such difficulty. But he could make it now. Finally, they were able to advance through the warren of tunnels and stairs toward some station near the surface.

The food had better be good after all this.

## CHAPTER TWENTY-SIX

Kezari bit into the warm bread and moaned when the spiced meat hit her tongue. It was a delightfully convenient meal, one she was happy to enjoy as they strolled along the tree-lined walkway. There were so many humans here—and some non-humans, she'd noticed a time or two—and thus a countless array of habitations and shops. And all the conveyances! She wanted to try out all of them, from the tiniest cars to the largest of the red buses.

But she couldn't bear to put Tynan through that. Guilt eroded some of her pleasure when she recalled the pasty shade of his skin as they'd exited their train. Was there anything they could do to mitigate his reduced shielding when near so much iron? The metal didn't bother her. Could she bolster her mate through their link?

She studied him out of the corner of her eye. His color had returned, and a hint of pleasure flowed toward her as he took a bite of his filled pastry. He appeared to be doing somewhat better above the surface. In fact, the return of his good nature lent a sparkle to his eyes as he glanced her way.

"What do you think?" Tynan asked.

"I like it," she answered, though she was speaking of him more than the food.

Light from the surrounding buildings and the street lanterns blended with the faded gold of sunset, lending his hair an amber glow and casting the dip of his muscles into shadows. She wanted to trace her finger along those darkened paths to feel the definition beneath. And if Delbin and Inona hadn't been strolling ahead of them, Kezari might have tugged him into one of those delightful alleys to do just that.

Tynan's brow lifted. "You should eat before your food gets cold."

As much as she hated it, he was right. There was no point in lusting over her mate when there was nothing currently to be done, but the delicious pastry was consumable *now*. So she scarfed it down—only to immediately wish for another one. Too bad they needed to return to the garden. For once, she'd found things of more interest than an ancient dragon.

Delbin pulled one of those rectangular phones from his pocket. "Let me see how far it is to the garden. We've been walking a while, but trains go pretty fast."

"Have you ever been here before? London, I mean?" Inona asked, a slight smile crossing her lips.

"Nope." Though his face was in profile, even Kezari could tell he was flustered. "You found me working at a carnival. I didn't exactly have the money for an international plane ticket."

Kezari sped up slightly so he could hear her. "Paying for flight? Is it expensive?"

The side of Delbin's mouth kicked up. "Oh, yeah. Maybe you should set up your own service. Though I guess one person at a time wouldn't be so lucrative."

Carry strangers on her back every day? Kezari shuddered at the idea. There wasn't enough treasure in either world for that indignity. "I suppose it's fortunate for me that you're happy to spend Ralan's wealth."

Delbin laughed, but Tynan let out a choked sound beside her. "What?"

Even Delbin and Inona glanced back at that, though they didn't stop. It left Kezari to figure out why her mate was staring at the last few bites of his pastry with growing horror. Had he found something terrible in his food? Had they added too much spice? Something was obviously bothering him.

"Did you find an imperfection in your food?" she asked.

"No. It's only... He spent Ralan's money on this?" His look of horror only deepened. "Does Prince Ralan know? Gods above. The clothes were bad enough, but to take advantage—"

"Relax," Delbin interrupted. "He knows. In fact, he added me to his account, so I'm even doing it legally."

A hint of relief eased the lines on her mate's face, but she suspected his worry wasn't entirely gone. "Why are you so concerned?" she asked.

"Priests are paid well enough, but I'm hardly royalty. Or even nobility," Tynan muttered.

Delbin nodded. "It's not easy being a regular guy in the middle of all this. A bit of advice? Just roll with it. Ralan was literally famous here. He could buy a house in the middle of this city without blinking, though I'd bet he owns one already. We could've bought out every food stall in the station, and he wouldn't have noticed."

Hmm, that had possibilities. Too bad Delbin hadn't mentioned that sooner, for she absolutely would have purchased as many pastries as she could carry. The air was growing cold, and she couldn't create herself a thicker shirt with long sleeves in the middle of a human street. Extra food would have at least boosted her metabolism—and warmed her hands in the holding.

At least until she'd eaten them all.

Delbin directed them over to the side of a building, out of the flow of the moving crowd. "According to the map, we're still a long walk away."

Kezari frowned down at the rectangle he held. Those phones

had maps? Though after peeking at the screen, she had to concede that they were not large ones. There were detailed street lines, but hardly enough space for entire continents. But she couldn't stop a flare of envy, regardless.

Tynan cleared his throat. "I'm not sure I can…"

Ah, he was worried about another trip through the tunnels. "What about another type of transport?"

"Let me see." Delbin pinched his fingers on the screen, then squinted down at whatever that had revealed. "There's a bus stop not far from here. Follow me."

She'd loved studying how the tunnels had been carved out, shaped, and decorated, but she was equally happy to experience a new type of conveyance. And why not? There was no way of knowing when or if she would ever return here. Lyr had been wary enough of sending her on a mission specifically for dragons. What if another opportunity never appeared?

A thought best left neglected.

ONCE THEY'D ESCAPED the miserable tunnels, Tynan had begun to enjoy this little sojourn to Earth. Though a mélange of emotions still battered his shields, it was worth the experience of witnessing such a different world. Neat buildings lined the streets, the structures towering over them at four or five or more levels high. Despite that, there were plenty of trees, enough to soften the effect of so many habitations.

A tangle of scents required decoding—the harsh acrid bite from the tunnels, the tangy spice wafting from the last bit of filling in his pastry, flowers dancing in window boxes—and the sounds were little better. Beeps and honks and countless voices. It was almost too much to process, but it was more fascinating than overwhelming. Unlike in that underground torture chamber lined with iron.

But when he climbed the steps of the bus, his shielding flickered and dimmed once again. Though a sheen of sweat dampened his brow, he continued down the aisle between the occupied rows. *Pull in energy. Reinforce shields. Repeat.* He could do this. Then his arm brushed against a man hunched low in his seat, and grief shoved forcefully into his head.

His defenses cracked, nearly shattering before Kezari's hand gripped his elbow. Her spirit surrounded him—or at least his mind—until the stranger's pain faded to a dull throb. But there was plenty waiting for the chance to crush him. Another accidental nudge, and the maelstrom rushed in. Frustration and fear *—they're out of Mum's medicine again, so what will—*No, it was victory. *No one thought I would get that promotion.* But then a lump of sadness closed his throat. *I should have been chosen.*

No.

*No, none of this is mine,* he insisted to himself.

As they cleared the more crowded rows, Tynan was able to beat some of the feelings back. Then desire hit him from a pair of women staring at him from the back. Kezari hissed like Emowa when her fur was ruffled, and his bonded must have been baring her teeth in a dragon's grimace. Fear scalded him, sharp and true, as both women blanched and then looked down at their phones.

How much more could he take?

Finally, he dropped into an empty seat beside the window, Kezari easing down beside him. Tynan squeezed his eyes shut and leaned his head against the cool glass. Was this bus lined with iron? Was the horrid stuff everywhere? He was nothing but a hindrance.

Aris should have come with Kezari, after all.

~

WHAT HAD SHE DONE?

Kezari had been so certain she could ensure her mate enjoyed this outing despite his misgivings, yet here she sat, helpless to aid him through the struggle of merely existing in this world. The way he hunched against the window as though protecting himself from a blow was enough to cleave her heart—a heart she hadn't been entirely sure was there. Metaphorically, anyway.

As Inona and Delbin took the seats behind them, Kezari rubbed soothing circles across Tynan's back. It didn't do much good, but he didn't appear to worsen, either. Still, how could she be so unable to protect him? To guard him from the relentless emotions pounding down on him? She could sense them now through their link. So many. Even after the bus lurched into motion, the deluge came, pouring from pedestrians and houses and shops.

Everything within her demanded she shift into her dragon form and pull her mate from this moving monstrosity to fly free on the wind. But force would not help. That would cause panic, and he would surely crack beneath the pressure, then. So all she could do was try to send him the same kind of comfort he provided so often. She wasn't particularly good at it, but she tried.

For him... Oh, for him, she would always try.

Her heart tipped over, and warmth rushed out. This was so different from the fires of stark possession or the rock-solid certainty of their belonging. It wasn't the instinct that urged her to frighten away any who dared look at her mate with interest. It was...

Well, she didn't really have a word, did she? Deep affection or love or longing—how was she to know? She'd never experienced the kind of love she'd heard the other mated people whisper about. It was as foreign to her as the sign flashing their destination at the front of the bus. But it didn't matter. For the moment, the tender rush of unnamed feeling was enough on its own.

Inona's head popped up over the back of Tynan's seat. "Is there anything we can do?"

Tynan rocked his head against the glass in denial, and Kezari clenched her free hand into a fist in her lap. "Hope this conveyance is speedy."

"I didn't think of the steel frame on this thing," Delbin murmured above her head.

Kezari didn't glance up. Instead, she closed her eyes and did her best to merge with Tynan, even though their link wasn't entirely formed. No, there were still rough edges where they hadn't fully merged. Would she be able to carry more of his burden if the ancient dragon told her how to complete this bond? There was no way to know if the Moranaian-style necklace would even work for her.

*"Let me share this,"* she sent softly.

*"Too much. You're not used to it."* Stubborn man. He trembled beneath her hand. *"How can one city hold so many unshielded people?"*

If there was a way to incinerate the problem, she would have done it. But no. All she could do was rub his back and pray her support would help him maintain control.

FEW THINGS in Tynan's life could compare to the pure relief that poured over him when they walked through the gates of Tarah's garden. Whatever shielding she used apparently dampened more than weather and sound—it dulled emotions, too. His protections had been strong enough before they left that he hadn't realized how much the garden kept at bay, but he wouldn't be able to forget it now.

"Oh, good!" Tarah said as she rushed up the path. "Caeregas and his brother are..." The guardian's steps ground to a halt, her gaze skimming him with obvious concern. "Did something happen?"

"Apparently, he's an empath," Inona explained. "That tube place did not serve him well."

Tarah groaned. "Oh, the Tube can be such a menace, at least for most elves. Had I known of his gift, I would have advised against it. I suppose we shouldn't go to my flat as I'd considered. We'll just have to cram into Caeregas's little guest house."

In the absence of so much emotion, energy filled the aching channels of his mind, and his body felt a little stronger. But when he tried to straighten, Kezari's arm tightened around his waist. He let her hold on as tightly as she wanted to. Though he hadn't been able to process it at the time, he'd felt her emotions on the bus along with everyone else's.

She cared for him. Truly cared. There were times he felt more like an acquisition. A replacement hoard, if that were possible. But the way her softer emotions had filled him left no doubt that his fears weren't true. He wasn't merely something to possess.

*"What a foolish thought,"* Kezari sent. *"You* are *mine. But not like an object. I am yours, too. I assure you I do not claim to belong to jewels or gemstones. It's not the same at all."*

Tynan smiled, but he was too exhausted to send back a thought. Although he did feel stronger, this world had depleted him too thoroughly to do much besides trudge along the carefully sculpted garden paths. What was it about this city? Did it do this to other elves? Or perhaps it was him, not the place itself. His shields had already been shaky before coming here, after all.

But why?

Nerves frayed, he retrieved his herb pouch from his pocket and lifted it to his nose. The scent alone triggered pleasant memories—days spent in the training room with his patient mentor as he learned to use his gift, sunlight streaming through the temple windows as he knelt in front of the altar, the absolute peace that had filled him during his ordination. So many years of goodness despite his early trauma.

Had he said his customary prayers before undertaking this journey? Guilt twisted within him, and he lowered the pouch before the scent could go sour. Truthfully, he couldn't remember. He'd been so stunned and consumed by bonding that he hadn't been able to think of much else. Quickly, he opened himself to Lady Bera for at least a quick prayer.

Except...

His blood ran cold, and his steps faltered. Kezari steadied him, but her firm grip couldn't relieve the terror screaming through him. The world faded to a blur as he scrambled within himself for that vital connection. But it was the faintest link, like a star nearly hidden by the clouds.

What had he done to earn Her disfavor? Was it the lack of prayer? His loss of control? Leaving Moranaia? What did he need to do to keep her from abandoning him entirely? Bera's love had been his foundation for almost as long as he could remember. He would never survive the loss of her regard.

*"Tynan, be calm,"* Kezari sent, the urgency in her tone hitting him with a snap. *"The gods of Moranaia do not hold sway here. That is likely all. Although now I must wonder if your goddess has bolstered your shields more than you realized. It would explain your current troubles."*

He scrabbled for those words like a lifeline—a curiosity to pull him free of imminent panic. The link wasn't gone. It wasn't. Even obscured from sight, a star was still there, after all. Had it been Lady Bera's light preventing disaster for most of his life? But why had he begun to struggle before leaving Moranaia? Nothing made sense.

*"I confess I do not know,"* he managed to send.

Kezari's hold tightened around his waist, but it was a comforting kind of pressure. Solid and steady like the stones she often shaped. He let the feeling seep into him, and a refreshing coolness calmed his spirit. It reminded him of the constant temperature inside a cave, a gentle relief in the summer and a brush of near-warmth in the winter.

He barely noticed the small structure they approached until their guide halted in front of it. The grimace she gave them held more than a little apology. "This was really only built for a bit of diversion when these were popular a couple of centuries back. There definitely won't be enough chairs for everyone."

Inona took Delbin's hand. "Why don't we stay outside? I'm

really only here to guide them through the Veil, and Delbin's job is to spend money as needed. We'll only be in the way."

"Fine by me," Tarah said, shrugging.

As the couple strolled toward a decorative bench farther along the path, Tarah opened the door and gestured Tynan and Kezari through. Kezari had to release him to enter, and surprisingly, a hint of those chaotic, outside feelings resumed their pressure as though waiting for him to falter. Had her presence aided his shielding? He did his best to brace himself before entering behind her.

*Not* surprisingly, she blocked his path just beyond the door, her shoulders back like mantled wings. Guarding him, of course. The wonder of that nearly made his current torment worthwhile —and it absolutely would have if not for the fierce, intense emotions swirling around the two other men in the tiny room.

One man glared—generally, not at Tynan personally—from a seat beside a closed door, and the second stood restlessly beside a narrow window. Either this house was small beyond even Tarah's estimation, or these men filled the space too thoroughly for anyone's comfort. The very energy in the room made his head ache terribly.

"Shield yourselves well," Kezari snapped, her voice as sharp as the door clacking shut behind them.

Both men's attention snapped to Kezari's face with palpable force, and the glaring one straightened in his seat with more than a little menace. Instinctively, Tynan froze. What was she thinking to antagonize two ancient dragons? Before now, she'd spoken of them with awe. Now, it seemed she wanted to alienate them.

But really, he couldn't deny the reason—it was all because of him.

# CHAPTER TWENTY-SEVEN

Her mate's vulnerability had Kezari too on edge, for only one thing had dominated her thoughts: protect. As soon as they'd walked in, she'd felt Tynan's tiny flinch in her own body, and the weight of others' emotions had become her personal burden, too. She couldn't have stopped herself from issuing that command if she'd tried.

Such power here, and unmistakably dragon. She wanted to bask in it, but she dared not. That very force had brought pain to Tynan's already aching head. So she held herself steady beneath the Ancient Ones' tense regard.

"You dare much," the red-haired one rumbled from his seat. "And it's doubly bold from a Moranaian dragon."

"Hold, Egrenneth." The other man had long, pale hair—and a more thoughtful demeanor. "I would hear an explanation for such an order before a greeting has even been made."

Suddenly, Tarah slipped in front of Kezari. "Our other guest is an empath."

Instantly, their emotions went muted.

The first man scowled, but the more reasonable one looked over her shoulder at Tynan. His eyes widened a fraction before narrowing on Kezari once more. "How are you only half-mated to this one? Have Moranaian dragons become inept at all skills?"

Heat traced over her skin, but before she could answer, Tynan stepped to her side. "I gave her my necklace, but she has nothing to give in return," he explained. "If anyone is to blame, it's me for beginning the process before she did."

Both dragons gaped at her—actually gaped. Then the paler one shook his head. "What of your red beryl?"

She had no mental image for such a thing, though it sounded like the type of name often used for Earth minerals and gems. "My...what?"

The one called Egrenneth sank back against his seat, his fingers half-covering his face. "It seems you haven't only abandoned *us* but yourselves, as well. I should never have let Caeregas talk me into this."

Shame burned in her stomach, but anger sparked in her heart. "If there is fault, it lies first with our so-called queen. Zevie."

The pale man frowned. "I have not heard that name. She was neither queen nor heir of the dragons on Moranaia."

Kezari had no response for that—there'd been few names at all in the histories she had read. Although it was known that Queen Zevie's mother had taken the throne well after the war with the elves, so it wasn't precisely a surprise. But wait. What if Zevie's family hadn't been the rightful rulers? It would explain so many of her poor decisions.

"Perhaps we should introduce ourselves." The blonde one inclined his head. "I am Caeregas of the Pine, son of the Guardian of the Frozen North."

The other man sighed, but he lowered his hand to stare at them. "I am Egrenneth of the Crag, also son of the Guardian of the Frozen North. Though these days, I'm more commonly called Ren Gough."

"Really? You have a modern name?" Tarah asked. "Did you say 'cough' or 'golf'? Wait, no, that's Welsh, right?"

"Yes," Egrenneth said irritably. "And of course I do. Unlike Caeregas, I didn't go dormant for a few millennia."

Kezari's breath caught. All this time, the red dragon had walked the Earth. If she could have traveled here at an earlier age, she could have asked him anything. But why hadn't he been investigating the poison that had been inserted into the wall holding back the magic?

"Enough, brother," Caeregas muttered. "What is your name, dragon of Moranaia?"

What name did she give? Suddenly, it wasn't so simple anymore. Ancestor's heart—this was going to be longer than Tynan's introduction. "I was born Kezari the Golden, daughter of Meyehza and Oethak. Now, I am called Callian iy'dianore tenah i Kezari Baran se Tynan nai Braelyn."

To his credit, Tynan's lips merely twitched at the irony.

"I've been given to understand that you are an exile from the Isle of Dragons, which your Moranaian name supports." Caeregas crossed his arms. "Based on what I was told, I decided to meet with you, but I do hope you are not attempting to deceive. To say that your queen has abandoned the old ways is a heavy charge."

Kezari stuck out her chin. "It is no charge, only truth. Queen Zevie commands all to sever or mute their connections to Earth. I refused, which nearly earned me banishment on its own. However, several months back, I detected a poison emanating from Earth's energy. I was told that to pursue it meant exile."

"Poison?" Egrenneth asked, his eyes narrowing. "There was something off before the wall shattered, but I was not sure what. My talents lie in fire, not ground, and my connection to that type of energy is...shaky. Still—"

"Then how did you pull power from beyond the wall?" Caeregas demanded. "Isn't that how you remained awake?"

A frown crossed Egrenneth's face. "Not directly. I said I found a way, and that way was through elemental fire. The burning core of the world, if you will."

So he'd avoided going dormant because of his fire. Kezari

pondered that cracked, poisoned gash in the wall holding back Earth's magic. It hadn't been a physical thing, exactly, but even in its alternate plane of being, there'd been the tone of earth energy. Not fire. If he'd pulled through his connection with elemental flame, might that have purified the power in some way? Aris's life magic had done much the same.

"There was an actual crack in the wall," Kezari explained. "Created by an exiled Moranaian prince. He injected a poison, one I can only assume was burned away for you, Ancient One."

Egrenneth winced. "Well, that's a talon's blow. I've lived forever, but I needn't be reminded of it. Please, call me Ren or Egrenneth. Really, anything but Ancient."

"Do you feel no urgency for anything but yourself, brother?" Caeregas asked, scorn ringing in his tone. "Understanding what went wrong and what *still might* go wrong is paramount, not whether you're old."

Ren waved a hand. "Paramount to you. I no longer care."

Kezari blinked at the heated exchange. No wonder it had taken Caeregas so long to return—she didn't want to know how he'd actually convinced his brother to come. Yet somehow, they managed to keep the force of their emotions to themselves, for she sensed no distress from Tynan.

"Do continue, Kezari," Caeregas said. "Pay no mind to my brother."

Hah. Like she would make that mistake. He was not the type to be ignored.

But she nodded toward the elder dragon all the same. "The poison spread through the energy. When I told the queen of my concerns, she ordered me to sever my link with Earth and ignore what I thought I sensed. So naturally, I retrieved my *skizik* and flew for the Moranaian gate, treaty or not. Only the most wretched wyrm would ignore our sacred connection like that."

"She showed no concern for the wall?" Caeregas asked.

Kezari shrugged. "She acted as though she'd never heard of it. But that's no surprise. Those who had heard the tale mostly believed it to be either myth or ancient history, not something active. Since they severed or blocked their link, they would have no reason to feel otherwise."

That sparked Egrenneth's temper, and suddenly, his stare burned into her. "So they *did* abandon me. The Moranaian dragons were supposed to stand as a pillar, same as the Unseelie king. They were supposed to ensure that Earth kept at least enough energy for us to maintain our guard. But instead, they *disconnected entirely?*"

That last ended on a dull roar that vibrated against the thin walls and made Tynan flinch again. Kezari edged in front of her mate once more. "Control yourself."

"How dare you even speak to me, much less deliver a command!" Egrenneth leapt to his feet. "I should kill every one of the Moranaian dragons for the harm they have caused."

Kezari's skin tingled from the scales rising to the surface. She made no effort to control them. "I am not your enemy, but I will become one if you threaten my mate, *Ancient One*."

His power was surely incredible, but she truly didn't care. She would burn in the core of the Earth before she saw her mate crumpled against the wall, buried beneath others' emotions, the way he had been on that bus. Never again. Her shoulders ached with the urge to extend her wings. If only there was enough room. Ancestors, how she longed to sharpen her teeth on Egrenneth's bones.

Then calm wafted through her—Tynan.

*"Lend me steadiness,"* he sent. *"And strength."*

Without question, she did.

Egrenneth nearly buckled beneath the onslaught of a sudden, horrid peace. Calm and light and quiet. Gods, how he hated such things. He'd spent millennia alone in such perfect placidity. Day after day, only tranquil nothingness stretching before him. Even through modern times, since he couldn't risk closeness lest his true nature be discovered.

Peace was merely loneliness with newly shined scales.

He'd told his brother he'd wanted to be left alone, but it hadn't taken long to realize it was a lie. When his brother had come to reclaim his hoard after waking from hibernation, that momentary conflict in a tiny pocket dimension in Cardiff had provided Ren with the most feeling he'd experienced in...how would he even know how long? He'd been tasked to protect the wall for more years than calendars could count.

"Cease your interference," Ren commanded the mind healer. He had never intended to harm the man, but if he continued this assault, Ren would have to reconsider. The healer appeared to understand, for the wave soon receded, allowing true emotion to fire his blood with life. "Never try to calm me again, or it will be your last moment."

Peace was decades—*decades*—of wandering empty hills and patrolling forgotten forests, no one to speak to but himself. A brief encounter, and then decades more. He would not be forced into something like that.

The young dragon hissed. "If you—"

"I admire your dedication to your mate, but I refuse to yield on this." Fire broiled his insides at the thought. "I vow to you and your mate that I'll do you no harm unless you offer me a threat. Using that power on me? I consider it a threat."

Before she could respond, the mind healer grabbed her wrist. "I will honor his request. It would be no better to cause him pain with my gift than for him to use emotions against me. I should not have done so without consent."

This time, the dragon scowled at her mate. "That makes no sense, Tynan. I could feel how his anger hit you. If you can avert that, you have the right."

The argument might have continued, but unfortunately, Caeregas lost patience. Glaring, Ren's brother dropped his arms and stepped between them. "I did not retrieve you for conflict," Caeregas said. "Not with me or with them."

"I'm surprised you retrieved me at all," Ren quipped, though it was truth rather than jest. Caeregas had always believed the worst of him. He'd even thought Ren would steal his hoard while he slept—a sour memory. "Perhaps we should get to the point so that I might continue my adventures and bother you no more."

Kezari's nostrils flared, but she nodded. Whatever friendliness she'd displayed before was clearly gone. Ah, well. Frustration was better than remoteness, and he was tired of hiding behind calm.

"As I said, I went to the Moranaians with my *skizik*, and for that, I was banished," the young dragon continued. "But with the help of Lyr and Prince Ralan, I was able to travel to the site of the fracture with my *skizik* before the wall shattered horrifically. We weren't able to fix the crack, so it was transmuted into a portal between that cave and Moranaia."

So that was what had happened during that blinding surge of power. He'd believed it to be the release of energy from the fallen wall. Interesting, but hardly vital. "And you are here now...why?"

Caeregas's scowl was delightful. "I requested this meeting, not Kezari. If more of our kind awaken here, there needs to be some accord between us and Moranaia. Most certainly, there needs to be a reckoning for this Queen Zevie."

"Oh, yes," Ren said. It wasn't often that he agreed so readily with his brother, but it was more than easy this time. "You should challenge your former queen, Kezari. With your connection to Earth and enough focus stones, you should be able to defeat her."

Kezari's lips turned down, and her nostrils flared again. "I have no focus stones. She gave my hoard to my cousin as part of my exile, though I was supposed to receive some part."

Just two sentences—that was apparently all it took to send his rage to satisfying heights.

Even better would be ripping the heart from a treacherous queen.

~

TYNAN HAD THOUGHT he had a decent understanding of dragons after his time with Kezari, but it seemed that was not the case. Of course, he should have known better. Dragons were as individual as any living being, not a single monolith incapable of differences. Even the two brothers acted quite dissimilar.

Still, he'd never had anyone—elf, dragon, or fae—react so harshly to his calming energy before. It had been like sprinkling water on a bonfire, all flash and hiss and steam. If Kezari hadn't been anchoring him, he would have been scalded, and that in spite of the dragon's formidable shields.

Who in the world hated peace?

Apparently, it was Egrenneth, whose skin was currently mottling with an impressive array of red scales. "Did you say she claimed your hoard?" the dragon demanded.

Kezari froze—even her energy felt poised for action. "Why does that enrage you? It is a standard punishment for someone banished."

"It. Is. Not." Egrenneth bit out.

"Indeed not," Caeregas added, anger hardening the planes of his face, too.

Tension filled the room until it buzzed like an insect against Tynan's senses—annoying, possibly menacing, but not currently causing pain. There was something deep here, though, and that might be the part to sting. Some horror hidden just beneath the fury. Out of all that the brothers had heard, why were they the most upset about this?

A hint of motion caught his eye—Tarah, who stood quietly where Caeregas had left her. Grimacing, she lifted her shoulders in the universal sign of "I don't know what's happening, either." And like him, she didn't ask. In fact, she'd remained largely silent through the entire meeting. Either she didn't care what happened, or she hadn't considered there to be a true threat. With the portal she guarded only a short walk away, he suspected it was more the latter.

"She must die," Egrenneth snarled. "There is no other way."

Those words snapped Tynan's focus back to the dragons. Did the ancient dragon mean Kezari? His heart skipped a beat, but before he could say anything, Caeregas replied, "No proper dragon queen would take another's hoard. That is profane."

Tynan released a slow, silent breath of relief. They were speaking of the queen, not Kezari. And to call the queen's actions profane? It seemed his instincts hadn't been wrong—this was deep.

The reason appeared to be unfamiliar to Kezari. A hint of confusion reached Tynan through their bond, a feeling echoed through her words. "I do not understand."

For once, the brothers appeared to be in complete, murderous accord. Fortunately, Caeregas, the more level one, was the one who spoke. "Every item in one's hoard is gathered and honed by oneself. With one's own energy. Even things acquired from one's parents have the new owner's energy added," he said. "Those items are attuned to you and your very spirit. It is the rankest theft that steals something built from your own soul. It isn't something that should be handed over to another."

A pulse of searing pain shot straight from Kezari into Tynan's heart.

Until that moment, he hadn't truly understood what Kezari had given up when she'd defected to Moranaia. He remembered when she'd made the actual decision—her pain and rage had pulled Aris into her link with Earth, requiring Tynan to calm Aris to prevent a breakdown. But she hadn't opened up enough for him to see the depth of her agony, and he'd been too preoccupied healing Aris to press. Now, he knew. He rubbed his palm against his chest as though it would soothe the ache.

Oh, how he knew.

And his rage could fell the dragon queen by itself.

# CHAPTER TWENTY-EIGHT

The loss of her hoard had become a newly healed wound, still aching but technically no longer fatal. She'd survived. She'd done her best to move on—or so she'd thought. But at Caeregas's words, such hope and rage spilled forth that she could only have been fooling herself. As he had said, her hoard was a part of her spirit. How could she recover from a loss like that?

"Returning to the Isle will create complications," Kezari found herself saying, though she hadn't consciously decided to go. "And there is more you don't know, besides."

Caeregas tilted his head. "Such as?"

"Not long before we left Moranaia, my foolish cousin contacted me, begging for help." Kezari scowled at the memory. "Bold reptile. According to her, the younglings and any others still connected to Earth have gone power-mad. I suppose they were unshielded during the surge caused by the wall's collapse, considering so few believed me in the first place. Anyway, the eldest amongst the affected attacked the fae village on the Isle before fleeing to another island."

She'd never imagined that two dragons so ancient and experienced could look so aghast. Then came the anger, a flash they quickly contained. This time, she said nothing, for it was clear the two worked hard to control their emotions. Could she create a shield like theirs around herself—or even Tynan?

A question she placed at the top of her mental hoard for later.

"That is…" Egrenneth shuddered. "That is catastrophic abandonment. I thought it was a lack of regard for Earth and those of us who remained that caused my woes, but this runs much deeper. I will travel to Moranaia with you when you return, and we will right the course of the dragons there. Forcefully."

Kezari stared at him, her throat clogged by the shock of the suggestion. Attack her former home? Confront Queen Zevie? Ancestors, but the thought was dividing. One part of her wanted to shake her wings in exultant victory at the very idea, but another part wanted to shrink down and hide. Her encounters with the queen had never been pleasant.

Tynan's hand brushed against her lower back. "I am with you."

No, he couldn't be. She shook her head. "You're so weak compared to a dragon. I can't risk it."

"You can't, but I will," Tynan said steadily. "It is my choice, too, Kezari. But no, I did not mean I would go with you into battle. You said the fae village was attacked? They may need a healer's aid."

The words turned her stomach, but he was right. Although they were mates, they were individuals, too. Neither had the right to steal the other's choices. And the fae might truly need a healer. Such distance had grown between their two factions that she had no idea what talents those in the village might possess. Burn it all. She released a long stream of breath, whispered a few curses in her mind, and then finally conceded.

Except— "What of Aris?"

Egrenneth frowned. "Who?"

"My *skizik*," she explained. "His mind is…deeply scarred by past experience."

Tynan turned to face her, his hand cupping her cheek. Worry

shadowed his eyes as he held her gaze. "We'll speak to him about it. If I have time to rest, I can bolster him with my magic during the journey. I know you'll want him with you."

Softening, she leaned into him. "Thank you."

"Hah," Egrenneth interjected sharply. "I don't believe we'll have time for resting. This must be solved now, and even if it didn't require haste, I doubt the elves would welcome me amongst them during the wait. We'll have to fly straight for the Isle."

Kezari had to tamp down on a sudden surge of anger as she spun in Tynan's hold to glare at the other dragon. "They are not what you believe."

Egrenneth lifted a brow. "Didn't the elves and dragons of Moranaia war against each other?"

"Sure," Kezari countered. "Nearly forty thousand years ago or so. And for what? The elves claim we grew greedy and territorial over the portal. The histories I've read say that the elves denied us access entirely. So who is correct? Does it even matter? Even amongst our long-lived races, the original combatants are no longer alive. There is no need to hold to old hostilities over a conflict that has lost its truth."

For the first time since defending Tynan, Tarah entered the fray. "Caeregas told me that Earth dragons and Moranaian elves are not in conflict. We dealt easily enough with Lord Lyrnis."

"Did you, then?" Egrenneth's lips pinched tight, and he glared at the floor for a moment before fixing his fierce gaze on Kezari once more. "It would seem to me that the elves' refusal to allow the dragons access to the portal contributed to our problems here. Your dragons were supposed to help maintain the barrier. At their failure, it solidified until far too much magic disappeared. There hasn't been enough for me to shift for four or five thousand years. Maybe you are biased since your mate is an elf, but are you truly certain they are benevolent?"

If that was so, it didn't speak well of the Moranaians. She'd had trouble getting to Earth herself. And yet—had the elves been the ones to block her? Not exactly. According to Lyr, the treaty had included provisions for dragons to use the portal. It merely required agreement between both monarchs. What would they have done had Queen Zevie made the request? Prince Ralan had been willing to make Kezari a citizen of Moranaia to help her gain access to Earth—that request surely would have been granted.

In fact, the elves showed no rancor toward the dragons. None. Selia had once told her that she'd never met anyone who'd seen a dragon. Why? Because the Moranaian dragons had willingly disconnected to everything outside the Isles. It had surely been millennia since one had requested passage through the portal.

Kezari hadn't considered that when she'd first flown toward Braelyn. She'd thought only of the histories she'd read, all full of anger toward the elves for denying the dragons control of the portal. Considering their link, the dragons were the most obvious stewards of the gate, so she'd thought it an unreasonable war. But her kind hadn't attempted to use that vital resource since, had they?

Not to mention that until she, Aris, and the others had created the direct gate at the outpost, there'd only been one known portal on the entire planet that linked their worlds—and any other worlds. The elves would have been just as trapped had the dragons taken over and denied them entry. Truly, there was no right side to that war, only an immense failure to coexist.

"None of us are benevolent," Kezari finally said. "Merely self-involved, as has been the case for millennia. And the more I learn, the more I realize I do not know. There is allowance in the treaty for dragons to use the portal, Egrenneth of the Crag. So why have none attempted to do so for so long that the elves nearly forgot we existed? I tell you this. From what I've seen of Lord Lyr, he will attempt to help us find that answer. He has done nothing but offer me a place when my own kind have not."

The anger didn't fade from Egrenneth's demeanor, but Caeregas gave a sharp nod. "There is much we do not know, brother. If you cannot proceed with an open mind, you should not proceed at all. Perhaps it is best if I accompany Kezari and her mate to Moranaia. I can destroy that foul queen as well as you can."

"No," Egrenneth snapped, drawing himself up taller. "Stay here with your possible mate and guard the skies. I feel a stirring on the wind. You won't be the only one to awaken, and they should be greeted by someone far steadier than I am. Not to mention kinder. I have little softness left in me."

While Caeregas peered at his brother, Kezari studied Caeregas. Steadier—that he was, perhaps because his element was earth rather than fire. But was he really kinder? There was a ruthless energy to both men that she couldn't help but admire, but other sentiments were more difficult to identify. Still, Tarah displayed no worry around Caeregas, who was apparently her mate, and they'd contacted Lyr easily enough.

He would be the safer choice of companion, at least when dealing with the elves. Yet Egrenneth...he seethed with the desire to make Queen Zevie pay. If anyone would insist on learning the truth about her reign and all the dragons' failures, it would be him, not his brother. Passion was far better for such a challenge.

"Lord Egrenneth should go," Kezari said. "Provided he vows not to attack the Moranaian elves and will attempt to negotiate with them fairly."

"Are you sure?" Caeregas asked.

Tarah looked dubious, but she wasn't the only elf in the room. As Tynan's hand settled more firmly against Kezari's lower back, she felt his agreement through their bond. "If those conditions are met, yes," she said.

The muscles in Egrenneth's cheek twitched, probably from grinding his teeth. Would he agree with her terms? Strained silence kept the answer uncertain, but finally, he inclined his head.

"Very well," he replied, his voice so tight she was surprised he could get the words out at all. "I vow not to attack the Moranaian elves, and I will negotiate with them fairly. I will even listen to their side, if that's what it takes to set things right. The misery of the last five millennia should never be repeated."

Kezari smiled, but not with happiness. Oh, yes. Answers would be had—and none of it would be a pleasure for Queen Zevie.

~

LYR TRIED to concentrate on his book, but he couldn't quite manage it. His eyes kept being drawn to Meli or to Arlyn where they sat with their own books, both giving up their time to help him. It was a bittersweet blessing—bitter because of the task at hand but sweet because of their very presence. He would far rather this time in the family room be spent on more carefree things, not researching the war with the dragons before a probable meeting with the Ancient One.

It seemed inevitable that Caeregas would come. With the queen here acting erratic, he wouldn't be able to resist. But even though Lyr had studied the war fairly extensively in his youth, five centuries tended to blur the details. What aspects of this situation could they be missing? More importantly, how had the Earth dragons sided during the conflict?

Arlyn closed her latest book with a snap, capturing his attention once more. "Just another summary. Dragons demanded dominion over the gate. Elves protested. War broke out. Why have three books in a row said essentially the same thing? Ugh. Be careful what you wish for. I'm never saying I want to research a subject again."

Lyr tapped his finger atop his equally useless book. "If you need a break, I understand."

"No, I don't. Not really." Arlyn's smile was wry. "What a time for *Elnaia* to be holed up in the healing tower with Lial, though. She would probably have this solved already."

That was true—his mother had trained in the royal archives and knew more about the library than he ever had. But he would not ask her to brave the snow in her condition, not without far greater need. For that matter, he would rather not risk Lial's wrath. The healer had never actually given him an unpleasant potion, but putting Lynia in danger was the most likely thing to inspire him to that action.

"I wish my runes were more help." Meli wrinkled her nose in the way that made Lyr want to kiss it. "Unfortunately, these all have vital information about the war. Just...the same information."

Arlyn lifted the next book and gave it a wiggle. "This one at least looks different."

As she bent over to read, Lyr flicked through his own book with a bit more haste—but not too much, lest his mother find out. The entire population of Earth's remaining dragons could be at the door, and she would still fuss at him if he wrinkled a page. Not that he didn't understand, of course. She'd used a great deal of energy over the centuries on copying and preserving these texts.

"Oh, hey!" Arlyn exclaimed. "This starts out before the war. A direct account, written by the first Myern's son. The Ayal, so I guess the second Myern, eventually. Wow, this even has some archaic lettering. I didn't even know I knew these."

Lyr smiled. "The spell I used shared my own knowledge of the language, and *Laiala* certainly wouldn't have allowed me to lack such skills, whether I needed to read ancient texts or not. I've been frequently grateful when hunting down obscure laws, for no few were ancient."

"Well, I'll see if I can get anything out of this," Arlyn replied, half her focus already on the book in her lap.

Meli frowned at the stack on her own side table. "And I'll look for journals and such, too. That sounds far more useful."

He had to concur, but he already knew that none of those were in his pile of books. He'd already considered the ones he'd grabbed and had placed them in order of possible usefulness. Now that he was on the third book, the quality had already declined significantly. Why wasn't there more mention of

Earth? He could recall learning that the dragons there had caused a great deal of trouble for the humans. But was it something he'd read? Been told? In addition to learning from his parents, he'd had various tutors, too. It could have come from anywhere.

His recollection mostly matched the account he now held. The dragons hadn't been serious about any early attempts at negotiation, and what few parlays they'd tried had been cut off far too early. Then a group of rebel dragons had staged a raid, killing quite a few elves in the process. A surprisingly long and bloody war had commenced, much of it between mages and dragons, along with the dragons' fae allies.

The estate's complex shielding had been born of that time. The key that allowed Lyr and his close family to know the location of each citizen had been vital to the first Myern in identifying friend from foe, and the enclosing shield Lyr had recently used to prevent the virus from spreading had also once kept dragons out. Even the spells that protected the ridge, trees, and structures from fire, decay, or collapse had first been cast as part of the war.

Gods, he hoped they didn't need to use any of them for their original purpose again.

But there was only so much he could do. If Tarah was to be believed, Caeregas held no ill will toward the elves—Lyr would have to do his best to keep that true. Then there was the Seelie lord Meren, concocting who-knew-what kind of plans. Lyr had Koranel locked in the dungeon even now, awaiting his pending "exile" to Earth in the hopes of gaining Meren's attention. Would that bring conflict, too? He had a feeling not even Ralan and Eri could answer that with any clarity.

"Damn, the first Myern sounds like an asshole," Arlyn muttered. At his questioning frown, she grimaced. "Harsh to say about an ancestor, I guess, but listen to this. 'Tensions grow increasingly strained, but Father does little to help. What matter is it to him that the dragons claimed a hunting ground in the southern woods? But he called them slavering beasts who deserved no hold on Moranaian ground. Food. They wanted food. I cannot abide this.'"

What? Lyr's frown deepened. He'd never read a single account of discord between the first Myern and his only son. "May I see?"

With a shrug, she slid the open book into his lap. Lyr kept the place marked with his hand while flipping back to the back cover. Sure enough, the family crest had been pressed into the bottom corner, an archivist's seal of confirmation beside it. Both were faded and nearly smooth, but they were there. This was an official account written in the second Myern's own hand, not a random, misattributed work.

He turned back to the spot where Arlyn had left off and began to read. With each word, a sick sense of horror grew until bile scorched his throat. Much of what he'd learned had clearly been a lie—or at least not the full truth. And his own ancestor bore much of the blame.

What was it the fairies had told Kai when he'd sought their aid with the virus? "Follow your past trouble to find future cares. Address every grievance, or Braelyn will see more bloodshed than it has in millennia." Well, here was one massive past grievance, written in the bold, angry stroke of the young heir's hand.

*Today, Father rejected the third attempt by the dragons for a formal meeting concerning the portal. To what end? Our people may have discovered this world first, but we've never denied access to any other fae who've come here since. Why create such conflict with the dragons? Rather foolish, considering their power. But it is obvious that Father wants them gone entirely. Day and night, he fills people's heads with stories of their brutality on Earth. What brutality? I've been through the portal recently, and while all is not peace, there is not such chaos as all that.*

*I fear what the dragons will do next, though I cannot say I would blame them. Recently, there have been more envoys from the Earth dragons, and there are rumors of an energy shift on that world. Naturally, the dragons here want to be free to travel there in case of trouble. I would not wish to be trapped here, that is for certain. Yet my brother had to bring up the possibility of treachery through those envoys, and Father is back to his rants again.*

Lyr paused to reread the last sentence. Brother? The first Myern had sired one son and one daughter, and the daughter had died as an infant. Why would the Ayal mention a brother? This time, Lyr flipped to the front to read the name signed there—but what he saw chilled his blood. Osieren Dianore. Simple enough, except for one thing.

In no official record did this person exist.

# CHAPTER TWENTY-NINE

As soon as Kezari stepped through the portal, all of her restlessness and annoyance returned. It was that inexplicable itch again—yet the source was no clearer than before she'd gone. No, it was merely more obvious after her relatively pleasant sojourn on Earth. But why? She might feel a connection to Earth, but Moranaia was still home. She'd spent far too much time in communion with the ground beneath her to feel otherwise.

"You can make it back to the estate, right?" Inona asked.

Kezari smiled gratefully at the guide. "It'll be a cold walk, but I know the way. Thank you for your help."

Though surprise flickered for a heartbeat on the scout's face, she returned the smile before bidding them farewell and pulling Delbin back through. Almost instantly, the swirling mists disappeared, leaving them in the clearing—just her, Tynan, Egrenneth, and the pair of guards stationed at the gate.

A dusting of snow covered the ground, but it had obviously been cleared recently. The drifts around the perimeter could have reached her breasts in spots. Kezari shivered and formed a cloak around her, only her arm left free since she still held Tynan's hand from the crossing. It was unfortunate that they hadn't gone through the outpost this time, for that gate opened beside the local portal that led straight into Braelyn.

And warmth.

Egrenneth, of course, showed no sign of a chill. Lucky dragon. Not that he showed much sign of anything. His blank stare scanned across the clearing dispassionately before his attention returned to her. Only then did he frown.

"Are you actually cold?" he asked incredulously.

She would not snap at the ancient dragon who'd traveled here to confront Queen Zevie. She would *not*. "I have recently found my mate," she reminded him. "My temperature shifted accordingly."

He blinked at her. "You...can shift it back with enough intent, you know. Unless you are or want to be pregnant, that is."

Kezari couldn't help it—her mouth dropped open like a youngling awaiting scraps of meat. But for far less appetizing reasons. All this time, she could have been warm? Traveling through this blasted snow without a care in the world? Feeling absolutely normal? Her breath hissed out in a frosty stream.

"I have never heard this," she said.

Egrenneth shrugged. "If you've lost all knowledge of the red beryl, there is no doubt plenty of lore around mating of which you're unaware. In any case, I doubt it is easy to override that kind of instinct. I wouldn't know."

"Isn't your brother in the process of mating?" she asked.

"We are hardly close enough for such discussions," the other dragon replied, his expression hardening. "But lying dormant for millennia would have lowered his temperature, regardless. It will take some time for his metabolism to return to normal if it hasn't bothered him enough to shift it consciously."

Tynan squeezed her hand. "Perhaps we could discuss this more once we've reached the warmth of Braelyn?"

Nodding, she led them out of the clearing and down the proper path, but all the while, her mind turned over this latest revelation like a jewel, each side shiny and new. Well, almost new.

She'd known that her temperature could be altered on purpose to produce young—she'd simply never done it. But with the mate bond, it had felt spontaneous. Uncontrolled. If it was caused by the bond, it had seemed to her that the effect would last until nature was satisfied. So to speak.

Apparently, that didn't have to be the case. Provided she could figure out how to do it, she could theoretically return her temperature to normal. Unless she was pregnant or wanted to be, he'd said. Hmm. She didn't possess the ability to know if she was, but did she want to be? She turned that over and over in her mind but still hadn't found an answer by the time they neared the front of the estate.

Tynan walked steadily at her side, no hint of turmoil in his energy now that they'd returned to Moranaia. Did he realize what she worried over? What did he think of having young? They hadn't spoken of it, which...wasn't well done considering they'd already slept together. What if she did already carry his child? Would she be able to shift?

Horror turned her blood to ice and froze her steps to the snowy path. How could she fly to the Isle, if that were the case? Elders' teeth. Had her impetuous nature messed things up yet again?

Just a single surge of dread, and Tynan tugged her against him, his arms circling her waist. "What is it?"

"Yes, what?" Egrenneth practically snarled from beside them.

Kezari gave Tynan's upper arms a squeeze before glaring at the ancient dragon. "A thought of concern. When I do bear young, will I be able to shift?"

Egrenneth closed his eyes in an obvious attempt to contain his temper. "You want to learn the *basics* of dragon reproduction *now?*"

*I will not eat him. I will not eat him.*

"If I find I am already with young, how am I to know if I can go to the Isle?" she asked sweetly—as sweet as the syrup she would drizzle over his bitter corpse if she did have to eat him.

Bleh. But as needs must.

"I cannot fathom this level of ignorance," the other dragon muttered. "Of course you can. Female dragons always produce shifters, and in the womb, they change form with the mother. Unless you're going to tell me that our biology has changed while living on Moranaia?"

She gritted her teeth together. Hard. Why hadn't she chosen Caeregas, again? "The fae and elves who originally accompanied us as *skiziks* live mostly separate now. There hasn't been a pairing between us and them since...truly, I do not know if there has ever been one on the Isle. I have no clue what you've been doing on Earth, but there is no point of reference here for me."

Egrenneth surprised her by bowing, his expression shifting to chagrin. "Forgive me. I take my own knowledge for granted. Though I've been the only dragon awake on Earth for millennia, I'm old enough to have lived with my own kind amongst the humans. It is difficult to imagine generations passing here in the same span."

So he *could* be polite. It was fortunate, really—she would rather not resort to cannibalism, and she wasn't overly fond of syrup, either.

Tynan's arms tightened around her waist. Reassurance or impatience? He smiled down at her gently, but there was a restlessness to him that suggested it was a bit of both. "We should go," she said. "The Myern is waiting."

*And isn't that meeting going to be lovely?* she mused, pulling away from Tynan.

As they approached the elaborate double doors at the front of the estate, she couldn't decide if she wanted to wince or grin. Here she was, bringing an even more unreasonable dragon into the estate. When had she become the one more likely to act as intermediary? Now, that was a frightening thought.

*"Isn't it?"* Tynan sent into her mind, his mental voice a teasing lilt.

*"Who would have believed it, right?"* she replied. But her

thoughts kept slipping back to other concerns. *"How long have you been listening to my litany of worries? You said nothing during my earlier musing."*

He fell silent for a moment. *"Long enough, since you weren't exactly quiet with your fears, but as the sharing wasn't intentional, I didn't want to interrupt. But if you're wondering... Kezari, I'll be honored to have children with you whenever you wish. Perhaps Lady Bera will show us a blessing with the proper timing."*

Kezari stumbled slightly over the threshold. *"Your goddess gets people pregnant?"*

*"Not alone, to be sure,"* Tynan joked, though there was a serious note beneath the amusement. *"And I doubt She oversees all. Even so, were you aware that She isn't only the goddess of healing? She also reigns over life and death, so if She wills it..."*

A shiver went down Kezari's spine, but it had little to do with children. *"Life and death? Is that why you said you learn about death at your temple?"*

*"That's right."* His nostrils flared. *"It's something often hidden beneath delicate sentiment, but it is there. Remember that when you're thinking of me as gentle and weak."*

She got a clear image from him, one of fierce protectiveness, but for the life of her, she couldn't imagine him hurting anyone. *"With your link to mind and emotion..."*

*"I would happily stop the heart of the woman who locked one of my last patients in a closet for a month. No light. Barely any food or water."* His mind was so closed in that moment that she received no hint of a mental image—only anger, dark and deserved. *"All for running away from the previous week's beating. After healing that child's mind, I assure you that whatever punishment the lady of the estate gave that woman, it wasn't enough."*

Kezari stared at Tynan's profile, so strangely neutral in comparison to his emotions. *"Aris never mentioned your penchant for..."*

*"Vengeful thoughts?"* Tynan shook his head. *"He wouldn't know. None of my patients do, for it would bring them no relief."*

She let out a soft *tsking* sound. *"Remember what I said about damming cave streams? You can't continue to seethe with this. Hmmm... Maybe I should try my hand at shaping pottery. You can break it against the cave wall, and I'll reform it again."*

His chuckle brought her great pleasure, though she hadn't been joking. Not entirely. There was no telling how many awful things swam in his memories, a sad consequence of his job. She'd seen enough from helping her *skizik*. How much worse to bear so many others? She couldn't fathom how her mate didn't want to burn the whole world.

The thought of fire had her eyeing Egrenneth over her shoulder. He wasn't a mind healer, but his attitude *did* scream "I want to cast everything into eternal flame." Had he lived through multiple traumas, then? It would explain his harshness, which was extreme even to her measure. She was beginning to suspect that he enjoyed making trouble for trouble's sake.

A snarky dragon who wanted to watch the world burn. Lyr would be thrilled.

Once again, she regretted not choosing Caeregas.

Tynan wanted nothing more than to pull his bonded into one of the rooms they passed and lock out everything else. Part of that was the newness of their joining, of course, but it was far from the only factor. First, he wanted to answer the question currently burning its way through his gut—was she pregnant? Bera's grace, but he didn't know what he hoped for in that regard. But the fact that he could satisfy both their worries with such a basic use of his healing magic ate at him most of all.

It wasn't the only thing. After their time on Earth, he could feel for himself the differences in her. She'd been lighter there. Happier to see everything that world had to offer. Why didn't she explore these lands with the same verve? He didn't want to consider that she might prefer that other world—one that he found nearly intolerable.

Now, there was a fretfulness to her energy. He'd sensed it building from the moment they'd stepped back through the gate. And though he liked Kezari just the way she was, he hated that some of her edges had been resharpened by whatever bothered her here. She deserved playfulness and light, too.

*"My grandparents were chased away from here after a terrible war,"* Kezari sent, proving that she wasn't the only one to unintentionally transmit their cares to the other. *"Exploration of these lands takes a bit more care. Anyway, it's mostly this strange…itchiness. But I still don't understand the source."*

As a guard redirected them to the library, Tynan pondered that bit of news. Now that she mentioned it, some of the difference he'd felt—that fretfulness—could be described as a sort of mental itchiness. It was like a loose thread in one's clothing or a shoe just a hint too tight. A minor annoyance, but an ongoing one.

*"How long have you felt this?"*

Kezari shrugged. *"I'm not sure, but I'd say it has grown more noticeable over the past moon's cycle. I couldn't even say when I first recognized it."*

A slow build, then. *"But you've detected no source?"*

Her lips twisted as her eyes cut sharply in his direction. *"Don't you think I would have flown off in pursuit if I had? Until our journey to Earth, I couldn't even be certain it wasn't coming from there."*

Tynan merely smiled in response. Truly, it had been a foolish question. If Kezari was aware of something that needed changing, everyone would know about it. But he couldn't think of it as a weakness. After all, that very trait had ultimately brought her to him, even if that had been more side-effect than cause.

Kezari halted at the library door to glare back at Egrenneth. "Take care here. They have books older than both of us, and that is obviously no small number."

The elder dragon laughed low. "I give my word that I have never incinerated a library, nor will I. No matter what rumors might suggest otherwise."

It was probably fortunate that neither Tynan nor Kezari had heard any rumors about the man, for Tynan suspected that final comment was less reassuring than it should be. But what could they do? If the Myern had left orders for them to meet him here, then he had to be aware of the risk. They were merely obeying.

But when they entered, it was obviously not to a staid meeting. Lyr, Meli, Arlyn, and even Lady Lynia were situated around a table stacked with books, more than a few abandoned open. Arlyn and Lynia sat side-by-side, each studying their own massive tome. Runes glowing in one hand, Meli shuffled through one of the stacks, and Lyr took the ones she shoved his way.

"This is a fascinating greeting from the famed elves of Moranaia," Egrenneth drawled, attracting every gaze but Meli's, who was too focused on following her runes.

Lyr inclined his head even as he accepted another book. "I hope you will excuse this terrible lapse in manners. However, the information we are searching for is both urgent and relevant."

Still raw from his time on Earth, Tynan opened his senses the tiniest amount, only to recoil at once from the near panic hovering in the air like fog. Did he want to hear what was important enough to cause a frantic search through the library by the four most powerful people on the estate outside the royal family? No, he did not. If nothing else, Lynia's presence told him that. She'd been set on remaining in the healing tower with Lial.

Tynan exchanged a confused glance with Kezari. "Shouldn't we do introductions?" she asked slowly. "Something excessively long and unnecessarily complicated?"

"Normally, yes," Lyr replied easily enough. But the hand he ran through his hair shook with apprehension. "But this..."

Tynan cleared his throat, then tried not to wince at the Myern's questioning look. "Would it be best if I did the formal introductions? I realize I am not the most senior in rank or age, but under the circumstances, I would be happy to offer aid."

Lyr shook his head. "Thank you, but even that would take too long. I am Lord Lyrnis Dianore, Myern of Braelyn. This is my soulbonded, Meli, my daughter, Arlyn, and my mother, Lynia," he said, gesturing to each in turn. "And our guest does not appear to be Caeregas."

"Absolutely not," Egrenneth said firmly, though his expression held humor. He bowed at the waist as he'd done for Kezari. "I am Egrenneth of the Crag, son of Deyriglair, who was the Guardian of the Frozen North in your ancestors' time."

Kezari's head snapped around, and Tynan had a moment's worry that she would shove him bodily out of the way to better stare at Egrenneth. "Deyriglair? You did not mention your father's name before. He is known in our legends."

"As in ours," Lynia murmured. "The one I'm reading now, in fact."

Egrenneth shrugged. "That is no surprise. After all, he was one of the main pillars of the wall, and his name is no doubt inscribed on your treaties. He told us all about his attempts to broker peace between the elves and the Moranaian dragons. Based on that, I am sure I will not be welcome here for long."

Shocked silence morphed into palpable tension. Why hadn't the dragon mentioned that little tidbit on Earth when he'd expressed his other misgivings? But the satisfied smile on Egrenneth's face suggested a truth they should have considered.

The elder dragon hadn't come to cause trouble to only Queen Zevie—he was happy to do so for everyone.

# CHAPTER THIRTY

On a surge of fierce anger, Kezari ducked around Tynan so that she was between her mate and the deceptive Egrenneth. "You withheld that information on purpose."

A smile flashed across his face. "Yes and no. My brother and I rarely offer our father's name, as we prefer to stand on our own authority. However, you're correct that I withheld his name with full intent."

"Why?" Kezari demanded.

"Would you have believed my promise not to cause harm had you been aware of this?"

She paused to consider the matter and had to concede that acceptance would have been less likely. But he still should have given her all of the facts before she'd made a decision. What else would he keep from her? "I am not sure I believe it now."

His eyes narrowed. "I do not give my word lightly. My mistrust of these elves will make no impact on that."

"I told you they—"

"He's right," Lyr interrupted. The haunted tone of his voice had her focus shifting to him, though she kept watch on the other dragon out of the corner of her eye. "It's the cause of our current search, actually."

Kezari had seen the Myern looking annoyed, frustrated, and even angry, but she'd never witnessed him so shaken. "He's right?" she asked. "About what? That you'll treat him poorly? That seems unlikely."

Lyr rubbed his hand across his face, only to lower it quickly to grab another book Meli shoved toward his chest. "No, he's not correct that I would treat him poorly. However...when I was looking through some of the old histories about the dragon wars, I found a journal. A *family* journal. It seems the first Myern actively worked against the dragons. And since the person who wrote this account disappeared from my family history, I have more than a little concern about how far the first Myern might have gone in his hatred. As such...yes, Lord Egrenneth has just cause to mistrust us. At this point, *I* mistrust Delvian."

Who in the darkest depths was Delvian? She couldn't recall that name, but from the surge of shock she felt from Tynan, it had some significance for the elves. The first Myern, most likely, though she couldn't fathom why Tynan would care about the ancient history of this estate.

"You're saying Prince Delvian hated dragons?" her mate asked. "But the Queen herself interceded for peace."

"Yes," Lyr said tightly. "But that doesn't mean her son agreed."

Kezari frowned. "Wait, the first Myern was a prince? Or are these two separate people?"

"Upon our founding, the queen created the nine branches as guardians of the nine sacred trees and placed one of her children in charge of each," Tynan explained. "So Delvian was both prince and Myern."

Lady Lynia glanced up from the book she'd been studying. "That is correct. And according to these records, he had only one child who survived until adulthood, a son who eventually became the second Myern. This tome lists every birth and death on this estate for the first thousand years, and there is no mention of anyone named Osieren being born to anyone."

"That's because his father was a spiteful bastard," Egrenneth said, his tone so harsh that Arlyn gasped and Lyr's eyes narrowed. "If casting aspersions on your ancestor offends you, I assure you, I don't care. Delvian was closed-minded, cruel, and spiteful. He was absolutely furious that his mother ceded Earth to travel here. When the dragons and Unseelie created the wall, matters only became worse. With so much less energy, he could not convince his mother to return to Earth, and he blamed the dragons for that most of all. I imagine when Osieren abandoned him for the Isle, he erased his son out of existence."

The Isle? Did he mean to say that a Dianore ancestor had left with the dragons? It was not a name familiar to her, but she didn't exactly pay attention to the surnames of their fae and elven inhabitants. She couldn't even recall Perim's, and that woman had been the one to capture and torture Aris. But how would Egrenneth know all this?

"You speak as though you were there," Kezari said.

He lifted a shoulder. "My father was quite clear in his warnings. Caeregas might have preferred to shirk his lessons, but I did not. Delvian attempted to discredit and then drive away the dragons all the way until the war, and he wouldn't have granted them clemency after it if not for his mother. He was a fearsome warrior. One who would not yield."

The somber quiet was broken by Meli, who blinked in confusion as her focus returned. "I...seem to have missed something."

"We all have," Lyr said with a sigh. Then he pulled his mate close to his side like a lifeline. "Thank you for your honesty, Lord Egrenneth. We will continue to search for more accounts, and I'll be reading the entirety of Osieren's journal myself. Though I do have to wonder what Prince Ralan knows about this. He would have learned more than I did about the war."

"He might *not* have heard of Osieren," Egrenneth said. "My father spoke of his defection with some relish, but there is less reason for that to be widely spoken of here."

Lyr pinched the bridge of his nose. "I suppose it doesn't

matter, at least not to our dealings with the current dragon queen. But I do wonder how this new truth might affect negotiations and whether we should reconsider decisions of the past. The dragons were clearly not treated fairly, and I must call into question anything said about them in Delvian's records."

Kezari grew still at those words, even her breath coming slower. He couldn't mean that to the extent it could be taken. Who would consider renegotiating a treaty that had stood for almost forty thousand years? Then again, if there was one thing she'd learned about the current Myern, it was how seriously he took his duties—not only the doing, but also the fairness of how they were done.

"You'll not be negotiating with Queen Zevie," Egrenneth said, crossing his arms. Probably to hide the hint of claw she'd glimpsed where fingernails should be. "Because I'll be executing her on sight."

Even Kezari could only stare at him in shock at that bold pronouncement. She'd thought any mention of ripping out the queen's heart had been...hyperbole, really. Maybe a solid life goal. But obviously, Egrenneth had been serious. His general attitude might annoy her, but reluctant admiration crept back in.

Viciousness was a boon when it was righteous.

The elves might not feel quite the same. Arlyn and Meli grew pale, even as their eyes widened. Lynia glanced up from her book, her mouth agape. And Lyr... In nearly every encounter she'd witnessed, the Myern had kept his implacable demeanor, but this time, his mouth moved wordlessly and for longer than she would have expected.

Finally, he shook his head as though uncertain of what he'd heard. "Did you just say you are planning to execute the queen of the Moranaian dragons?"

Egrenneth smiled, and she could imagine the sharpness of his teeth in dragon form. "It is not a plan. It is a reality. She has broken some of our most sacred laws, and there is no coming back from that."

"Wouldn't she set the laws for her own kingdom?" Lynia asked, her brow furrowing with curiosity. She was probably already composing an entry for her records.

"We dragons do not tend to follow gods. Rather, we drift with the universe and become one with its energies," Egrenneth said, and his words struck against Kezari's heart with their truth. "However, we have maintained a strict code of conduct from our earliest days. All of us, no matter where we live. This Zevie has perverted that code. Upon her death, the Moranaian dragons must be put back to rights."

A horrible, unthinkable, impossible worry sidled its way into Kezari's heart. Who would take Zevie's place? Would he expect it to be *her*? To Kezari's knowledge, no one on that island was capable of setting anything to rights, not with their connection to Earth compromised or broken. All of them had been complacent with the queen's plans, the current rebellion owing itself to madness more than justice. So who did that leave to assume command?

"I am not taking her place," Kezari said, baring her own teeth in a dragon's smile.

Tynan's hand suddenly gripped hers, and she could feel his worry like her own. The elder dragon's grin didn't make that any better. But she didn't dare turn away to comfort her mate, no matter how much she wanted to assure him that she did not want to live on the Isle of Dragons, much less rule it.

"I should think not, Young One," Egrenneth said sharply. "I shall do so. That wasn't my plan before I stepped through the gate, but the energy is lovely here and the need is strong. Now. Myern Lyr. If you could direct me to the appropriate hunting area, I would be appreciative. I'm given to understand that Kezari's mate needs time to rest. Then, we have a reckoning to plan."

Kezari stared at him, her admiration going up another notch.

Her kin on the Isle had no idea what was coming for them.

~

STEPPING into the cold but empty clearing in front of the estate relieved Tynan's senses despite the frigid wind that seemed to cut through his cloak. Better the harsh chill than the relentless pounding of so many emotions. The last couple of days had given new appeal to living in Kezari's cave, that much was certain.

Aris hurried up the path as Kezari and Egrenneth were preparing to shift. The elder dragon sighed, but he made no complaint when Kezari instead met her *skizik* a couple of paces away. Tynan eyed Aris carefully, searching for any signs of increased agitation, but the time he'd taken to recover from his latest incident must have done him well. Aris greeted Kezari with joy, and he even gave her a hug—a quick one, but a hug all the same.

"I'm glad to see you returned safely," Aris said. "I meant to be here upon your return, but I was helping locate someone who went missing in the snow. It took time to see her safely to the healer's tower."

"Are you a scout now, then?" Kezari asked with a teasing smile.

Aris grinned in return. "No. Merely an adventurer who can find the spark of life. Though in truth, I might do well as a scout once I've recovered. My thirst for exploration has been much quenched."

"Perhaps. But you should come to Earth with me if I get another chance." Some of the eager happiness returned to her expression. "You would enjoy riding the humans' speedy conveyances, at least the aboveground ones. Well, if the iron humans use in the construction isn't too disturbing. Tynan struggled greatly with that."

A pulse of discomfort throbbed in Tynan's gut, and he could be honest enough with himself to admit that it wasn't really the mention of his weakness. No, it was an unfortunate mixture of insecurity and envy. It even made sense. Tynan had already known that Aris would have been the best choice of travel companion had he not been struggling with his trauma. This merely confirmed it.

"I'm not sure how I'd fare with ambient iron, but I suspect it would be worth it." Aris's gaze shifted to Egrenneth. "And you brought another dragon, I see."

Kezari launched into a quick introduction, but Tynan paid little attention to the words. He couldn't look away from the admiration that gleamed in her eyes each time she looked at the other dragon. He could feel it through their link, and it rubbed against his heart like the roughest fabric. Did she regret their bond? Perhaps she would have rather held out for the powerful future king of the Isle.

By Arneen, she deserved that.

She pinned him with a single, amused glance. *"What is Arneen?"*

*"Ah..."* She wanted to learn about his religion now? *"It is said to be the place where the gods fully revealed themselves for the first time. The royal palace was built not far from the spot."*

*"Well, if you doubt my dedication to you as mate again, I will happily drop you there for a conference with them."* Her mental voice held a snap her expression did not. *"Though I can sympathize with the jealousy, it is foolish in this case. Stop it."*

Oddly, desire flashed through him at her rebuke, along with a more reasonable pleasure. He'd never imagined himself the type to enjoy possessiveness, but then, he'd never stayed with anyone long enough to care so deeply. And he did care, for the thought of her with Egrenneth made him want to rage, too.

"How long do you need to rest, healer?" Egrenneth asked. "Will you be sufficiently prepared after our hunt?"

Forcing his focus back to the conversation at hand, Tynan shrugged. "If Lial is available to offer aid and your hunt is a long one, I might do well enough. But if you'd like me at full strength, no. I hardly slept last night for helping Lial and...other reasons. I can barely maintain my shields here."

"Fine." Egrenneth's lips pinched closed. "Sleep as much as you need, and we will leave soon after you wake. It shouldn't take long to formulate a plan. We can do much of that on the wing."

Kezari looked up at the sky. "Though it's only midday, it'll be sunset in three or so hours."

"Are you afraid to fly in the dark?" Egrenneth snapped.

"No, but—" Kezari huffed. "We can discuss this later. I'm too hungry to argue, and my mate needs rest."

The other dragon looked like he wanted to refute her dismissal, but instead, he spun away and strode across the clearing toward the ridge that descended to the village below. Before he reached the edge, Egrenneth shifted—one moment fae, the next a dragon shining like a ruby in the sun. Answer enough, Tynan supposed. As did Kezari. She surprised him with a quick kiss before stepping back.

Only to freeze, an abashed expression crossing her face. "Egrenneth said I could shift regardless, but I don't know if…"

An awkward moment passed before her meaning sank in. They hadn't had a chance for him to confirm if she'd conceived, unlikely though it was so soon after they'd slept together. Though he couldn't help but flush beneath Aris's curious stare, Tynan moved to Kezari. He hesitated only a moment before pulling her into his arms—a position that would look more like an embrace than an examination to their observers. Anything else felt far too obtrusive.

Cuddling Kezari close, he sent a tendril of his magic into her, as little as he could manage to avoid the telltale glow of his energy lighting up the area. His hands trembled against her back as he finally scanned her womb, uncertain of what he would find. Unsure of what he wanted to find.

No baby, he discovered at once. He sagged a little. Was it relief? Disappointment? He couldn't say. But really, his surprise shouldn't have been so acute. Her temperature had just changed, so he should have realized that she wouldn't have had time to ovulate. Would Kezari be upset?

As his magic faded, he met her eyes. *"Not yet,"* he sent softly.

She released a long sigh. *"I'm not sure how I feel."*

*"Nor am I,"* he admitted. *"But I suppose we should take more care until we figure those emotions out."*

Kezari nodded almost solemnly, but then she gave him a sudden smile. *"We'll all be happier if I warm myself back up until spring, especially if I'm hauling you and Aris around on flights. It's rather uncomfortable up there for the rider during winter, even with my usual warmth. I'm not sure how miserable it would be without it."*

Tynan shivered at the thought. *"Good to know."*

*"Go sleep."* She patted his shoulder. *"I've a* daeri *to catch."*

He watched her until she took to the sky, her golden wings carrying her away beside Egrenneth. It seemed there was a longing inside them both for children, if not at this moment. But he had a feeling it would not be easy. Many elves struggled to conceive, as did dragons. How long would they have to try together?

Aris stepped up beside him. "Dare I ask what that was about?"

"Only following a bit of your previous advice on considering the future." Tynan kept his gaze on the distant line of trees. "We were careless last night, and Kezari worried about shifting in case of any...consequences."

"Ah, children." Aris chuckled. "If you'd asked, I could have told you that I sensed no additional life. Well, if you're disappointed, you could ask for one of Lial's new fertility potions. I imagine he'd like to see if it works. On a woman this time."

Tynan grinned. Lynia had given one of those to Lial when he'd been infected with the virus to see if the life magic imbued within would help cure him. Lial claimed it had played no role in Lynia conceiving, since it had been designed to work on the womb, but it was far too easy to tease the grumpy healer about it, no matter the facts.

"I suppose Kezari and I will talk about it." Tynan turned away from the ridge—and hopefully toward sleep. "I've been advised by a reliable source that we should do more of that."

Aris's laughter followed Tynan down the path that would circle around to the observation tower, and the healing sound brought lightness to his steps. If Aris could laugh, there was hope for all of them.

# CHAPTER THIRTY-ONE

By the time Lyr summoned her to the library a couple of hours later, Kezari feared she might have to plan another assassination. For Egrenneth-call-me-Ren-until-I'm-king, of course, not Lyr. It was a definite relief to fly back to the estate, for if there was a way for Ren to annoy her, he found it. The *daeri* weren't as plump as Earth deer. The cold was too harsh—but not as bad as Greenland in the dead of winter. A cold, green land? It made no sense.

And of course, she was not sufficiently skilled—in anything.

As Kezari landed in the clearing at the front of the estate, Ren dropped down beside her, and they both shifted at the same time. Still, he frowned at her. "Can you shift as you land?"

Would Caeregas of the Pine hold it against her if she pitched his brother off the side of the ridge? "Naturally. Can you?"

"Your hunting methods are...fascinating," he observed. "Who trained you?"

She hadn't had much success with changing her temperature during flight, so the wind bit into her flesh with painful insistence. But ancestors forbid she form a cloak again around *this* one. "My parents died when I was too young to remember them, but I imagine they did at first. Then my aunt and uncle, when the whim struck. If you find me inadequate, you'll want to visit their cave to discuss it."

His brows drew together. "Do you think that's why I question you? I must know the extent of knowledge lost, and you are not inclined to admit such things without prompting. Otherwise, you wouldn't be shivering. You'd be confessing your lack of learning so that I could instruct you on temperature regulation."

"I am not your experiment or your information source," she said, glaring. "Nor am I your student. I've seen nearly four hundred turns of this world and am far past my fledgling years."

"So old, then?" Ren scoffed. "I lost count of my age sometime around my six-thousandth year. Bravado serves nothing. It only kills you, you know. Fools die at the hand of false wisdom and feigned pride."

Kezari bit back a curse. Only she could have chosen a self-determined dragon-sage to accompany her to Moranaia. "Not all of us learned at the wing of our legendary parent, Ren Gough. Truly, I feel for any mate you might find. I hope you stumble upon someone more knowledgeable than you. For *their* sake."

His expression hardened. "At least I have a red beryl when I do, hmm?"

Without another word, Kezari spun on her heel and marched off. She was supposed to be meeting Lyr in the library, not killing his guest. Besides, the sun was setting, she was tired, and the argument was foolish. She was too sensitive, and he was too obnoxious. It made a poor combination amidst so much stress. No doubt if Tynan had been there, he would have attempted to defuse it.

Not that his previous try had gone well on Earth. Maybe she should reconsider escorting Egrenneth to the Isle, for he obviously struggled with simple calm. He was volatile, in fact. That had been well and good when the plan had been to punish Queen Zevie and restore order. But as king of the dragons? That could cause her dragon kin a great deal of harm, and no matter what they'd done, she didn't wish that.

"Kezari, wait," Ren called from just behind her.

She didn't stop walking.

"That was beyond the bounds," Ren said. "I'm sorry."

Fine. She would at least slow down. "I should not have mentioned your potential mate, either," Kezari conceded, though she *did* feel bad for that unlucky soul. "However, your desire to annoy and criticize does not bode well for you in the future. I tire of it. I'm supposed to meet with the Myern, anyway."

Ren sped up until he reached the front doors at the same time she did. The guard at the door frowned as the dragon placed his hand on the wood to prevent Kezari from opening it. "One moment only."

She glared at him. "One."

"Do you know what it's like to be alone for millennia? With nothing to do besides guard a nearly failed barrier forgotten in ancient times? I could never be anything but silent and stalwart." He grimaced. "I suppose my enjoyment of expressing true emotion was destined to go awry."

Her anger faded a little. "Is that why you detest calm?"

"Loathe it," he said, nodding. "But I did not mean offense. I really do want to help. And here...I am both needed and free. Can you imagine the joy in that?"

Unfortunately, she could. Living at Braelyn had given her a taste of freedom, even if she was often afraid to grasp it. But that didn't give either of them the right to be so...so rude. She—Ancestors, she'd been just as annoying as Egrenneth with her scorn of elven etiquette and tradition, hadn't she? She had the sudden urge to apologize to everyone she'd spoken to after her arrival for causing them this kind of angst.

"Here's some advice for *you*," Kezari said. "Your joy shouldn't cause others pain."

Something she would do well to remember herself.

TWENTY MARKS—THAT was how long Kai had stood watch after his father's surgery, waiting for a sign of true life. Of course, it was obvious that Naomh lived. His chest rose and fell at a steady rate, and—possibly the most telling—Lial paid him little heed. The healer would have done far more than a few cursory checks if anything had been amiss.

But fuck, Kai had been through so much. Technically speaking, he'd survived far worse physical trials with fewer aftereffects, but his body didn't seem to agree with his assessment of severity. His muscles ached as though he'd been training for hours, and his mind had the hazy feel of exhaustion. Stress and grief *hurt*—though standing at attention beside his father's bed for more than twenty marks didn't really help.

He hadn't even eaten.

Somehow, Lial hadn't noticed, but he hadn't precisely been idle. He was treating another frostbite patient now, this one a woman from the village who'd strayed from the trail in the worst of the snow. Poor woman—and poor Lial. He'd barely cleared the last case from Tynan's room upstairs, and now there was another to treat.

A sharp gasp from the bed pulled Kai's attention immediately to his father. Naomh's eyes were open, but a touch glazed with shock. Had his mind sustained damage? Kai had heard Lial say time and again that the brain's complications often required wakefulness to detect. Heart pounding, Kai knelt beside the bed.

"Naomh," he said softly, hoping his voice wouldn't startle his father.

Naomh's head turned oh-so-slowly until he finally fixed his eyes on Kai. At first, there was no recognition, but after his father blinked a few times, some of the blankness faded. "Kai?"

"I have kept watch, just as I promised Caolte."

"Where...?" Naomh licked his lips. "Where is Caolte?"

"Keeping your realm from collapsing," Kai answered.

Naomh frowned. "Yes. I remember now. The one who sent me to sleep said..."

Gods above, but his father was weak. Kai hurried over to the divider blocking much of the room from view and peeked around. Yep. Lial was still bent over the woman's feet, blue light glowing around her toes from his healing power. He was in too much of a trance to have heard their soft conversation.

Kai grabbed the untouched mug of water that Lynia had left on the side table before Lyr had escorted her back to the estate for research. Ah, family secrets. First Kai's birth family, and now his bonded one. At least Arlyn's emotions weren't engaged by the news of their mystery relative. For her, it was more curiosity than a question of honor.

Not so for Lyr, who'd grown up with tales of their family history.

Cup in hand, Kai knelt beside his father once more. Naomh eyed the cup and then grimaced. "Can't..."

With the iron gone, his father's wound was fully sealed. Kai had watched the entire process, then confirmed the results with Lial. Even so, he hesitated a moment before slipping his arm beneath Naomh's shoulders to boost him up a little. Not much, but his father was able to manage a few sips before losing his energy to drink.

"Do I still have a realm?" Naomh asked, but his voice was too faint to convey the emotion that might be behind the question.

"I would assume so." Kai hesitated, but there was no use in hiding the truth. "However, according to Kezari and Tynan, you'll need to do a fair bit of landscaping. Or rather...a lot. Caolte is..."

"A fire mage." Naomh's smile held a great deal of affection—more than he typically displayed, in fact. "How did you get him to stay?"

Kai carried the cup back to the table. "There wasn't really a choice. Lial was unwilling to risk going there, since his beloved is pregnant, and Tynan didn't have the right skill set to perform the needed surgery. You had to come here. But Caolte could barely manage the realm while actually there, much less from a distance."

"He needs to stand on his own," Naomh murmured, his eyes slipping closed. But apparently not to sleep. "I want to touch the ground."

Kai blinked. "What? Why?"

"Elerie," his father said.

Simple. Absolute. A universe in a single word.

"Did Tynan—"

"No, he neatly evaded." Naomh's voice dropped to the barest whisper. "It was others I heard. Said she's alive."

Kai cursed beneath his breath. What was he supposed to do now? His father barely had the energy for this conversation, much less the journey to Oria he would inevitably insist upon. But Kai didn't want to lie. There'd been enough of that for all of them.

He sighed. "It's true, but she's unconscious. I've only known for a day or two."

"How?"

"My—" Kai swallowed. "Allafon pushed her down the stairs, but it seems the healer hid my mother away in the dreaming. She told no one."

"Why...?" His father licked his lips again. "Why is she still unconscious?"

How would Naomh take the shock of this news? No, Kai didn't want to lie, but how much could his father take in this condition?

"Just tell me," Naomh said, a hint of the usual bite returning to his tone.

"She will live, but she requires a great deal of healing." Kai ran his fingers through his rumpled hair. "She might not walk again, in fact. Oria's healer left her spine untreated for too long, it seems."

Naomh's eyes snapped open. "Why would she do such a thing?"

Kai dropped into the nearby chair. Had he been alone, he

would have put his head in his hands. "To save me, apparently. Allafon would have murdered me if the ruse had been discovered."

His father muttered a curse, but Kai was too afraid to ask if it was directed toward Allafon—or at him.

～

WHEN KEZARI and Ren reached the door of Lyr's library, a guard stopped them. "Pardon me," the woman said. "I am tasked with escorting Lord Egrenneth to his guest tower."

The other dragon smiled wryly. "For containment, I suspect."

"You would have to ask the Myern," the guard replied, her demeanor neutral. "He gave me no orders in that regard."

"I'm sure he knows he doesn't need to. I can take a hint." He inclined his head at Kezari. "Until later."

But even after Ren and the guard departed, Kezari hesitated. Lyr obviously wanted to speak to her alone—or at least without Egrenneth. Was he angry at her for bringing the elder dragon back with her? She hadn't thought to ask permission, and she was well aware how much leaders hated that. But he shouldn't have expected anything else, should he? Her nature was hardly a mystery at this point.

Steeling her spine, she knocked on the door, and at Lyr's immediate call to enter, she strode through with no sign of her initial hesitation. It would do no good to appear weak or uncertain. She'd followed the best course for the dragons, and she'd even remembered to consider the elves, too. She shouldn't be faulted for that.

Instead of awaiting her in front of his desk, he sat behind it. A book was open atop a small stack of the papers as though he'd been working on something else when he'd stopped to read. Was *Lyr* avoiding work? But then she remembered the journal he'd mentioned. Perhaps he had found something there to warrant this summons.

Kezari halted in front of his desk. "You wished to speak with me?"

Frowning slightly, Lyr placed a marker between the pages of the book. "Yes, but I assure you that it's nothing you've done. If you're concerned I'll be upset that you brought Lord Egrenneth here, don't be. It saved us another journey."

"You would have requested him?" she asked, her brows rising.

"More likely Caeregas, but you are a better judge of which brother the dragons most need than I am." Lyr ran his finger over one of the pages. "Either would work as far as I'm concerned. Did you know their father was king of *all* the dragons before some chose to travel here with my ancestors? He remained such on Earth and even chose the new royal family here when we decided to settle on this world. That's why he was so integral to the treaty's success."

Kezari had the sudden urge to snatch the book away so she could read about the legendary dragon for herself. Deyriglair— The Peacebringer. But little was known about him aside from his help in securing the treaty, for many records had been lost in the difficult journey to find a new home. The elves might say the dragons had "flown off to the Isle," but it was far more complicated and painful than that.

"I did not know," she simply replied. Lyr had enough to read without an extended history lesson on the dragons' migration, although recounting what she'd heard of the tale to Lynia might be a good idea. Once they were less busy, of course.

"If Osieren's musings are correct, that gives Egrenneth power in this situation," Lyr said. "He could rightfully claim rule through his bloodline. But Kezari...what do you think of him? Will this prove a boon or a disaster?"

Before Ren's attempt at explaining his rude behavior, her answer would have been succinct and pithy. Possibly using a few choice words in her native language that she would rather not translate. But although she still didn't like the other dragon, she now understood him better. He'd lost all purpose and meaning over the millennia; this challenge had sparked his heart anew. She'd had a similar drive after she'd detected the poison, and she'd arrived at Braelyn with a similar obnoxiousness.

"I can't answer the last question, really," Kezari said slowly, choosing her words with care. "On a personal level, I would happily toss his trussed body from the observation tower and smile as it bounced. But it was his very fierceness that prompted me to choose him. The complacent dragons on the Isle need someone to provoke them, and he will not cower despite the odds. For the dragons there, that is a boon. But for us? I cannot guarantee he won't cause future trouble for you or the kingdom."

Lyr rested his steepled fingers against his chin. "Hmm."

What was that supposed to mean? Did he agree with her summary or not? Or maybe he was concerned about her loyalties. "I will not side with them," Kezari said quickly. "Here, I have my mate, my *skizik*, a future home, and a job. Even friends, perhaps. I do want to travel to the Isle to save the younglings and to retrieve my hoard, but I will return here when that is done."

"I was merely thinking, Kezari," Lyr said with a low chuckle. "There's no need to defend yourself. But what was that about your hoard? I thought it was forfeit."

"It should not have been." She tried not to let her mind linger on the details, lest she fall back into anger. "According to both Caeregas and Egrenneth, claiming another's hoard is a grave offense. I suppose Ren's help with the reclamation is one solid reason not to shove him off the tower."

Lyr smiled. "Indeed. As for the rest, I suppose only time will tell. There will be chaos enough when I recommend changes to the treaty. I'll be chatting informally with Ralan about that before I broach this with the king."

She'd wondered earlier, but... "Truly?"

"Oh, yes." Lyr's smile became more of a grimace. "I'm not even finished with the journal, but I've already seen enough. The terms were far too harsh. Delvian would not yield on some things, despite the queen's command."

"He disobeyed the queen during negotiations?" It shouldn't come as a surprise, since Kezari had disobeyed her own, but the elves seemed far more...rule-bound. "And he remained the Myern?"

Lyr shook his head. "Recall that he was the queen's own son, and there were far fewer noble families, since many of the sub-branches hadn't been established yet. I have to wonder how many other ways he abused that power. And against whom. There could be a good reason why some of the other founding families have greeted me with greater reserve than others. But that's irrelevant to the current issue."

Perhaps so, but Lyr's concern about the overall problem warmed her in a way she couldn't define. Had she grown so accustomed to complacent injustice? Or maybe *complicit* was a better word. Far too many of the dragons were willing to participate, so long as it benefited them. *They* wouldn't be sitting here wondering if their ancestors had been fair.

"What changes are you considering?" she ventured to ask.

Lyr frowned thoughtfully. "As I've yet to make any decisions, I hesitate to say. But passage here for any of the fae living on the Isle for certain, and likely a method for other dragons to become a citizen as you have. Otherwise...I don't know. Greater access to the portal seems reasonable, but there are many complexities, especially with the state of modern Earth. It would be unconscionable to release countless dragons into a world that no longer believes in them, and with no preparation on either side's part."

After what she'd seen of Earth, the mental image that conjured had her nodding at once. "That would be a nightmare. But this may be one way that Egrenneth is a boon. He has apparently walked Earth in his humanoid form for millennia, so he'll be well-equipped for such preparation."

"I appreciate your insight, Kezari," Lyr said. His sigh fluttered the book's pages. "In any case, I'm sure we'll speak of this again in the future. I have much to consider."

That was the beginning of a dismissal—she *was* learning some of their cues. "If that is all, I will go rest with my mate now."

Lyr inclined his head. "I believe he is in the observation tower."

Kezari could feel that for herself, but it was polite of the Myern to tell her, nonetheless. "Thank you. Even if I'm not grateful for another walk through the blasted snow. Why you haven't created tunnels connecting the buildings is beyond me."

"The cost of so many mages to carve out and then maintain..." He straightened, a look of surprise crossing his face. "Ah, but a talented earth dragon would be able to do such a task with far more ease. I believe you may have hit upon your next job, once the other tasks are complete."

*Scratched by my own talon,* Kezari muttered to herself.

Though really, she didn't mind. Another reason to belong and a way to avoid the horrible snow—both would make the effort worth the trouble.

# CHAPTER THIRTY-TWO

*E*ven stirring from a deep sleep, Tynan recognized Kezari when she tucked herself against his back. He sighed with pleasure as she curled her arm around his waist, her warm breath brushing his neck. The sensation was nearly ticklish, but he didn't mind. It simply meant that she was there.

"I assume no one died," he murmured.

She snorted. "It was close, but we managed to hunt without killing each other."

He smiled softly at the annoyed indignation in her voice. He'd felt her surges of anger along their link, tiny tremors that shook him periodically from sleep. But somehow, they hadn't caused him the turmoil they once would have. Those little hints of emotion had become more of a comfort, another sign that she was near and well.

Angry, maybe, but well.

Blessed Lady, but his body was still so heavy. "How long have I slept?"

"It's only sunset," she replied. "We've time until dinner, and I want to rest. Go back to sleep."

He wrapped his hand around hers where it rested against his chest and let himself drift.

When he came to awareness again, the room was completely dark, and Kezari was breathing slowly and steadily behind him. He should activate one of the mage globes and check the water clock, but he couldn't bring himself to care enough. The rest of the world would just have to go on without them for a little bit longer. Once they left, they would be heading into danger, and even if everything went well, there were no guarantees.

Not for them.

He should savor this moment of peace, but dread eroded his contentment like the water dripping down one of the stalactites in Kezari's cave. Or maybe that was too subtle and natural a thing. It was more a scab that he couldn't help but tear open if he moved the wrong way. Every time he thought it had healed, he found that he'd been painfully wrong.

He just couldn't rest easy about their bonding. The simple explanation was that Kezari hadn't completed her part of the bond, but the full truth of any problem was rarely one simple thing. No, in the quiet dark, he could admit what had been bothering him since Egrenneth's revelation in the library: Kezari's dedication to their bonding made no sense. Tynan might no longer fear that she hated him as he'd once believed, but she wasn't in love with him, either. Yet she slept against him so sweetly. Why? She could be anywhere else.

And *why* remain with an elven healer-priest when she could become a dragon queen?

"Because I would soon be executed for murdering the king," she grumbled, startling him. "The dislike I have for him is not the kind that hides attraction. Trust me."

"I didn't know you were awake."

"Surely." Her hand twisted beneath his. "Where is Arneen again?"

Should he laugh or hide? He had the definite desire to do both. "I actually wasn't thinking of you marrying Egrenneth. If enough people on the Isle see that you were right, you could have support for your own sake. But having a Moranaian elf for a mate would be a hindrance."

She remained silent for a moment. "Are you power hungry?"

Tynan frowned into the darkness. "No. Why would you think so?"

"Because you seem rather fixated on rulership. I can't imagine why else you believe I have such a goal."

It wasn't that he thought her power hungry. His fears were more complicated than that, but he couldn't think of a way to explain it that wouldn't see him dropped at Arneen for the gods to sort out. This blend of envy and insecurity and desire undercut everything, and it was insecurity dragging him down the most. Although she'd grown so dear to him in such a short time, there was no reason for *her* to feel the same.

Nevertheless, he wanted her to share his feelings, and he refused to let despair claim him. Maybe it lingered deep, ready to spring out at the slightest weakness, but that dark emotion couldn't stand up to the bludgeon of his hope. If Kezari didn't have a reason to share his feelings, he could give her one. As he would tell one of his patients...he was worthy.

Flawed, but worthy.

Releasing her hand, Tynan rolled over to face her, but he could barely make out her form in the dark. The moons must not have risen or the clouds must be thick, for no hint of light streamed through the windows. With the barest flex of magic, he activated the nearest mage globe just enough to discern detail but not to blind.

Kezari's lips turned down. "I dampened the light on purpose, you know. I sleep best in caves, not out in the open."

"And I wanted to see you." He stroked his finger down her nose in a teasing motion, then ran the pad of his thumb across her full lower lip. "I am *not* accustomed to caves."

Her frown only deepened. "This is not fair."

"What isn't?" he asked, lowering his hand uncertainly.

"I have the urge to mate with you again, but I haven't worked out my temperature yet."

His mind blanked with surprise, but his body responded enthusiastically—and rather inconveniently. "*Clechtan.*"

"I really should have asked King Annoyance, but he'd already criticized enough." Kezari blew out a sharp breath. "Perhaps... perhaps you should start preparing for our journey while I sink into a trance and try to figure it out. Otherwise..."

Otherwise. He had plenty of mental images about the forms *that* could take.

"I suppose it would be best," he said.

But he could only stare into her eyes, molten gold with her desire. He slipped his hands to her face, his thumbs caressing her cheeks as he lowered his head to kiss her. Not with the heat of his body, though—this was the tenderness welling in his heart.

Kezari gasped as his lips left hers, and now, he could barely discern the glow of her irises in her wide eyes. "Tynan."

At his wrist, he could feel the way her pulse pounded frantically at her throat, and her nipple had hardened beneath his arm. He was not helping. A reckless, possessive part of him didn't care —he could take and she would give. But she had expressed her feelings on the matter of children, and he would not override it. He'd seen enough how such things brought pain.

Groaning, he rolled away from her and lurched to his feet. With his back to her and his eyes closed, he cycled through a litany of unpleasant thoughts until walking would no longer be so... uncomfortable. But he didn't dare look over his shoulder at the way she sprawled—no. Not the best line of thought to follow.

Focus on the necessary tasks at hand. Travel. What would he have to do for travel?

He needed to wear his sturdiest, warmest clothing. And not his priest's robes, either. Not only would they be uncomfortable during the long flight, but they might not be useful. Here, they announced his profession, which granted a certain level of respect, but that probably wouldn't be the case on the Isle. The dragons didn't follow the same religion, and he had no idea what religion the fae there followed. Yes, simple clothes would be best.

What else might he need? He had yet to unpack the small bag of healing and survival supplies from their last journey, so he only had to grab that on the way out. He wouldn't carry a weapon, except for perhaps a knife. He wasn't trained in sword or bow, and his Kezari was better protection than either. What else? He couldn't think of a single thing to pack.

But if he were to stop himself from turning back to their bed, he had to do something, and there was one essential he would not forget again—his prayers. He may not ever learn if he'd angered Lady Bera, but he would not risk the possibility of offending Her again. She'd been with him during his darkest moments, and he would never abandon Her.

He grabbed his bag and headed toward the window seat to create an impromptu altar.

KEZARI COULDN'T FOCUS, much less figure out how to shift her temperature. Her heart raced like frenzied prey, and her body was aflame with desire—not natural heat. But more distracting by far was the tenderness welling within her. Had she ever been looked at as though she were treasure? She'd almost pounced on the man again, and forget the consequences.

She had to cool her desire if she hoped to accomplish anything. But even after naming every gemstone she'd ever seen until her mind was clear and her heart rate steady, she struggled to sink within herself well enough to find the source of her inner heat. Perhaps the bed was a poor place to meditate?

Quietly, she slipped down to the stone floor, resting her back against the opaque, crystalline wall. Tynan was setting up candles on the bench seat across the room, but his movements didn't falter enough to suggest that he'd noticed her shift in position. Good. She pinched her eyes closed before the sight of him prompted another gemstone recitation and connected with the stone behind and beneath her.

It wasn't the same as joining with her cave, not by any means, but the tower at least connected with the bedrock deep beneath the soil. There was enough resonance. Should she shift to dragon form? But no. That could be the wrong approach. Her desire for mating began in this body, and she'd already tried to adjust her temperature earlier when she'd been in dragon form.

She must have searched her body forever before she finally stumbled upon the trigger within herself. Unfortunately, it was no instant thing. It required pressure and intent, a constant prodding that warmed her by agonizingly slow degrees. But little by little, her body flushed with heat until she finally had to magic away the extra clothing she'd added beneath her thin gown.

The stone warmed with her skin until she could almost imagine she was cradled in a narrow cave. A dragon's cave was always that little bit hotter than normal, after all, especially if the chamber was small enough to retain more body heat. All she needed now were her wings to curl around her.

So peaceful had she grown that the sudden mental push caught her by surprise—but not for long. Scowling, Kezari strengthened her shielding against Tebzn at once. She'd forgotten her cousin would be able to reach her more easily outside the greater protections of the shielded cave. After Kezari's last threat, she could hardly believe the wyrm had dared to contact her at all.

Kezari opened her mind the slightest amount. *"I do not wish to kill my kin, no matter what you've done. But you test my patience."*

*"I'll give you the hoard if I must,"* Tebzn practically shrieked. *"Just come. Now. Please come."*

If her cousin was willing to relinquish her ill-gained goods, there must be disaster, indeed. *"Slow down. What has you in such a panic?"*

*"The dragonlings attacked again. The injured are everywhere."*

Images came with the words—the fae village aflame, bodies

scattered, even a fallen dragon. Kezari's stomach lurched. *"How many dead?"*

*"I don't know. I don't know. I fled to my cave."* Of course she had. *"The queen has ordered a full attack. Not to capture. To kill. Any of the renegades are to be killed on sight, youngling or not. Why would she do such a thing?"*

The lurch in her stomach became a full-on roil. *"I will fly your way soon, but I am uncertain I can stop this."*

*"Hurry,"* Tebzn insisted.

Kezari severed the link without reply, for she didn't want her thoughts to trickle through. Though something within her had wanted to console Tebzn by telling her of Ren, Kezari didn't dare. There was no way to know whether her deceitful cousin would go straight to the queen, and the ancient dragon's presence would be best as a surprise.

Killing the dragonlings. Kezari shuddered, nearly losing grip of her newfound heat. They didn't have time for elaborate plans; they needed to leave. She opened her eyes to call for Tynan, but he knelt before his little altar, clearly deep in prayer. Her heart raced again, though not in pleasure. How long should she give him?

The time it took her to contact her *skizik*, at least. What would Aris say? She hadn't had a chance to talk to him about going to the Isle, and there were no guarantees he would agree. Although his magic would be a boon, she wouldn't force him. He'd suffered too much in Perim's little cave of torture.

Kezari gave him a mental nudge and then waited.

It didn't take long. *"What's wrong, Kezari?"*

*"A message from Tebzn."* Quickly, she shared what she'd learned, and his horror joined with hers through their mental link. *"I hate to ask this, but I must. Are you recovered enough to go?"*

His revulsion hit her like a blow. *"I...I don't know. And there's Selia. Iren. I..."*

She should have considered his family. No, this was too much. *"You should stay, skizik. Dealing with the wall on Earth was enough danger for one with young. I wasn't thinking."*

*"I will discuss this with Selia,"* Aris sent. *"And do some soul-searching myself."*

*"I've thought better of this. You should not—"*

*"You've always been there for me, Kezari,"* he interrupted firmly. *"I promise to work within my own tolerances, but I will not let this go without serious thought."*

And as she had with Tebzn, he cut off the mental link.

~

IF RALAN CIRCLED her one more time, Cora was going to puke. "Would you stand still? Please?"

It wasn't a particularly nice "please," a point Ralan was wise enough to note. He came to an immediate halt, but his distant, almost dazed expression brought her a new worry. He wasn't pacing around the sitting room for nothing. Had he had a disturbing prophecy, or was there another problem?

"Did something happen when you slipped over to Earth?" Cora asked. "Did the bank catch on to Delbin using your debit card before you could add him? Or maybe a new tabloid story speculating about you and Eri? Maybe you should stop pacing and start talking."

Ralan's eyes sharpened on her face, and he frowned. "You're pale."

"Yes, well, I was already a little queasy, and then *someone* kept pacing circles around my chair," she said archly. "So go grab my potion and then tell me what's wrong."

Nodding, Ralan hurried into their bedroom, returning a moment later with the vial Lial had given her for her morning—more like all day—sickness. She would have retrieved it herself if movement wouldn't have threatened her stomach further. Gods, she would be happy when this part was over. She was around four Moranaian months pregnant, so a little over two and a half on Earth. Surely, the sick part would be over soon.

Cora took a sip of potion and closed her eyes for a moment

while it worked its magic. Blessedly, it was quick. By the time Ralan sat down in the seat beside her, looking at him no longer made her want to vomit—a thought that made her lips quirk up. Really, that sounded far worse than she'd meant it, though in a sense, her current state was partly his fault.

"I get the distinct feeling I don't want to connect with your thoughts," Ralan said wryly.

She chuckled. "Probably not. But I'm not upset at you, so nothing deadly."

He reached for her hand, twining their fingers together between their chairs. "I'm sorry I made you ill with my pacing. It wasn't anything I saw on Earth. Nothing on that trip, at least. The futures..."

"Prophecies, then." Her heart twisted at the turmoil on his face. "Can you tell me?"

"For the most part, I can't tell *me*," he grumbled. "Remember when I said dragons cause me problems in that regard? Well, this involves a fuckton of them."

She shouldn't smile, but his curse reminded her fondly of her time on Earth and the cleverness of human language. At his lifted brow, she smoothed her expression. "Sorry. A fuckton, huh? Metric or standard?"

Ralan snorted. "Whichever is bigger. Trust me, I want to laugh, but I'm not joking. I'm sure everyone is expecting me to pop over and tell them the best thing to do, but there are a good thirty future strands before Kezari and Egrenneth even leave. Who should go with them? I don't know. They're flying into... hundreds of dragons. Maybe thousands? I can't even begin to count them, much less all the possible strands. Yet at the same time, I know it's important, because my Sight is being inundated with the coming conflict."

A major event that her bonded couldn't predict—his favorite. It was a wonder Eri hadn't gotten involved. Speaking of... "Where's Eri?"

"Playing with Iren," he answered at once. "I believe he wanted to show her some illusions Selia taught him to make. And before you ask, she doesn't appear to be as affected as I am. Which means the goddess is shielding her."

"Which also means there is the potential for dark happenings," Cora added, frowning.

"Oh!" Ralan squeezed her hand, drawing her gaze. "Tell Maddy to close the shop two Saturdays from now, if she wasn't planning to already. She should have her father close the jewelry store, too."

Alarm coursed through her. "Why?"

"There's a protest planned that day. A group demanding answers about magic." The muscle in his jaw twitched. "It will likely be uneventful, but there's a chance for things to go poorly. I need to contact Dria about ways to avert some of those, but I've been trying to get a clearer picture. Regardless, I would recommend anyone with non-human blood stay clear of the area."

Alarm turned chill with fear. "A protest concerning magic? Oh, no."

"Yeah," Ralan replied, scrubbing wearily at his face. They'd both lived on Earth for enough centuries to have seen where that could go. "But I suppose it has been too quiet after the magical energy returned. So many things could topple Earth from peace into chaos that it's impossible to predict which event will spark it. Just...talk to Maddy. It might be an excellent time for her and Anna to join Fen at the Unseelie palace for an extended trip."

The edge to that last statement suggested it was more than an idle suggestion, but for whatever reason, he thought it best not to explain. If she wanted to hear another diatribe on how knowledge of the future could affect it, she could ask.

Yeah, she would pass on that.

"Will do."

Ralan released her hand and shoved to his feet with a sigh. "And I need to contact my father before we walk over for dinner. Lyr is going to ask me about a relative of his whom I've never heard of, and I don't feel like searching the strands for the eventual answer. At this point it would probably be obscured by hordes of dragons. Damn dragons."

He stomped into their bedroom where they kept the mirror that connected directly to the palace, and she smiled after him despite the worry his words had caused. Being bonded to a seer was...unusual, but she was beginning to adapt. When it didn't end in her standing in the cold for hours, anyway. At least this latest prophecy hadn't included *that*.

With her own sigh, she headed for the small mirror that she used to contact Maddy. A rough time calculation told her it was probably the middle of the night there, but she had an uneasy feeling that she shouldn't wait. Ralan wouldn't have told her now if it wasn't important. Ah well. Maddy was young enough to deal with a little lost sleep.

# CHAPTER THIRTY-THREE

Once Tynan had completed his standard prayers, he paused, uncertain precisely what to ask for. He'd already expressed regret for forgetting to pray before his last mission, and he'd requested strength and aid during their coming journey to the Isle. There shouldn't be anything else, yet the comforting ritual felt somehow incomplete.

Perhaps part of him hoped She would speak to him again. But did he really deserve such regard? He was relatively new to the priesthood in comparison to his peers, and he was far from the most important. That She had taken any interest in him at all was honor enough. With faithful service, he might earn an increase in favor.

Tynan opened his eyes as he gave one final prayer of thanksgiving, then began snuffing out the candles with a hint of magic. He saved Lady Bera's for last. The single flame reflected against the window in a mesmerizing dance, and he had to jerk his gaze away before he lingered. Lady forgive him, but he could not tarry. It couldn't be long until they needed to leave.

Suddenly, his vision flashed white. *"LONG HAVE I CARED FOR YOU AND LONG WILL I STILL, BUT YOU MUST*

*SEEK YOUR OWN STRENGTH. DO NOT BE COWED BY THE COMING STORM."*

*"Have you...have you been bolstering my shields, my lady?"* he ventured.

*"ONLY WITH YOUR OWN POWER."* The goddess hesitated, a universe of energy in the weighted pause. *"ELF AND DRAGON AND FAE, ALL MUST STAND TOGETHER. MEDIATE. AND DO WHAT YOU MUST TO GUARD YOURSELF AND YOUR ALLIES. I WILL MEET THE SOULS OF THE FALLEN."*

As abruptly as She had appeared, the goddess was gone, but although Her presence cut off, Tynan's vision didn't quite clear. It rather darkened.

Until it cut to black.

~

ONE MOMENT, her mate was extinguishing candles; the next, he crumpled.

With a furious cry, Kezari darted across the room, but she wasn't fast enough to catch Tynan before he hit the ground. She knelt at his side and leaned over him, her focus instantly on his head. Had he hit it against the window seat as he fell? But a quick probe found no injury. No blood. No forming knots. She rolled him to his back and checked his side.

As far as she could tell...clear.

Should she call for Lial? Dispelling the spell dimming the light, she peered out the window at the sky and saw silvery moonlight, not pitch-black darkness or snow. If the trails had been cleared, they should still be passable. Surely, the healer was accustomed to such summons and could navigate here in these conditions.

"Kezari?"

Her eyes snapped down at her mate's soft voice to find him blinking up at her. "I thought you were *praying*," she said. A bit too forcefully, but she couldn't stop the words from pouring out. "What kind of religion do you elves practice to require such a thing? Do these gods steal your energy?"

"Kezari," Tynan said again, amusement entering his voice this time. "Calm down. This isn't a normal part of prayer. The goddess spoke to me, longer this time. My mind was not prepared for the force."

"You could have hurt yourself," she insisted. She ran her fingers through his hair, searching his scalp again.

He grabbed her wrist. "I'm fine. The goddess of healing would not leave her priest injured from a communication mishap."

Though he was clearly correct, Kezari couldn't slow the pounding of her heart. His religion was a remote thing to her, something she didn't understand but accepted. It had never occurred to her that it might take him from her. What if his goddess didn't heal him? What if she used and discarded him at some godly whim?

"Did she demand something of you?" Kezari asked.

"Yes and no." He frowned up at her. "Could I sit up?"

"Oh!" she exclaimed, leaning back. "Sorry."

Tynan shoved himself to a sitting position, his legs crossed and his hands in his lap—until he reached out and linked their fingers. "Lady Bera bid me to mediate between the elves, dragons, and fae. I'm assuming she means the fae still on the Isle, but I'm not positive. However, She also told me to do what I must on the mission. She didn't exactly tell me I could kill if necessary...but at the same time, She did. Whatever we are facing on the Isle, it can't be good."

If a goddess of life and death said such a thing, then no, it wasn't good, especially combined with Tebzn's latest call. Kezari's skin itched with a hint of scales. "My cousin dared contact me again. There was another attack on the village, and the queen has ordered any of the maddened dragons executed if found. Even the dragonlings."

He blanched. "But that's..."

"Yes." She tugged at his hands. "We need to go retrieve Egrenneth. I spoke to Aris, but when I thought of Iren, I urged him to stay. We are likely to be on our own."

Tynan kissed her fingers before releasing her. "We'll make do."

She picked up one of their packs and waited as he checked his altar. Since all the candles were already extinguished, he only grabbed his little pouch of herbs. Kezari smiled. She had to admit that she was growing fond of the scent herself.

They would need all the comfort they could get.

ARIS HAD to make a decision quickly, but it was no easy matter.

Though Kezari had changed her mind and told him to stay here, he couldn't shake the feeling that he needed to be there. But how could he face that awful place again? Even if he avoided the cave where he'd been held, just being there could shatter his sanity once more. Had he worked hard enough? Healed enough?

"Oh, that looks just like a *camahr*," Eri cried, and Aris smiled at her joy over Iren's illusion.

His son's talent for that was modest, but he delighted in showing off each new creation he mastered. That morning, Selia had helped him create a passable *camahr* and a variety of early winter flowers she'd had him study in the garden a couple of weeks back. He'd already shown Eri enough to fill a garden of his own, if what he'd created was truly real.

How could Aris leave his son again?

Selia sat down beside him, and for a moment, they watched the children on the other side of the sitting room. But finally, she spoke. "This is hard. I...I can't bring myself to offer an opinion either way. The last time I urged you to go on a journey..."

His ship had wrecked, and he'd washed up on the Isle of Dragons, only to be bound and tortured by his potential soulbonded. Oh, how he knew. But it wasn't Selia's fault. She'd merely encouraged him on his explorations.

"I've told you I do not blame you," he murmured.

"I know." Her hand settled just above his knee. "Is it strange that I want to go with you? Maybe it's anxiety or the urge to protect you, but it's strong, regardless. My magic could be useful."

Aris stared at her. "What?"

Her gaze remained on Iren. "It's foolish. One of us should stay, and you're Kezari's *skizik*. If there were imminent danger, like the collapse of Earth's wall, it would make sense, but it's rare enough for parents with young children to undertake something so risky even then. I doubt Lyr would approve it."

He didn't know what to say to that. It *was* rare, and Lyr seemed especially conscious of the risk. Not to mention that Aris hadn't decided if he should go. Had he? Maybe Selia knew him better than he knew himself. He simply couldn't stop thinking about how Kezari might need his aid. She'd pulled him from literal torment to become family.

But he had family here, too.

Iren's illusion faded, but instead of casting another, he met Aris's eyes. "You must go, *Onaial*," his boy said, softly but firmly. "I don't want you to, but honor demands it. You'd be able to detect every lifeform in the area, right? Tracking down dragonlings and the injured would be easier with you there. And maybe you could purge whatever drove them wild."

"The surge of energy from the wall's collapse did it, Kezari said. Which..." Realization struck with sudden force. Could some of the poison have reached them through their link with Earth before everything had been purged? "Gods. I do have to go."

Eri shifted in her seat, and her serious expression made his heart thump. How had he forgotten the young seer was there? "Dragons make things hard to See," she said, almost sadly. "It's really not worth trying, but I want to. Iren's going to be so worried. Ugh. I can't even tell if Lady Selia is going. Probably not.

But maybe? If I try to search so many strands again, the goddess is going to put me on time out."

Aris wasn't positive what a "time out" was since it was an Earth term, but he could take a guess—blocked Sight. The little girl had stepped in far too often during other situations, so he didn't want to think about how many possibilities there were now if exploring them would get her in trouble with the goddess of time. It seemed a very high threshold.

"It's fine, Eri," Iren said. "I didn't become your friend to hear about the future. You never have to tell me anything."

A smile broke across the little girl's face, and Aris's heart warmed with pride. Selia had done such a fine job raising their son during the years he'd been captured. Iren was only eleven, but it was already obvious that he would grow into a fine man. Whatever happened on this mission, Aris would do his best to return in one piece. He wanted to be here to see for himself the man his son would become.

TYNAN'S HEAD still rang a little with the remnants of the goddess's favor, but he felt stronger, too. Yes, she'd bolstered his shields—with his own power. That meant everything he needed for this mission was already within him, waiting for him to grasp it. All his life, he'd been afraid to access the full extent of his magic, and that had been what had stood between him and complete control.

Even hurrying to follow Kezari's near-dash across the slippery paths couldn't prevent him from chuckling at himself. Wasn't that so like the advice he would give one of his own patients? *Don't let fear hold you back. Reach for your own power. Create new memories to help the mind form new, more positive channels of thought.* All of which he'd failed to do, or he would have more tools to fight against unexpected surges.

Many expected healers to be the healthiest in all ways, but

healers were usually the worst at seeing—and treating—problems for themselves. A joke immemorial.

"*Sbezie*, let's go," Kezari called over her shoulder. "Ponder later."

Tynan frowned at her back all the way through the door and beyond the entrance to the library. What in Arneen had she called him? During his training, he'd spell-learned quite a few languages, but he'd never met anyone—besides Kezari, of course—who knew the dragon tongue. Was *sbezie* a curse, endearment, nickname? Maybe it actually meant "let's go," and she'd merely translated it for him.

She snorted. "It means 'mate,' which I'd thought would be obvious."

She wasn't looking his way, but he lifted his brows anyway. "Obvious how?"

"It's similar enough to *skizik*, isn't it? And that's the word for a magic partner."

Tynan shook his head at that logic. Aside from a few shared letters, he didn't find them particularly similar at all, but there was no use arguing the point. Why would he? She'd called him mate in her own language, which felt far more...intimate. Closer to the heart. Pleasure spread through him at the thought of that.

They rushed into the dining room, but Kezari stopped so quickly that Tynan almost crashed into her. Had something horrible happened? He moved around her, only to find that the table was close to empty. Of all the usual guests, three people were there—Lyr, Meli, and Arlyn. None of them appeared distressed, though. He opened his shields and found mostly surprise.

"Where is everyone?" Kezari asked.

Lyr smiled. "Kai is still at the healing tower with his father, and Lynia returned there to be with Lial. Otherwise, I have no idea. But we have a few moments yet."

A peek at the water clock showed that it was a quarter past the mark. "Did the usual time change?"

"No, but on chaotic days like today, I abandon all thoughts of punctuality," Lyr said wryly. "Not even our guest has arrived with the guard I sent to invite him, nor have I received a refusal."

Kezari stiffened. "Are you sure he is still here?"

"According to the estate key, yes," Lyr said, lifting his shoulder in a slight shrug. "Are you going to sit?"

A visible tremor went through Kezari, and Tynan settled his hand soothingly on her lower back. "We must go," she said. "I heard from my cousin again, and the news isn't good."

"Of course it isn't," Arlyn muttered, and across from her, Meli sighed.

Lyr didn't so much as blink. "Go ahead and tell me."

As Kezari recounted the full conversation, Tynan's own ire rose at hearing the details spelled out. Why would the queen have gone to such extremes? There could be no possible excuse. Not even protecting the fae village could justify murdering innocent young.

The Myern vehemently agreed. "I'll have Egrenneth summoned with more urgency," Lyr concluded. "Is Aris going to accompany you?"

"I...don't know. Though I told him he shouldn't, he wanted to consider the matter," Kezari replied. Her gaze shifted to the place where Aris usually sat, and Tynan's heart twisted at her obvious sadness. "I'd hoped he would be here already, but I suppose he's still deciding."

It would be no easy choice for the life mage. Had there been more time, Tynan would have suggested a consultation. They could have discussed the matter in the training room, where they might explore any potential difficulties while under the protection of that room's strong shielding. Unfortunately, that wasn't possible. If Aris did come along, the only time they would have to prepare was during the flight across the ocean.

Provided Tynan was in any shape to help at all on his first time in the sky.

First portals, now flying. He gave a little shudder.

Kezari frowned at the motion, but voices echoed into the

room a couple of drips before chaos descended. Ralan, Cora, Eri, Iren, Selia, and lastly Aris all streamed through the door in a chattering line, and the room suddenly felt tiny despite the walls full of windows that made the space seem like part of the snowy night. But only Ralan, Cora, and Eri took their places at the table.

It appeared to be time for Aris's decision—and it didn't take long to deliver.

"I'm going," Aris said, almost stubbornly.

Kezari's response clarified why. "No. You have young to consider."

"As do a great many dragons."

Tynan studied Aris's face as the two of them bickered. There was fear there, but it was a healthy one, no small amount of reasoned calculation in the mix. The life mage fully understood the risks, and he'd accepted them. Did that guarantee success? No. But that awareness heightened the chances that he would withstand the worst of the trip.

"He should come with us," Tynan said, interrupting one of Kezari's retorts and earning himself a glare. "I'm sorry, but I think it is time. Perhaps he needs to face the Isle as much as you do. Besides, his family stands here in support."

Selia nodded. "I thought about offering my services as a mage, myself. I'm still not certain that I shouldn't."

"No," Ralan said, earning everyone's immediate attention. But just as Tynan was about to look away, the prince groaned. "Maybe? Fucking dragons."

Even without their bond, Tynan would have felt the way Kezari bristled beside him. Quickly, he rubbed a circle along her lower back. "It sounds like your options are open," he said politely to Selia.

He hadn't intended it to be funny, but the observation earned a laugh. An edgy one, to be sure, but the tension in the room eased a notch.

Still chuckling, Selia drew something from her pocket. Or two somethings, he saw when she opened her hand—a crystal and a necklace. "I made these for you," she said to Aris. First, she lifted the crystal. "This holds my dragon-immobilizing spell, but there's only enough energy for a couple of uses."

"I suppose freezing two dragons is better than none," the life mage answered with a smile.

"Oh, it puts out a rather large field. Kezari should fly a good distance away if you need to use it." Then Selia held up the necklace, the blue stone on the end swaying gently. "This activates a portal home. I set the terminus in the training room, and only your energy can trigger it."

Tynan's breath caught as she draped it around Aris's neck and smoothed the chain against his chest. It was plain to him why she had done it—so that Aris would never be stranded far from home again. Tenderness and love and healing filled the room like a balm, and for one brief moment, they all reveled in it.

Then Lyr stood up, so quickly his chair scraped across the wood. "Well, then. According to the guard, our guest decided to shift to dragon form in the front clearing. Since I was going to offer the local gate to portal up to a closer estate, perhaps we should stop him from flying away."

Kezari muttered a dragon-sounding word that undoubtedly *was* a curse before they all sprang into action.

## CHAPTER THIRTY-FOUR

If that obnoxious reptile had deceived her, Kezari would hunt him down and make him pay. And to think that she'd been eager to meet the ancient dragons of Earth. What a terrible waste of enthusiasm that had been! She would have done better to remain on Moranaia all along.

"I'll contact Lord Ikwen, the Botsal of Tasan," Lyr said as they neared the door. "Meet me at the interior gate."

She didn't know who or what any of that was, and she wasn't going to stop to ask. They needed to move faster. Glancing back from the doorway, she saw Aris hugging his son close as he bid his family farewell. She couldn't begrudge him that. Her gaze landed on Tynan, who'd followed Lyr through first. Somehow, the thought of leaving him without so much as an embrace twisted her insides with unhappiness and revulsion.

No, she couldn't begrudge her *skizik* that time.

They were nearly to the front door when Aris caught up to them, a bag slung over his shoulder to rest against his sword. "Sorry," he whispered.

Kezari smiled at him. "Don't be."

But any tenderness that had stirred in her evaporated at the sight of the massive red dragon at the edge of the ridge. What was he thinking? A line of *sonal* stood between him and the estate, their arrows trained on any soft spot in range. No doubt, there were more guardians hidden in the trees on the edge of the clearing. While most of the arrows would bounce off of Ren's scales if fired, the elven warriors were unlikely to be ignorant of how to kill a dragon. No doubt their ancestors had passed along their war-gained attack methods as part of general training.

"Do you want to be king, or do you want to be dead?" Kezari called as she and Tynan approached the line of *sonal*.

Kera, the new captain of the guard after Koranel's recent removal, intercepted them a short distance away. "He was told to remain in his guest tower if he did not wish to join the Myern at dinner, but he refused."

"Idiot," Kezari muttered, staring up at Ren. Then she raised her voice again. "What are you doing?"

*"Their cries scrape at me,"* Ren sent abruptly into her head. *"Can't you hear them?"*

Did he mean the younglings? Frowning, Kezari searched within herself, but she didn't find that same call. Only that awful restlessness that had long plagued her. Could the cries he heard be the source of her discomfort? Perhaps part of her had detected the growing distress amongst the dragonlings. Even so, it was nothing like Ren described.

"Come with us," she yelled. "The Myern is securing us passage farther north through the gate. It'll save us nearly two days of flying."

*"I doubt those elves would let me through."*

Kezari pinched her nose and counted to ten. "Fine. You start flying toward whatever you sense. You can meet us there after we've solved the problem."

When steam curled up from his nose, her entire body went on alert. She tended to be resistant bordering on impervious to flame, but a fire dragon's flame burned the hottest. From an ancient, it might actually singe her, and Tynan and Aris wouldn't stand a chance. Resigned, she prepared to shift so she could stand as shield for them.

But suddenly, Ren shrank into his humanoid form. Sighing in relief, Kezari leaned toward Kera. "Let him through. Lyr really did tell us to meet him inside at the gate."

The captain nodded and issued a few short commands. Instantly, the *sonal* slipped back into the trees, fading from sight with impressive ease. It might be night, but that many guards shouldn't have been able to practically disappear. Truly, Ren underestimated them at his own peril.

Kera escorted them to the door, her focus on Ren. As was Kezari's, but for a different reason. The ancient dragon looked... different. Not physically. It was his demeanor. He'd been almost careless in the way he acted before. Curious and energetic, to be fair, but not concerned in quite this way. Now, the intensity of his focus could burn all on its own.

Once inside the entryway, they found Lyr waiting beside the gate. His expression held a dubious quality when he looked at Ren, but he gestured them forward. "Lord Ikwen has granted you passage, but do *not* shift until you are told. We're lucky enough that I'm on friendly terms with him. He is more wary of dragons, his estate being one of the closest to where they might attack. In fact, the Botsal will not be greeting you personally. This is to be passage only, not a diplomatic event."

The fact that the elves would even consider having that kind of event in a crisis...well, she'd promised herself she wouldn't be so rude about their traditions. "Excellent. Thank you," she replied, deciding simpler was better.

Lyr's lips twitched, but he gave no other sign that he was amused by her uncharacteristic restraint. "Lord Egrenneth, will you abide by the rules? I am trusting you not to create an incident for me by shifting before it is allowed."

"And how long will that take?" Ren snapped. "I cannot abide any delay."

"Then stop delaying your agreement," Lyr replied, his tone

level but firm. "A guard will lead you to a clearing just outside the estate to shift. No more, no less."

The ancient dragon scowled. "That leaves the chance for ambush."

*Is he serious?* The stubborn way he scowled at Lyr suggested he was. Now. When they needed to go.

Kezari's restraint cracked like a *daeri*'s spine. "Ren. *Shut up.* You're a guest from Earth, and I'm a Moranaian citizen, as are Tynan and Aris. *Why* would they ambush us? We're the ones heading to the Isle to put a stop to all this trouble. Do you think Lord Whoever wants a bunch of crazed dragons spilling onto his lands? No. They'd far rather us solve the problem for them. So make the promise and get moving, or by the ancestors' desiccated balls, I will leave you here to fend for yourself."

Ren stared at her in shock for several long heartbeats before reluctant admiration crept across his expression. "You'll do, Kezari. Very well. I promise not to shift until given permission." He bowed, his arm sweeping toward the portal. "After you?"

As Lyr activated the proper spell, she caught the sound of Aris's low chuckle, and she felt Tynan's amusement well enough through their bond. But there was no hint of mockery to it. Maybe...camaraderie? Whatever it was, it allowed her to loosen up enough to cast away some of her aggravation. She was even able to walk past Ren without a single verbal barb—or the harsh shove she'd enjoy delivering.

But the other dragon's behavior shifted again as soon as they crossed into the other estate. Once again, he grew sober and self-contained, which really wasn't a bad thing. Perhaps he would remain quiet enough to keep himself out of trouble. Would he be able to avoid shifting? The guard stationed by the door was bundled in so many furs they could almost be mistaken for prey, but Ren didn't act as though he wanted to hunt.

Stark, unadorned stone made up the entire room, a drab place containing only the portal, the guard, and the door. But a quick probe with her magic told her much. These walls were thick, with dirt packed the length of her arm between two layers of solid stone. In a place that used magic to heat and cool their habitations, that meant one thing—it was going to be a frigid wasteland out there. That explained the ridiculously thick clothing.

"Greetings," the guard said. "If you'll follow me?"

By elven standards, the welcome was both curt and undeniably rude. Even Kezari could recognize that, but a quick glance at Aris and Tynan confirmed it. Both men studied the guard with surprise—Tynan's mouth was even slightly agape. She sighed. They were probably going to regret leaving her to do the talking.

"Sure," Kezari said, once again reminding herself that simpler was better.

Without another word, the guard led them through the door. Kezari expected the corridor to be less...utilitarian, but the stone was the same dull, unembellished brown. There weren't even windows. What proper estate looked like this? She hadn't thought anything could be worse than that monstrosity called Oria, but at least that place had windows.

*"Is this a small habitation?"* she sent Tynan.

He lifted a brow her way. *"Absolutely not. Tasan is a major estate guarding one of the nine trees, that of Petoren, God of Winter. Didn't you hear Lord Ikwen's title? Botsal. That's roughly the first duke, you might say."*

Ah. So of the major families along the Callian branch, this one held the first spot, while Lyr was third down as a Myern. But was their god of winter also a god of tedium? *"This does not look like a major estate. Did they drop us into an outbuilding?"*

*"No."* Tynan grinned. *"But I understand where you'd get the idea. I came here once to see the Great Tree during my early training. We entered at a different spot, but it was just as austere. The entire bottom floor is like this. During the height of winter, this level is buried beneath the snow and is largely unused. But on the upper stories, there are windows and fine stonework. At least the small part I saw."*

Kezari had a feeling that she wouldn't get a chance to view

that for herself. The way the guard was dressed, they were surely headed straight out the door to the outside. But how long would it take to get there? Though she felt Ren seething with alertness behind her, she ignored him to peek over at Aris to see how he fared. Pale, probably because of the enclosed nature of the space, but not nearing panic.

"So," Kezari said aloud. "Who's riding whom?"

Missing a step, Tynan jostled into her. "What?"

Did he really think she was talking about mating? She wrinkled her nose at him. "When I'm a *dragon*. Normally, I only carry my *skizik,* but I would do the same for my *sbezie.* However, unless I learn to fashion a new saddle, someone will have to go with Ren."

"You'd better be thinking of design plans," Ren said from behind her. "I carry no one. Ever."

She glanced back at him. "Do Earth dragons never have *skiziks*? I know you take mates, since your brother has one. And you've bragged enough about your beryl."

His glare could cut through the thick stone wall. "Do not speak so casually of that. As for the other, I have no intention of working with a *skizik.* My complement is generally water, and I have no desire to be quenched."

Kezari faced forward again, resolved to ignore him. He thought himself so perfect, so dauntless. Maybe even invulnerable. Well, no one was invulnerable. Why did he even claim to be lonely? He saw a companion as someone who would dampen his glow, not widen his range. Though maybe his concern wasn't entirely unfounded. If she were the mage who had to work with him, she would douse his sorry hide, too.

She was still grumbling to herself when they reached another door. When the guard opened it, Kezari squinted to see what was beyond, but she couldn't make out anything except *white.* Were they going to have to dig themselves out? It wasn't completely solid, though, because cold poured in, so frigid and biting that Kezari recreated the pants and cloak she'd worn before readjusting her temperature. Tynan let out a shocked *oomph*, and Aris groaned.

"I forgot how awful the north is in winter," Aris said.

The guard stared at him with a gaze as cold as the unrelenting white behind them. "You should have better prepared."

Kezari's temper flashed red, and her shoulder blades tingled. She stepped forward, but Tynan's hand wrapped around her wrist to stop her. "We are in a rush to help those in need," he said calmly. "I'm sure Lady Bera will bless all in Tasan who aid in my healing mission to the Isle, whether I help dragon or fae. I go on Her orders, after all."

Simple but effective—what little could be seen of the guard's skin turned a bright pink. "I did not realize you were a priest of Bera."

"It should not matter," Tynan retorted, earning a deeper blush.

After that, the guard hurried to provide Tynan and Aris with several layers of furs and warmer cloaks and then bowed toward the door. As Kezari neared the wall of white, she could finally discern greater details. A hint of translucence, sharp angles... It wasn't a wall—it was a set of stairs carved from solid ice. No wonder it had been white beyond the door. The stairs they climbed ended well above the lintel.

Once they reached the surface, Kezari had to lift her hand above her eyes to block the unexpected brightness. Ice and snow covered the entire landscape, and moonlight reflected off of every surface. Sparse, evergreen-type trees did little to break up the ice-crusted snow stretching as far as the eye could see. Behind them, the more elaborate levels of the estate did rise, just as Tynan had told her.

"I hope it's at least nice here during the summer," Kezari said beneath her breath.

The guard actually smiled a little. "Flowers dot the green fields now buried under the snow, and the temperatures remain pleasant, unlike places farther south."

At least that sounded lovely. Kezari had arrived at Braelyn in the autumn, but if it got as hot in the summer as the others said, she might have to fly up here for relief.

"Where should we shift?" Ren asked, clearly unimpressed.

"Over there." The guard pointed toward a large clearing beside a thin crescent of spear-like trees. "There's enough ice beneath the snow that it should hold your weight. Do your best not to damage it."

Well, then. One more trudge, and they could fly free.

Kezari's heart leapt. She could hardly wait.

FLIGHT WAS AN UNEXPECTED JOY, thrilling Tynan more than he'd expected—even if fear did thrum through him in equal measure.

Ahead, there was nothing before them but the glimmer of moonlight on water. Tynan leaned around Aris to watch the land disappear completely behind them, and his breath caught with wonder. For only a moment. Kezari dipped a little with a gust of wind, and for a terror-filled heartbeat, he scrambled for balance. Aris gripped his upper arm to steady him without comment.

Maybe not quite equal measure.

The double saddle was a little awkward, with Tynan sitting in front of Aris, but Kezari had shaped two distinct scoops so they wouldn't be crushed together with every movement. Aris never would have borne the contact, which might have forced Tynan to use his healing magic—and thus his energy—before they reached the Isle. But there was a downside. Kezari's range of motion was more limited. He'd worried that she wouldn't be able to take off at all.

*"Stop moving,* sbezie,*"* she grumbled. *"This is hard enough thanks to Ren's useless hide. Look at him, soaring as he pleases."*

Tynan couldn't tell a great deal about dragon flight, never having seen it so closely, but Ren did seem to be gliding with a bit more verve. As Tynan watched, the dragon tilted his left wing down, which made him turn away from their path. But then he tipped the other wing down until he circled back to them.

*"I'm surprised he isn't doing flips,"* Kezari added.

Like a bird? That seemed far too difficult at a dragon's size. *"Completely upside down? Is that possible?"*

*"Oh, yes."* Kezari's head bobbed, and the saddle shifted uncomfortably beneath him. *"You seem to fly well enough. Maybe someday I'll take you up alone and show you, since it would be far too risky with more than one rider."*

He couldn't decide if that sounded amazing or horrifying.

They flew in silence for some time, only the occasional slap of wing against air and the whine of wind sounding between them. The light dimmed with the first moon's setting before he finally sensed Aris's presence at the edge of his mind. Tynan took a moment to gather his thoughts and emotions before opening the link.

*"You're doing well,"* Aris sent.

*"Kezari said something similar,"* Tynan replied. *"Though my stomach was uncertain at first."*

Aris's soft chuckle was whipped away with the wind. *"Mine still is at times. But not tonight, somehow. I find I might have preferred that to this growing fear, though. What if this is too much, and I end up causing more harm than good?"*

*"I worry about the same for myself,"* Tynan confessed. *"I can only imagine the amount of emotion that is about to crash into my empathy. But I believe we'll make it, Aris. It's almost as though we've been chosen for this very task."*

A flicker of surprise. *"Do you mean that as a priest? If so... Well, wouldn't that statement mean that the gods chose for us to suffer in preparation of this moment? We couldn't have reached this point without the pain, and I find that difficult to reconcile with my faith."*

Though tempted to give a quick answer, Tynan carefully considered his response. Based on the interference of both Lady

Bera and Lady Megelien, it was clear that at least some of the gods were involved in current events. But responsible for *causing* so much misfortune? Ah, he was tempted to hand them that responsibility, but he couldn't. Generations of choices had led to this point, and he, Aris, and all the others were merely the closest people at hand who might be able to solve the present crisis.

*"Chosen is not the same as created,"* Tynan finally answered. *"Think of all the future strands Ralan and Eri See. Our own actions make those, while the gods seem to simply guide them. If they have picked us, it is because of how we've followed those strands to become stronger. Better suited."*

Aris pondered that for a moment. *"Perhaps you are right, though I suppose none of us can say for sure."*

*"That is true."* Tynan closed his eyes and savored the wind flowing around him, the cold eased to coolness by the two dragons' heat. *"Lady Bera didn't say when She spoke to me, but I do know She is with us. And if you're still worried, I will do my best to bolster you."*

*"Heal any others first,"* Aris said solemnly.

*"No,"* Tynan said at once. *"You are as worthy as anyone else there. I will not shuffle you aside like an afterthought."*

Between their mental link and his empathy, Tynan could feel for himself how conflicted that statement made Aris. Pleased but wary—doubtful but hopeful. It was difficult for someone who'd suffered such trauma to be seen and respected, so Tynan said nothing else on the matter. Insistence would only push his patient away from acceptance.

*"Then will you allow me to provide you with life magic?"* Aris asked.

Tynan's hands clenched on the saddle. Once again, his own advice came back to haunt him. But was this instinctive pinch of fear reasonable? Yes, he'd almost lost control beneath the weight of unexpected life magic while treating Aris, but when Aris had provided that same energy to heal Lord Naomh, Tynan had come to no harm. He simply needed more positive experiences to outweigh the first one.

"*I suppose so,*" Tynan conceded.

Aris laughed again. "*Perhaps we will manage, after all.*"

Kezari turned her head slightly to peer at them. "*Good. Settled. Now I need to pull Ren into a mental link so we can discuss the lay of the land. We'll have hours to ponder what to do with that information and come up with a plan. Unless you think you can sleep? Rest is useful, too.*"

Tynan glanced over her side at the shine of the water, dimming as the second moon neared the horizon, and he shivered at the thought of slipping into its depths. "*I am not skilled enough at this to risk sleep.*"

Planning was definitely favorable to a frigid swim—and subsequent death.

"*As if I would allow such a thing,*" Kezari sent with a snort loud enough to reach him over the sound of the wind.

Then she connected them with the ancient dragon, and the real fun began.

# CHAPTER THIRTY-FIVE

soft thud brought Kai to instant awareness. He straightened in his seat, searching for the cause, but he didn't have far to look. It was his father, who stared at him from bed—*sitting up* in bed, to be precise. That thud must have been his feet hitting the floor.

But wait—Naomh wasn't looking at him at all. His gaze was too distant and unfocused. Could he be moving around in his sleep? Then his father let out a kind of low, choked moan Kai had never heard from him before. Not even when first learning of Kai's birth and Elerie's death. Or apparent death, in this case.

Maybe it was a nightmare.

"Father?" Kai said, rising from his seat.

Naomh flinched, and awareness returned to his gaze. Blinking hard, he swung his legs back onto the bed. "I felt her. Connected with her, if lightly."

He had to mean Elerie. Kai's heart pounded with sudden dread. "Did you wake her?"

"No, thank the gods." His father's hands trembled as he shoved the fall of his pale hair away from his face, highlighting the lines of stark despair. "She is so weak. So broken. I doubt you know how much. But even with my slight healing gift, that connection revealed much."

Kai's pulse pounded in his ears at those pain-filled words, but he forced himself to calm. He had to think rationally. This sounded bad, but Lial had said she would live. Even Ralan had confirmed it. She wouldn't recover to her full strength, but what did that matter? She hadn't died. She was here.

"Are you upset that she will no longer be perfect?" Kai found himself asking.

Naomh's eyes jerked up. "I do not deserve such a foul accusation."

"Then why do you sound as though you're about to go to her funeral pyre?" Kai asked. "I've seen her. I know very well she is weak."

"I'm…" His father sighed. "I'm afraid she won't survive. To lose her again without even being able to speak…"

So it was fear, not certainty. Kai lowered himself back into his seat on shaky legs. "Both Lial and Ralan have said that she will live."

"Yes," Lial said as he rounded the divider. "With much work, provided you do not disturb Lady Elerie too soon."

The healer glared at them both in equal measure, and Kai lifted his hands in innocence. "He woke while I was napping. I would have told him not to check on her yet had I been aware of his intentions."

She…her… Why was it so difficult for him to refer to his mother by name? It was hard to think of her as *Laiala*, and definitely not as *Onaiala*, the more informal and intimate word for mother. But he supposed that until her eyes opened, until they spoke, Elerie was really more theory than fact.

A sad thought.

"It's the middle of the night," Lial fussed as he stood in front of Naomh with a hand outstretched. The blue light of his power glared through the darkened room, but it only lasted a moment. "Your energy is still very low, though you are recovering more quickly than I expected considering how close you were to death."

Naomh frowned. "I would regain my strength even faster if I could be connected to the living earth. Plants in particular."

Lial pointed at the high window, and a few flakes of snow drifted past as if on cue. "Do you work with ice, too? Because all you're connecting with out there is a bed of snow. Even the early winter flowers wouldn't have survived this."

"I should return to my realm, then. I—" His father let out a choked sound. "No, I cannot. That would mean leaving Elerie."

"You'll need a bit more time yet, but you'll have to go soon," Lial said. "It will be weeks before Lady Elerie is well enough to awaken, and that time will be longer if I'm spending all my effort healing you, too. Although from what I understand, you should consider going somewhere besides your realm if you're hoping for regeneration."

Naomh's breath hissed out. "I should speak to Caolte."

"I already told Caolte you are well," Kai said, hoping to ease his mind.

"From here? How?" Lial demanded.

"That is not sufficient," Naomh snapped at the same time.

With a resigned sigh, Kai pulled the small mirror from the pocket of his tunic. "I attuned this in my free time. There isn't a great deal to do while watching over someone who's asleep."

Naomh held out his hand. "Let me contact him."

"No," Lial insisted. "You cannot afford the energy expenditure."

Kai stared at the two, taken aback by his father's forcefulness in the face of Lial's ill temper. If Naomh weren't careful, Lial would render him unconscious for the next week. But would that really be for the best? A moment's reassurance would likely help more than an extended argument or forced sleep.

"I'll hold the link," Kai offered. "Though I'm tired, I'm not drained. But I'll only do it if you promise to keep your conversation short."

"Done," Naomh said. "I give my word to keep the discussion brief."

Lial's eyes narrowed on Kai. "Did I not order rest?"

"Do you think he'll sleep without speaking to Caolte?" Kai asked in turn.

After glaring at him a moment, Lial waved his hand in dismissal. "Fine. I'm returning to bed before another patient shows up. If your father collapses, you're responsible."

Kai waited until he heard Lial stomping up the stairs before he activated the spell on the mirror. "He might not answer," Kai warned. "I don't know what time it is there."

"He'll answer," Naomh said. His gaze sharpened on Kai. "Boredom seems too simple an excuse to expend such effort. Why did you really create that device?"

Kai studied his own tired expression in the mirror. "I knew you would want to talk to Caolte, and I didn't feel like hauling the bigger mirror here from my room. Even with a levitation spell, I'd rather not transport a mirror in the snow."

Which was true—but it wasn't all of the truth. The rest he could hardly explain to himself.

"Hmm," his father said, but before he could question further, the spell clicked into place.

Caolte's face filled the glass. "Has something happened?"

Kai gave his uncle a quick smile before handing the mirror to Naomh. He could no longer see Caolte, but he heard his exclamation of surprise when Naomh righted the glass in front of himself. It might have seemed a foolish luxury to Lial, but Kai knew better. These brothers were closer than some twins he'd met.

"Caolte," Kai's father said. "How is my realm holding up?"

"It...still stands," Caolte answered, the wince clear in his voice. "I have done my best, but I know it is inadequate."

"You knew about Elerie," Naomh said flatly.

"Yes. I learned of her survival during your treatment for the virus." There was such a wealth of emotion in that simple statement that Kai's spark of anger at the answer faded quickly. But his father's frown did not disappear even as his brother continued. "I dared not tell you, not even to inspire you to live. There was too much risk that you would fight to reach her when you weren't able."

"But you did not know before then?" Naomh demanded.

"Upon my honor, I did not."

His expression must have matched his tone, for Kai's father relaxed somewhat. "How bad is the damage to the realm?"

"I recommend building your energy before you return," Caolte answered. "But it is less dire since Queen Ara lent her aid."

Was he talking about Fen's mother, the Unseelie queen? Kai leaned forward a little, though he could hear well enough from where he sat. His father didn't miss the motion. He gave Kai the barest nod.

"Why was the Unseelie queen visiting my home?" Naomh asked.

"To warn. According to her spies, Meren is in Ireland. She believes he's looking for the secondary entrance, which I've been careful to guard." Caolte paused. "It was not an official visit. According to my sister, the queen has been at home getting acquainted with her son and now his mates, who just arrived. There's not a single rumor of her visit here."

Naomh's nod was more pronounced this time. "Good. Their recent troubles are best not entangled with our own. Now, I promised my son I would not speak for long. He holds the link, and I intend to send him to get some rest."

Kai shook his head. "I gave my word—"

"With Naomh this aware, you should go sleep," Caolte said. "Since your task is largely done, I release you from that promise."

"Then we'll all sleep," Naomh proclaimed—and it did sound more like an order than a request.

In only moments, he'd bid Caolte farewell and handed the mirror back to Kai. Naomh fixed Kai with an unyielding look. "I did not jest. I've kept you from your soulbonded for long enough, and I would wager you'd far prefer to sleep with her in your arms."

That he would. "Thank you. I'll leave this mirror on the table since I have one in my room. Send a mental call if you need something, and by the gods, please sleep. Lial is mad enough at me as it is."

Although his father didn't appear fazed by that, Kai gave an uneasy glance toward the stairs once he'd slipped beyond the divider. But there was no healer waiting to eviscerate him. Nothing but quiet emptiness. Lial truly had mellowed after winning Lynia's heart.

A blessing, that.

~

KEZARI FLEW straight toward the dawn as the sun pierced the sky. If not for the light-dampening spell she embedded in her shields, it would have been blinding. Dragons' eyes might be a little more resistant to sunshine, since they were adapted to fly high, but they hadn't exactly evolved to head straight into it without pause.

It wouldn't be long before they spotted land on the horizon. She'd debated stopping at the tiny island to the southwest of the Isle that she'd found while escaping with Aris, but the jaunty joy had long ago left Ren's wingbeats. He'd told her that he'd only taken a few short flights since the return of Earth's magic. Now, the cries he heard had grown intense enough to cut through his exultation at flying completely free for the first time in millennia.

They needed to hurry.

Ren planned to head directly to the queen's cave at the top of the highest mountain, but Kezari couldn't imagine they would get far before someone stopped them. There was shielding in a wide swath around the Isle preventing easy escape—not that it couldn't be thwarted, as she well knew—and as soon as they crossed over it, the others would sense them. If the dragons were already searching for the younglings, they would rush to confront Kezari and Ren.

*"This is a foolish plan,"* Kezari sent, not just to Ren but to the others, as well.

Tynan's exasperation hit her. *"We've debated for most of the trip, love. I'm beginning to wish I'd attempted sleep."*

*"Direct is the only way,"* Ren insisted, just as he had all night. *"Neither of us are inclined toward stealth, so there's no use trying it. Just cut away as soon as you can. If you protect Tynan and Aris while they work to heal the injured in the village, I'll take care of the queen."*

And by "take care of," he clearly meant "kill with all haste."

When Kezari thought of all the times the queen had called her to her cave—or even in front of the entire chamber full of her useless council—she couldn't feel a hint of regret about what Ren would do. For as long as she could remember, the queen had been borderline cruel, correcting her over the most foolish things. *Because you lost your parents so young, Kezari.* Hah. They weren't even related. Why should Zevie care?

To the north and east, a hint of darkness shadowed the horizon. They'd decided to swoop in from the south, though it brought them closer to the southern continent than she would like. *That* place was cursed. Her ancestors had tried to settle there first, but they'd lost nearly a quarter of their population in the attempt. The legends were perhaps overblown, since she couldn't imagine dragons actually dropping dead without cause, but her stomach tightened at the very thought of getting close to that awful, impenetrable land.

*"Truly?"* Tynan asked.

Ah, she'd forgotten how closely they sometimes tracked each other's thoughts. *"If our oldest histories are to be believed. Why else would we have chosen an island? And why haven't the elves gone there? I think there's even another landmass south of yours."*

*"Our ships are not built well enough to handle this planet's seas,"* Tynan replied, but she caught the hesitation behind his

words. *"From what I understand, Aris's ship wrecked despite being the newest and most advanced. It's as though there's some element here that we can't entirely comprehend."*

*"It bothers me."* Kezari studied the distance to the island and silently directed Ren a touch more south. *"If Arneen is the place where the gods revealed themselves to you, then they were here first, right? Why? Perhaps they are the ones who do not wish you to explore the entirety of this world."*

He recoiled, mentally and physically. *"I am a priest of Bera. I'm aware of your distaste for our religion, but I cannot believe my goddess has dark intentions."*

*"Did I say they did?"* She huffed. *"The dragons did not fare well on our own, so your gods may have a good reason to keep you in one place. But I do wonder how they came to be."*

*"I...don't know,"* Tynan admitted.

Now she'd done it—she'd questioned her mate's faith right before a major conflict when he might need his belief the most. Brilliant. But she'd meant nothing by it. As Ren had said, dragons tended to flow with the universe, and in doing so, she'd felt deep presences that might have been called gods. Their great trees absolutely held their own power. Why would she deny that? She simply didn't connect the way the elves did.

*"I didn't intend to inspire doubt,"* she sent softly.

*"My faith is not so shallow."* Tynan patted the side of her neck. *"Don't worry. I am not a philosopher myself, but I've heard similar questions debated at the temple. It's only that the not-knowing doesn't bother me much. I commune with the Lady, and I am content. Do you find that unusual?"*

*"Maybe."* She bared her teeth in happiness. *"But I like you anyway."*

He shared his joy like a smile, and she let herself glory in it. Best to take such moments as they came. Soon enough, it was time to turn north.

The sun was a talon's length above the horizon by the time they flew through the shield. It was far enough out that she could still barely see the island, but she felt Aris's legs tense around the base of her neck from sensing the shield alone. Her poor *skizik*.

Tynan's calm radiated around them, earning a growl from Ren, but Kezari gnashed her teeth at him in warning. He'd been told that Aris might need this, and she would not compromise on it. She'd led him to the island quickly; he could deal with a moment of his hated peace.

It didn't last long, anyway. Three dragons approached at speed—two pale blue dragons and one a reddish brown. Kezari peered at them, hoping to identify them before they were in range, but they were nearly upon her before she managed it. Noqi, Zofho...and Tebzn. Huh. Her lazy, no-good cousin had actually flown out here herself. The only thing that would have surprised Kezari more would be Baza crawling out of his cave.

*"Hold on tight,"* Kezari sent to both Tynan and Aris.

As soon as they complied, she slowed, finally pounding her wings to maintain a hover. It pitched her upper torso up enough to cause her riders real trouble, but there was no avoiding it. Fortunately, she sensed that they were both secure.

"You came!" Tebzn shrieked in the dragon language. Ancestors, had her cousin always sounded this annoying? "Oh, please hurry. The young ones approach from the north, and the queen herself is intent on hunting them."

The *queen* was doing the hunting? That did not sound right.

"You are responsible for this...this traitor being here?" Zofho demanded, snarling.

Tebzn's head swiveled toward the young air dragon. "Surely you do not want to murder our dragonlings? Otherwise, you'd be hunting them, too."

"No, but I do not need *her* aid." Zofho hissed at Kezari. "Back with her stolen goods, and Perim has disappeared, besides. No doubt murdered. And with a strange dragon."

Quiet Noqi didn't glance at Kezari—her focus was for Ren. "Who are you?" she asked.

Kezari had expected some kind of speech. Instead, Ren tipped his head back and breathed a stream of elemental fire up into the sky before glaring at the three dragons hovering in front of them. "I am your new king."

That was it? No name? No explanation?

"See?" Zofho said. "Enemies."

A reasonable assumption, if Kezari were being honest. However, the strength of Ren's fire should have made it clear that he was no average dragon. Not that Zofho's reason stretched that far. Oh, no. Instead, she had to prove herself the most foolish dragon on the Isle.

Zofho actually attacked.

# CHAPTER THIRTY-SIX

With each hiss and snarl that he couldn't comprehend, Tynan berated himself for not having Kezari spell-teach him the dragon language. The way he was hunched over her neck, he couldn't see more than two of the newcomers speaking, and he wasn't adept enough at reading their body language to tell how it was going. But there was no mistaking intent when one of the dragons breathed a stream of fire toward Egrenneth and then dove toward him.

Tynan tucked himself as close to Kezari as he could, his head against the surprisingly smooth scales of her neck. Her roar vibrated through his entire body, and Aris's hand dug hard into his arm in reaction. But that couldn't compare to the veritable explosion beneath him when Kezari breathed fire of her own. Though he turned his head away, his ear still rang from it.

The attacking dragon had attempted to swipe at Egrenneth beneath the cover of her flame, but she hadn't counted on Ren being unfazed by her fire. He bit down on her outstretched forearm long before she made contact. The sickening crack echoed around them a heartbeat before the horrific screech of pain cut into Tynan's ringing ears.

He expected the ancient dragon to let her go—he didn't. Ren

twisted his head, sending the other off balance, and then jerked her into range of his talons. Before Tynan could blink, Ren shifted position and sank his teeth into the other dragon's neck, one talon digging into her injured forearm and the other locked on the spot where wing joined back.

Abruptly, Kezari dropped altitude and then tilted. Tynan pinched his eyes closed as her wings beat furiously and the air whistled around him. But when another, louder scream sounded, he couldn't resist looking back. They'd moved away, but around Aris's shoulder, Tynan could just see Egrenneth dropping his prey, her wing bent at an impossible angle.

The ancient dragon didn't look down as his attacker crashed into the water.

Gods above.

Tynan's hands went numb against Kezari's neck, and shock kept his gaze locked on Ren as he shot fire into the air in a terrifying stream. What about the other two dragons? Would he kill them next? Despite all the darkness Tynan had seen while healing others, he couldn't stop shuddering now.

*"It is difficult to witness death firsthand,"* Kezari sent. *"I am sorry,* sbezie.*"*

He turned his attention forward and tried to focus on the sensations around him to calm his body's reactions. The rise and fall of Kezari as she flew hard toward the distant island. The warm breeze, so much more pleasant than the weather they'd left behind. His own breath. But then he also felt the tremble of Aris's hand where he still gripped Tynan's shoulder.

Tynan opened his senses enough to detect the barely controlled panic rioting through the life mage's mind, and just like that, he shoved his own discomfort aside. The sudden violence had hit Aris in a different way—not for the action itself, but for the way it cracked open his darkest memories.

A wave of calm would not be enough. Carefully, he connected to Aris's mind. *"Shall I help?"*

"Yes," Aris gasped aloud.

Then Tynan became too occupied with rerouting or dulling the life mage's worst mental pathways to pay attention to what the dragons did.

Kezari would see them protected.

EVEN KEZARI WAS surprised by Ren's quick, brutal kill, though not as profoundly as Tynan and Aris obviously were. The ancient dragon's attack had been both beautiful and terrible at once, and she still couldn't decide how she felt about it. He'd defended himself without compromise. But did that mean there was no yield in him?

She'd had no time to prepare Aris for that level of violence, and that bothered her most of all. As she flew ever nearer to the Isle, she could only hover at the edges of both men's minds as Tynan worked with Aris. It was amazing, really, the way her mate helped her *skizik* redirect his thoughts themselves, away from the unending path carved by trauma.

Not permanently, of course. If new, deep channels of thought and pattern weren't dug, the mind tended to drift back into old habits like a temporarily diverted stream. She'd watched that happen to Aris, but she hadn't understood it fully until now, when she could see the process from both perspectives. Had she realized sooner, she might never have dived upon Korel when he'd made Aris uncomfortable with the dark magic within him, causing another trauma.

How did they persevere? Both her mate and *skizik* were amazing men. Surely, she'd done nothing in her life to deserve such good fortune. Though perhaps the universe had no intention of letting her off easy—she might spend years yet, earning such grace. Assuming they survived this mission at all.

Wingbeats approached, and she flicked a glance over her shoulder. Tebzn, Noqi, and Egrenneth all followed. Apparently, those two had yielded to whatever Ren had commanded, for he flew behind them easily. She wasn't surprised by that. Tebzn would cower at the slightest show of force, and Noqi was a clever, thoughtful dragon.

*"What have you done, Kezari?"* Tebzn whined into her head. *"He made me swear fealty without knowing more than his name."*

Kezari turned a cross eye on her cousin as she drew up beside her. *"His full name?"*

*"Of course. I'm not so silly that I wouldn't demand that."*

Kezari's snort clouded the air. *"Did you even recognize it? I'm sure Noqi did."*

*"Ah…"*

*"Son of Deyriglair? The Peacebringer?"* At Tebzn's blank look, Kezari tossed her head. *"Elders' teeth. We were taught by the same family. How could you not…?"* She sighed. *"Never mind. Deyriglair was our king before we left Earth, which means Egrenneth has a legitimate claim on the throne. And he's thousands of years old. He knows the ways of our kind better than we do."*

Tebzn huffed. *"Maybe our current ways are fine."*

*"And maybe we've lost an entire generation of young to those ways, while our queen offers death instead of help,"* Kezari pointed out. *"What are we even doing out here, Tebzn? We have lost our purpose."*

Her cousin fell silent, and Kezari didn't ask what she was thinking. Either she would fall in line or she would not. Kezari had ceased to care the moment her cousin had betrayed her, pretending not to remember Perim instead of hunting her down as she'd sworn she would. And for what? Extra stones in her hoard? Those gems weren't even attuned to her power. Such a waste.

Though speaking of… *"Tebzn. Did you know that by ancient law, taking another dragon's hoard is punishable by death? Both sons of Deyriglair agree on that point. Even the nicer one."*

She pretended not to see the fearful look her cousin cast Ren.

*"Death? I… The queen…"* Tebzn whimpered low. *"I already told you I would give your hoard back to you. Not that I kept it.*

*Clearly, it was never mine. Oh, I am such a fool. I never wanted to betray you, Kezari, but the queen ordered silence. And between her and Baza…"*

"*I no longer care,*" Kezari snapped. "*You have lost my trust, and I cannot imagine a way for you to regain it.*"

Yet she couldn't claim her emotions were entirely disengaged. The closer they flew, the clearer the island became to her sight, and with each detail she discerned, her heart pinched a little more. Her old cave entrance was out of view, but she could see the gentle peaks of the three mountains she'd always used to mark the way. And the mouth of the river that split the island glimmered in the morning sun, reminding her of the sunny days of her youth.

She could make out the forest where she preferred to hunt, the tall trees sheltering a glorious variety of tasty game. More types than there should be on an island, probably. Her ancestors had carried over some of their favorites in mating pairs to feed their growing population. There wasn't much risk of a species taking over when they were constantly being eaten.

Her least favorite sight, though…that was the fae village that sprawled out along the coast, between the river and the ocean. Or at least it had. She squinted, trying to discern the buildings. But instead of neat stone structures with their dull tile roofs, she made out only rubble. Smoke rose like little tendrils of fog from piles of stone.

What was that brown lump beside the river? It took a few more wingbeats, but finally it clarified. Fire burned in the back of her throat. That was a dragon. Alive or dead? She couldn't be certain, but it didn't look good. Not at that angle.

"He died defending the village," Noqi said aloud from Kezari's other side. "That's why the queen roused herself to join the pursuit."

Hmm. Other dragons had been hurt or killed over the years, but the queen had shown little reaction. Only…Oh. That deep brown. It must have been Eknen, Zevie's estranged lover. They'd fallen out a couple of centuries ago over her lack of care for the fae, and some believed she still had feelings for him. Apparently, they were right.

Zevie would have even less sympathy for the fae now that her love had died defending them.

"Did no one else try to stop this?" Kezari asked. "Those houses were made to resist fire for obvious reasons. That kind of destruction took intent."

"There's said to be a mage amongst the oldest of the renegades," Noqi replied sadly.

A barely trained dragon mage destroyed a village full of fae, many of whom could do magic? Something didn't seem right about that. Yet the closer they drew, the more undeniable it became. The younglings had destroyed the village. Almost all of it.

Above the distant mountains, dragons circled, and a few flashes of magic caught her eye, making her wings itch in reaction. Those dragons had left the village abandoned, the fae expected to fend for themselves. It was an obscene breach of the agreement between them. This community was all that remained of the elves and fae who had chosen to accompany their dragon allies at the end of the war, and this was how they were repaid for their loyalty? Smoke streamed from between her teeth.

She didn't need to hear Ren's agreement—fire blasted out above and to her right, directly over Tebzn, who yelped and dove out of his way. In spite of her anger at the village's destruction, Kezari flashed her teeth in a satisfied grin. Her complacent wyrm of a cousin would learn quickly to mind herself around the ancient dragon.

Or she would join Zofho in the ocean. Either way.

As Kezari prepared to descend, Ren's mind brushed hers. *"I'm going for the queen. I ordered the other two to stand guard with you over the healer and your skizik. If they even appear to be betraying you, kill them. Though seeing how the Moranaian dragons treat their allies, I'm not sure who deserves to live."*

*"Much change is required,"* she agreed.

Shame weighed her down as she angled toward a bit of empty

coast, though she hadn't been the one to do this damage. Really, had she been much better than the dragons he castigated? She'd given little attention to the fae and elves who lived here, at least until she'd sensed Aris when the waves had carried him beyond the shields and onto the island. She'd been so oblivious that she hadn't understood the scope of Perim's deception.

At the heart of things, that type of negligence was the cause.

Egrenneth's path continued toward the dragons to the north, and Kezari could practically feel the relief oozing from Tebzn and Noqi. They didn't even glance toward the conflict raging in the area where Ren headed. Oddly, Kezari had to force her attention away so that she could safely land. Each time her gaze strayed that way, the itchy feeling she'd grown accustomed to suddenly intensified. But she still didn't hear any cries.

She landed softly on the wide stretch of beach, but the flurry of wingbeats from three dragons sent the sand flying around them until it obscured her sight. Impatiently, Kezari connected with the ground and tugged the dust down with a flex of her magic. In the sudden clarity, Tebzn and Noqi stared at her in shock.

"Have you felt uneasy lately?" Kezari asked.

Both dragons blinked at the unexpected question.

"Who wouldn't be upset about the dragonlings?" Noqi asked slowly, her head tilting in confusion.

"Not mere emotion," Kezari tried to explain. "A sort of itchy feeling that you can't describe. Or a cry you can't identify."

Tebzn's wings folded tight against her back. "You're speaking oddly, and we're supposed to be rescuing people."

She would take that as a no.

Kezari swiveled her head until she could see Tynan and Aris, both sitting so still. Tynan's eyes were closed, but Aris's gaze darted around the beach like a sand lizard. He'd washed up not far from here, where Perim had carried him away—into literal years of agony. Her claws dug into the sand at the thought. He was here reliving this torture for her.

"Skizik," she whispered into his mind. *"I can carry you back to that tiny island. The one we stopped at before. There is no need for you to suffer this."*

Thankfully, the eyes he turned her way hadn't lost all reason, though it was a near thing. *"No,"* he answered, his mental voice almost a whisper. *"I must conquer this, or I will never rest easy again."*

She fell silent. Helpless—she was helpless. Unable to do anything but watch as Tynan worked frantically to help Aris. Only a few moments passed, but it felt like an eternity before her mate's eyes finally opened. And he smiled at her, completely unbothered by all she lacked.

She tried to think of something to say, but both men slid off of her back before she managed it. As the two elves tugged off their heavy cloaks and furs, Tebzn lowered her head to peer at them, and although Noqi tried to pretend she wasn't curious, she failed entirely. Why hadn't the men remained safely in the saddle until the other two were gone? They could have cooled themselves down later.

Glaring, Kezari placed her body between the other dragons and the elves. "Guard the skies, as Egrenneth ordered," she snapped.

Tebzn and Noqi hesitated, but the memory of Zofho's sudden death must have made an impact. They actually complied without complaint.

She mantled her wings over Tynan and Aris while the two dragons took flight, kicking up sand once again. And once again, she ruthlessly pulled it down. Only when Noqi and Tebzn circled high did Kezari shift into her elven form.

The first thing she did was pull Tynan into her arms.

BEFORE HE'D HAD time to process the shift, Tynan had an armful of Kezari—fortunately as an elf, not a dragon.

He gathered her close, savoring the feel of her against him. She nuzzled his neck, and he buried his face against her hair. Instantly, her spicy-sweet scent filled his nose, better than the pouch of herbs he so treasured. They were nothing compared to her, of course.

She was everything.

When Kezari tugged against his hold, he was slow to release her. They'd only had a few moments. A single precious pause. Unfortunately, they couldn't afford more. Gods knew how many dead and wounded they would find, and Aris was barely holding it together. Already, Tynan had expended more energy than he ought while helping him.

"There is much to do, *sbezie*," she whispered against his ear.

Sighing, he kissed her softly and then let her go.

As Kezari peered around the area, Tynan turned his attention to Aris. The life mage stood stiffly, but his eyes lacked the wildness Tynan had felt during the healing. Fortunately, Aris had managed to keep his energy steady despite his fear, so together, they'd contained the worst of it. On the less fortunate side, there was no telling what horrors they were about to encounter, and that might undo all their hard work.

Aris took a deep, shaky breath that was probably loud enough to reach the dragons overhead. Then he drew his sword from its sheath, and green flashed and danced around the blade. Though the mage's knuckles were white against the hilt, he nodded toward the nearest pile of stones.

"Let's go," Aris said. "If I'm to crack, it will at least be while I'm helping."

Tynan couldn't say he was unhappy to have the two with him, despite the possibility of Aris breaking. The first plan Egrenneth had proposed had required Kezari to drop Tynan off alone while she and Aris continued on to find the dragonlings. But Kezari had adamantly refused to leave her mate behind.

Thank Bera for that.

Kezari marched toward the first crumbled house, but a quick search revealed no sign of people, living or dead. Nor did the second house. Had the maddened dragons carried them away like prey? Tynan's stomach lurched with revulsion at the thought. Hopefully, there was a better explanation.

*Please let there be a better explanation.*

"Do you sense anything, Aris?" Kezari asked.

Jaw clenched, the life mage turned in a slow circle, but his eyes didn't focus on any of the rubble. It was his magic that trembled through the air. Just the lightest brush, but Tynan would never be able to mistake that glorious taste of pure life for anything else.

"Nothing in the ruins," Aris said, his voice remote. "But...that way. There's life that way. Also pain. Someone must have directed them to evacuate."

In silence, they picked their way around tumbled stones and the smoldering remnants of fallen trees. Blood dotted some of the rock in sickening splatters, and a rancid, charred scent nearly made him gag until he dug the pouch of herbs from his pocket. For once, even that barely helped. This kind of devastation could only be called a nightmare.

They found a trail on the other side of the ruined village, and Aris directed them to follow it, Kezari taking the lead. But they hadn't gone far before the mage's steps slowed. "We should be cautious," Aris said. "If they have—"

"State your name and purpose quickly." The high, sharp voice crashed into them like a blow. "Or I'll kill you where you stand."

Tynan peered around the empty forest surrounding them. Where...? But he only needed to follow Aris's gaze to find a woman perched in a nearby tree. Her tattered leather clothes blended into the bark, but the short, silver hair fluttering around her pointed ears did not. Nor did the lines of bright red streaking her cheeks.

"I am Callian iy'dianore tenah i Kezari Baran se Tynan nai Braelyn, formerly of this very Isle," Kezari said, her voice ringing with pride. "I am here with my *sbezie* and my *skizik* to offer aid."

"You're a dragon?" the woman cried—in oddly accented Moranaian. She lifted her hand, and water gathered in a ball above her palm. But just as suddenly, her eyes went wide. "Wait. Did you say 'iy'dianore'?"

Tynan didn't need to be an empath to sense the depth of her surprise. What he wasn't sure about was the cause.

But the unusual cadence of her words certainly gave a hint.

# CHAPTER THIRTY-SEVEN

Kezari tensed, her body bracing to shift, when the woman dropped out of the tree only a couple of paces away. Water still danced around the woman's hand, and her expression was far from friendly. But for some reason, Kezari remained in her elven form despite the potential threat.

"How could a dragon be connected to the Dianore family?" the stranger demanded.

Kezari took a slight step to the side, ensuring she was in front of Tynan and Aris. "I was adopted into that House when I was banished from the Isle. If you've heard of some foul, betraying dragon, that would be me."

The woman's eyes narrowed. "Were you the one who confronted Perim about her so-called bonded? I didn't see the commotion, since I rarely come into the village."

"So-called?" Kezari studied the stranger for signs of any similarity to Perim, but she found none. Still, she was the first to express doubt about Perim's claim. "What do you know of that horrid woman?"

The stranger's lip curled. "I found her shielded cave a few months back. At first, I thought it was empty, but I saw her with a sad-looking man there once. She said he was her bonded and that they sought privacy for a time. I didn't believe her, but others did. But just as I found a way to unwind her shielding, a dragon carried him away. Not that anyone would admit that once Queen Zevie got involved."

Silently, Aris stepped around Kezari. His pain and anxiety echoed along their link, but his expression was closed as he faced the woman. "That was me."

The stranger's mouth dropped open as she studied him. "You're looking...well," she said. "I'm sorry I couldn't help you then. My magic was ill-suited to counter such a shield, and when I tried to report it, I was scoffed at. There's a reason my family didn't live in the village."

That was a curiosity. Kezari hadn't been aware of any fae settling outside the village. Or in this case, elves—most dragons tended to conflate the two since most of the original settlers had been fae who'd traveled with them from Earth. It wasn't as though there were many physical differences. Although...could there be more elves who'd chosen not to live with the others? Was that even within their laws?

It wasn't explicitly forbidden. Not that she could recall.

Beside her, Aris shuffled his feet. The silence had grown almost awkward. Was he even going to speak?

"It is not your fault," Aris finally said. "She was a master of manipulation, so I'm grateful that you saw the truth and attempted to help at all. Whatever the others have told you after our departure, Kezari saved me." He shifted his tunic aside to reveal the dragon-shaped mark their link had formed on his chest. "I am her *skizik*. And against my own best interests, I've returned with her to help."

Kezari sensed Tynan's intentions a moment before he eased around her, and she couldn't stop herself from placing her uselessly small arm in front of him. "I'm a healer," Tynan said, amusement in his voice. "And as you can see, Kezari's mate."

The woman stared at them for so long that Kezari considered shifting just in case, but after a moment, the stranger's posture lost its tension. As the water evaporated from her hand, she inclined her head. "I am Osere teni i Iskedai Dianore."

Dianore? Well, that explained the elf's odd behavior after hearing Kezari's title. But what were "osere" and "teni" supposed to mean? Those were not words she'd learned as part of the Moranaian language. Wasn't the first thing in the title supposed to be the name of a branch? Callian, Riere, or Taian. Those were the choices. Kezari looked at Aris and then Tynan, but neither man appeared any less confused than she was.

"Osere is not a branch," Aris said carefully.

Tynan took Kezari's hand in his, lowering the arm she held in front of him. "Do you use a different method of naming? It has been a long time since your family left Moranaia."

"*Your* portion of Moranaia," the woman pointed out. Then she sighed. "You're right that Osere isn't a branch, because I don't belong to one of yours. My great grandfather passed along what he could, and so we named our little sapling of a family after him. And before you ask, 'teni' means 'keeper of the dragon bond.' Not that there's anything left to keep."

Kezari had never heard any of this. As far as she knew, none of the other fae on the island went by special titles in the Moranaian style. "So you are called Iskedai?"

The woman shrugged. "I go by Iski. Now. What is this about helping?"

"We brought one of the ancient dragons with us. He's taking care of the queen," Kezari explained. "My mate is a healer-priest of Bera, and my *skizik* is a life mage. We'll care for the fae of the Isle, as the other dragons should have done."

Iski's measuring gaze swept across them one more time before she nodded. "Follow me, then. But I'll warn you. Almost all of them are injured in some way. They're only lucky I live out in the woods, or there'd have been no one to help them evacuate."

Kezari squeezed Tynan's hand as they followed. That itchy, uneasy feeling buzzed across her skin and hummed in her mind, and she couldn't help but fear that it foretold something dire. Was it connected to the injured villagers? Whatever they were about to see was no doubt worse than they already imagined.

And Tynan might harm himself trying to help them all.

~

THE TERROR and agony and hysteria reached Tynan well before the tinny scent of blood. The mass of it pounded against his shields until he feared they would crumble, and his awareness faded to nothing except Kezari's hand in his, the movement of his feet, and relentless emotion. How would he ever bear getting close to anyone to heal them?

His own emotions rose to meet the maelstrom knocking at his shields. Like a host welcoming guests, he could take those emotions in. Use them. Amplify them until the world became a screaming agony in his path. It was what would happen if he lost control. He'd seen with his own eyes the damage he could cause.

*"Did you lie when you claimed your goddess used your strength to make your extra shields?"* Kezari demanded harshly, her mental voice snapping into him like the whip of her tail.

*"That was what she said, and I believe her."* Tynan shivered as another wave of fear hit. *"But do you feel how much…?"*

Kezari's hand tightened around his. *"I don't think it was ever me who caused your control to slip. It was your lack of trust in yourself. You're afraid of getting too close to others, aren't you?"*

He gritted his teeth against that truth. *"Now is not the time for self-analysis."*

*"But* sbezie, *that's your job,"* she said sweetly. *"I heard your earlier thoughts, you know. About how you needed to embrace your full power instead of hiding from it? You can trust that I will not let you forget."*

Tynan wanted to groan, but really, he had no defense. He *had* come to that conclusion, and it *was* his job. Now, he had a bonded who would not allow him to neglect his own mental state. How had he ever thought that Kezari was his greatest weakness? He'd been so very wrong. She was more like the column that supported his weight.

And he could not allow himself to become a burden.

Ignoring the others, even the strange Iski, Tynan halted in the middle of the path. His instincts urged him to keep walking, to answer those pounding emotions, but for a moment, at least, he had to stand firm. But it would be impossible to fight off those feelings—that wasn't the solution. He had to open himself enough to process and release them. He had to stop trying to make them his own.

"Hold me," he murmured.

He didn't have to explain the comment—Kezari understood. Her spirit held his as he lowered his shields enough to let those emotions trickle through. Instinctively, he flinched as pain slammed into him first, so acute he couldn't tell if it was his or another's. *Not mine. I am unharmed.* With his power, he gentled it and let it flow into the ground at his feet.

But as quickly as he solved one, countless other emotions pounded to get in, threatening to overwhelm the channel he'd opened to allow them. How had he thought he could handle this? His fear surged, and his vision blurred. He tried to stifle his fear, but it kept building until he thought it might consume him. Or worse, explode from him.

*No. No. I can't let that happen.*

Nearly desperate, he reached down and up—in and out—hoping for enough energy to form the shields Lady Bara had once wrought. Instead, something seemed to click in him. A connection he couldn't describe. It was almost as though he could see the nearby emotions without feeling them himself.

*"The universal flow,"* Kezari whispered into his mind.

Was this how she saw things when she did magic? He'd sensed her spirit almost blended with the stone, not standing above watching it. That made no sense.

*"Observe and then join,"* she explained. *"Join and then shape. It is ever thus."*

Tynan watched the unending sea of agony and pleasure, dread and joy, and couldn't imagine rejoining it. How could he consider hefting that mantle of fear waiting in his own heart, much less any of the other emotions? It was safer to look, wasn't it?

But there was no such thing as safety, and he refused to continue hiding. As heedless as Kezari on a sudden dive, he leapt back into the chaos and let it become his strength.

Only then did he understand how to shield and still feel.

IGNORING the incessant crying in his head, Egrenneth counted a mere five dragons as he swept closer to the group on the north end of the island. Was their population that small, or were these the only ones the queen could muster in her defense? While it was true that Earth dragons had stopped settling in such numbers as the human population grew, there was nothing holding them back here. This large island with its plentiful forests and mountains could support at least a hundred, though more might be a strain.

As he neared, the group slowed and then stopped, their wings snapping against the air as they hovered. "Who dares intrude upon my lands without my permission?" the green dragon in the center demanded.

Ren sized her up and found only one thing—average. Average size, average power. "I am Egrenneth of the Crag, son of Deyriglair, the Guardian of the Frozen North and Regnant of All Dragons. Who are you to demand anything of me? You are not of the bloodline given rulership of this place."

He suspected Kezari might be, though distantly. He sensed a slight kinship with her, and the original king here had been a cousin. Unlike this pretender, who felt like the Mescenai line. An honorable enough family on Earth, if a little weak.

"Deyriglair's son?" the other dragon demanded, as the other

four swiveled their heads to stare at her. "That's not possible. The gate is closed to our use."

"Not to mine. Or did you forget that Earth dragons are not bound by your treaty?" he demanded. The discordant cries pounded with more intensity in his head, and he bared his teeth in reaction, making the queen's wingbeats briefly falter. "I have learned what a miserable excuse of dragonkind you have become, and that was *after* you neglected your obligations to us on Earth. Did you think your failure would never be discovered? Now, I'll give you one more chance to identify yourself. Do not expect further mercy."

She hissed with anger—but she complied. "I am Queen Zevie of the Isle, daughter of Mecal, the previous ruler."

Ren scanned her more deeply with his magic at the claim, and what he found—or rather, hadn't—sent anger and triumph surging through him in equal measure. The so-called queen hadn't neglected her responsibility to maintain the wall. She'd never been linked into it in the first place, and it was unlikely Mecal had been, either.

"You are queen of nothing. No wonder your society has fractured. Your parent might have seized power by some underhanded means, but they didn't find the link. They didn't understand the core of it. Nor do you."

He expected fury, but what he saw in her eyes was fear. "A bizarre claim. You have no proof."

"Step down or die," Ren said. "Those are your choices."

Zevie shrieked, the piercing sound echoing against the mountains. "Did you hear that threat?" she snarled at her attendants. "Defend me!"

Ah, he'd been hoping she would do that. Grinning, Ren released a long, rolling stream of steam, a precursor to the hell he was about to rain down. She'd committed so many crimes that he would have had to order her execution, anyway. This would save him a step.

Then he could claim the throne and figure out how to save the younglings.

And he wouldn't have a moment's peace.

~

THEY'D JUST REACHED the outskirts of the scattered, haphazard camp when a shriek rent the sky. Kezari's head snapped up, her eyes already searching for the source before she'd even paused to think. Unfortunately, there were too many trees to see much of the sky, and she was too far away to get a clear view, anyway.

At the sound, new sobs filled the air, and despite his improved shielding, Tynan flinched beside her. He was learning to process those stray emotions and direct them into his own defenses, but it was a new skill, far from mastered. She couldn't be focused on the conflict between Ren and the queen. She needed to help her mate.

Reluctantly, she forced her attention back down to the fae huddled next to one another in groups beneath the tree cover. Here and there, bits of fabric were strung between the branches like open tents, inadequate for true protection but some help against the weather. There were no fires. No signs of food, either. Only terrified people gathered in scattered clumps around the most injured.

"I don't know where to begin," Tynan said.

Though visibly shaken, Aris stepped up beside Tynan. "I can tell which are closest to death. I'll guide you."

Before she could think of what to offer, the two men hurried away. Some of the fae didn't seem to notice, their eyes blank with shock, and some others flinched at the elves' passage. A few more followed Tynan and Aris with avid attention. Unwilling to be caught unawares? Hopeful? Both? After being betrayed by their own guardians, Kezari couldn't imagine there was much in the way of hope.

"Do they not have a healer?" she asked Iski.

The elven woman grimaced. "She was crushed beneath her house in the first attack. Her apprentice is still young, but she's done her best to bandage what she could. The child's healing magic isn't trained or mature enough for much more."

Tynan and Aris reached one of the larger groups, and after a brief conversation, they parted to reveal a pair of fae stretched on the ground, a girl kneeling over one of them. There was a hint of energy around her and tears coating her determined face—the apprentice, no doubt. The comment on her age hadn't been based on experience. The girl *was* a child.

"How old?" Kezari asked.

"Ten, I believe." Iski shook her head. "Poor dearling. I was helping her until your group struck my shields. I hope your healer can give her some relief."

As Tynan sat beside his new patient, Aris knelt beside the child and held out his hand. A tiny green ball danced over his palm, and the girl stared, entranced.

"What is he doing?" Iski asked sharply.

"Life magic," Kezari replied. "Healers can use it to augment their power."

Iski's fierce blue eyes seemed to pierce her. "It's difficult to believe he's a life mage. How could Perim capture someone of such power?"

Kezari could understand the doubt. Truly. But she would not allow anyone to disparage her *skizik*. "He was barely alive when she found him, and she was his potential soulbonded. Do not call his competence into question."

"She was telling the truth about the bond?" Iski asked, eyes wide.

"I said *potential*. She demanded. He refused." Her fingertips burned for her claws. "And so she tortured. More than that is none of your business."

A visible tremor went through the elf. "I am sorry."

"Do not ask Aris for details," Kezari warned. "Or I'll be happy to give you a demonstration in pain. He isn't fully recovered, and being on this island is difficult enough."

"I won't," Iski said quickly. "Even without your threat."

There was a youngness to Iski in that moment that almost made Kezari inquire about her age, too, but it seemed wrong to ask after telling the elf to mind her own business. Maybe it was simply how different she was from the Moranaian elves. Wilder and less polished. Iski's leather clothing was roughly made, utilitarian, and well-used, and the two lines of red painted across her cheeks appeared both deliberate and impromptu somehow. The lack of perfection, perhaps.

Catching Kezari's gaze on the markings, Iski tapped her finger next to one of them. "Kill marks. I took out two of the invading dragons myself."

Kezari glared. "You killed our young?"

"What?" Iski snapped. One of the villagers yelped, and the elf lowered her voice to a furious hiss. "Why would you accuse me of that?"

"I was told the village was attacked by dragonlings, driven mad by their connection to Earth." Kezari scanned the treetops as though a new threat was waiting to appear. "So it is a logical conclusion."

Iski shook her head. "I'm not sure about the first attack, since I wasn't there. During the second, I did see young circling the beach, but it was a dragon mage and five others who attacked. Eknen tried to scare them away, but clearly, it didn't work. He only managed to kill one before he was slain. Did you see his body? I left it, since I wasn't sure if the dragons perform any special rites."

The queen's ex-lover and one of the few who'd still defended the fae—the former made it difficult to believe anyone would attack him over the latter. "Did he kill the mage?"

"No." Iski's nostrils flared. "The mage was too strong, so he managed to get away. I tracked them and managed to defeat two of the others. That leaves two and the mage still out there."

Noqi had claimed there was a mage amongst the oldest of the renegades, but little of what that dragon had said matched Iski's account. Had Noqi and Tebzn been the other two in that group? But what about Zofho? Had she been involved?

"Too bad elves don't speak the dragon language," Kezari muttered. "I could use a name or two right now."

Iski's sudden smile could nearly be called a smirk. "Who says we don't? My family passed that knowledge along from my great grandmother. Though in this case, there wasn't much conversation. Eknen called the mage Baza when asking what he was thinking. Baza invited him to join in a rebellion against the queen after they 'torched the useless fae.' Eknen refused, and that was that."

Baza.

*Baza* had roused himself from his cave to form an uprising against the queen? He was despicable enough to betray the fae—but like this? And if the dragonlings had been nearby, he'd likely helped corrupt them, too.

She was going to cut him into tiny pieces, roast him in the depths of the earth, and then feed his carcass to the fish. Or not. She actually liked fish.

But somehow, Baza would pay.

# CHAPTER THIRTY-EIGHT

Egrenneth immolated the first two dragons who charged him, their charred bodies falling from the sky to land somewhere below. Understandably, that caused the other two attendants to hesitate, and Zevie retreated like the coward she was. The remaining dragons would not burn so easily, however. Water and air—one could douse fire, and the other would either extinguish it or send it to greater heights. He didn't have time to deal with either.

"Ancient elemental fire burns hotter than a normal dragon's flame," Ren said, hoping the attendants would not guess their own power. "Submit now, or I will kill you."

The air dragon bowed her head. "I yield."

Alas, the water dragon was more knowledgeable. "You'll not defeat me as easily as those two," they snarled.

So it would be another battle.

Before anything, Ren noted Zevie's position and couldn't hold back a snort-laugh. The fool had stopped not far away to watch. Did she truly have some expectation of victory? He bobbed his head mockingly in her direction and then sprang into action.

He blasted fire at the water dragon, but he didn't bother to augment it with his magic. Elemental flame would burn the other dragon, but it wouldn't injure them enough for Ren to bother. Instead, he used the same trick that had worked on Zofho. As his opponent dodged the blast, Ren let himself drop in altitude and then swooped up with a flurry of wingbeats.

Crunching into the dragon's lower leg with his teeth, Ren gave a violent tug. His enemy faltered, their wings pumping frantically as they attempted to stay aloft. A blast of cold water rushed down Ren's back, chilling him, but fury warmed his body soon enough. This dragon's water wasn't nearly as strong as others he'd fought.

He jerked his head back and tilted his body until he could rake a claw down the other dragon's soft belly. His opponent screamed in pain, but instead of countering with a blow, the water dragon tipped their body back to glance down at their wound. Had they never trained in combat? Ren dug his lower talons into the other dragon's stomach, then slashed his enemy's throat open with his upper claws.

A quick blast of elemental fire burned the water dragon's wing beyond all hope of use, and Ren shoved the useless wretch away with a victorious cry. But he made sure to watch the other dragon until they crashed in a broken heap into the base of the mountain far below. He would rather not have another blast of water.

Rage could only warm one so far.

Annoyingly, Zevie had taken advantage of his distraction to fly away, her wingbeats carrying her rapidly east toward the highest mountain. It would have been more convenient had she not wised up.

He turned his head to study the remaining dragon. "What is your name?" Ren asked.

"Eh...Elzalel," the young female gasped. "Please, son of Deyriglair, I do not wish to die. My grandmother told me tales of your father. I am not silly enough to challenge you."

"Swear fealty to me, then."

Elzalel nodded her head. "I give my loyalty to you, King Egrenneth."

"Then you may prove it by helping me track Zevie," he ordered. "I'm sure you know how to find her cave."

The other dragon nodded. "Yes. Follow."

It could be a trap, but Ren doubted it. Even the dragons who'd guarded their supposed queen appeared to be untrained. Though he would remain on guard, he couldn't find enough respect for them to anticipate such a complicated plan. It would probably take him centuries to sort this lot out.

He bared his teeth in a smile. Once the situation stopped being appalling, the work was going to be wonderful.

Although his bonded's turmoil tugged at his focus like an invisible string, Tynan managed to stabilize his current patient before he withdrew from his trance. A fine sheen of sweat coated his brow from both the effort and the growing heat of the day. It was far from summer here, but the warm ocean breeze didn't mix well with the remaining layers of clothing he hadn't removed while they were on the coast.

Ignoring his discomfort, he looked toward the spot where he sensed Kezari. She still stood at the perimeter beside Iski, but something had obviously happened. Though her emotions were muted by her carefully layered shields, rage danced around her like waves of heat from a sunbaked stone.

Instantly, he connected. *"What's wrong?"*

Her gaze found his across the distance. *"Baza was the dragon who attacked. He's a formidable mage, skilled beyond his innate element, but typically lazy. Or so I thought. I long to hunt him down."*

*"And we are stopping you,"* he sent softly.

She glared up at the tree limbs. *"This place is not secure, and I will not leave you and Aris unprotected. I cannot be certain that Tebzn and Noqi won't betray us. They may be allied with Baza."*

A few paces away, Aris caught his attention. "The next one is over here."

Nodding, he hurried toward a young woman with terrible burns covering half her body. But what should he tell Kezari? It was true that they weren't safe here, but they might fare no better if this Baza caught them by surprise. As he dropped to his knees beside the woman and extended his hands over her, he sent his conclusion to Kezari.

*"You should take to the skies and do some scouting, at the least. And if you get the chance to defeat the mage before he returns here, it would be best. Only do not risk yourself."*

Then he sank into yet another healing trance.

KEZARI'S BODY trembled at those words. *You should take to the skies.* But did she dare? The two most precious people in her world were here. Soft and easily damaged—even killed. They were both skilled men, but could their talents counter a dragon mage? An entire village of fae hadn't stood against Baza's magic.

"You know the dragon responsible, don't you?" Iski asked.

"Unfortunately." Kezari studied the trees once more. "Have you detected his presence again after the last attack?"

Iski shook her head. "The dragons have left us alone since."

If Baza intended to rebel against the queen, then the fact that she was on the move would draw him away. Had he intended to destroy the fae entirely, nothing would have stopped him after Eknen's death. Surely not Iski, who might be talented but was still only one elf. This really might be the ideal time to hunt the wyrm down.

"I'm going to scout the area and possibly pursue Baza," Kezari said. "Is there an ideal place to shift? Somewhere that won't cause panic?"

After a quick glance at Tynan and Aris, Iski's brows drew together. "You're leaving them here?"

"I know nothing about healing." Kezari swallowed against the lump of dread in her throat. "My skills will better serve them above."

Though the elf's frown didn't fade, she shrugged. "Very well. I'll show you to a clearing where you shouldn't startle anyone."

Kezari followed Iski away from the camp and around a thick stand of bushes. Beyond that, they took a curving path that circled between a line of trees. Sure enough, the clearing nestled beside that line was large enough for a dragon to take flight. Barely. If they augmented their leap with a hint of magic. But it would serve.

Iski left her with a worried smile, and for the first time Kezari could recall, she didn't want to shift. Her heart pulled her back to the camp where her mate and her *skizik* were working. Her instincts urged her into the fight—to rend and kill. To protect. And that was the problem. It was impossible to know the proper course, and both goals overlapped and conflicted.

She could only guess—and follow her sometimes-questionable impulses.

A prickle swept across her skin, and for the first time, a sharp, defined tug came along with the uncomfortable sensation. North. She was needed to the north, where the dragonlings had flown. Where Ren had gone to confront the queen. Unwittingly, Kezari stepped into the center of the clearing.

Should she finally heed the call?

Aris's mind brushed hers. *"I will watch out for him. Go."*

*"And yourself?"*

Amusement flowed in with his words. *"Yes, dearest sister. I will take care of myself, too."*

Her lips curved up in a wry but happy smile, the latter mostly because of the endearment. *"See that you do."*

Releasing their mental connection, she shifted into dragon form on a breath. Power rushed through her from the ground below, her link with earth stronger in this form and more focused now that she was alone. It was then that she heard it—the slightest mental whimper, a bare moan she wouldn't have caught from the other side of the world. How had she not noticed it when she'd landed on the beach?

It was hardly the crying Ren had described, but it was surely related.

With a surge of power, both physical and magical, Kezari leapt into the sky, her wings carrying her upward until she caught sight of Tebzn and Noqi circling above the village. They seemed to be obeying Ren's command, but were they poised to betray him? Had they been the two who'd attacked the village with Baza?

Kezari couldn't follow that strange mental cry without satisfying that question first, so she flew their way. Both dragons drew back into a hover at her approach, and their heads tilted in confusion at her low warning growl. She didn't want to kill her cousin, but the roiling in her gut reminded her that she might have to.

"Where is Baza?" Kezari demanded.

Tebzn flinched. "Oh, not that one. If I knew, I would try to kill him myself."

Kezari peered at her cousin. She might be telling the truth— she'd said she would *try* to kill him, and that admission was too close to reality to be one of Tebzn's typical lies. "I thought the two of you were friends. You had no problem working together to lie to the queen and steal my hoard."

"But that's just it!" Tebzn cried. "He told me you were as crazed as your *skizik*, and Perim *did* seem distraught, and I didn't want to cause more trouble, and the queen was so angry. *So angry*, Kezari. She would have kicked me out, too. Then who would have guarded your hoard, including those gems passed down by your parents? And Baza said he sensed no problems from Earth, but that he would protect me if he was wrong. Then when the dragonlings lost their senses, he threatened to kill me if I so much as mentioned you. Lately, he's abandoned me totally. He led me astray, that rotten reptile."

Kezari blinked at her cousin. Was that lightning flash of a diatribe finally over? Not that it hadn't been enlightening—Baza had obviously used her cousin for his own gain. "But why would he bother? I've had no real argument with him. He barely leaves his cave, and he even rejected a place on the queen's silly council. It makes no sense that he now seeks power, nor that he would use you to do it."

"He wants you dead," Noqi said quietly. "I overheard Perim offering to kill you if he told her how to escape the island. He gave her directions to a tiny, forming rift to the Veil that's off the east coast of the Isle."

Tebzn's head snapped around. "And you didn't tell me?"

Noqi hissed. "I thought you were part of the plan. You sure handed over those earth crystals quickly enough."

Well, that explained how Perim had reached Earth to try to kill Aris while they'd been forming the permanent gate and restoring Earth's magic. Aris had been forced to confront Perim during that working, and the rancid piece of *zeznit* had been too dead to interrogate when Kezari had returned to awareness after shaping the cave system.

"Those crystals were not from the family portion," Tebzn said to Noqi, continuing their useless argument. "So they were not important."

There really wasn't time for this.

"Forget about that for now." Kezari detected no hint of subterfuge in these two, but it was impossible to believe them. Particularly Tebzn. "According to one of the fae below, it was Baza and four others who destroyed the village, not the dragonlings. Two of his allies were defeated, but two escaped. Curiously, there are two of you here now."

The spines around Noqi's eyes tilted down in anger. "I dislike that insinuation. We've been scouting the southern side of the Isle with Zofho, so if you want to confirm our innocence, just ask —Ah, *verzen*. You can't ask Zofho, thanks to our crazy new king."

"She did attack an ancient," Tebzn pointed out. "Foolishness. Made me regret not staying hidden in my cave."

Kezari released a thin stream of smoke and then pulled in a calming breath. "Swear on your elements that you are not allied with Baza or any other attempting to harm me, the fae, or the elves who came with me and that you will do your best to protect the fae and elves below."

Noqi agreed easily enough, but it took a bit of grumbling before Tebzn complied.

Despite their oaths, Kezari glared at them both in warning. "Betray me, and you will suffer. It won't be a quick death by the Ancient One, but it will *absolutely* be brutal."

Promise delivered, Kezari angled her body to the north and flew as fast as she could. All the while, she scanned the skies in search of other dragons. All clear. Whatever Ren had done, there were no dragons circling the mountains now. But on the wind, the harsh scent of charred flesh reached her, and she scanned the skies with her senses.

She was no air dragon to excel in that element, but she could tell there was no one, burned or otherwise, near her in the sky. Remnants of a battle? She peered down at the ground, her sharp eyes focusing as though hunting for prey, and noticed a thin, wavering tendril of smoke. Then another. There—a charred lump that might have been a dragon. A few wingbeats away, she spotted another.

Next, it was the acrid smell of blood that reached her on the breeze. Not prey. This had the bite of dragon's blood. Kezari studied the sparse trees covering the base of the mountain and still almost missed the blue-and-red clump of another fallen dragon lying unnaturally beside the river. The red was blood, not scales. A dead water dragon.

Had Ren done this? She couldn't imagine it was any other. Bile burned up her throat, hotter than her fire, and she had to fight against a wave of sudden doubt. Had she been wrong to bring him here? Would he murder them all?

But no. He hadn't killed Noqi or foolish Tebzn, and the latter probably deserved death a couple of times over. Could these dead dragons have been with the queen? The first two had been too burned to identify, but the water dragon might have been one of the queen's council members. If all of them were part of the council, that meant three of the five of those were dead.

That would leave two more—and they could be after the dragonlings.

Kezari picked up speed.

# CHAPTER THIRTY-NINE

Tynan's hands shook as he swept his hair out of his face to examine his latest patient. The child was younger than Eri, and his pitiful, dirt-covered face made Tynan's heart ache. Even unconscious, the little boy whimpered, and that was in spite of the pain block numbing the nerves in his shattered legs. But this wasn't physical pain. Tynan did his best to ease the channels causing the child's nightmare, but it would be impossible to do a good job of it unless he woke the boy.

"Is he still hurting?" the child's father asked, tears tracking lines down his dusty cheeks. "Is he too far gone to save?"

"He should live," Tynan assured the man. "I stopped the internal bleeding and set the bones. Thanks to my assistant, his legs are bound to splints in case you need to move him, but I recommend keeping him unconscious for a couple of days while the bones knit. I'm afraid I can't spare the energy to complete the process myself."

The father grabbed his wrist. "Wait, what if you leave? How will I wake him?"

"My spell will wear off in a couple of days," Tynan promised. "He may cry out with bad dreams, though. I implore you to let him rest, no matter how difficult that may be. Stroke his brow.

Whisper to him. Whatever simple comfort you can give without disrupting the spell."

Though a new tear followed the trail of grief on the man's face, he nodded. "Very well. Thank you, healer."

When Tynan stood, the young healing apprentice rose to her feet, as well. The girl silently tucked a roll of bandages into her pouch, and she said nothing as she trailed him on his way back to Aris. Tynan still didn't know the child's name, but he understood her trauma. Even for a healer-in-training, the little girl had seen too much.

"I am primarily a mind healer," Tynan said softly as they neared Aris. "I will help you when you are ready."

The child nodded, but she didn't speak.

A wave of dizziness spun through him, and Tynan dropped heavily onto the log beside Aris. He'd only stabilized the worst of the injured villagers, yet exhaustion already weighted his limbs and dulled his thoughts. It didn't help that he hadn't done more than doze lightly on the long flight over. And when was the last time he'd eaten? Aris had nabbed a bag of bread and cheese from the dining room when they'd left Braelyn, but they'd finished that off somewhere over the ocean.

"You need to take a break," Aris said, his concerned gaze sweeping over Tynan. "I'm not sure if even life magic would make much of a difference at the moment."

He wasn't sure, either. At this point, numbness had swallowed the relentless sea of emotions bobbing to and fro around him. He was simply too exhausted to connect, much less amplify. Truthfully, the effect disconcerted him a little. Could he have done harm to himself or to his gift by opening himself too much?

"Tynan?" Aris asked. "Are you too bad off to speak?"

Tynan sighed. "Merely tired and hungry, I think. Sorry."

"I'm afraid I can't help with the hunger, but I can provide energy if you want to try it."

Shaking his head, Tynan let his eyes drift closed. Life magic was easier to process than energy received from others, but all external magic required one's body to convert it to match one's own energy signature. Life magic needed such a negligible amount that Tynan hadn't noticed the cost at the healing tower. But now? Even the slightest strain on his internal reserves required great thought.

"Too bad we don't have Lial," Tynan muttered. "My talent for physical healing is so much weaker and the cost so much higher. He would be able to help far more."

Aris *hmm*'d beneath his breath. "What was it you said? If we've been chosen, it's for the strength we've built? I think you underestimate yourself. Besides, you've helped in ways you do not see. The very calm of your energy has brought so much peace. Look around."

Prying his gritty eyes open, Tynan did as Aris suggested. Sure enough, there was a greater ease to the people around him. Not a great deal, considering their trauma, but a hint more laxness to their postures and less fearful wariness on their faces. Best of all, the haze of shock had cleared just a touch more.

Iski walked over, a basket draped over her arm. With a slight smile, she handed it over. "There's a little food in there. Mostly dried game, unfortunately, but it's better than nothing. I've had the hardiest of the adolescents raiding the ruins of the storehouse on the outskirts. The fresher stuff would be scattered in the rubble of houses, and being out in the open like that seems too risky."

"Thank you," Tynan said, cleansing his hands with magic. "This is blessing enough."

It was no lie. Tynan was so hungry and depleted that the first bite of the dried, stringy meat tasted better than the finest meal. He devoured three pieces before he bothered to dig deeper into the basket where he found a pouch of seeds and a bundle of dried fruit. Equally delicious. But after a bit of each, he returned to himself enough to consider Aris and the girl.

Abashed, he held out the basket. "There's plenty, and both of you must be hungry, too."

Aris dug in readily enough, but the child was slower to grab some of the meat and fruit. Tynan had a feeling she wouldn't have accepted it at all if the basket hadn't come from Iski. There was too much wariness behind the child's searching gaze and hesitant hand.

Iski offered a water pouch next. Tynan gulped down several mouthfuls of the clear, cool liquid before handing it back. He didn't have time to rest, though. There were far too many injuries to heal, and the more people of sound body, the better chance of everyone's survival. Sound mind...well, that would take far longer.

He and Aris had just started toward the next-worst patient when a roar rent the air from the direction of the village, followed promptly by a loud *crack* and then a shriek. Several of the fae screamed in fear, and more than a few moaned. But when a deep thud boomed through the trees and trembled in the ground, Tynan considered joining them. That sounded like a dragon crashing into land.

Kezari. Had she been felled?

His heart leapt, the sudden pounding of his pulse filling his ears until the cries around him faded to nothing. Kezari had gone up there to scout. Had Baza slipped around to attack? He'd spent so much time worrying that he would hurt her with his emotions, and now he might have sent her to a physical doom.

He didn't *feel* anything wrong. Would he? They were bound, but the link wasn't complete on her end, not without that gemstone. Would that affect his ability to sense her pain? No, that didn't make sense. Incomplete bonds were more unstable, increasing the likelihood that both would die if one did. Pain would surely be more intense.

A hand gripped his shoulder, drawing Tynan to a sudden halt. When had he started moving? *No matter.* He spun around to face the new threat, but it was Aris who stepped back with lifted hands.

"What are you doing?" Aris asked.

Some of Tynan's terror cleared, and the path beyond the fae

camp clarified in his view. He'd darted after Kezari without a moment's thought. His entire body shook, and his lungs burned from his frantic gasping. A panic attack. He bent at the waist, bracing his hands against his upper thighs and staring at the ground as he sucked in slower, deeper breaths.

"It is not her," Aris said quietly. "We both would have felt her injury. If my senses are correct, it's her cousin, and she's not yet dead."

Finally, Tynan was steady enough to straighten. "I'm not sure why I panicked to that extent. Perhaps the ambient emotions during the—" A new worry made his blood run cold. "Tell me I didn't send that out to the others."

"You didn't," Aris assured him. "Whatever balance you found with your shields, they held."

Relief eased his clenched muscles and soothed his fear-twisted heart.

Then another *crack-thud-boom*, this one too distant to send more than a vibration through the ground. His hand darting out, Aris gripped Tynan's shoulder. Hard. "Still not her."

Tynan nodded, that truth clearer outside the deluge of fear swamping the camp. Nevertheless, he had to return there. He had no idea how to heal a dragon, but the vulnerable fae needed him and Aris to help keep them safe. If nothing else, Tynan could channel a hefty dose of terror into the heart of any intruder.

If said intruder showed themselves.

UNEASINESS SANG the same discordant tone as the incessant whimpering in Kezari's head. She was nearly to the tiny island where the renegades had retreated, and she'd yet to encounter anyone. If any of the queen's council had come to kill the dragonlings, they'd either succeeded or fled. Kezari saw nothing to indicate battle or even habitation.

But the increasing moan told a different story.

Finally, she understood the terrible *wrongness* that had overcome Aris when he'd detected Korel, whose blood had been loaded with a spell-created virus. That sense that something good, pure, and natural had been perverted by dark magic...it tore through her insides until she nearly vomited fire. What *was* this?

On shaky wings, she landed on a long stretch of beach. Though it looked peaceful, the ground beneath her feet cried out with its own horrified voice. It almost reminded her of the poison that Kien had used on Earth—yet not. This sickness held as much attraction as repulsion, and it had a nexus.

That central point probably rested somewhere beyond the cave entrance that opened like a trap in the side of the island's long-dormant volcano. A cave would be a perfect place for an ambush, and that would explain the absence of others. If Baza was using the dragonlings to get to her, they would all be waiting inside.

Kezari shrank herself to the same small form she used at Braelyn to dart between the massive trees. Then once again, she took flight, doing her best to scan the area while trying not to throw up. She circled the island twice. If there'd ever been any game here, those animals were long gone, but otherwise, nothing appeared to be physically out of place. There was only the cave left to check.

But as soon as she neared, dragonlings poured out like a colony of bats. Kezari drew into a hover. Should she shift to her full size for protection? If they were maddened... Yet the swoops and dives and cries weren't aggressive as they swirled around her.

"Are you here to defeat the darkness?"

"Did you bring food?"

"Only the youngest can go in. You look young."

"Even a little *daeri*?"

"All this power is useless when you're hungry."

"Hush. Baza's bringing us food when he's killed the dark sorcerer."

Cracked claws, but they talked more than Tebzn. Unfortunately, their words made even less sense. Darkness? Power? Sorcerers? What was going on here?

Kezari scanned them for signs of ill health, but although they were a little thin, they were far from mindless and crazed. In fact, their energy glowed with the vitality of a full link to Earth. What they *had* was an excess of exuberance, since clearly no one had taught them how to channel all that power.

So why were they on a creepy island in the middle of the ocean?

"I don't have food, either," Kezari said, trying her best to sound young. "Baza said to wait in the cave."

"Grrrrr, that's what he always says," a light blue dragonling moaned. "Well, we are supposed to keep the sick ones safe until the sorcerer is dead."

Sick ones. That didn't sound good. Dread weighted Kezari's wings as she followed the flight of dragonlings into the dark cave entrance. The musty smell held some comfort, but not enough to counter the growing sickness of approaching...whatever this was. An effect not heightened by the half-rotten bones abandoned here and there along the tunnels, the steadily increasing heat, or the strange, frantic chattering of the young ones. Hunger, darkness, and sorcerers apparently made up their whole world.

The tunnel finally opened into a vast cavern, all but a few columns smoothed away from a strange pillar in the center. To the right, several dragonlings huddled together in a pile, only a couple of them bothering to raise their heads. She didn't have to scan to see that they were sick. Deathly sick.

An angry scream jerked her attention to the left, but there was no immediate threat. No, it was more horror—someone had formed bars across a small cavern full of dragonlings. Hissing, snarling, raging ones, too. So Tebzn's claim of maddened young hadn't been entirely wrong.

"Baza didn't say what I was supposed to do," Kezari ventured.

"Guard. Give energy," a dragonling chirped happily. "Only we are strong enough to protect the crystal after the surge."

The crystal? Kezari peered around the room, but it was a real challenge not to linger over the afflicted young. At least until her gaze passed over the pillar and then caught. In the middle sat a perfectly round stone of deep green shot through with veins of blue. It hummed and pulsed to the resonance of that awful whine, but it shouldn't have.

Because that was one of *her* own stones.

She nearly shifted to her full form at once, but she forced herself to wait. Though her body didn't bear the softness of a youngling, they weren't observant enough in their current state to realize that. If she resumed her usual stature, they would no doubt attack, and she would end up hurting them—and receiving injury, too. Most were too small to use much magic, but there were a lot of them. All with teeth, claws, and an even worse grasp of impulse control than she possessed.

So Kezari drifted with the slower young ones as they circled the cavern in manic loops. Fortunately, there was a benefit to her age—multiple points of focus. She'd flown so long that it required little thought, so she was able to turn her energy and attention to the stone.

It still bore some of her energy signature beneath Baza's attempt at possession. But he'd gained enough control of the powerful gem to use it as a focus for two intertwined spells. One pulled energy from the dragonlings, and the other...dug? Magically speaking. There was something buried deep beneath the floor of the cavern, but it was surrounded by strong shields. Baza was using the gemstone to crack through them.

Her curiosity over the mysterious treasure blazed so brightly she considered leaving the spell alone, but only a heartbeat passed before she regained her senses. That spell was killing the dragonlings, and that *drec* Baza had set the young ones to guard their own doom. Oh, she wanted to gut him a thousand times. How long had he lain in wait with this plan?

It had been guile keeping him in his cave, not laziness.

No wonder he wanted her dead. She was one of the few

strong enough in earth magic to unwind this mess, especially with her own stone and energy part of the mix. But she needed to do it fast. If Baza was hunting food for the young, he wouldn't be gone long.

Reduced size or not, he would recognize her at once.

# CHAPTER FORTY

Tynan and Aris had barely made it back to the camp when the voice blasted through. *"Send up Kezari with her mate, or I will burn this entire forest to the ground."*

Sobs and cries rang out around him, and some of the uninjured fae scattered from the camp and into the deeper forest. Others sat frozen where they'd huddled, too terrified to flee. Neither group would fare well if the woods were set aflame. Tynan peered up at the bits of sky he could see between the branches. No dragon directly overhead, but the source of that voice was probably close.

"There are three of them," Aris murmured. "One has a powerful lifeforce, the kind often seen in mages. I'd bet it's Baza."

Cold apprehension trickled down Tynan's spine. "And he wants Kezari and *me*. How does he know she has a mate?"

A blinding flash forced him to cover his eyes, and thunder rumbled so hard that his chest reverberated with it. In the silent lull after its passing, wood creaked and then snapped, landing somewhere with a thud. Tynan cautiously lowered his arm and spotted a large tree limb across the path. In the space where the limb had been, he glimpsed the red-gold glimmer of dragon scales in the distance.

Iski rushed up beside them. "It seems Kezari didn't find him. That's the same dragon and his friends who attacked last time."

Before he could reply, wind swept through the trees. The harsh slap of it tore at hair and clothes and toppled supplies. Another branch crashed down, nearly landing on a couple crouched beside a trunk. A charge filled the air, too, and Tynan's skin prickled in reaction. More lightning?

*"Where are they?"*

The limb covering the path burst into flames, and a wave of pure terror crashed into him along with the cries and moans from behind him. Tynan's shields bowed beneath the weight. *Lady Bera, help me hold it,* he prayed, scrambling to reinforce his only protection. Then Iski flicked her hand, quenching the flames with her water, and the distraction eased the villagers' panic enough for him to regain control.

For the moment.

He had to get out of here, or his empathy would defeat him before the dragon did.

"I need to lead him away. I'll try to reach Kezari, but I'm not sure my range is good enough," Tynan said to Aris. "Stay here and try to contact Kezari, too. He doesn't seem to know about you."

The life mage scowled. "That's neither safe nor wise."

"Do you think I can withstand a village-worth of panic?"

He couldn't stop the tremble that swept through him, but even as Aris debated, another tree burst into flame. Then another. A scream pierced the air—this one from above—and a moment later, a pale blue dragon skimmed just above the tree line, sending hailstone crashing down atop the camp. Terror smashed into Tynan with equal force, and for the first time since his earlier working, a crack formed in his shield.

Panic nearly stole his breath.

If he lost control, who would help him regain it?

No other priests.

No other mind mages.

*Lady Bera, help.*

*"Aris,"* he managed to send.

"Go," Aris said. "Run through the trees bordering the path, and you'll find Kezari's cousin. She might be able to reach Kezari if I can't."

After a nod, Tynan dashed toward the trees, letting the panic fuel his flight. If he could get far enough from the fae camp, he could unleash the emotions pounding through him, but now? Right now, he could kill. Better Baza receive the force of that.

Lady Bera *had* said she would greet the souls of the fallen. It was up to Her to dispense punishment or reward after that.

THE SPELL WOULD DEFUSE if Kezari could disconnect it from the stone, the stolen energy returning to the dragonlings. Which... might not be the best for the maddened handful scrabbling at the bars between fits of hissing and snarling. Was it having their power drained that caused the illness, or would the rebound only make things worse? She was no healer to know, but there wasn't another choice.

Connecting with her own energy still imbued within the gem, Kezari gradually increased the force of her own power. She'd found and excavated the stone, then shaped and smoothed it in the heart of her energy. As any earth dragon understood, stone remembered. It held entire histories in its depths, and this particular gem held more than others. She needed to apply very little pressure for it to recognize her.

Baza's spell shattered with an audible crack, and a blinding amount of power exploded through the small cavern. The force of it buffeted her until she struggled to stay aloft, and the shrieking younglings fared no better. When the flash of light cleared, the never-ending, itchy, awful whine no longer echoed in her head.

And Kezari was one of the few still in flight.

Worried, she darted around the cavern, checking on the dragonlings who'd tumbled to the floor. But the young were softer and rounder for a reason. Aside from a few bruises and strained wings, none were hurt.

Across the cavern, the huddled clump of lethargic dragonlings stirred, heads poking up and wings flapping as though testing the air. Kezari turned to the barred room, and relief stalled her wing-beats for a moment at the sight of the younglings sitting on the ground. They blinked at each other, then out into the chamber. She would wager they had no clue where they were.

"What happened?"

"Was the sorcerer defeated?"

"I have even *more* power!"

"I want to go home."

"This place is boring. What am I doing here?"

"Isn't anyone going to bring me some *daeri*?"

Kezari smiled at the cacophony of voices, as exuberant as ever. But no longer under Baza's control. Already, they'd stopped gathering around the central pillar. Some hurried over to their waking brethren, and others flew up to the barred room. Curious, Kezari landed on the pillar and waited. Would they care that she was so close to the gemstone?

"Wait. Why is Meyzen locked up? Who would do such a thing?"

The more Baza's spell wore off, the angrier the dragonlings became. Now, their frenetic energy shifted to a new goal—justice. And *daeri*, of course, but mostly justice.

Kezari leapt into the air, shifting her size as soon as she'd cleared the pillar. Though the cavern wasn't large enough for her to safely assume her full form, the dragonlings squeaked in alarm, regardless. At half her usual size, she settled on her haunches and curled her wings against her back. They would only remain shocked for a moment.

*"Baza trapped you here,"* Kezari sent through the room. *"He's been stealing your power for some dark purpose, and he's had some of the younger adults helping him."*

Silence. Then the noise—ancestors' bones, the *noise*. Cries and screams and demands. So many questions. So. Many. Had she thought them exuberant before? Hah. That chattering had been nothing. Kezari liked dragonlings in general, but nearly twenty of them upset at the same time?

No.

So she did the only thing she could think of.

Kezari roared, and in the void of the sound, quiet finally reigned again. "Everyone thinks you attacked the fae village, so it isn't safe for you to fly home," she said aloud. "The queen would have you killed."

A little, golden dragonling hovered in front of her. "Oh, no. We didn't do that. But there was this sorcerer...I think..."

Kezari's heart softened at the confused tilt to the young one's head. "It was a lie, I'm afraid. I need to find you a safe place to hide until the adults have the misunderstanding all cleared up."

But where could she take them? She'd already been gone longer than she'd like, leaving Tynan and Aris vulnerable. Maybe one of the tiny islands to the west of the fae settlement? With enough shielding, it might be safe enough. What else could she do?

"Wait for me outside," Kezari said. "I want to make sure Baza's spell is truly gone. Then, I'll find a place for you to stay."

With a flex of her power, she opened the bars trapping the confused-but-now-docile dragonlings in the other chamber. Then she waited as the young ones flew out. Based on how weak some were—or battered from hitting the wall—several of them would struggle to fly so far west and south, but it would be better than staying here. Even if Baza didn't return, there was always the chance that one of the queen's minions would.

Once the last, chattering youngling was well beyond the cavern, Kezari examined the ground beneath her feet. What had Baza been so desperate to retrieve? Now that the dragonlings were safe, she couldn't resist taking a moment to find out. But first, she reclaimed the green-blue gemstone from the pillar. Its smooth weight was perfect in her talon's grip. Absolutely perfect. She let out a sigh of pure joy.

Now to store it somewhere safe, far from Baza's reach.

Thankfully, she'd already planned a spot for a new hoard—there was a secure chamber hidden in the wall of her cave at Braelyn. Though she was loathe to release the stone, she sent it to safety with a pop of magic. She could check it for damage later.

There was no visible sign of possible treasure on the cavern floor. No marks or mystical symbols. But now that Baza's spell no longer hummed through the room—nor the moaning of the injured dragonlings—Kezari could sense the immense power lingering far below.

She connected with the cave, sinking her consciousness deep into the stone around her. Echoes of dark magic lingered, but the energy pulsing deeper had no connection to that. What was it? Carefully, she drifted closer until she could almost touch the outer shield. This was what Baza had tried to crack through. But why had he needed *her* gemstone imbued with *her* power to do it?

With a tentative mental hand, Kezari gently probed the shield —only to recoil in shock. This was familiar. Not quite her own energy, but so close that...

Her mother.

Her mother had buried this here.

His claws digging through scales, Egrenneth perched atop Zevie and roared. Blood, both hers and his, rolled down his chest to plop against her back, and when she squirmed, he tightened his hold. One rip of his right talon, and he would sever the joint between wing and back. A sharp enough twist of his left, and he could crack her spine.

They both knew it.

But the curious thing? None of the dragons ringing the broad cavern made the first attempt to defend her. Not even the one who'd been on Zevie's council. Apparently, she did not have the loyalty she thought she did.

"Where is the Monarch's Hoard?" Ren demanded, pressing a little harder on her wing with his claw. "Your mother surely claimed it."

"Gone. Only a rumor," Zevie gasped out.

"Is that so?" he pinched his claws together another inch and waited for her scream of pain to fade. "That would mean your family pretended to lead this colony for, what, six or seven thousand years? It's fortunate for you that your negligence drained Earth's energy too much to allow dragons to shift, for had we discovered this, you would have been dead long ago. You should have known that one of Deyriglair's line would hunt you down for usurping the throne."

"Few remember you or Earth," Zevie snarled, twitching restlessly in his hold.

Ren flicked his tail and tried not to wince at the burst of pain from a slash she'd scored. "I'm sure that's on purpose. It's easier to control dragons who have no understanding of their history or their true power, isn't it? Ancient or not, I should have been torn to pieces long before I reached you, their so-called queen. Fair but unyielding. That's how our kind should be."

Zevie had no rebuttal for that, and in the lull, silence consumed the room. It was too quiet. Ren scanned the area for signs of attack, but there was no hint of such in the dragons' horrified stares—not for him, but for their pretend queen. She'd done an excellent job of obscuring their history if they hadn't realized she wasn't part of the original ruling line.

But if there was no immediate threat, then why was he so edgy? Wait, the cries. At some point in the middle of battle, the relentless screams of the young had cut off. Was it for good or ill? He'd left Kezari to help heal the fae, not tackle whatever spell had connected with the Monarch's Stone. Had she found it on her own?

"Present the Monarch's Hoard to me to prove your legitimacy, and I will let you live." An easy promise, since he didn't think she had it. "Fair but unyielding, just as I said. Fail to comply, and I will snap your neck for the crimes you have committed."

Zevie shrieked. "What crimes could a *queen* commit?"

"There are some laws beyond nations," Ren said, his left claw tightening on her neck. "A universal decency. You've failed in the monarch's sworn duty to uphold the ancient laws, which is bad enough. But to order these dragons to disconnect from Earth's energy? That's their origin point, one that allows them access to the universal flow. It's like cutting off their soul. Which is the same, I might add, as stealing or revoking another's hoard, something formed with a dragon's soul energy. Those are crimes against all dragonkind, and I mean to see them rectified. Present the Monarch's Stone. Last chance."

"My mother never found the hoard, but Baza is looking for where they hid it," Zevie cried out in a rush. "He thinks he's found it. Now that he has Kezari's earth crystal, he's been able to—"

*Crack.*

With teeth and talon, Ren severed her spine. He'd found out what he needed to know—not only did Zevie not have the hoard, she'd never possessed it at all. But it was hidden somewhere on the Isle, and with it, the crystal given by his father to the first king. The Monarch's Stone, sealed with Deyriglair's blood to link the rightful ruler here with the dragons of Moranaia.

And to Earth's former wall.

∿

T YNAN'S HEART raced faster than his feet as he ran beneath the too-sparse trees.

Once he'd cleared the camp, he'd sent a challenge into the sky —*this is Kezari's mate. Come find me.* Two of the dragons had answered, one red-gold and the other silver, but for some reason, they hadn't attacked. Only followed. Were they waiting for him to reach Tebzn so they could finish both of them off? He'd tried to stay beneath cover as much as he could, but so far, not even a stray leaf had fallen along the path.

From the direction of the camp, he heard another scream. Had Baza not been satisfied? Was there some other danger? As Tynan leapt over a rock and darted around a thin tree, he reached for his link to Kezari. And he felt her—alive, but intensely focused on something. Yet no matter how much he tried, he couldn't connect telepathically. Either she'd flown very far, or his gift for mental speech was too weak.

Aris. Maybe Aris would be close enough.

*Please be in range. Please.*

He'd almost given up when the connection clicked.

*"I haven't connected to Kezari yet,"* Aris sent, urgency slipping through with the words. *"That ice-wielding dragon hasn't relented, so Iski's directing another evacuation. The fae are scattering through the forest so there's more than one location to target."*

*"They* aren't *attacking me,"* Tynan replied. *"Am I close to Tebzn?"*

*"Yes. I'll try for Kezari again, but a dragon might have better luck."*

The link cut off, and Tynan cursed as the silver dragon skimmed the branches above his head. Bera's heart. They were playing with him like he was prey—feeble prey, at that. Why did his telepathy have to be so weak? Perhaps if their bond had been complete, he might have reached Kezari across the distance, but there was no way to be sure now.

His only hope was reaching Tebzn, his bonded's potentially treacherous cousin. She'd been able to reach Kezari on the other side of the world. If she could do the same here, then Tynan could rest easy. Help would be on the way for the others.

And if he lost control, only his enemies would suffer.

# CHAPTER FORTY-ONE

$I$t was no good. Though Aris could sense Kezari, he simply couldn't form a mental link with her. Which was unfortunate, because Baza didn't seem to care that Tynan had offered himself as bait. Why would Baza relent when he had an ice dragon who could launch spears from the sky?

The few healthy fae who had darted from the camp had returned to carry litters holding the injured, but the evacuation was far too slow. If Aris were close enough, he could suck the spark of life from the dragon and send it to the ether. Killing with his power was a horrid experience, but he would do it to save others. From here, though? Accuracy would reduce at such distance, which meant he might pull the spark of life from others, too.

"Can no one here cast adequate shields?" he asked when Iski skidded to a halt beside him.

She shook her head. "The best mages died fighting Baza in the first two attacks, and the rest are too drained. I'm not sure what else we can do besides scatter. My water magic won't do well against ice."

The other elf darted off again. Ice slashed down between the canopy of leaves, and Aris dodged out of instinct. It hit so close that frigid shards prickled his face before melting. He gasped at the shock, staring at the deadly point of the icicle melting into the ground. Wherever Kezari was, it would take far too long for her to save them from this.

His hand closed around the crystal in his pocket. According to Selia, there were enough charges on it to immobilize dragons in a wide swath once or maybe twice. But at what distance? And had she been counting on dragon *mages*? Kezari hadn't known a counter, but she was an earth dragon. If Aris tried and failed to contain these dragons, this entire camp would be annihilated.

They needed help, and he knew exactly where to find it.

Ancient treaties could fall into the ether.

Slipping between evacuating fae and dodging a few more spears of ice, Aris dashed toward a thick stand of trees on the quieter end of the camp where few had fled. After a quick glance up to confirm that the dragon hadn't seen him, he pulled the chain from beneath his tunic and wrapped his hand firmly around the crystal. Gods knew what time it would be on the other side of the world.

But Selia would come. He simply knew.

SELIA STARED into the still darkness outside her bedroom window and prayed for the dawn. For Aris. And Kezari and Tynan. Even for the dragons. Anxiety made a feast of her stomach, though, no matter how fervently she prayed. Were they safe? How long would they be gone?

"You should have gone, *Onaiala*," Iren said softly behind her.

She spun to face her son and wanted to weep at the dark circles hollowing his too-old eyes. When had he begun to look at her with the shadows of manhood in his gaze? It seemed like only yesterday that he'd smiled at her with nothing but a child's joy.

"There was too much risk that we might not return." A terrible, sobering thought in light of the worry pinching her heart.

Would Aris return? "You've been through too much, my love. And if you were orphaned... Well, I know how much you hate the strictures of your grandfather's home."

The smile he gave now held nothing but sadness. "I could go to the Citadel early. Not that I want to lose you or *Onaial*. It's just...some battles must be fought, and we can't always choose when to fight them. Like the time I had to throw a fireball at that intruder to save Arlyn. It was awful, but I would do it again."

Mature gaze or no, Selia pulled her son into her arms and buried her face against the top of his head—which was surely too close to her own. When had he grown so tall? His arms curled around her waist in a tight squeeze, and she recognized then how worried he must be to let her hold him. This from the boy who groaned when she tucked him in.

When he finally stepped back, a hint of tears welled in his eyes. "I hope he's okay."

Selia opened her mouth to offer assurances she didn't exactly feel, but a warning ping from the training room shields froze her. The portal was forming. Aris had to be alive to use it, but that didn't mean he was in good condition. If he needed help, he would already have to wait several drips for the long-distance gate to form.

"Go," Iren said.

She frowned over her shoulder at him as she darted to the box where she kept her energy crystals. "Did you key yourself into the shields again? I told you—"

"Lecture later," Iren interrupted, lips twitching. "Go. Do whatever needs to be done. I'm not five anymore, *Onaiala*. I *know*."

Selia could see that he did—and quite well. Aside from stopping the attack on Arlyn, he'd been with them on Earth when Aris and Kezari had helped form the permanent gate. He'd witnessed Perim almost killing her, too. Not to mention the glimpses he'd seen of his father's torture. Her poor, sweet boy was far too aware of the darkness in the world.

"Here." Iren waved his hand, and a thin, wavering—but passable—gate sprang to life.

Though she could barely see the door to the training tower on the other side, Selia hurried toward it, stopping to look at her son before continuing through. "I love you, Iren. I'm proud of you."

"I love you, *Onaiala*," Iren said. "I'm proud of you, too."

Tears clouded her eyes as she walked through the gate into the bitter cold. But she had to tuck away the ache in her heart, or she would be no help to anyone. Selia shoved her free hand into the pocket of her dress for warmth and sent a mental call to Lyr as she opened the door. He responded at once—at his desk, of course—but there was little for her to report. She had no idea what she would find.

The warning spells on the training room shifted from a ping to full alert as the edges of the portal formed. Selia hurried through the door toward the image taking shape on the far wall, but something tugged at her skirt. A paralyzing spell sprang into her hand, but before she could cast it, Eri swung around to stand in front of her.

Or...not Eri. Not entirely.

"The treaty must be reformed since the dragons have no ruler now. Go save our lost kin. The lord here must send warriors through." Her little mouth pinched into a thin line, and then the haze of the goddess dimmed a little in her eyes. "Only a royal can authorize this, and that's me. Have the injured brought into this room, by the authority of Moranai Aldiaberen i Erinalia Moreln nai Moranaia."

"Your father..."

"Will ground me to my room for a month," Eri said, her voice full of tired resignation. "It's okay. Grownups just don't have the patience to look through that many strands. Or maybe it's the free time. I probably wouldn't have either if it wasn't for Iren."

The portal finally solidified, at least as much as it was going to over such a distance. Aris stared at her across the space, his brow pinched in indecision. If he crossed through, the gate would collapse, and it would take her a massive amount of energy to reform it. She needed to go.

"Now," Eri said. "*Onaial*'s going to wake up any minute. Oh, don't forget to keep the portal open, and send the worst of the injured through."

"Very well." Slipping around the child, Selia dashed toward the gate. "Take care of Iren for me," she called over her shoulder.

"Nah," the child replied. "He'd better be able to take care of himself."

On that odd note, Selia stepped into pure chaos.

TYNAN FOUND Tebzn's crumpled form atop a broken tree branch. Her chest rose and fell with breath, but the eye he could see remained closed. How did one wake a hurt dragon without getting eaten? Most injured beings lashed out when in pain, and he didn't want to be mistaken as a threat—or a snack.

He sent a wave of calming energy to surround her and waited. No response. So he scanned her with his healing magic to see how she fared. He was in no way trained in dragon physiology, but that wasn't exactly a requirement in this case. Her wounds were all-too-obvious. She had five broken ribs, and several of the bones were snapped in the wing she'd landed on. Some internal bleeding that had nearly stopped on its own. And a concussion. Of course.

Suddenly, a blood-curdling scream of rage slashed through the sky. Lightning crackled in an endless dance, leaping and snapping between rapidly building clouds. Tynan crouched low and prayed the underbrush would give him some cover, at least from being seen. He wanted no part of whatever had caused that cry.

He focused on doing what he could for Tebzn. He dared not attempt to knit her bones, especially not in her wings, without her being awake. With an elf, he would prompt natural healing with his magic, but if that prompt wasn't the same for dragons, he could ruin her ability to fly again.

Instead, he did his best to ease the swelling around her brain. Still risky, but not as much so. It didn't appear to help a great deal, for she still remained unconscious. What should he do? He needed Tebzn to contact Kezari. This was far too much for he and Aris to handle alone.

Between one breath and another, a dragon hovered above the tiny clearing. The red and gold one. *I should kill you now, but I won't. She will come for you.*

"Baza, I presume?" Tynan asked.

*"Precisely so."* Steam rolled from the dragon's mouth. *"Call your mate, or I'll change my mind about killing you."*

Under that predator's gaze, Tynan couldn't move. A single bite, and he would be gone. Sheer terror shook him. But it was all *his* emotion—he detected nothing from Baza. Would Tynan's fear alone have enough of an effect if it was pushed into the dragon's mind? Could he break through any shields to do so?

Something squeezed around his body, forcing the air from his lungs. His blood burned and his mind raced as he tried to suck in air. What was it? What was killing him?

*"Leave him alive,"* Baza snapped.

The pressure eased enough for air, at least, and that allowed clearer thoughts to slip through. Something held him. When Tynan dared to glance down, it was to find himself in the grip of a massive silver claw.

He averted his gaze, and in that motion, he saw a hint of hope. Tebzn's eye had opened the tiniest crack. Would she be aware enough to understand? He didn't have much choice but to try.

"I can't reach Kezari at this distance," Tynan said. "I was hoping to find a dragon who could, but this one is almost dead."

Baza bared his teeth. "How about we take you closer, hmm?"

Before he could ask what the dragon meant, Tynan's world went black.

~

WORRIED-SOUNDING dragonling voices echoed from the tunnels as Kezari finally hovered the treasure out of its hiding spot. The boulder was half the size of her head in full dragon form, but otherwise, it was only a smooth, solid slab of milky gray stone. What was so special about it? She scanned it with her earth magic and then gasped. The outer layer was sedimentary rock, but it wasn't a type she'd found here. No, she'd last encountered this when carving and shaping the outpost on Earth.

And it was hollow.

The chattering drew nearer. Not much time. Quickly, she parted the top layer of stone and peeked inside. Atop a rainbow of gems sat a massive, deep red sphere of pure, raw ruby. Had she been in her elven form, the stone would be almost as large as she was. As a dragon, it would take both talons to hold. The rarity of such a piece was beyond all reason. She nearly touched it with an outstretched claw, but it hummed and pulsed with so much magic that she didn't dare.

"Did she abandon us?"

"Maybe it was a trick."

"Not if everyone got better, right?"

Dread turned her stomach as Kezari resealed the rock over the priceless gem before the young ones could see it. This had to be kept safe from Baza. Though the outer shields on the hiding place had been forged by her mother, the magic of this hoard held a different energy. She had to hide the treasure until she could consult with Egrenneth, and there was only one place she could think of—her cave at Braelyn.

Thank the ancestors that she'd prepared to gather a large hoard, since this would take up a great deal of space. As tiny wing-beats snapped nearer, she activated the spell to send the rock to her hiding place. Then she closed the hole in the cavern here, smoothing the floor over just in time for the dragonlings to round the bend.

"We waited and waited," the golden one said.

Kezari nodded. "There was a lot of magic to safely clear, but I'm finished now. Let's gather outside."

She shrank to follow the young ones out, and despite the worry creeping through her, she smiled a little at the chittering laughs of the dragonlings at her change in size. It was a magic they would only master as they grew, for one could only shrink to a size one had already been. As such, it never failed to amuse the littlest.

Once outside, Kezari resumed her full form, and a few of the young ones chirped in surprise. "Oh, you are old," the brave golden dragonling said.

Kezari's breath puffed out on a chuckle. "Not quite four hundred, you know."

"Will I ever be that old?"

"That's forever!"

"My grandfather is nine-thousand-years-old, so that four hundred doesn't sound too bad."

"Did he see the planets shaped?"

"Ancestors' snouts, we have history older than that, idiot. Pretty sure planets are older than dragons."

Shaking her head, Kezari stretched out her wings and gave a warning flap. *Prepare for flight.* But as the dragonlings took to the air and spread out to allow her more room, Tebzn's voice crashed into her like a tumbling dragon.

*"Baza is here. He's carrying your mate away, but I'm too injured to fly. No clue what happened to Noqi. Come back, come back."*

Her cousin's voice faded as though she'd run out of strength.

But Kezari was too overcome with rage to care.

# CHAPTER FORTY-TWO

Egrenneth had barely cleansed the blood from his scales before he'd taken to the sky again. He'd demanded and received blood-and-magic-sworn oaths over the pretend queen's body, but there was still a chance of betrayal. If so, he would deal with it when he had to. He needed to fly north to see if Kezari had found the Monarch's Hoard, or he wouldn't be the full, rightful king, either.

The scent of salt had just started to strengthen in the air when he sensed the stumbling approach of another. He glanced quickly over his shoulder. Was that one of the first they'd met? One that he'd ordered to guard the village? He swung back around to see.

Soon, he recognized her—Noqi. Her wingbeats were unsteady, her body wobbling as though she might crash at any moment. He flew as quickly as he could to meet her, but instead of hovering in flight, she circled him. Unable to balance herself, then.

"Baza attacked," she said. "Kezari went out scouting, and I don't know if Tebzn is dead. He got her first, and she crashed hard."

Ren cursed. Which direction should he go? Help save the dragonlings or the fae villagers? Both were rather pressing matters.

But before he took the time to decide, he pinned Noqi with a fierce stare.

"Your message is delivered. Land somewhere safe and take care of yourself," Ren ordered.

She gasped. "But you might need help!"

"Dead allies aren't allies anymore," he pointed out. "Land before you do real harm to your wings, and do not question my orders again."

Though she gave him a quick, searching glance, she nodded and cut away instead of continuing to circle him. Normally, he would have watched to ensure she complied, but he didn't have time. Instead, he angled to the northwest. He would need to fly south and west to reach the village, so at least he would be moving in *one* proper direction. After scouting the coastline in search of the dragonlings, he would turn south.

Then a pained cry resounded from the north, and he forced his tired wings to move faster.

INSENSIBLE, Kezari launched herself into the sky. She could see nothing but the sharp lines of Tynan's face. The full curve of his lips when he smiled. His vulnerable pain and regret when he'd told her of his past. Beyond that childhood mistake, what had he ever done except try to help others?

Nothing, but still he suffered.

Was he hurt? Could she save him?

Deep inside, she found their bond and held it tight, her greatest treasure. He was alive. She felt it. But when she tried to reach his mind with hers, there was only darkness. Again, she roared out her grief.

Little moaning cries rang out around her. The dragonlings. She hadn't even realized they'd followed her. What was she to do? They would never be able to keep up, and she couldn't bear to slow down. There had to be a place for them to go.

"What's wrong?" the golden one called.

"My mate was taken," Kezari snarled.

She couldn't focus on the chatter that followed. It was approaching midday, and the wind had picked up with the rising heat. Her very heart followed the currents that would best lead her back to the fae camp. Nothing else mattered besides that.

From time to time, she thought she felt a flicker along their link, and not long after, her earlier dread bloomed into fear. Not fully hers, she recognized. If his emotions were leaking into hers, was she getting close enough for speech? Tebzn could reach her through the ground, but Tynan didn't have that advantage.

A deep red, nearly the same shade as the ruby she'd found, glinted on the horizon, approaching at speed. Ren. She turned south to meet him, but several of the dragonlings cried out in fear.

"Who is that?"

"Scary, scary, scary."

Kezari snorted. "He's an ancient one from Earth. If anyone can keep you safe, he will."

"Ooooh, ancient!"

"If an old person says someone is ancient, they have to be near death."

This time, Kezari's terror and rage burned too bright for amusement to make a spark.

*"What happened?"* Ren sent before they were close enough to each other to stop.

*"According to Tebzn, Baza captured Tynan,"* she replied. *"I will not pause, so don't bother asking. Just ensure the young ones' safety. I'd thought to take them to an island far west of the fae village, but they'll never keep up."*

He sent a mental hum of assent. *"I would never ask you to stop. But did you find the Monarch's Hoard?"*

*"If you mean a giant Earth rock hiding a ruby even Ralan couldn't afford, then yes."* Kezari ground her teeth together at the thought of that stupid treasure, the cause of her current woes. *"I*

*spell-sent it to a safe place at Braelyn. Find me once the dragonlings are safe, and I'll retrieve it for you."*

As Ren neared, Kezari ordered the dragonlings to follow him. Then ordered them a few *more* times before they complied, being young ones. The golden one was the last to pull away with Ren to the west, and she kept giving sad glances over her shoulder. Kezari did her best to ignore the bold dragonling.

She had destruction to rain down on a certain reptile to the south.

~

TYNAN STIRRED SLOWLY TO AWARENESS, but even when he opened his eyes, the world was dark. He reached for his healing magic to scan himself for injury. It didn't comply. His heart thumped hard, the relentless beat the only thing he could hear. His shields? Gone. His energy? Dispersed. Only his dratted empathy still sputtered emotion into his head.

Triumph and glee from his left. Rage and hatred from his right.

He took stock of his physical condition. His entire body ached, more acutely where sharp points dug into his side from the surface beneath him. Something cold and heavy dug into his wrists and ankles. The burn of it against his skin sent suspicion sinking hard through his stomach.

He was bound with iron. Somewhere dark, like a cave.

Oh no.

"Well, well, it seems our new friend is awake."

Sudden light blinded him, and he squeezed his eyes shut. Though he wasn't sure he wanted to see, he cracked his eyelids open a slit as soon as his vision adjusted. A young, silver-haired man stood over him, his triumphant grin suggesting he was the person to the left. The silver dragon? From the knife in the man's hand, he certainly wasn't an ally.

*"No torture,"* another voice sent. *"Yet."*

Tynan tilted his head up a little to get a better view of the room. His stomach heaved. He'd never been here, but he recognized the place with horrific clarity. He'd seen it all-too-clearly through Aris's worst memories.

"Perim wouldn't let us play with her toy before she abandoned us, Baza," the silver-haired man said. "I'd hoped to grab one of the fae who'd abandoned our cause, but you killed them all. I can't see a reason not to take a few slices now."

Sick—that was the only word for the twisted emotions pouring unfiltered into Tynan's mind. He cried out from it, and his captor laughed.

"See? Only the threat has him moaning. Let me torment him a little, and he'll call his mate sooner rather than later."

*"And bring her here already insensible with rage?"*

Tynan nearly laughed. As soon as Kezari found out what happened, there would be no escaping that.

A surge of raw anger burned through his head, and a foot connected hard with his lower back. Pain bloomed with breathtaking force. "You dare smile?"

For endless time, Tynan shivered against the frigid stone, trying not to move. If he did, he would throw up. Too much pain, from his no-doubt-bruised kidney and the searing bite of constant empathy that he couldn't stop. But with his energy drained by the shackles, he couldn't seem to gather the emotions and send them back out.

*Lady Bera, please let help get here soon.*

~

THE CRYSTALLINE CRACK of ice against shield vibrated through the air, but the dome Selia had cast over the camp held. She'd learned a great deal from helping Lyr with Braelyn's protections. Even so, the ice dragon wasn't giving up, and the drain on her power would soon grow costly.

Sword in hand, Aris stood beside the fragile portal and

poured his energy into the crystal to sustain the gate. That wouldn't hold much longer, either. Luckily, the worst of the injured had already been carried through. Would it create a diplomatic nightmare? Probably. But child or not, Eri had given an official command.

Selia could have wiggled out of it if she'd chosen to, of course, much as she would an "official command" for extra sweets.

But she hadn't.

And neither had Lyr, apparently. Heavily armed scouts—twenty in all—rushed through the portal. The one at the head of the line halted in front of Selia and tapped his fist against his chest.

"Lady Selia, Lord Lyr sent us to help. What do you need?"

"Help get these people to safety," she replied. "Then I'll need support. Once I drop this shield, I'll have a furious dragon out for my blood."

While the scouts leaped into action, Selia studied the area around them. Soon, the camp would be clear of all but the most determined fae—and chief amongst them was the woman named Iski. Surprisingly, the elf had refused to leave for any reason, even after the others had been evacuated. But the woman wielded water magic, and that would be a help.

More ice shattered against the dome, and a screech sounded from above. Selia scanned upward for the dragon, but she didn't have to search far. The dragon hovered just above them. Carefully, Selia studied her opponent's shields. Fairly standard and elemental in design. This dragon was no mage, simply skilled in her innate element.

Fire, then.

Selia pulled two crystals from the pouch at her waist—one with extra energy, and another with a dragon-immobilizing spell. She'd prepared several of the latter with Iren's and Arlyn's help after Aris and Kezari had left on this mission. In case the dragons flew to Braelyn to retaliate, she'd reasoned. But maybe her heart had told her she would end up here all along.

She marched over to Iski, who was waving the last of the evacuating fae through. "If you're not going, I could use your help," Selia said.

The elf's brow lifted, and something in the motion reminded her oddly of Lyr. "With what?" Iski asked.

"I'm about to melt a little ice. Please redirect the resulting water."

At Iski's assent, Selia hurried away from the portal to the other end of the dome. The water mage followed for part of the way, but she slipped behind a tree several paces away. Selia waited. Then the portal closed, and the scouts spread out in an arc in front of her.

Her breath came fast, but her hand was steady as she summoned fire into her palm. After one deep breath, she dropped the domed shield with a thought. Then she cast the fire upward to catch the dragon's attention.

It certainly worked. Across the clearing, the dragon lowered her head and breathed a stream of ice crystals directly at Selia and her line of guards. She melted the ice with her flame. And while Iski pulled the water away, the scouts loosed their arrows, a couple hitting true on the dragon's soft underbelly.

The resulting shriek was enough to make Selia's eardrums pop, but having raised a toddler, she barely winced. Now was the best time to act. As the dragon reared her head back for another blast, Selia lifted her crystal and sent forth the spell. Almost instantly, it caught, and the dragon tumbled from the sky, landing with a thud and more than a few painful-sounding snaps.

Selia ran forward, the scouts moving with her to surround the dragon. Aris met her beside the dragon's head, and he gave her a quick once-over before relief crossed his face. Sword in his hand, he took a step toward the dragon, but Selia held up a hand. Tiny ice crystals danced up with the dragon's breath, so Selia cast a warming field around the immediate area.

Only then did she gesture him forward.

A few paces forward, and her husband had the tip of his

sword at the soft underside of the dragon's jaw. The green that flowed around the blade sparked and sizzled at the contact as though eager to plunge through flesh. Was it a reflection of Aris's mood, or did life itself rage for justice against the dragon's deeds?

"Where did they take Tynan?" Aris demanded.

Selia flinched. "Who took Tynan?"

"Baza and his companion," Aris said, fury tightening his voice. "I no longer feel his lifeforce near."

*"How do you know he isn't dead?"* the dragon mocked.

Concerned by the cold look on his face, Selia eased closer to Aris. "Because he would make a better captive than a corpse," Aris said. A drop of blood welled up around the tip of his blade. "I've severed the life of my own potential soulbonded. Tell me now, or you'll follow her to the ether."

Gods, this was a disaster. She'd never considered that Tynan hadn't gone with Kezari, but Selia had hardly had a chance to discuss things with Aris amidst the chaos. When had the healer disappeared? Why hadn't Aris sent her after him immediately?

*"You'll love this, then,"* the dragon sent, smug despite her blood dripping onto the ground beneath her. *"Your elf friend is at Perim's cave. I'm sure you'll have no problems retrieving him."*

Aris went stark white, and his hand trembled on the hilt of his sword. She had to end this before he lost control. Gently, she wrapped her hand over his and lowered the blade. Then with a snap of her magic, she sent the dragon into a deep sleep.

A few more binding spells on the wyrm, and she would go after Tynan herself.

Finally, she could pull that whole awful cave down—and melt the remains.

# CHAPTER FORTY-THREE

ezari was almost halfway back before she managed to connect with Aris. *"What happened? Where's Tynan?"* she sent as soon as the link was established.

Instantly, she realized her mistake—Aris's mind was a finely wrought thing, ready to shatter at the slightest touch. She pulled back slightly, but his low hum of distress struck against her growing panic until she vibrated with it. It must be terrible news for him to be so close to the brink.

*"Baza took him to the cave,"* Aris answered, every word slow and measured against the thick weight of pain.

The cave? Oh. *The* cave. Her breath hissed out at the echoes of horror ringing through that one word. *"Tell me you aren't there, too."*

*"No."* A wave of nausea rolled into her. *"But Selia and I are heading there now. She was going to go alone, but I couldn't allow it."*

*"Selia?"*

*"I had to open the portal. Baza and two others attacked, and the ice dragon stayed behind when he chased after Tynan. Most of the fae went through to Braelyn before Selia captured the dragon. The ice dragon is the one who told us Tynan..."*

Kezari sprayed a stream of fire into the sky. Maybe she should burn every last thing on this island, then turn the very stone in on itself. If Baza hurt her mate, she would do that very thing.

*"He's not dead as far as I know,"* Aris said quickly. *"But that location. If they used the...the same shackles...any telepathy..."*

Her poor *skizik* could barely talk about it, but she understood well enough. The iron shackles she'd removed from him had been enchanted to stifle magical abilities and drain energy. If Baza had used those on Tynan, he might not be able to reach anyone telepathically. Including her.

*"I will find you soon. Do not go in without me."*

As soon as Aris assented, Kezari disconnected. He didn't need to be exposed to the deadly rage that pounded her wings faster, toward the line of mountains she knew like her own claws. For there was one stop she needed to make before anything.

She needed some of the gems from her hoard.

Kezari arrowed through her cousin's caves without a second thought, shattering the pathetic shields like cobweb. Tebzn was not creative—her hoard was easily found in a barely concealed side cavern that required only a slight shifting of rock. And sure enough, Kezari's own gems were piled in a neat stack beside Tebzn's. Hah. All mixed together, her tail.

She wrapped them in her magic and sent them to their new home at Braelyn, except for one handful of tiny stones. These were for focus, mostly, some with Earth names but others not. Most had come from her parents, and after the trove she'd found hidden by her mother's magic, she suspected these little gems were also from Earth.

Two were red—could one be a red beryl?

No way to know. She scooped them all into a pouch she formed around her neck and darted back out, barely remembering to resecure Tebzn's hoard behind her. Her cousin had done many terrible things, but Kezari could forgive her for all of them for sending warning about Tynan.

She focused on her link with Aris, following it until she found him and Selia just north of the destroyed village. She landed in a flurry of dust and fury, and she formed the saddle on her back before her wings had stopped beating. Though pale and shaky, Aris ran toward her, Selia keeping pace beside him.

"I'm sorry, Kezari," he said, true pain lining his face. "I was supposed to watch out for him, and now..."

Were she in elven form, she might have hugged him, but there was no time for shifting now. *It's not your fault. Baza has clearly planned this for some time.*

"But—"

*"Get on. You can explain what happened along the way."*

"He should not go there, Kezari," Selia said. "Take me with you, instead. I'll be able to counter Baza's spells."

Before Kezari could answer, Aris swung up into the saddle and held his hand down to help his wife. "You know I will not stay, even if it breaks me."

A new concern among many, but she could feel his resolve for herself. He believed himself responsible—of course he wouldn't stay behind. Selia seemed to come to the same conclusion, for she let Aris tug her up behind him.

Kezari boosted herself back into the sky and prayed to Tynan's goddess that they wouldn't be too late.

ECHOES OF ANGER—AND not his own—plagued Tynan's every thought. He was too exhausted for anything but fear for himself. This was like whispers behind a nearby door, almost clear but not quite. Was it Kezari? Their link was steady and true, but no matter how hard he tried, it slid away from his hold when he tried to grasp it.

Even so, it was his fragile lifeline, and he sought it out with single-minded focus. No spell could break their bond. Muffling his telepathy would make communicating through their link almost impossible. But that was *almost*. If nothing else, he might be able to send his emotions through so she would know for sure he was alive.

"Are you going to go after Vexen?" silver-hair demanded.

*"For what? She failed,"* Baza sent.

Sent.

Why would he hear the dragon's transmitted thoughts if his telepathy was stifled? Why could he feel the emotions that came in, but he could send nothing out?

Then it hit him—Perim had wanted to be able to give pain that way, too.

Bile scalded his mouth, but he managed not to move.

"You have few allies, to treat her so casually."

A low growl. *"Her wing is broken, and I'm not a healer. Vexen said that Perim's former toy and some mage from a portal did this. They're on their way here, so once we've defeated them, we can retrieve Vexen."*

Tynan winced. Perim's toy...that was probably Aris. But a mage from a portal? Had Aris used the necklace Selia had given him? If so, Selia herself was no doubt the mage. But Aris would never be able to tolerate stepping foot in this cave. Gods above. If his mind shattered here, Tynan's would, too. He would have no defense at all.

He had to find a way to get free.

"You know that's a lie," Silver said. "Then it will be Kezari you must pursue, and after that, the dragon who killed the queen."

Frustration tinged with anxiety floated out with those words, straight into Tynan's head. For the first time in his life, he longed to let them explode from him like a bolt of grief-filled lightning. He tried grasping the thread of emotion with a mental hand and pulling, but it only earned a new spear of pain through his battered mind.

Or so he'd thought.

Like unfurling wings, new emotions sprang free from the elven-form dragon. Deeper and harsher ones. "Why should I listen to you when you have so little regard? I need the taste of blood, and you would deprive me."

*"Zorteth!"*

Was that Silver's real name?

Suddenly, there was a sharp tug on the chains at his wrists, and then fire consumed his side as he was dragged across the floor, the jagged stones digging furrows in his skin. A thousand times worse than a kick. And the malicious glee pounding into his skull... He tried not to scream, but it was impossible.

Silver jerked him upright and slammed his back against the wall. Tynan panted as pain burned through him—and he hadn't even been tortured yet. Across the cavern where he hadn't been able to see, a red-gold dragon crouched, eyes narrowed to angry slits. The sight did not help the panic sawing through his lungs.

The shackles fell away from his wrists, and Silver slammed his arms above his head where yet another set of shackles waited. Maybe if he struggled, he could fight free. But then a hint of energy trickled in, and Tynan froze. The bindings around his ankles didn't prevent his gifts from working, and his allergy to iron was too mild to stop *all* energy from coming in.

He needed a distraction. Now.

He scrabbled for the thread of Baza's anger—and gave a sharp jerk.

This time, Baza roared something aloud, the word rumbling the ground beneath Tynan's feet. Silver snarled, and scales danced down his arm and across his face as he half-turned to face the other dragon. Perfect. Though their emotions burned his mind like boiling water, Tynan yanked at them as much as he could.

Anything to keep them off balance.

All the while, he did his best to suck up energy, difficult though it was with the iron around his ankles. But he only needed to gather enough power to fully use his gifts, either healing or empathy. With enough magic, he could kill with either.

His wrist stung, and a line of wetness rolled down his arm. Silver's claws, probably. As the growled words intensified, Tynan squeezed his eyes shut and reached for his link to Kezari. This time, she connected. This time, she poured through.

Rage and all.

*"No anger,"* he hissed into her mind.

Her shield slammed up, easing the burden. *"What have they done to you?"*

*"Scrapes and mental torment so far. I can't shield my empathy."* Another claw dug into his flesh, and he bit his lip to hold in a cry. *"Do not let Aris in here until I can do so. I will not survive it."*

Kezari didn't miss the pain he tried to hide. *"I will dig caverns in his flesh for every mark. Who is it?"*

*"A silver dragon. Zorteth, he was called. I think."*

She muttered something dark-sounding in the dragon tongue. *"I should have known. Who else?"*

*"Only Baza, I think."*

Silence for a moment. *"I'll have Aris stand guard outside. As soon as I can release your remaining bindings, run."*

*"Wait!"* he sent as she pulled away a little. *"Don't close the mental connection."*

He couldn't bear to be alone here.

*"I won't,"* she assured him. *"I promise I won't leave you."*

And so he stood there, shivering against the stone and gathering his strength. Waiting. She was close.

Any moment now.

～

"HE KNOWS YOU TWO ARE COMING," Kezari sent as Aris and Selia climbed down from her back. "You should both stay out here."

"You mean me," Aris said tightly.

Kezari nodded. *"Tynan is unshielded, and his empathy is open. What do you think will happen when you go inside?"*

Aris leaned against her forearm, and she could feel his body shaking just from the sight of the cave entrance on the other side of the clearing. He sighed. "I must face this, Kezari. I killed Perim myself. I should be able to go into a cave."

She turned her head to glare at him. *"Do it when my sbezie isn't at risk of madness."*

"I will," he relented, though he didn't look happy about it. "Call for me when it is safe."

He straightened, stopping only to give Selia a kiss. Then he crept from tree to tree until he could take position beside the entrance, his stiff posture betraying his nerves.

"I should enter first," Selia murmured. "If Baza doesn't know you're here, he won't expect it when you finally strike."

With a thought, Kezari shifted into her elven form. The pouch around her neck weighed more now, the gems inside the size of her palm in this body. She wrapped her hand around the cloth and let the power within flow through her.

"What are you doing?" Selia whispered.

Kezari shrugged. "Pretending to be an elven mage. If I slip in like this, they'll think I'm you."

Selia's brows drew up. "They won't recognize you?"

"I rarely shifted, and never around Baza or Zorteth." Kezari dropped the pouch and stared down at her clothes, adjusting them to look more like Selia's. "I've lived with the elves long enough to pass as one of you to another dragon, I think. Will your immobilization spell work on me when I'm in this form?"

"I don't think so." Selia's frown deepened. "But there are no guarantees."

Kezari gave a sharp nod. "Let's see, shall we? Creep in behind me, and at the first chance, use it. If I'm frozen, free Tynan."

Then without a second thought, Kezari marched forward.

# CHAPTER FORTY-FOUR

Kezari loathed setting such a weak foot into this nightmare cave, but pretending to be Selia was the best plan she could think of. If she blazed into the room in her dragon form, either Baza or Zorteth would kill Tynan without a second thought. So she put on her best elf expression, activated one of her focus stones, and hovered a ball of rock above her palm like a mage would before marching through the last bit of tunnel and into the cavern.

At first, none of them noticed her. How insulting. But Baza and Zorteth were too busy arguing, Baza in Dragonian, and Zorteth in some broken mix of Dragonian and Moranaian—the dragon language was too difficult to speak in elven form. Her focus narrowed on Zorteth, his scale-covered arm pinning Tynan against the wall. At the sight of the blood covering her mate, she had to clench her teeth to keep from baring them.

She took advantage of their distraction to part the iron around Tynan's ankles with her magic. His gaze met hers across the distance, and his eyes widened. *"What—"*

*"I'm Selia,"* Kezari sent before he could ask about her form. *"And I'm about to create a distraction. When Zorteth releases you, run."*

Baza's head swung toward her then. *"Look, Zorteth. The little mage has arrived. Didn't I tell you?"*

The silver dragon twisted away from Tynan a little more, and his hold appeared to loosen. "Where's the other one?"

"My husband could not bear to come in here," Kezari said, doing her best to sound like Selia. "But I'm a talented enough mage to confront you alone."

Baza snorted. *"Your husband is a weak fool, as are you. I can't imagine how you defeated Vexen with a rock and a few pitiful shields."*

Vexen was the ice dragon? Oh, that burned. She'd been one of the kinder dragons, and not one Kezari would have expected to betray them all by forming an alliance with Baza. But she couldn't reveal that reaction, or they would realize she was no off-Isle elf.

"Perhaps my shields are too complicated for your feeble understanding," Kezari said instead.

A bluff—hers were no better than any other earth dragon's would be.

Baza's huffing laughter sent a haze of smoke rolling across the floor. *"Not true."*

As a red dragon, his strongest element was fire. Was he powerful enough to melt stone? She wouldn't have thought it, but she hadn't anticipated any of his actions to date. It seemed there was only one way to find out.

She *did* need a distraction, after all.

Kezari poured more magic into the rock above her hand until the stone was the size of her torso, then tossed it at Baza's head with a flex of power. He laughed again as he easily caught the stone. As expected. While Zorteth smirked at the rock now in Baza's grip, Kezari connected with the earth beneath the silver dragon's feet.

She softened the stone, sending him off-balance, but she didn't merely close the rock around his feet. Instead, she surged it upward, forming twin columns around his legs. He released Tynan with a yelp.

Zorteth's useless air magic pounded against the solid stone, and in his panic, he forgot that he could shift rock, too. Not as well as she could, but he could escape eventually. Really, given time, he could also erode it with wind, but she would never allow him that.

"Disrupt the spell!" he shouted at Baza.

Baza's eyes narrowed on the stone. The game would be up soon, for he would realize in moments that this was a dragon's elemental magic, not a mage's spell. Kezari met Tynan's gaze again and jerked her head to the side.

*"Run,"* she sent.

But like a dragonling, the fool man didn't comply.

As soon as the shackles fell away, Tynan sucked in energy like a root during spring's first rain. And the first thing he did with it? Reformed his shields. The pounding tangle of emotions eased, and he let out a long breath. *Thank Bera.* Kezari caught his eye and told him to run.

That would be wisest, but he couldn't. Baza's head swiveled toward her, and Silver had given up on breaking the stone creeping around his waist to glare at Kezari, too. The air he'd gathered to destroy the rock coalesced in a silvery ball around his palm, but Kezari's attention had returned to Baza. She was vulnerable in this form, and both dragons were poised to attack.

Before Tynan could linger on what he must do, he slipped behind Silver and gripped his neck tight. Life and death, that was what a priest of Bera guarded.

This time, it would be death, but that would guard so much life.

Without a qualm, he sent his healing gift through. Not to repair. An audible crack sounded as he severed Silver's spine at the base of his skull, and at the same time, he stopped the dragon's heart. No chance of regeneration. No last spell.

Only a quicker death than the torture-happy wretch deserved. *Lady Bera, greet his soul, your own judgment to take.*

Kezari gaped at him. *"Did you just…?"*

*"Yes. Pay attention."*

Baza released a stream of fire at her, but she only dodged it. She didn't shift. What was she doing? Surely, she didn't intend to fight the dragon mage in her elven form. Yet she dashed toward Tynan, her hand digging into a pouch bound around her neck.

*"Kezari,"* Baza sent. *"I should have known you would act so oddly. It is beneath a dragon's dignity, as usual for you."*

Tynan hurried to meet her, skipping over one of the chains before he could trip like a hapless maiden in a terrible bard's song. *"Why don't you shift?"* he demanded as she skidded to a halt in front of him.

*"Selia's in the tunnel, ready to cast the immobilization spell. If it still paralyzes me in this form, run for it."*

He snorted at the very idea. Every bit of his body ached at this point, but he would never leave her helpless on the ground. *"You'd better stand close so I can grab you."*

*"You dare to ignore me?"* Steam hissed from Baza's teeth, and he took an earth-shaking step forward. *"I know you broke my spell, Kezari. I felt it. Hand over the stone you stole, or I'll roast your weak mate alive."*

*"So you can be king?"* she called out.

The spines around Baza's eyes rose. Surprise? Amusement? *"Of course. Your parents died after re-hiding that treasure. Zevie was close to finding it when they interfered, so she ordered them killed. But she was a fool, easily led, and Perim made it simple to force you out of the way. Perhaps if you give me the stone, I'll let you leave with your mate."*

Tynan frowned. The dragon's tone suggested it was indeed amusement, but a quick brush with empathy said otherwise. Fury, bright and painful. Very painful. Tynan exhaled sharply at the burn in his head, and Kezari stiffened. *Miaran.* He couldn't distract her, not now.

But he didn't have to.

Selia stepped into the cavern, and her spell was instant and brutal—and not one that immobilized. Light flashed around the dragon, and as a *crack* shook handfuls of stalactites loose to rain down upon them, Baza shrieked. The dragon's shields—they were gone.

A ball of fire shot Selia's way, but the mage countered with a blast of water. Gods. A battle in a cave this size could send the whole thing crashing down on them. Baza had little room to maneuver as it was, though that gave them some advantage. A physical attack would be harder for him to perform.

Abruptly, Kezari grabbed Tynan's hand and pressed something smooth against his palm. "I think this is the red beryl. I honed it with my power alone, and now it's yours. As is my heart. Take both and run."

Kezari kissed him, hard and fast, but power rushed through them even as she eased back. The few still-ragged edges of their bond snapped tight, and for a moment, pure happiness poured into his heart at the full joining. He'd feared this for so long, but nothing had ever been more perfect.

Aside from the dragon and mage battle, of course.

With a huff, Kezari took the stone from his hand and formed it into a pendant with her magic. Then she dropped the chain over his head and gave his shoulder a shove. "Go."

A slow smile spread across his face.

Not a chance.

THE STUBBORN MAN clearly wasn't going anywhere, which meant she would have to shift if Baza blasted fire their way. She might need to anyway if Selia didn't cast her spell soon. The dragon's attacks were relentless. All the elf could do at the moment was counter.

As Kezari merged with the earth, a whip of lightning made it through Selia's defenses, drawing a yelp of pain from the mage. And in the moment between Selia crashing against the wall and Baza's next spell, Aris darted into the tunnel with a cry of pure rage. The blazing green of his sword brightened every shadowed corner—both a blessing and a curse.

Like a flight gone suddenly wrong, Kezari couldn't stop the coming crash. She could only watch the pain rushing first through Aris as he finally processed his surroundings and then spilling straight toward Tynan. Her mate's shields held against the worst of it, but he hadn't regained enough energy for this. Uselessly, she flung herself in front of him.

Aris sank to his knees as the memories flipped through his mind, holding him in a cruel thrall. Kezari longed to gather her *skizik* close and fly him away from here once again, but she couldn't. They had to defeat Baza, or none of this would ever end.

While Baza laughed low, Selia rushed to Aris's side. Light flashed again, and the laugh cut off, though the dragon's mouth still gaped. Unmoving. The immobilization spell.

Finally.

Selia sank down next to Aris, but she didn't make the mistake of touching him. "She's not here. You can do this."

Aris didn't respond, his focus on the chains stretched across the floor. His mind was locked in an impossible battle, one neither she nor Selia could fight for him. Kezari's claws sprang free with the urge to rend Baza's sorry hide, but she felt Tynan shudder beside her. There was no hint of calm drifting from her mate now. He wouldn't be able to hold out, either.

Baza's mental voice rang through the room. *I'll break this soon and kill you all."*

There was far too much glee coating the horrid words.

Tynan grabbed her hand, tugging until she met his gaze. "Hold me," he said.

She frowned. What—

Then he dropped his shields, and she understood.

～

With Kezari anchoring him, Tynan grasped the burning strand of Aris's pain and drew it through his already-shrieking mind. But he didn't try to disperse it. It wasn't his, but he gathered it in his mental hand anyway.

So much horror. So much agony.

All of it, he tossed straight at Baza.

Only a gurgle made it past the dragon's frozen vocal cords, but the screech from his mind—Tynan slammed his shields up against it, but some still whipped through. He moaned with it, and beside him, Kezari growled.

"Kill him," Tynan said aloud, unable to tolerate the slightest mental link to send the suggestion.

Though her spirit still bolstered his, Kezari released his hand and ran forward, shifting as soon as she could. The gold of her scales tinged green in the light of Aris's sword, the effect oddly beautiful. He couldn't look away as she pounced on Baza's outstretched neck and dug her claws in tight.

*"You will not be queen,"* Baza sent.

Tynan shivered from the pain of it, but the words gave him pause. The treasure Baza had wanted from her was connected to the ability to rule. If she'd found it, she had claim to the dragon throne. Would she want to stay here?

She bared her teeth at him across the distance. *"I don't want to be queen."*

His relief far outpaced the ache telepathy brought.

Near the entrance, Aris shoved himself to his feet, his body visibly quivering. But with his darkest emotions temporarily purged, the life mage was able to glance around the cavern without crumbling. He took one shaky step toward Baza and Kezari. Then another.

"Aris..." Selia began.

He shook his head. "He helped Perim," Aris said tightly.

The life mage stumbled forward, his wife at his side. Tynan's breath caught. He might have pulled those awful emotions away, but he couldn't rebuild new memories from the rubble. Only Aris could do that.

Aris lifted his sword, the tip a hairsbreadth from Baza's eye. Then he looked up at Kezari. "Which of us has more right?"

Kezari's answer popped loudly through the cavern—she'd snapped the other dragon's neck.

She perched there a moment longer, but as soon as the light faded from Baza's eyes, Kezari hopped down and shifted back to elf. Before he realized it, Tynan was halfway across the room to meet her. He longed to pull her into his arms more than he wanted to breathe; unfortunately, he was coated in blood.

"It doesn't matter who had more right," Kezari said. "You will not bear another moment's pain in this place, *skizik*."

Sighing, Aris sheathed his sword. His solemn gaze swept around the terrible cavern, with its chains and bloodstains and dark, awful crevices. Then he shuddered one more time before turning his back on it all to limp toward the tunnel leading out.

"*Sbezie*," Kezari said, catching Tynan's gaze. "Would you go with him? Selia and I have things to take care of in this place."

Suspecting what some of those things might be—destruction, mostly—he nodded and spun away to follow. He was several paces away when he heard Kezari mutter, "Now he listens." Though his body was a mass of blood-covered pain, he smiled. She hadn't imagined a dragon ever needing the aid of a healer, so he doubted she would admit how much he'd helped.

The battle had surely ended faster for it.

Outside, he followed Aris to the nearby stand of trees. In silence, they both leaned against a tree trunk and stared at the entrance. High up the mountain, smoke streamed out from several ventilation holes, only to be blown away on the breeze. But it wasn't more danger, not if the satisfaction he sensed from Kezari was anything to go by. She was probably immolating Baza.

Then the ground vibrated softly beneath their feet. "Selia has long wanted to destroy that place," Aris murmured.

"How do you fare?" Tynan asked, finally facing his patient. He tried to open his senses to check for himself, but the swift surge of pain disabused him of that notion. "I'm afraid my channels will need healing before I can offer help."

Aris's lips twisted—wryly but not with displeasure. "Don't you think sucking up a breakdown's worth of emotion was enough? Thank you, Tynan. Truly. I'm shaken, but I...I think I'll be fine."

They fell silent again, watching as Selia and Kezari emerged from the cave entrance. Dust whooshed out behind them a moment before the last remaining bit collapsed in on itself. Tynan nearly cheered. Instead, he smiled as Kezari smoothed the side of the mountain into something none of them would recognize.

Healing, it seemed, took many forms.

# CHAPTER FORTY-FIVE

Kezari stared at the side of the reshaped mountain with something like...closure? Though the echoes of the past never truly went away, this was the closest to that feeling she might ever get. Of course, there was also Vexen to deal with, so the battle wasn't finished. This part, though. Knowing that no one could ever use that cave again did something suspiciously warm to her heart.

"Good riddance," Selia said.

Dust coated the mage from head to toe, there were scratches on her cheek and left arm, and she drooped with exhaustion, but satisfaction gleamed in her eyes. Selia might not have experienced all of her husband's memories, but she'd seen enough. Kezari hadn't even considered stopping her from helping with the destruction.

Tynan slipped up beside her, and Aris eased around Selia to stand close to the wall. He touched his sword to the stone, and vines rolled up from the ground, climbing and climbing. Soon, the entire mountainside was consumed by verdant life.

"They won't last more than a season growing on stone," Aris said softly. "But I suppose it's a good reminder. All things end. Even pain."

There wasn't much anyone could say after that truth.

In silence, they turned down the path to the destroyed village and the camp beyond. It was a long walk, especially in this body, but Kezari was far too tired to come up with a saddle for three people. Much less carry them. She'd flown so much in the last day that her shoulder blades ached even as an elf.

They hadn't gone far when Selia pulled a crystal from her pocket. "I'm making us a gate."

The mage was obviously tired, too, but not a single person protested.

When the clearing clarified beneath the narrow, glowing gate, Moranaian scouts instantly formed a ring in front of it. Wait, scouts? Kezari tried to recall the details she'd learned about Selia's arrival, but they were long lost beneath the haze of battle. And rage. Lots and lots of rage.

"I...suppose we'll be needing a new treaty," Tynan said.

Apparently so.

As soon as they stepped through, the scouts relaxed. "Is this the person you were looking for?" one man asked.

Selia nodded. "The very one."

Kezari examined the nearly abandoned camp, searching for Vexen. It didn't take long to find the dragon stretched out on the ground on the distant edge. But...not breathing? Then she saw Ren, standing to the side in his elven form with three dragonlings flying circles around his head. The ancient dragon glared at Iski, who was gesturing at Vexen's body.

One of the dragonlings chirped and headed her way—the golden one.

"Oh, Kezari! He said you're actually the dragon, and you're called Kezari. The other ones stayed on the island, but I could not. Do you see? King Ren killed the sorcerer after all! And that silly Baza thought it was some fae. Nope. Ren swooped down just as Vexen was gathering some ice in her mouth."

Kezari's lips twitched, but she let the youngling lead her toward Ren like it was some kind of prize. So much for being called Egrenneth when he became king. He'd made the monumental mistake of providing a nickname to the dragonlings.

He would be King Ren until he died.

"You can't burn the body," Iski was insisting as Kezari and the others neared. "That's an honor, and she does not deserve an honor."

Ren folded his arms across his chest. "We're dragons. We burn everything."

Iski blanched. "The spirits of the dishonorable should not be set free on the wind."

Oh. Kezari winced. It would be best not to mention that she'd fried Baza to ashes only a few moments ago, then, wouldn't it? She gave Tynan a sidelong glance. *"Is that no longer a tradition for Moranaians?"*

*"No, it is,"* he replied. *"But only for elves. We have no rules about how dragons dispose of their dead, though it appears that isn't the case for Iski."*

Still glaring, Ren strode away and then shifted to dragon form. With a growl, he opened a massive gash in the ground with his magic and then shoved Vexen in with a bone-jarring crash. Kezari had to admire the smooth way he closed the dirt back over the traitor's form, not a sign of disturbance remaining on the grass.

He didn't look back at Iski as he stomped—literally—into the center of the clearing. *"I've had your cousin carried to her cave to heal. Come to the council chamber, and bring the stone,"* he sent before launching himself into the sky.

Kezari sighed. It had been a long day, and like the unflagging sun on its path along the sky, there was still more to go. She hadn't even thought about poor Tebzn. Fortunately, Ren had. Of course, he'd had a longer break since *his* last battle.

She strode toward the clearing to follow.

～

TYNAN SLUMPED across Kezari's back and let the cool air soothe his tired body. Aris and Selia had remained at the camp. Selia had claimed she needed rest before creating the portal back to Moranaia, and that was probably true. But the heartsick exhaustion in Aris's eyes had no doubt contributed.

In a way, it was a relief.

Now that his link to Kezari was complete and the walls between them were gone, her presence soothed his empathy instead of aggravated it. All that doubt and fear and hiding—gone. He could simply be with her, and she with him. He would have needed to shield far more heavily if Aris and Selia had come.

By the time they landed in the massive cavern, a worrisome number of dragons had gathered around the perimeter. This... Well, it would be a terrible but swift way to die, charred or eaten by an angry mob of vengeful dragons. It took all of his willpower to slip off of Kezari's back.

He winced as his barely healed flesh pulled with the motion. He'd found enough energy to repair the worst of it, but even that had split his head open with pain. He'd barely noticed when Kezari had reformed his clothes. Now, he had a moment's worry about what she'd made, but it was a silly concern. The dragons weren't going to care.

*"Calm down,* sbezie,*"* Kezari sent, laughter in her mental voice. It was almost enough to soothe his incessant headache. *"I promise no one will eat you, nor will they demand you demonstrate your knowledge of fashion. Now, link more closely with my thoughts so you'll understand what's being said."*

Grimacing at the pinch of pain, Tynan merged more deeply with Kezari as Ren approached and nodded his head toward her. "You defeated Baza and retrieved the Monarch's Hoard. Present the treasure. And if you wish to challenge my claim to the throne, do so."

The spell was so quick that even enmeshed with her thoughts, Tynan hadn't sensed its spark before the massive stone appeared between the two dragons. Where had she been hiding something like this? He could use it as a bed and still have room to spare.

Only the hissing of countless dragon breaths echoed through the cavern. Then Kezari tipped her head toward the boulder, and with a surge of magic, she...opened it? He caught sight of the deepest red gleaming from the top, but there was no way he was going to move closer for more detail. Not with a cavern of dragons looking at the thing.

Kezari lifted her head and stared straight into Ren's eyes. "I do not wish to be queen."

"Are you sure?" Ren demanded. "Your mother was of the blood, as are you. It is a bit distant, but there."

Tynan held his breath, though he could feel her resolve through their connection. This was her birthright, and he would not influence her decision about it. Except—*miaran*. He'd bonded with the dragon equivalent of a princess, hadn't he? He'd spent so long dancing around royalty and nobility, and technically, he was now one of them.

The goddess no doubt laughed.

Amusement spilled from Kezari into his heart. "I am a citizen of Moranaia now," she said to Ren. "The Isle is no longer my home, and I do not wish to rule it. If you want to lead this mess, then do so."

Tynan couldn't help but release a relieved breath.

Ren inclined his head. Then he reached both talons into the boulder and lifted out a massive red gemstone the color of his scales. Gods above. The thing would crush Tynan if it fell on him. Was a gem that size even natural? It seemed impossible for such a flawless stone to be so large.

*"It's rare,"* Kezari confirmed.

A glow built in the stone's heart, intensifying until the room turned a sickly shade of red. Tynan closed his eyes, but the back of his eyelids still seemed coated with blood from the flash of it. The gathered dragons cried out, tempting him to look, but since Kezari remained calm, he resisted.

Then it was done.

Whatever it was.

"You may always feel a tug if there's a crisis," Ren warned Kezari. "It still holds the old spell to your bloodline."

Kezari's sigh warmed the air. "Then do a good job, would you?"

Ren laughed. "I suppose I must. The dragonlings will hold me to it if you won't."

The few young ones that had accompanied the new king flew in a dance overhead, happy chirps lending a lightness to the cavern. At Kezari's signal, Tynan climbed back into the saddle at the base of her neck. Instantly, his tension eased a notch at the safer vantage point.

"When you have things settled, send a messenger to Iski at the fae camp. We'll be working with her to return the fae who want to rebuild here." Kezari hesitated. "A new treaty must be made. However, not all of the elves and fae will wish to come back. I hope there will be no retribution before the new treaty is done."

The new dragon king snorted—rather unregally. "I have no desire to keep prisoners, for that's what they ended up being. It will be their choice."

After a few more words, it was finally time to go. *Thank Bera.* Tynan clung to Kezari's warmth and finally let himself doze as she carried them back to the camp—and the portal home.

THOUGH THEY STEPPED into another kind of chaos, Kezari smiled to see the familiar walls of the training tower. Sure, pallets of injured fae covered the floor, and Lial hurried around like his robe was on fire. But it was home now, and she could think of nothing better.

Iren threw himself against his parents with a happy cry. "You made it!"

Joy filled her heart, but Kezari averted her eyes to give them privacy. Besides, she had a mate to fix. She tightened her hold on Tynan and half-carried him across the room to Lial. The other healer took one look at her mate and sighed.

"Of course," Lial muttered.

After checking to make sure Aris was distracted, Kezari leaned close. "He was held in chains in Perim's cave. Take it easy on him."

Lial blanched—he was one of the few to have seen Aris's memories during her *skizik*'s healing. Without a word, he directed Tynan to a chair and bent over him, blue light surrounding his head. Lial probably couldn't spare the energy for a full healing, but at least Tynan wouldn't be in so much pain.

The healer's *camahr*, Emowa, picked her way around the pallets on her way to Lial. Her tail was held high, blue light glowing from the jaunty tip, and the fae children who'd huddled together over to the side laughed softly and pointed. Although the *camahr* coiled around Lial's ankles without a care, she cast a few, preening glances their way.

Then Lyr marched in—if one could call his tired stride such. At his approach, Selia and Aris joined Kezari to greet him. "What a mess," Lyr said before any of them spoke.

Selia stood straighter. "Eri gave the order, but I followed it."

"Relax." Lyr rubbed the bridge of his nose. "I followed the command, too, and I would do so again. My ancestors didn't deal fairly with the dragons or their fae allies, but I will."

Aris chuckled. "We met a relative of yours. She stayed behind for much the same reason. Though I tried to convince her otherwise, she wants to be the one to deal with the new dragon king."

Interest sparked in Lyr's eyes, but he shook his head. "There's a year's worth of reports in all this, but none of us have the energy to pursue that now. Go rest. I've requested additional healers, and as we don't require *mind* healers this time, we'll have help soon. We'll figure out who goes where, and how, later."

Tynan picked his way over, and as soon as he reached her, he slipped his fingers between hers. Linking them, as they always were. "Lial has ordered me to sleep on threat of forced unconsciousness."

Lyr waved his hand toward the door. "Don't let me stop you, lest I suffer the same fate. We'll figure everything out."

By silent accord, Kezari and Tynan exited the training room and headed down the path to the observation tower. She formed a thick cloak around her mate and adjusted her own wavering temperature in the blasted cold. The paths, at least, were clear. Not all of the fae had fit in the first room, so there was a constant stream of motion between there and the main part of the estate.

Wearily, they climbed the stairs. When they reached the top, light glared in, and Kezari frowned. This was a terrible place to sleep, but it had never been intended for such. Unfortunately, she hadn't had a chance to make a new home yet. But panels wouldn't go amiss, would they?

She lit the mage globes. Then circling the room, she formed a thin line of stone beneath her palm and stretched it wide across the windows. It took a bit of energy and work to make them moveable rather than permanent, but when she returned to Tynan, the warmth in his eyes made the effort worthwhile.

"I love you, Kezari," he said softly.

She slid into his arms and closed her eyes, content. "I love you, too."

Silly man. Didn't he know a dragon never let go of her treasure?

**THANK you so much for reading Maelstrom. I had a great deal of fun living in a dragon's head while writing this, and I hope you enjoyed it, too. Of course, The Return of the Elves series isn't over. Danger rises in the Unseelie court, and together, Ara and Caolte must confront the threat.**

Legacy is currently a work in progress, but turn the page for a sneak peak from the rough draft. Be on the lookout for the Legacy pre-order, coming in early 2025.

477

FROM LEGACY

Despite the bathwater's warmth, Ara's skin prickled with awareness, a knowing honed by centuries of vigilance. Someone had entered the room. She attuned her earth magic with the floor, the stone as familiar to her as one of her limbs. What...? Ah, there, it was. The airy weight of a levitation spell pressing where feet should be. A Seelie trick, that. But this uninvited guest had to be inexperienced not to realize how readily she would sense it.

As Ara scrubbed the cleansing cloth along her arm, she opened her shields enough to unfurl her other senses—a predator's instincts. Her hearing heightened until she caught the sound of a ragged exhale. The slide of flesh over...wood as fingers tightened and shifted. So the blade had a wooden hilt this time. The last person Meren had sent to kill her had shown up with a solid iron throwing knife.

Did he think her as fragile as a Sidhe? Felshreh—blood elves—weren't so easily felled by iron.

The would-be assassin crept nearer, and the frantic pounding of their heart drummed in Ara's ears. She pretended ignorance of the stranger's approach, at least until she heard the rustle of fabric followed by the whistle-hiss of a descending blade. Like a trap, she sprang into motion, twisting and lunging so quickly that she sank her nails into the attacker's arm before the blade made contact with her skin.

A man's cry rang out, and he jerked against her hold. Ara grabbed his wrist with her other hand and sank her fangs into his forearm to release his blood—and unlock his energy for her use. He screamed again, this time from the pain she didn't bother to dull. An assassin didn't deserve the usual courtesies.

When he wavered on his feet, she sealed the wound on his arm so blood wouldn't drip into her bath and then shoved him away from her. Even as he toppled over, she sucked his energy away. His little levitation spell winked out from lack of power, allowing him to thud onto the ground with a satisfying thump.

Ara leapt from the bath, cursing beneath her breath at the shock of cold. Then she straddled the man's back and gripped his hair. Water soaked the man's clothes until he trembled from the chill, too. Well, and from fear. He stank of it.

"Who sent you?" she snarled.

A useless question, of course, but confirmation of her suspicions wouldn't go amiss.

He made a feeble attempt at bucking her off, but he was already weak from magic loss. "I won't tell you."

Scoffing in annoyance, Ara took a greater hold on the blood link, opening it the slightest bit until she could suck more of his energy through. Power pulsed through her, enough to reshape the entire stone bathing chamber with barely a blink. She smiled. Her son, Fen, might enjoy regaling her with the humans' vampire myths, but blood itself wasn't the Felshreh's greatest strength. Their food was the magic that blood unlocked.

And she never had turned away from a good meal.

"Would you like for me to drain your power until you can no longer sustain your own life?" she asked sweetly.

The assassin paled. "He said you were helpless around water."

"Meren?"

Although the man refused to answer, his subtle flinch and

widened eyes told enough. "Let me go, and I will serve you," he offered.

Did he really think she would believe that?

Ara's laugh bounced around the room with deceptive cheer. "No, you won't. Anyone who attacks the Unseelie queen does one thing. Die."

She'd threatened to drain his energy, but she wouldn't—not unto death. The dark stain of that...no. Instead, she claimed as much of his magic as she dared before twisting his head to bare his throat. Then she released the blood link and let her fangs finish the task.

Ara had learned the hard way that softness only ruined one's life.

Caolte glared at his brother's image in the glass. He absolutely could not have heard those last words right. "A week at the outpost? On Earth?"

The hiss of Naomh's aggravated sigh brushed against the small communication mirror he held. Unlike the large wall mirror that Caolte stood in front of, Naomh had only the hand-sized one that his son had enchanted for him, but it was sufficient for their needs. Which in this case appeared to be the delivery of nonsensical news. His brother did his best to hold to the ancient ways, and one of the Sidhe's oldest oaths was to never step foot on the surface of Earth.

And as he'd just pointed out, the outpost was *on Earth*. Directly and irrefutably.

"Before you ask," Naomh said. "I assure you that my injury has not muddled my mind. Rather, it has cleared it."

Had his brother not looked so gaunt and worn down, Caolte might have argued the validity of that point. "I told you that you'd need to regain some energy before returning here, but I thought you would do so on Moranaia with your son as guard."

"Meren caught me by surprise once. *Once,*" Naomh hissed. "I know you take your promise to our father seriously, but I am a—"

"Yes, I'm aware that you're a powerful Seelie lord." Caolte lifted a brow. "But you're also rash at times. Making an alliance with Kien? Imprisoning your own son? Need I go on?"

His brother scowled, but he didn't bother to argue with the statement. But then, it wasn't the first time they'd had this disagreement—not that an outsider would believe it. With Naomh's element being earth and Caolte's fire, most assumed that Caolte was the spontaneous one, when it was actually the opposite. His fire kept him contained, for never in his life had he been able to fully lower his guard. Not unless he wanted to incinerate everything around him.

"Don't worry, brother," Caolte said. "I won't tell Kai where he gets it from."

Surprisingly, Naomh smiled at the quip. "I doubt he would believe the comparison."

His nephew would figure it out soon enough without any aid. No matter how good Naomh was at feigning steadiness, his reaching nature always revealed itself in the end. Like the vines that bolstered his power, he quietly crept where he willed, regardless of what—or who—he might cross. Fortunately, it was a slow process that Caolte had long ago grown adept at spotting.

And redirecting. Most of the time.

Caolte blinked, and the weight of his ever-present weariness settled in a fraction deeper. He needed to close this link before he wasted even more of his finite energy. "We can argue it later. It's only been a day or two since your healing. What kind of healer would send you off to a place where you won't even touch the ground?"

"Oh, I'll touch it." Naomh's expression hardened. "I'll forego honor if it means a quicker recovery."

The air around Caolte warmed, a sign of his loosening control. "Heal on Moranaia."

"It's winter here. Nearly midwinter, in fact," his brother

snapped. "I need greenery for natural regeneration, and Lial is busy tending to refugees from the Isle of Dragons. Though it's autumn at the outpost, there's still enough life to be the better option."

"The queen—"

"Can argue as she will. She owes her life to Unseelie royalty, one of whom is mated to the leader of the outpost." Naomh shook his head. "Stop fretting, brother. The outpost is heavily guarded, and I'll be able to regain my power more quickly. Or at least enough of it to resume charge of my realm. Perhaps not my realm's repair, but that will come in time."

The bitter tastes of anger and guilt coated Caolte's tongue. Yes, he'd failed to properly uphold the magic here, but at least his brother had a place to repair. Their father had left Caolte nothing —save an oath that grew heavier with each passing century. Or day, as was the case lately. To some, duty seemed a gift. A reason for being. But it could also prevent a person from living.

"Caolte?"

He ran his fingers through his short hair and winced at the tingling sparks that never managed to burn his skin. Now his brother would know he was agitated. "I grow weary. I'll end the communication link now, lest the strain on my energy damage your realm further. Let me know when you've reached the outpost safely."

He cut the connection even as his brother's mouth opened in some kind of retort. Caolte had nearly given his life for his brother twice—not that Naomh knew—and would do so again. But that didn't mean he couldn't find the man exasperating. Now that the initial relief of his recovery was wearing off, Caolte couldn't deny the growing urge to throttle him.

Ara jerked the bedroom door open and glared down the long corridor. There should have been a guard stationed in the center, but he was suspiciously absent. The rotten *sremed* had better pray he was dead—or at the least gravely injured. If he'd turned traitor, there was nowhere in this realm or any other that he could hide. Especially since he'd left Fen in danger. Her son and his mates were in residence directly across from where the guard should have been standing.

Before her heart could trip more than once in alarm, her son's door opened, and Maddy poked her head out. A strand of her bold, red hair tumbled down her thin robe, but despite her rumpled state, she froze. The girl's eyes widened with a hint of horror as she stared up the hallway at Ara.

"Umm. Queen. Your Majesty." Maddy cleared her throat. "Are you aware you're...umm...naked? Except for..."

Ara glanced down at herself and grimaced. She was indeed still naked, save the blood blotching her skin like nightmare's freckles. Ah, well. Nothing to do but brazen it out. Shrugging, she met Maddy's gaze. "Yes."

The young woman blinked. "Oh. Okay, then. Do you... I don't know, do you need something? This honestly wasn't what I was expecting when I heard a noise."

"I imagine not." Ara bit back a smile. "I don't suppose you've seen the guard who should have been near your door?"

"No, only you," Maddy said.

A low grumble of annoyance heralded Fen's arrival as he slipped up behind Maddy. "Anna said you..."

Like Maddy, he froze at the sight of her. Fen's mouth dropped open before he abruptly spun away. In typical fashion, he knocked his forehead dramatically against the doorframe while muttering curses. Had the human world made them so exceedingly modest? Granted, she wouldn't have been thrilled to see her own parents naked, but the fuss was a bit excessive.

"Do I even want to know why my mother is standing in the hallway in her birthday suit before the sun has even risen?" Fen groaned.

There really was nothing for it. Ara stiffened her spine and marched down the hall toward them. She didn't have time for another bath, not until the missing guard had been tracked down and the corpse removed from her bathing chamber. She needed to solve matters now. Heckling her son was merely a bonus, if a self-defeating one. But it hardly mattered. He'd written off any hint of a relationship already.

"Do forgive me for not being properly dressed after fending off an assassin," Ara said, the hurt from her thoughts lending a chill to her words that she hadn't intended. "Regrettably, he didn't allow me time to leave my bath and garb myself appropriately."

Fen's forehead cracked against the doorframe with a decidedly louder snap. "Fucking hell," he yelped, rubbing the welling bump as he spun to face her.

"Don't do childish things, and you won't have childish consequences," Ara pronounced dryly.

As usual, he missed the wry humor buried in her tone. "Thanks for the sage advice. I'll be sure to order your 'World's Best Mom' cup next time I'm on Earth."

The bitter barb cut her more deeply than the assassin's blade ever could have, even though she didn't entirely understand the insult. "Fen. I didn't come out here to argue. There should be a guard outside your door, and you should all be on your guard while I figure out why there isn't."

Though Fen hated her, she had finally brought her son home, and she would kill anyone who threatened him. Never again. Never again would he be left unprotected while she worried over the throne and the endless court schemes. Staying away hadn't saved him last time, and she refused to take that risk again.

"I'll go and find—"

"No," Ara snapped. "You will return to your rooms with your mates and bar the door. I've already killed one person before breakfast, and I'm annoyed enough to deliver retribution to any others."

Maddy sidled closer to Fen. *Fabulous. Now I've scared one of my son's mates,* Ara grumbled to herself. But she wouldn't back down. Not in this.

Unfortunately, Fen was unaffected. "There's no reason we can't help search."

"It is too dangerous."

He rolled his eyes. "An assassin made it into your bathroom. Where the hell are any of us supposed to be safe?"

Ara pressed her fingertips into her temples and recited the Order of Nobles in her head until she could regain control over her temper. Sadly, it would take naming every noble House in the kingdom to fully stifle her aggravation, but at least by the time she'd made it through the royal cousins, she was able to proceed with the conversation. Such as it was.

"My door was not barred," she said. "Yours will be."

*Thump.*

Her attention jerked to the door across from Fen's. The noise had come from there.

*Thump. Thump, thump, thump.*

Waving the others aside, Ara rushed to investigate. But as she grasped the doorknob, a loud moan echoed through the wood. A moan of *pleasure.* She froze—or rather, burned—from the force of the rage that swept through her. Had she really had to kill an assassin and march naked down the hallway because her guard couldn't help but fuck someone while on duty? He'd better hope she was mistaken about those sounds.

She shoved through the door, and her breath hissed out at the sight that greeted her. Her guard had a woman bent over a chair, her upturned skirts the only thing blocking Ara's view of the man's thrusts. Both were lost in the moment, their eyes pinched closed in pleasure. But the man was a bodyguard. Shouldn't he have noticed her presence?

The fool.

With a flex of power, Ara softened the floor beneath their feet, then whipped tendrils of the stone around their ankles like vines. The woman yelped, and the guard stumbled behind her, nearly falling until he caught the side of the chair with his hand. Finally, he saw Ara, and the blood rushed from his face so abruptly that he was as pale as a *Felshreh*.

Ah, it was Scalanis. She should have known.

"Your Majesty," he gasped.

Ara's bare feet slapped against the floor as she crossed the space between them. "You dare to neglect your duties for your own pleasure?"

His companion showed no fear—no, it was annoyance in her gaze as the guard pulled free of her and shoved her skirts down. Scalanis didn't notice the scowl the woman transferred to him as he tucked himself back into his pants. He was too busy trying to combine syllables into something resembling words to actually look at the woman he'd just been buried in.

"A...a moment," Scalanis managed. "There couldn't have been much harm done while I was..."

Ara gestured at the blood drying in patches on her skin. "Does it look as though all was well during your little diversion? And to bring a stranger into the royal wing is an unfathomably bad lapse in judgement."

The guard shook his head. "No, no. She's a maid here. Nothing ever happens while I'm on duty, so I thought there'd be no harm in a bit of fun before she cleans the room."

Before Ara could retort, the woman straightened with a sharp, scornful laugh. "What a worthless fool. Couldn't help me find my pleasure and couldn't identify a trap when he was fucking one."

"But—"

"She doesn't work here," Ara said through gritted teeth. "You should have learned during your training that seduction is a common ploy for assassins."

"Usually my favorite one, too." The woman glared at Scalanis again. "When they're *good*."

Above the guard's muttered curses, a chuckle sounded from the doorway—Fen, of course. Why had she expected him to return to his room with his mates? He ignored nearly every instruction she gave him. Had she raised him from the start, perhaps he would have obeyed without question, but he had no respect for her and thus no reason to heed her directions. Otherwise, he wouldn't have stepped into a dangerous situation without a care.

She needed to end this quickly.

With her earth magic, Ara gathered more stone from the floor and twisted another layer around the assassin's feet and legs. Surprisingly, the woman laughed again. Her hand whipped up, and before anyone could react, she'd buried a knife in Scalanis's throat. His gagging, gurgling breaths sliced through the room, an announcement of his pending death. There was no way a healer would arrive in time to fix that.

"I would have advised him to improve his technique, but it won't be a concern for him anymore," the assassin said.

Then in a flash of magic, she disappeared.

**I hope you enjoyed this snippet from Legacy, which is currently a work in progress. Legacy will be available for pre-order soon at all retailers.**

# CHARACTER LIST AND DICTIONARY

<u>Characters</u>

Allafon – Previous Lord of Oria, an estate under Lyr's command. He betrayed Lyr and was eventually brought to justice after Arlyn's arrival.

Anna – Mate to Maddy and Fen. Anna once believed herself to be human, but after the barrier fell, allowing magic to return to Earth, her fae blood began to awaken. Ann is a descendant of the Gwragedd Annwn, Welsh fae.

Aris – Selia's husband and Iren's father. Aris is a life mage who can connect with the essence of living things and manipulate them. Once presumed dead, he returned to his family after the dragon Kezari rescued him and was instrumental in destroying the barrier.

Arlyn – Half-blood daughter of Lyr and his potential soulbonded, Aimee, who he met on Earth. Arlyn traveled to Moranaia after her mother's death to confront her elven father and quickly bonded with Kai. After helping Lyr and Kai defeat

Allafon, Arlyn decided to stay on Moranaia and train as her father's heir.

Baza – A dragon mage on the Isle of Dragons

Caeregas – One of the ancient dragons previously dormant on Earth. He has recently awakened to discover that magic has returned to Earth.

Caolte – Brother of Naomh and Meren. Caolte was born of an affair between his father and an Unseelie woman, making it difficult for him to fit in with either faction. Caolte is sworn to protect his brother, Naomh.

Cora – Ralan's soulbonded. Originally from Galare, Cora fled to Earth after a failed betrothal put her in danger. To pull power from an environment, Cora must bond with that particular place. When Ralan was almost killed defeating Kien, Cora saved him by linking to Moranaia.

Delbin – A young elf exiled to Earth one hundred years prior in order to escape Allafon's machinations. Now that Allafon is dead, Delbin is able to return to Moranaia. He is often sent on missions requiring knowledge of modern Earth.

Deyriglair - A legendary dragon who once ruled over all dragon kind. He was known for brokering the peace treaty between the elves and the dragons on Moranaia.

Dria – Youngest child of King Alianar and Enielle. Dria was sent early to the Citadel, the place where the highest-ranking mages train for battle. At 317, Dria is one of the youngest to complete her training and take her place within a mage troop.

Egrenneth – One of the ancient dragons, although he did not go dormant like his brother, Caeregas. He has instead wandered earth in human form for millennia.

Elan – A lower-level healer who acts as Lial's assistant.

Eri – Daughter of Prince Ralan and a human woman. After nearly dying from energy poisoning, her father brought her to Moranaia from Earth to be healed.

Fen – Mate to Anna and Maddy. Son of Ara and a human man. Fen was abandoned on Earth, where he got involved with Kien's group of outcasts. To atone for working with Kien, Fen helps repair the damage he'd once contributed to creating.

Inona – A Moranaian scout most frequently assigned to check on exiles banished to Earth. After finding Delbin, she is often sent on missions to Earth with him.

Kezari – A dragon from the distant Isle of Dragons on Moranaia. Kezari rescued Aris from captivity and returned with him to Braelyn to fix a problem she detected with Earth's energy.

Kien – Son of King Alianar and Enielle. Power-hungry and determined to someday claim the throne, Kien plotted to kill his brother Ralan, a seer, first. When he was ultimately discovered, Kien was banished to a distant planet but managed to escape to Earth. He finally made his way back to Moranaia and was killed by the king.

Koranel – Former captain of Lyr's army

Korel – One of three bodyguards assigned by the previous captain, Norin, to protect Arlyn after she first arrived. Of the three, he was the only one banished by Lyr for failing to stop an attempt on Arlyn's life. He died from the virus unleashed in SOLACE.

Lial – The primary healer at Braelyn, Lyr's estate. Lial is renowned for being both highly skilled and easily annoyed.

Lynia – Lyr's mother. A researcher whose magic lies in books and knowledge. Lynia was almost killed during Allafon's attempted coup, but Lial saved her.

Lyr – Lord of Braelyn. Son of Lynia and soulbonded of Meli. Forced to leave his first potential soulbonded on Earth to find his father's murderer, Lyr expected neither a future mate nor children. But after Arlyn's arrival and the subsequent upheaval, Lyr has learned to stop expecting anything—unless it is unusual. Now he lives with his daughter, Arlyn, his new bonded, Meli, and an odd assortment of people he never thought could coexist on a single estate.

Maddy – Mate to Fen and Anna. Maddy lives in Chattanooga, Tennessee and is currently buying her friend Cora's shop, The Magic Touch, after Cora moved to Moranaia. Maddy is half Seelie Sidhe and half human. Maddy helps any fae who need to integrate with humans.

Meli – Lyr's soulbonded. One of the rare Ljósálfar (Norse elves), Meli guided her king's ambassador to Moranaia to ask for help with the energy poisoning affecting their realm. She ultimately bonds with Lyr and remains on Moranaia.

Meren – Brother of Naomh and Caolte. Meren is the oldest of the brothers but diverges sharply in ideology. Believing that the Seelie Sidhe should leave their underground realms and reclaim the surface, Meren will do whatever he deems necessary to achieve his goals.

Naomh – Brother of Meren and Caolte. Kai's father. Naomh once worked with Kien in a misguided attempt to keep his people from returning to the surface. Now, he tries to stop Meren from causing further trouble.

Ralan – Son of King Alianar and Enielle. Eri's father. Soulbonded to Cora. Now that Kien has been defeated, Ralan is helping establish a secondary palace to monitor the new gate Aris and Kezari created to Earth.

Tebzn – Kezari's cousin who claimed her hoard after Kezari was banished.

Tynan – Mind healer and priest of Bera. He temporarily traveled to Braelyn to help Aris with his trauma.

Zevie – The queen of the dragons on Moranaia

<u>Common Terms</u>

- ahmeeren – Unseelie for my darling or dear
- Bera – Goddess of the afterlife, protection, and healing
- Braelyn – Lyr's estate
- camahr – An animal on Moranaia that is somewhat between a fox and cat in shape and disposition. It can use the tip of its tail to detect impurities.
- clechtan – A Moranaian curse word similar to 'damn'
- daeri – deer
- drec – A Moranaian insult. Someone who defiles nature or the natural order.
- elnaia – Moranaian word for grandmother
- Eradisel – One of the nine sacred trees, symbol of Dorenal
- Felshreh – Unseelie word for blood elf

- Gwragedd Annwn – Welsh water fae, said to inhabit lakes.
- inai – DNA / builders of life
- laial – More formal Moranaian word for father
- laiala – More formal Moranaian word for mother
- Meyanen – God of love and relationships
- mialn – Beloved (used for mate or lover)
- miaran – Iron (literal). Used commonly as an expletive
- onaial – Moranaian word for Dad
- onaiala – Moranaian word for Mom
- orlayak - Second father / step-father
- peresten – Elvensteel
- sbezie – "Mate" in the dragon language
- skizik – An elf, fae, or other dragon with complementary magic who links with a dragon to join skills
- tieln – Beloved (used with a child, sibling, or parent)
- zeznit - A dragon term for a rancid corpse. Often used as an insult

# MORE BY BETHANY ADAMS

The Return of the Elves Series

Book 1: Soulbound

Book 2: Sundered

Book 3: Exiled (Novella)

Book 4: Seared

Book 5: Abyss

Book 6: Awakening

Book 7: Ascent

Book 8: Solace

Book 9: Maelstrom

Single Titles

The Mage's Curse

Written as Willow McCain

The Fae Kings' Bargain

For updates on new releases and sales delivered straight to your email, you can sign up for my newsletter on my home page at bethanyadamsbooks.com.

Want to be among the first to see snippets, cover reveals, and other fun? Join my Facebook group, The Worlds of Bethany Adams, and come chat whenever you like.

# ABOUT THE AUTHOR

Ever since finding a copy of *The Hero and the Crown* in her elementary school library, Bethany has loved fantasy. After subjecting her friends to stories scrawled in notebooks during study breaks all through high school, she decided to pursue an English degree at Middle Tennessee State University. When not writing or wrangling her two young children, Bethany enjoys reading, photography, and video games.

facebook.com/writerbethany

x.com/bethjadams

instagram.com/willowreve

bookbub.com/authors/bethany-adams

tiktok.com/@bethanyadamsauthor